GRID Traveler Trilogy: Distant Reality, Alien Shores, and Lines Crossed

I0658819

J Carrell Jones

Mythical Legends Publishing

GRID Traveler Trilogy is a work of fiction. The characters, incidents, and dialogs are products of the author's imagination and are not to be construed as real. Any resemblance to actual events or persons, living or dead, is entirely coincidental.

A Mythical Legends Publishing Mass Market Paperback

Copyright © 2013 by J Carrell Jones
Published by Mythical Legends, 2013
GRID Traveler Distant Reality and GRID Traveler Alien Shores
Copyright © 1993, 2012 by J Carrell Jones
Publisher@mythicallegends.com
http://mythicallegends.com

ISBN-10: 0962783528
ISBN-13: 978-0-9627835-2-4

Printed in the United States of America

9 8 7 6 5 4 3 2 1

DEDICATION

To my brilliant and beautiful daughter Nicholette, you are the future.

To all those who believe it can happen.

ACKNOWLEDGMENTS

I mainly started writing because of a handful of friends who have graced my life tremendously. None of which played a minor role in my development. I am forever grateful:

Patricia Williams
T. Le Roy Birdine
Kenneth Strickland
Jay P Hailey
Brenda Gilmore

I'd also like to acknowledge some of the writers who grabbed my attention and never let go:

Robert A Heinlein
CJ Cherryh
Arthur C Clarke
Isaac Asimov
Ray Bradbury
David Gerrold
Frank Herbert
Larry Niven
Jerry Pournelle
Michael Crichton
L. Ron Hubbard
Eric Van Lustbader
F Scott Fitzgerald
Elizabeth Moon

ACT I:
Distant Reality

In a person's life-time decisions are made, some good, some bad, some of no immediate consequences. A person frets over some little unimportant detail when the big picture stares back. A choice is not always made under the best of circumstances. The only thing a person hopes for is an outcome that is remotely close to what is hoped for. Thus, a decision begets a consequence.

Chapter 1

Sean Blakemore stared blurrily at the picture in front of him. The picture frame weighted in his alcohol weakened arms. Why he kept the damn picture all these years was beyond him. Why he held it in his hand more so. He was an idiot for yet again torturing himself like this. Idiot, idiot, and idiot. He squinted once and sighed heavily. "Damn you!" he hissed. "God damn you to hell!" He screamed and flung the picture frame across the room. The frame broke and the glass cover shattered into small pieces. He slammed his glass at the shattered remains. Liquid spotted a torn photograph of a beautiful woman. He stood up and walked over to the bathroom sink. The remains of his last eaten meal still clogged the drain. He stared into the mirror. "You bastard! You ought to walk out in space right now." Sean, at this moment hated himself and a decision he made years ago. The man in the mirror stared back with eyes that spoke of disappointment, pain, suffering and shame. Sean thought that if he were The Buddha his eyes would show him his duhkha. Instead, they reflected a man in deep pain.

"Excuse me Commander," a disembodied voice said.

Sean looked over his shoulder. "What is it now?"

"Commander." The computer said.

"I know my rank!"

". . . You have a call coming in from headquarters."

Sean stared at himself again and rubbed the day old growth on his chin. Not too long ago Sean enjoyed receiving calls. It was always that hint of the unknown that gave him a reason to serve GRID Command. Now . . . he didn't feel one way or another. A call was just that: A call.

"I'll take it in my Ready Room."

"Yes Commander." The computer said.

Sean walked the walk of a man trying not to show his inebriated state. He entered his Ready Room and sat heavily into his chair. He faced the computer terminal and pressed a 'ready' button on the keyboard. The screen sparkled a moment, then a shaped solidified. Sean blinked. He cleared his throat and said, "Yes, sir. What may I do for you?"

The man on the screen stared intently at Sean for a moment, as if he could literally read what was on the younger officer's mind. Then he smiled. "Sean, you look like shit!"

"I feel like shit." Sean smiled and raised an eyebrow, "A mission?"

"Yeah Sean, you got a mission and what a mission it is."

Sean chuckled softly to himself, "Good, patrolling asteroids is not my idea of fun."

The Admiral laughed. He knew all the details over the incident. When it happened he shook his head in astonishment. The man sacrificed a promotion for a fellow officer. Sean had been on the fast track to Commodore. Everyone he came into contact with believed it. Sean believed it. There was no stopping the progress. Except something did stop the progress. It was emotions, or if one was a direct witness of the events then it was lust. Maybe love, but lust definitely and loyalty, trust and belief. Sean had put all that into a person. He momentarily stopped thinking about his original goal in joining GRID Command, "To be the best damn anything I put my mind to." In letting his emotions steer him away from the main path he got side-swiped and it resulted in a very nasty ugly collision with an alternate destiny. Sean disobeyed a direct order from a commanding officer, a commanding officer with ties to the military measured in centuries. After the dust had settled and cleared, and the body count recorded, only one person stood. Unfortunately, it was not Sean. The fellow officer had won a commendation, a commission, and a promotion. GRID Command is an institution where discipline, duty, loyalty, and honor are held in high praise – when applied to the right side. Sean picked the wrong side and he was a casualty of a bruised ego. In one felled swoop ten dozen bodies littered the streets of revenge and embarrassment. He figured that as the walking wounded he'd be rescued. He wasn't. His wound was deep.

Sean Blakemore walked onto Top Deck. He stepped just outside the elevator doorway. The elevators doors hissed closed behind him. He stood for a moment listening to the beeps and low tones around the room. 'Top Deck Chatter,' Sean thought. The beeps, the hushed conversations, background noise and voices coming from the intercoms, the clicking sound from keyboards, all this was Deck chatter. It was a sound that all hands grew to believe, no felt, synonymous with the autonomous functions of the brain. Quiet the Deck chatter and the ship is dead. Rumor had it that if you silenced Deck chatter for a minute all hands would suffocate.

"This is the one thing she can't take from me."

"Commander?" A young ensign asked. "Are you alright?"

Sean stared down at the youth. He was young physically, but his mind was old. He noted the smooth skin and wished that his scarred and hardened face could recapture that long ago look. "Nothing Ensign," he smiled, "I'm okay."

"Okay, sir." The ensign said, turned and walked off to other assignments.

Sean walked over to the command chair and sat down. He swiveled over to look at a CRT on his right. He punched in his pass code and read the scrolling information on the screen. His eyes widened first with excitement, then narrowed with anger. His assignment was going to put his ship under HER command. He swore loudly.

The personnel on Top Deck turned to see their Commander in a foul mood. He ignored them for the moment; his only concern was the data he was now reading. "Incredible! They want my ship as a damned escort vessel!" Sean looked up suddenly and saw many startled faces. Deck chatter was an octave lower.

Sean sat for a full minute before he moved. 'Damn,' he thought, 'God hates me.'

"Mr. Foster," Sean said, "get us to the nearest GRID point, we're going to Flashpoint."

"Aye, aye sir." The Lieutenant said. He fingers played over the control panel. Sean watched as his helmsperson worked the controls. He noted the long dark colored fingers dance from one button, control, slid, to another button, control, slid. He noted the crooked nose on a long face with small eyebrows over almond shaped eyes. Medium lips that occasionally spread wide and thin in a smile.

"Course laid in, sir."

Sean sat back and pressed the 'Comm. button'. "All hands, all hands, travel stations, repeat, travel stations." He pressed the button again. His second-in-command sat next to him in the XO chair. Sean swiveled to the left. "Well, number one. Ready?"

Dawn pressed several keys on her terminal, read the scrolling data on her CRT. "Yes, Commander."

Sean Blakemore cleared his throat. "Mr. Foster, proceed!"

The GRID Ship Battlecruiser Reginald L. Johnson's engines flared into action, thrusting the massive battle ship into motion. Her destination: A GRID Point. An artificial point that created a measured amount of gravity within dark matter. GRavity InDuced points, in space, allowed a mobile object the ability to travel to another GRID point. The Johnson approached the grid point at a controlled angle. The helmsperson eased the ship into a jump point.

Sometime in the three-quarter 20th century scientist speculated about the fate of the Universe. Some said that what was seen in the heavens was all there was. Others argued that the visible Universe was about 4% of what was really out there. Early in the 21st century "dark energy" was discovered. It was in complete contradiction to Einstein's gut feeling that "there was no such thing as ether." But, like all things scientific, some gut feelings must give way to observable facts. Succinctly put, the visible Universe was but a pinch in a hand full of existence. We lived in a place of great mystery as others called folly.

GRID travel was possible because of dark matter and energy interactions with "normal" direct observable matter and energy. The basic idea behind GRID travel was that space-time is a very thin extremely strong, durable and self-healing rubber sheet. This sheet was made in such a way that pulling or pushing a section does not disturb neighboring sections. The sheet remains strong. GRID travel involves creating a wave with several crests and valleys. The base line of each crest and valley intersects with a section of this rubber sheet. A GRID capable ship just rides this wave as far as it can. And as things are, some ships are faster at riding the wave than others. Battlecruisers were able to produce a GRID wave that skips several sections of space-time before it intersected space. A ship able to travel a long GRID wave effectively traveled many times faster than the speed of light.

Sean sat back, watching the main viewer.   The signal
beacons bleeped on and off marking the boundaries of the
grid-point.

Mr. Foster said over his shoulder. "Ready to enter, Sir."

Sean stared. His mind was on the encounter he was about
to face. The bleeping of the signal beacons broke the thoughts
of someone he once loved.

Mr. Foster waited.

"Proceed, Mr. Foster."

GRID Ship Johnson's engine's pulsed.   The huge ship
labored forward into the grid point.   It accelerated, then
vanished between two beacons that flashed on and off in a
relentless job of signaling a GRID slot.   The ship was gone,
toward another grid-point to another point, to another point,
to another point, until it reached its destination.

Mr. Foster checked and rechecked the pattern flow across
his CRT. He knew the drill: Pick a point, lock in on it, pick
another, and lock in on that one also.   Keep doing it until you
were where you wanted to be. He knew the drill, but to make
sure he checked and rechecked.   "ETA in ten minutes, Sir."

Sean looked up from his CRT, "Noted Mr. Foster." He
swiveled his chair to the communications section.   "Mr.
Kirkland."

Mr. Kirkland pulled the Comm. plug from his ear, "Yes,
sir."

"When we get to Flashpoint, contact the Webster. Let
Webster know that we're ready for rendezvous."

"Aye, Sir." Kirkland placed the Comm. plug back in his
ear. He listened intently on the comm. traffic over the grid
net. He picked up bits of messages from the Outlands. He
dialed in a tighter signal. His panel beeped that his designated
target was in communication range.   He typed in a brief
message and sent it to the Comm. Officer of the Webster, a

friend.

Sean just sat and stared those last ten minutes away. He snapped out of his dream state, "Mr. Kirkland . . ."

Kirkland looked up from reading a text message that flashed across his screen. His friend had just sent a message explaining that the crew was on edge. Webster's Captain was going to command Johnson and she wasn't too happy. "Yes, sir?"

"Are we in contact with the Webster?"

"Yes, sir. Just reading a message from the Comm. officer now . . ."

"Good, please ask their Captain to contact me at her earliest convenience."

Sean got up and started walking. "I'll be in the conference room. Dawn, please accompany me, I have things to tell you."

Dawn followed Sean through the sliding door. To the Top Deck crew the door hissed closed rather tightly.

Kirkland began typing out the message to the Webster.

> *Beginning of Message*
> Commander of Johnson wishes Captain of Webster to contact him at earliest convenience.
> *End of Message*
> *** Commander is in a bad mood - think maybe blood is still bad between them? ***

The reply came back,

> Commander of Webster acknowledges message. Information on rendezvous follows immediately.
> *** Yep, blood is still bad. The Captain cursed up a fit when she received the orders. ***

Sean sat down behind his desk. He turned the chair around so that the expanse of stars swept by the view wall. This was his place of ease. Dawn sat just in front of the desk and turned her chair likewise. She watched the stars streak by. She waited a few moments – Sean seemingly was in awe with the view, cleared her throat.

"Sir, is there something wrong?"

Sean broke his gaze from the window and turned his chair to Dawn. "Yes, very much wrong." He paused.

Dawn waited.

"Captain Spaarin will be taking command of the Johnson for the duration of this mission."

Three seconds ticked by.

"The fucking bitch!"

Sean wanted to laugh. Dawn knew all the details. She was absolutely loyal to him and he was certain of that. During that time Sean gave her an order and she followed it. She believed in that order; she still believed in the order and she felt Sean had been given a raw deal. It was absolutely political. Dawn had heard rumors that someone high up had taken a liking to Captain Spaarin. This someone had shielded her from all the meltdown that occurred from her disobeying an order and everyone else was collateral damage. The only good thing that came out of the whole mess was that Sean was given the command of the Johnson, but not given a captain's rank. The SI war ended with humanity victorious but left humanity wondering what it really meant to be human. Many lost their lives – many commanding officers died. Ranks had to be filled. The Johnson's leadership position was filled but without a promotion – and that smacked as a slap in the face to Dawn, increased responsibility but not an increase in pay. What better form of humiliation and punishment could be exacted on a person?

Dawn reiterated, "The fucking bitch!"

Sean nodded, "Wish it could be someone else."

"Damn! What is GRID Command thinking?" Then Dawn frowned. "What is our mission?"

"Don't know yet. I only know that Robin . . . Captain Spaarin will be commanding Johnson."

"Bitch!"

"This is why we are talking right now."

Dawn looked Sean straight in the eyes. Sean stared back and said, "I'll effectively be her number one and . . . "

"That is total bull shit!"

Sean nodded. He being number one meant she was out of a job. She would have to be temporarily reassigned. This mission sucked for everyone involved. He continued, ". . . and I'm keeping you as XO."

Dawn clamped her jaws tight. "Yes, sir. I knew I wasn't going to like this one bit."

Sean nodded and understood. During the 'fallout' Dawn was up for court-martial. Sean took absolute responsibility over the incident. Sean "saved" about a hundred personnel.

Dawn sighed, "Anything else, sir?"

Sean smiled, "Nope, I dropped that second shoe."

Dawn smiled back, "By your leave then sir."

He nodded and Dawn got up and walked out.

Sean sat there for a moment staring out the window. He remembered the first time he had been in space. It was a feeling that would always be with him. A sense of awe, and wonderment mixed with fear and anticipation. It never left him. Even now, amidst this mission Sean still took in the expanse before him. Space, Sean told himself, was something to always be in awe.

"Commander . . ." Kirkland's disembodied voice said.

"Yes?"

"Captain Spaarin is on comm. line three."

"Thanks," Sean replied, swung his chair around and hit a

comm. button marked 'three' on the terminal on his desk, "Commander Blakemore here." Sean listened. He stilled himself for the voice he knew would come."

"Yes, Commander Blakemore . . ."

Sean's heart skipped a beat.

"Put it on visual, Commander."

Sean hesitated. He really didn't want to see her face. Hearing her voice was painful enough. He hit the visual button. A beautiful face sparkled solid. A beautiful face he hadn't seen in five years, a face that reminded him of bad times – and good. He set his jaw, tensed, then relaxed. "Yes, Captain, do you see me now?"

The face was small and round, light hair, with dark eyes. The lips were full and every time Sean chanced the stare, emotions of lust would wash over him. He shook himself and remembered that this woman was the one who placed him where he is now, maybe not purposely, but nevertheless a result of the fallout from her actions. Sean never forgot, and for that he hated her.

Spaarin sat back and smiled thinly. She remembered Sean better looking five years ago. She stared into his eyes, and wished he had been stronger about the whole ugly affair they had. It wasn't her fault that he became too emotionally attached. She warned him, but by that time she was ready to make a career move. She had used Sean as a stepping-stone and she felt certain that he hated her. She sighed and said, "Yes, I see you Commander. Nice to see you after all these years." It was a lie, but she had a courtesy to lie, rank, position, and respect and all that in the service.

Sean nodded; he wasn't going to make this easy.

"Sean, we have a problem . . ."

"Yes."

Spaarin hesitated a moment, then, "I will be taking command of the Johnson . . ."

"The Johnson," Sean snapped, "is my ship. Just tell me what to do . . ."

"No Commander, I will be coming aboard. We will then proceed with the mission." She saw that Sean was grinding his teeth and clenching his jaw.

Sean stared intensely at her. He knew he couldn't fight it. His orders had been specific, 'Follow the orders of Captain Spaarin.' "Yes . . ."

She dared to push, "Yes what?"

"Yes . . . Captain Spaarin . . . I will make arrangements." He wanted to scream 'you bitch I'll arrange my boot up your ass! You messed up my career, and I took the fall for you.' But he stilled his tongue and swallowed his pride. He hit the off button, turned his chair to the view wall and lost himself in space. She, at least, can't take his last moments as commander of his own ship, the last moments that would allow him to be alone.

Captain Robin Spaarin looked at the now blank screen. She bit her lower lip and swore, "Damn!" She was not going to like this assignment, not one bit.

Sean sat in the dark staring off into the black void. He let his mind drift on nothing particular. His ship was being taken and he couldn't do a damn legal thing.

Captain Spaarin sat in her chair. She stared at the contents on the desk in front of her. The assorted mish-mash of stuff lay upon it. She reached out and picked up a picture frame. She held it close to her heart and sighed heavily. "I'm so sorry Sean, it had to be done." She looked at the photo and pursed her lips together. She laid the photo down face up.

It is the small things that command the most attention. Ego, pride, and shame are sprung from the same fountain of emotion but to differing degrees of appreciation. The sin that causes the most pain is not necessarily the sin most presented.

Chapter 2

Sean stood in the hangar bay watching Captain Spaarin's shuttle dock. His stomach twisted up in knots in anticipation. The docking rings locked into place and the green "all-clear" light, flashed. The hangar door hissed open and Captain Spaarin stepped out. She was met by a small contingent: Sean, Dawn, and other officers.

Robin saluted, "Captain Robin Spaarin here to take command of GRID Ship Johnson." She held her salute and stood stiff. It was only a moment but it felt like forever minus one hour.

Sean waited. He slowly stiffened and saluted back, "GRID Ship Reginald L. Johnson is temporarily in your command."

Robin nodded and dropped her salute, Sean did likewise.

"You'll be moving into my quarters. I'll move into the VIP."

Robin searched his face for distress she found none. "That won't be necessary Commander. The VIP room will do nicely. The Johnson is your ship and my stay on board will be brief.

Sean held himself in rigid control; he would not give her any reason to feel superior. Sean nodded once. "Follow me, Captain." He turned and walked out before she could reply.

The walk was more for his sanity then for her benefit. He wanted her to following him for once. He knew the Johnson, she didn't, and she would have to admit that.

She picked a spot at the back of his neck and stared. She could feel his tension, his stress, he was giving up his ship and that in itself had to be stressful. It didn't matter she knew he hated her. She resolved not to let it impair her decisions. She was in command now, at this moment that was the only thing that mattered. Robin cleared her throat. "Commander, take me to the Top Deck first please."

Sean stopped short, "Yes, ma'am." And entered the nearest lift.

"Top Deck." He spoke when everyone was in the lift.

The computer replied, "Yes, Commander."

The door opened and a flood of deck chatter washed in. Robin held her breath as she stepped out into the 'Top Deck.' Immediately the chatter stopped. Robin froze as she realized that she was a complete stranger to this particular Top Deck. Eyes stared at her from all corners.

Sean stepped from behind, said, "As you were people. Superior officer on the deck." The Top Deck sighed; Robin released the breath she held. Sean walked down the ramp to the command center and sat in the XO chair. Robin walked from station to station observing. The situation was indeed awkward. She pushed the thought of uneasiness aside. The Johnson was hers, for now, but only on a word. Sean was in command she was just sitting in his chair. That was the important thing to remember. Robin walked to the commander's chair and sat heavily. She reached for the CRT and typed in several keys. The computer blinked with access denied. She caught a quick glance from Sean. He was trying not to watch, but was failing in concealing his curiosity. She typed in another combination of keys. 'Access denied' again.

She looked up and over to Sean.

"Commander, may we talk in private please."

Sean nodded, got up and headed for the conference room. Robin got up and followed.

Just before the conference door hissed closed Robin snapped, "What the hell do you think you're doing?" Top Deck heard, "What the hell . . ." and the rumors would fly.

Her cheeks bright red from the anger she no longer held back.

Sean stared and kept his mouth shut. He had an idea what she was talking about, but he wasn't going to give her the satisfaction of pushing it out of him. He cleared his throat and said, "Captain, what am I doing?"

Robin placed herself in check. What had he done? That was his chair out there, not hers. He sat there and conducted ship's business very well.   In fact, he was getting a commendation. Then what had he done? He shut her out, his ship, his chair, and his people.   He shut her out and was not going to give her easy access to any of them.   She realized she was going to have to earn her place. Robin looked at Sean. His forehead was wrinkled in a frown. Yes, she was going to have to earn it from now on. "Commander, please give me access to all command systems."

Sean smiled, "I was . . ."

"But."

"Never had a chance to finish the process. You sat in my chair and started typing away."

Robin nodded.

"May I do it now, or do you have anything else you want to talk at me about?"

Robin stood in silence musing over the many ways she could handle his request. She sighed slowly, said, "Yes," and grinned.

Sean frowned, "Ah, yes to which question?"

"Which one do you want first?"

Sean looked into her eyes, eyes he remembered not too long ago he was happy to wake up to. Now he wanted, wished, he could forget them. Too much pain too much sorrow. "I'm sorry, Captain. I'll give you access now, may I go?"

Robin nodded.

Sean sat in the command chair, stared at the CRT and began typing. He gave her access to all his files, all the ships files, and everything else she may think she needed, he didn't care.

"Mr. Foster," Sean said, "please call Commander Dawn to Top Deck."

Robin stared out the view window. She thought of Sean and the life they would have had. She thought about her career, and how satisfied she was for making the choice she made. Life had been good to her. She turned and stared at the beige bland wall. 'Oh, Sean, I am sorry for what happened, but life goes on.'

A paradigm is a worldview unique to each person. Change the rules you change the outcome. Change the outcome changes the paradigm. The universe does not take kindly to changing the rules.

Chapter 3

Robin sat in the command chair, getting a feel for how Sean seated himself. She noted that he sat with his back flush against the rest. "Mr. Kirkland."

"Yes, ma'am?"

"Send a message to the Gallant. Tell them that all is well and we'll be proceeding to rendezvous point immediately."

Kirkland adjusted the Comm. plug. His fingers danced over the keypad. He placed in his routing codes and sent the message.

> *Comm. Officer of the Johnson sending a message to Commander of the Gallant. Message follows: Proceeding to rendezvous point immediately. No ETA given by commander. Please reply upon receipt of message. Signed Comm. Kirkland.*

Kirkland waited. He didn't know the Comm. Officer of the Gallant but a friend from the Trailblazer spoke highly of Gallant's Comm.

"Message sent, ma'am."

Robin nodded. "Mr. Foster, set a course for . . . "she keyed in a set of numbers and sent it to his console, "I want us there in two hours . . ."

Two hours, ma'am?"

"Was I making a suggestion or giving an order?"

"An order, ma'am."

Mr. Foster nodded and started his task. He called up the Nav. Map and took notes. Thirty-five grid jumps! By the book it would take a little over three hours. He cut it down to twenty-seven jumps. It wasted fuel and would be bumpy. He keyed in the codes, looked over his shoulder.

"Ready, ma'am. One hour fifty-seven minutes. Best I can do and keep our lunch down."

Robin smiled. Sean kept a good ship. "Proceed, Mr. Foster."

With a nod, Foster started the sequence of grid jumps that would take the Johnson to whom knew where. He watched his panel, and did what he did best: Navigate.

Robin punched the intercom button, "Commander Blakemore, please report to Top Deck conference room, please report to the Top Deck conference room."

Sean drifted in a sea of smooth colors, soft fluids, and faded lights. He dreamt of nothing but patterns. His dream-state body floated in complete relaxation, no worries, no hassles no fuss. A cloud of mixed colors covered him. It was soft and pleasant. Sean rolled in its cool and changing patterns. Another cloud drifted by, its collision marked by the increase in flowing colors splashing around him. Several more clouds drifted into the already chaotic patterns that were produced by the previous encounters. Sean's dream state sensed something wrong. He tried to relax and will the colors and patterns to smooth out, but more clouds gathered, their colors and patterns dark. Sean gasped as he tried desperately to stop his dream from its inevitable conclusion. "No!" He silently hollered, "No! I want to dream!" A cloud crashed into him. The force knocked his dream state in a spiraling fall into nowhere. Another cloud slammed into him, and another, and another and another.

Sean woke up sweating. The sheets were moist from the perspiration that gleamed on his body. He looked around. No clouds.

"Commander." The computer spoke.

"Yes, what is it?" Sean said, burying his face into his hands.

"Captain Spaarin requests that you see her in Top Deck Conference Room."

Sean got out of bed and dragged himself over to the sink. He stared in the mirror, studying a face that didn't sit right with him.

"Commander, did you get the message?"

Sean snapped, "I got it." Then, "Send the Captain an acknowledgment message to the Command CRT."

The computer remained silent.

Sean grabbed his clothes got dressed and headed out the door.

Robin sat waiting for Sean. Now was the time she would tell him, tell him the secret. The door hissed open and Sean walked through.

He looked at her, said nothing and sat down across from her.

Robin sat back and stared.

Sean stared back. He would meet her on her terms.

"Sean, did the Admiral tell you why he gave me command of Johnson?"

Sean shook his head, "Nothing important."

"Have you heard of Necronomicon?"

Sean frowned and shook his head.

"Have you heard of Magick?"

"Magic? Why," Sean blurted, almost regretting his tone, "are you asking me about magic?"

"Because, I want you to understand."

An eyebrow shot up. "Understand?"

"Yeah," Robin began, nodding her head slowly, "Understand that this is serious."

Sean sniffed, "Serious?"

"Suppose Earth was visited in the past by Aliens . . ."

"Excuse me, Captain, but is this speculation?"

"Pardon?"

"We've been out here," he waved toward the window, "for more than two centuries. The only aliens we've encountered were the ones we scattered ourselves."

Robin blinked and frowned.

Sean continued, "I would like to believe in 'em, but the only proof we have is broken pottery and markings in dirt."

Robin cleared her throat. "Have you heard of Magick?"

"Yeah, and?"

"I mean, really know of it? Not just something you grew up with, but have you seen it?"

"Just in movies and books. Why?"

Robin sat back and smiled. She pursed her lips in thought, took a deep breath. "Earth was visited long ago."

Sean huffed. "You turning my ship into some damned ghost hunter?"

Robin ignored the question. "Dr. Loggar will be joining us from the Gallant. She will conduct the investigation . . ."

Sean raised an eyebrow. He heard of Dr. Loggar. Pretty high up in GRID Command. "Shadow chasing?"

Robin thought a moment; Sean was very cynical as well as skeptical. "An investigation, the proof is beyond scary."

"How so?"

"Dr. Loggar was working out in the region we will be heading into. She and her group found artifacts and equipment, computer equipment Sean! Equipment that is still working."

"Working! Alien computer equipment? Impossible!" Sean said.

Robin shook her head. "No, it's not. The equipment is working. Hardcopy manuscripts detailing how to operate it. The manuscripts were preserved for over 1,000 years." Robin's eyes welled up with tears. She softly shuddered at the thought of this information. My Goddess, she thought, it still makes me shake when I think about it. She cleared her throat. "Sean," she began softly, "think of it, a connection between another intelligent race and ours. Suppose we are their people."

Sean sat uneasily in the chair. The information Robin was giving him was shocking, if not difficult to assimilate. Aliens, maybe real proof. "Is the evidence real? Any chance of fraud?" Sean knew the answer. GRID Command would never send a trillion credit ship on a whim. The evidence had to be exact and overwhelming.

Robin shrugged, "Anything's possible. After Dr. Loggar made the discovery, GRID Command placed armed ships in the area. She took some stuff to Earth for further analysis. She thinks the stuff is real. The Gallant is going to meet with us. We'll take her aboard and proceed to the system." Robin hesitated. "She asked specifically for you."

"Me! I don't believe in magic, or in aliens!"

"How can you say that, and really mean it? Earth has had a lot of unexplained occurrences throughout our existences."

Sean huffed. "Fraud, practical jokes, massive EM surges."

Robin thought a moment. She never really considered that Sean would totally deny evidence. Yet again he hadn't *seen* the evidence. She had and it scared her. A handful of scientist who think they've found something so profound and utterly old that it has to be from 'someone' else? As Sean put it, 'markings in dirt'. Maybe humans were the only ones in the galaxy. Robin slowly shook her head. "This place is much too big for just humans to exist." Robin said. "We can't be the only ones here."

"All right," Sean started, "suppose we're not the only ones in the galaxy, or the universe. The all important question is why have we not been contacted."

Robin opened her mouth to answer, but Sean cut her off.

"Because, maybe there is no one else." Sean said casually as if it was the hundredth time he said it.

"Maybe," mused Robin, "they've had some form of a Main directive regarding life forms. We have one."

"You see, you sound like all the other UFO . . ." Sean paused to consider his words, then continued with, ". . . believers. We've been in space four hundred years now. We've traveled to hundreds of planets. We've settled tens of then. And in our centuries of populating the galaxy we've made war with ourselves. Yeah, we've found some evidence of intelligent life, but we've *never* encountered it. I'd like to believe in 'em, but the truth is we are it. We've mapped 125 cubic billion light years and nothing. No encounters, no proof of existence now. Nothing, nada, zero, zilch."

"Sean," Robin retorted, "that is less than one percent of the total volume of the Milky Way."

"Robin, we've had this discussion before."

Robin stared.

"Look, scooping up an 8 oz. glass of ocean water is by far less than a millionth of a percentage of the total volume of water, but you'd find it full of life." Sean waited a second. He was giving Robin a chance to counter. "We should have found something by now."

"Wait and see what Dr. Loggar has."

Sean smiled, "I will. I'd also like to know why she asked for me."

Robin shrugged.

The room was silent for several seconds.

Sean cleared his voice. "If you'll excuse me, Captain."

Robin picked up on the formal tone, "I'm through. You

have other duties to perform."

Sean nodded sharply once, got up and walked out.

Robin turned her chair around to the window. A star streaked its elongated self slowly by. We can't be alone Robin wished, and hoped. This universe is much too large for it to be wasted on us.

Sean walked back into his room and sat down at his desk. He thought about what Robin told him and immediately got scared. He cursed himself for the sudden emotional turn. Why am I scared he thought. We are alone, are we? I grew up all my life believing that humankind was it. And if there was life 'out there' then it happened a long time ago, right? Sean got up and walked over to the bar and pulled a bottle out. He stared at the clear contents for a few seconds, pursed his lips and put the bottle back. I am scared. I'm also excited. What if, life, other than humans is out there? That would be something. "Computer?"

"Yes, Commander?"

"What do you know about Dr. Loggar?"

"Dr. Kathy Loggar, is currently GRID Command Exobiological/Anthropological coordinator."

Sean chuckled at the word exobiology. We humans will always hope, including giving degrees for things we can only speculate on. "Is she married?"

"At the last known query, no. Dr. Loggar is single."

"Do you have any documentation on her life?"

"I have documentation of all individuals of prominence and importance to GRID Command."

"How about answering with a yes or no?"

A pause, then, "Yes."

"Thank you." Sean walked over to his couch and sat down. "Tell me about her please. Dim the lights also."

The lights dimmed and Sean relaxed as the computer began.

Encounters are the very basis for being human. Our society and our culture is based on our interaction between one another. We think and wonder on the dynamics of the outcome, but in the end the results are from actually meeting. Speculation is usually a preparation for a physical encounter.

Chapter 4

Robin sat and waited. The shuttle glided to a smooth soft landing in the docking bay. Robin approached the shuttle as its side door opened. A tall slender woman of about forty stepped out. She walked with an air of arrogance, but with an obvious naiveté of presence – Loggar seemed to be thinking about something other than the present day now.

Robin held out her hand. "Dr. Loggar."

Dr. Loggar nodded and shook Robin's hand briefly. "Are we ready to proceed Captain?"

"Yes," Robin answered, "As soon as the shuttlecraft is clear, we'll proceed to the coordinates you gave us."

"Thank you, Captain." Dr. Loggar hesitated a moment and cleared her throat. "Is Commander Blakemore, here?"

Robin smiled. She looked knowingly at Loggar and spoke slowly. "Yes, he's on the Top Deck."

Loggar breathed a small sigh and pursed her lips. "Good." She uttered softly. "Good."

Robin turned, "Please follow me Doctor. I'll show you to your quarters. The trip is going to take several days."

"Yes I know." Loggar said with a heavier and more audible sigh. "I know. So far away, but faster than the transports GRID Command give us."

"Yes, Cargonaughts."

Loggar nodded, "You understand then?"

"Yes, perfectly. I started my career on a Cargonaught, the Cargonaught Surprise. Slow as hell."

Robin giggled a secret inside joke to herself. "Shall we?"

Loggar nodded and followed Robin.

Robin remembered that the Surprise had a colorful history attached to it. She remembered one day while on deck watch when the ship came within visual range of a space station, the Comm. Officer from the station yelled over the audio band channel "Surprise! You made it!"

Dr. Loggar drifted in and out, her thoughts dancing back and forth to things serious and things whimsical. She shivered under a feeling of embarrassment.

Robin stared straight ahead. She knew that Dr. Loggar' asking for Sean was something more than professional. The other woman exuded nervousness and anticipation. Would Sean pick up on this? She shook her head. 'Probably not' was her thought, but then again, at times he was good at reading people. He would have possibly been in line for fleet captain if not for an incident a while ago.

"Something wrong, Captain?"

Robin looked at Loggar. "Sorry Doctor. I was drifting."

"Oh," was the simple reply. "How long will it actually take us?"

"Considering we have no GRID points out to where we're going, we have to do long jumps."

"Long jumps? I'm afraid I'm not too up on the terminology."

"Quite all right." Robin paused and considered her next words. "Think of it this way. Since we don't have any heavy field generators strategically placed, we have to create our own."

"Create our own?" Loggar frowned.

Robin nodded. "We have heavy gravity induction probes. We drop one off behind us, and then we literally ride a gravity wave generated by the probe."

Loggar frowned again. "I think I get it. Is there a way you could show me the process? It sounds fascinating. If my studies hadn't taken me to biology I probably would have fielded engineering."

"I have just the person to give you a," Robin paused, nodded, and grinned widely, "class in gravity induction."

"You do, whom may I ask is it?"

Robin stopped at a door. It slid opened and Robin walked in. Loggar followed. The room was spacious. The light was set at low luminosity to give it the effect of appearing much bigger than it actually was. "Lights on." Robin said. She turned to face Dr. Loggar. "Commander Blakemore himself will take up the task."

Loggar blushed and quickly turned away. "Thank you, Captain, b-but I couldn't possible take Commander Blakemore from his important duties."

"No problem at all, really Doctor. You're an honored guest here --."

"Oh, I do hate that." Loggar had recomposed herself and turned around.

"Could I be treated as a regular guest? Nothing fancy you know."

"No problem." Robin backed out the door. "I'll have Commander Blakemore look in on you later on, say in about three hours?"

"Thank you."

"If you have any questions, direct them to the computer," Robin pointed at a CRT, "and it'll answer your questions. If it can't then it will contact me or Commander Blakemore."

"Thank you, Captain."

Robin took a step, then stopped and looked at her

timepiece. "It's Afternoon's watch, now. How about dinner at Dog's watch six bells?"

Loggar blinked.

"7:00 pm, about six hours from now.

Loggar nodded.

"Relax and enjoy." Robin did a quick nod, turned and walked off. The door slid closed.

Loggar turned to a window that faced out. She watched a star glide by and marveled at its beautiful passage. "Computer?"

"Yes, Dr. Loggar?"

"May I have a glass of water?"

A panel in the wall slid out and produced a glass. "An outlet is over in the kitchenette, Dr. Loggar. A tap will provide you with whatever your taste desires."

Loggar walked over and retrieved the glass. "Thank you, Computer." She held the glass in her hand. A Battle cruiser was definitely much better than a Cargonaught. She mused about her first encounter with Commander Blakemore. 'A bath, I need a bath.' She spoke out loud.

"Water is being drawn in the tub, Dr. Loggar. Please specify temperature."

"Ah, 37 degrees, please."

The computer beeped.

Loggar looked around and spotted her luggage. How efficient this crew is. She hummed to herself as she opened up her suitcase and held up a plain, solid red dress. "You're going to have to get a more colorful selection of attire." She smiled and walked into the bathroom.

Betrayal is a very powerful and destructive weapon. Its use can do considerable damage to all those involved. But it's most powerful when used in secrecy. The damage is everlasting.

Chapter 5

Sean sat still. His face was held in rigid contemplation. He wondered about Dr. Loggar and her findings. He wondered about Robin Spaarin. And he wondered about himself. Had he been wrong in finger pointing at Robin? After the trial he waited for her. He was a bit confused over the whole proceedings. It was amazing. Robin had disobeyed a direct order to fire on an unarmed jump ship. He and Robin had been junior officers on the Dreadnaught Hornet, a massive ship the size of a small asteroid. The Hornet had just moved into a suspected enemy position. Her Commander, Admiral Quail, ordered the entire area sprayed with missiles and artillery. Several hours later the Hornet moved deeper in. Robin had been on deck watch. It was three bells first Dogwatch. Sean was early – just making the rounds. He was next up. Sensors picked up the ship first. Communications picked up the mayday. The message said that an Ambassador and his staff had escaped enemy fire, but the ship was crippled badly. Life-support was failing. Robin called general alert and informed the Admiral. The Admiral said it was a trick and ordered her to destroy the ship. His orders were not subject to debate. Robin clicked off. She informed Sean that she was going to disobey the order. The Hornet had no reason to fire upon an unarmed crippled ship with important delegates onboard. Sean agreed, but since his watch was coming up the responsibility would fall on his shoulders. Change of duty was a funny thing within GRID Command. Robin received the order first, but since she openly disobeyed it, the responsibility to carry it out would fall on Sean's shoulders. Instead, he also failed to obey those orders and further executed a plan of rescue, on his watch.

During the trial Admiral Quail had been relieved of space duty. He retired a month later. The Admiral had endangered the lives of civilians. He disregarded proper protocol and was irresponsible in the execution of his duties. Robin was seen as a hero. She received a slap on the wrist, a commendation and a promotion. Sean also received a commendation, but since the Admiral's family had been deeply entrenched within GRID Command he was reassigned, suspended for a month. He did not inform the Admiral of the conspiracy, thus exacting a harsher punishment, later given command of the Johnson but denied promotion pending further investigation. Everyone was stunned. After the rescue, Sean had discovered evidence that the Admiral knew the Ambassador was in the area. Sean also discovered that the Ambassador had been pressuring the Admiral to retire years earlier for a debacle that jeopardized an entire system. The Admiral refused and threatened the Ambassador. All the evidence Sean uncovered had been tossed out and made classified. Robin's defense team distanced themselves from his. There was rumor on secret meetings in the judge's chamber.

After the trial and fallout, Robin informed Sean that she would be moving on. She thanked him for a great time but that was all it was. She had her eye on something bigger, something better. Her phallic symbol was advancement. For a long time Sean had been confused. He figured she would eventually come around to his way of thinking. He was firm in his convictions. He knew he was right. Robin would realize the mistake she had made when she dumped him. Sean waited. Counting off the days, counting off the weeks, then, in frustratingly painful realization, he counted off the months. The pain and frustration didn't subside as a year went by, then another, and another. The memory just got easier to deal with. Only in his moments of lapse did the pain come back.

The Top Deck door opened, and Robin walked in.

Sean looked over and grudgingly got up. "All is well, Captain." He reported.

Robin looked around. Several stares quickly shifted back to control stations. Maybe I'll be accepted, someday. Robin thought. "Very well, number one." She immediately regretted saying it. Sean had been Commander of the Johnson for years and voicing his new title was at best an insult. Someday seemed like forever now.

Sean cringed, but he locked his gaze on Robin. 'You bitch!' was his only thought.

Robin ignored his discomfort and sat in the command chair. Sean was about to sit when Robin broke the silence. "Commander, Dr. Loggar requested that someone give her some guidance in understanding GRID traveling." Robin paused, waiting to see if Sean would pick up on the hint. He didn't, or wouldn't show that he did. "Please assist her in whatever she needs."

Sean gritted his teeth. He spoke is a slow and measured tone. "Am I relieved from standing duties?"

Robin reflected. "Yes, Commander Dawn may temporarily perform number one duties. I want you to personally see to her needs, she --"

"Begging the Captain's pardon," Sean started with that same slow measured tone, "but shouldn't a protocol officer be assigned to her?"

"Any other guest, yes. For Dr. Loggar, no. You will assist her. I told her that you will be calling on her in about three hours. Beside, this is a good excuse to find out why she asked for you specifically."

Sean sat in the number one chair and thought about it. "Very well, Captain."

Robin called over her shoulder, "Is the shuttle cleared?"

"Yes, ma'am" came a voice from behind.

"Mr. Kirkland, please give the Gallant's captain my compliments."

Kirkland typed on his keyboard and listened to his ear comm.

"Message sent, ma'am."

"Thank you," then, "Mr. Foster."

"Ready, ma'am."

"Good, you have the Doctor's coordinates?"

Mr. Foster nodded.

"Your staff has been instructed on how we are to proceed?"

"Yes, ma'am." The reply was curt and formal.

Robin punched the intercom button. "Now hear this, now hear this, prepare for long jumps. Prepare for long jumps." She pushed another button. "Dr. Loggar?"

After a few seconds pause, "Yes? Is that you Captain?"

"Yes it is. Please make yourself very comfortable. Each jump is extremely bumpy and rough the first hour."

"Thank you, Captain. I shall."

"Since you've never experienced long jumps, I'll leave a transmit only comm. to your room. If you get tired of listening, just ask the computer to disconnect."

"Thanks again, Captain, I do appreciate it."

Robin tapped out a few commands on the Command CRT. She turned her attention back to command. "Mr. Foster, please proceed."

Foster punched in several sequences of keys. "Aye, aye, ma'am. Coordinates locked in, computer has 'a confirm' panel is green, condition is green."

Sean typed out a command on his CRT. "Confirmed, ship status is green, condition is green. Ship is ready Captain."

Robin said, "Mr. Foster, bring Johnson along path. Start when ready."

"Aye, Aye, ma'am. Johnson is along path. Probe launch, three seconds. Stand-by."

The Johnson's main engines flared. The GRID ship banked away and headed off into the void. A small round object emerged from the hindquarter of the ship. It glowed with intense brightness not seen by mortal eyes. The hulking vessel pointed away from it would respond to the radiate energy it produced, energy creating a gravity wave strong enough for the vessel to surf its way into the under-folds of space and time. The Johnson's engines flared, the ship disappeared into the under-folds of the space-time continuum transcended distances too incredible to comprehend, too far to measure with mortal life spans.

A flight of imaginary fancy sprinkled with hopes of varied reality.

A gift is something that holds a surprise inside. Usually it is given between friends, family or intimates. It is a symbol that transcends mere simple feelings but speaks of an underlying strong bond. It's very much a surprise when one's enemy gives the gift.

Chapter 6

Dr. Loggar looked at the strange mix of colors outside her window. Weird shimmering patterns danced about. Her door chimed. She turned, "Enter." The door opened and the figure in the door way caught her breath. Loggar had forgotten that Sean Blakemore would call on her. He stood in the doorway, in the flesh, finally. She had waited a long time to meet him and here he was. She regained her composure. "Commander Blakemore. I'm so glad you can assist me."

Sean leaned in. He looked timidly to the sides, and then stepped inside fully. The door closed. "Then, I'm not disturbing you?"

Loggar walked over and extended her hand, her offering of friendship.

Sean accepted . . . and quickly held his surprise. Loggar fingered his palm!

"No, not at all, Commander. I do have to admit my awkward feelings in having to be instructed on the workings of GRID travel and by a Commander at that."

Sean smiled. That was a mouthful. "How so?"

She motioned them to the table. "One would think that being with GRID Command I would have picked up on how GRID travel is done." Sean shrugged, "Maybe, maybe not. I don't know anything about exobiology and anthropology myself."

Loggar laughed cutely and smiled wide. She looked into Sean's eyes for a moment. Trying to see what the window into his mind revealed. As a trained anthropologist she picked up on what Sean didn't say, didn't do.

Sean became uneasy. Loggar' stare was piercing. She locked gazes with him. "Ah, how should we start?" Sean mildly choked out, breaking the horrid fear that was creeping over him. If he didn't know better, he would swear that Dr. Loggar wanted to get to know him. Really get to know him. He glanced quickly at the dress she was wearing, bright Red. Odd for a scientist he supposed, but he approved. She looked nice for a scientist. He noticed her skin. It was smooth and flawless, no wrinkles or scars. And her eyes, those piercing gray eyes that had -- what in the hell was he thinking? She was a scientist, a very important scientist, maybe a bit nutty in thinking aliens lived out there, but nonetheless important. He did wonder at why she asked about him. What he had been thinking was out of the question. Robin would have a field day if she found out that a VIP from GRID Command had literally palmed him. He wiped the thought of her piercing gray eyes, the curvature of her form, and her nice legs --.

"How about the history." Loggar said, interrupting his thoughts.

Sean, you dog, he told himself, back to business. "The history, sure, good start."

Jealousy is an animal that roams freely and with many disguises. Its true form can be a complete contradiction of its perceived form. Jealousy, fear, anger, wonderment, amusement, all part of the same family tree. Different roots from the tree but part of the same family.

Chapter 7

Robin looked at the display readout for the third time. It said the same thing it did when she looked at it the two previous times. She sighed and looked at her timepiece. Sean and Dr. Loggar had missed dinner. Robin thought about calling them - to see if they had forgotten, but thought better of it. Suppose they were indisposed? She stared at the display a fourth time. Same thing, nothing.

"Computer?" She called out.

"Yes, Captain Spaarin?"

"Is it possible to check on Commander Blakemore and Dr. Loggar without them being notified?"

"Is this a priority override request, Captain?"

Robin paused and reflected for a bit. "No, I suppose not. Maybe they're still talking?"

"Unable to speculate without further inquiring."

"No, I suppose not. Forget I asked about checking on them Computer."

The computer beeped an acknowledgment.

Robin sat and wondered. This is what she had hoped for, wasn't it? The Doctor did specifically ask for him. Robin subconsciously bit the side of her middle finger. Years of such biting created a thick layer of skin. 'Am I jealous?' was the thought that rang through her mind. 'I like Sean, but I made my decision. But then again, do I feel guilty?' Robin sighed, pursed her lips, got up and straightened out her uniform. She purposefully walked out the room.

Sean lay on the couch with a glass of colored liquid on his chest. Dr. Loggar was hunched over a CRT gazing intensely at some readout.

"Sean," She called out, "is this to mean that the power output is proportionate to the mass?"

"Yeap." He got up and walked over to Loggar. Her glass was empty. "Shall I?"

She looked up and caught Sean smiling at her. A forgotten feeling almost welled up. "Oh, my beer. Please."

Sean took their glasses over to the tap. "Computer, Beer, please." When her glass was full, he drained his and filled it up. "Beer." He said handing the glass to her.

Loggar took a sip. "Is that why the ship transverses roughly the first hour?"

Sean looked at the readout and smiled, and whistled softly. "I never had a student like you before. No wonder GRID Command listens to you when you speak."

She shrugged, "Sometimes, sometimes not. I'm a little fortunate, though. Picking a field that is just starting to make some waves." She stared Sean in the eyes for a long time. The thing that amazed her was that he was staring back. His eyes were warm and delightful, if not a bit out of focus from the alcohol.

Sean couldn't believe he was falling for a scientist, especially a scientist as renowned as Dr. Loggar. He stirred a little and reluctantly moved his gaze over to the read out. He nodded, "Doc, you're right, that's why it's bumpy the first time . . . the first hour."

Robin stood outside the door to Dr. Loggar's room. She

listened, nothing. She pressed the chime button and waited.

The chime rang.

"Who could that be?" Loggar mused.

"Oops, I bet it's the Captain. We didn't exactly excuse ourselves from dinner. It's my fault."

"Dr. Loggar, Cmdr. Blakemore?" Robin's disembodied voice called out.

"Enter." Sean spoke and straightened himself for the stare. "I'm sorry Captain. I should have . . ."

Loggar interrupted, "Sean, I should be the one to apologize."

Robin silently worded 'Sean.'

"It is my fault Captain, you see, when I get interested in something, I become obsessed . . ."

Robin leaned forward.

Loggar's statement struck Robin as both amusing and disturbing. Loggar was obsessed with Sean. She wondered when she would tell him. She wondered if she would if either of them ever asked. ". . . I was just very interested. I hope I didn't get the Commander in trouble?"

"No, not at all Doctor. I did relieve Commander Blakemore from his temporary duties to help you. I should have reminded you about dinner."

"Is it too late? Dinner I mean." Loggar asked.

Sean replied, "No, we could have it in here or in the galley, The Johnson has 24 hour service."

Dr. Loggar ran her hand across her stomach. "I am a bit hungry and I suppose I should put something in my stomach besides adult beverage." She turned to Sean, "Commander, I don't suppose you could show me to the galley. I'm sure the food is much much better than from a Cargonaught."

Sean nodded, "Beggin' your Captain's permission," and enjoyed Robin's slight discomfort. He had a feeling that this particular exchange of words and set of happenstances was not boding well with her.

Robin nodded once, and watched as Loggar followed Sean down the corridor. The Doctor had used the word obsessed. Robin thought, 'Sean heard, I heard it, and the Doctor realized we both understood. Loggar is someone you should watch out for.'

They faded off in the distance giggling. Robin had never known Sean to giggle! The door hissed closed.

Robin turned to the CRT Dr. Loggar had been looking at. It displayed advanced formulas of GRID jumping and power conduction equations. She noticed two equations that didn't belong to GRID calculating. Several symbols were foreign, but don't scientists often invent new ways of saying the same thing?

Robin said, "Computer?"

"Yes, Captain Spaarin?"

"Copy Dr. Loggar's 'text' from this CRT to primary TEMP region."

"Done Captain, anything else?"

"No . . . yes! Priority override. Mask my request to copy Loggar's text to primary TEMP region."

The computer beeped an acknowledgment.

Robin looked around and noted the near full glass of beer and no-doubt Sean's glass of toxins he liked to drink. She walked out and the door hissed closed shutting out a scene that made Robin feel guilty, upset, angry, and scared.

The answer to a question comes in two fold; an answer given and the truth contained within the answer. Also, the question asked comes in two fold; the actual truth and a truth hoped for.

Chapter 8

The mess hall was near empty. Sean picked out a table. They sat for a second before an ensign walked over.

"Good evening, Sir, ma'am. May I get you something?"

Loggar leaned back holding her stomach, "A sandwich, turkey and cheese?"

The ensign smiled, 'This must be the Doctor?'

"One turkey and cheese sandwich, ma'am, and you, sir?"

"Clam Chowder, hot, please."

The ensign nodded, walked away.

Loggar leaned forward, "You have waiters?"

"So to speak, it's one of the many duties new ensigns and Non-commissioned Officers have to go through. A pay your dues thing."

"Oh, I see. This is Grid wide?"

Sean nodded and Loggar frowned.

Loggar had never considered the use of lower ranks duty structure. "Did you have to go through that when you first joined?"

Sean nodded, "Yeah, hated it too. I mostly did the recreational areas, but it's something you get used to. And when they pin that new strip or you get that shiny bar it makes a whole big difference." Sean noted the frown on her face. "I don't suppose exobiologists have to go through the same thing?"

"As a matter of fact, we do, except ours was doing research for the head staff, and carrying out the manual labor tasks. I guess it's a thing that is done everywhere. You know, we did all the background work while everyone else up front basked in the glory."

The ensign brought their order and left.

Sean ate his chowder as Loggar silently chewed her sandwich.

"Dr. Loggar, may I call you Kathy?"

Loggar almost choked on a halfway chewed bite. "Yes, please, I'm sorry. I never said you could?"

Sean smiled and slowly shook his head. She was looking quite lovely in that instance – caught off guard and being speechless. One of the most vocal voices of GRID Command choking on a sandwich because she forgot to say it was okay to get friendly. He saw her blush and stammer and it pleased him.

Loggar smiled back and brushed a strand of hair that fell in front of her eyes. She knew she blushed. She just about cursed herself for such a simple silly mistake as to not have Sean call her by her first name. She was about to go into a slight panic fit when she realized that Sean's smile was genuine. 'I'll be damn,' she thought, 'a real smile.'

Sean took a deep breath, "What are we going to find?"

Loggar paused. She wanted to be very careful about her wording. "Historical Alien life that has some commonality to prehistoric Earth."

"Historical? As in the past? Nothing now, the present?"

Loggar nodded, "Historical, written history, in this case, electronic written history." She wondered if he was going to ask, and it frightened her that she might answer him.

"I never really believed in Aliens. I figured with all this time out here we should have found some really good evidences or hints, or something and not just "eye-witnesses" from past records. It just smacked too much like science fiction."

Loggar giggled, she was a little relieved that Sean took this approach to squish his curiosity. She was certain he knew that she specifically asked for him. "I remember reading books about far off lands and adventures. My favorite series was the STAR WARS™ saga . . ."

"Star wars?" Sean blurted out.

Loggar nodded, "I always wanted to be like Princess Leia. I read all three hundred and twelve books.

Sean beamed, "Han Solo was my favorite. I read them all, too. Han and Leia married and had kids. . ." His voice trailed off.

Both paused for a second, looking into each other eyes. The second went into two seconds, then three. Sean coughed lightly into his hand. "I have to ask."

Loggar leaned forward, smiled and softly replied, "I know."

"Me, why me? I'm just a commander of a GRID ship. I don't, maybe I might now, believe in Aliens. I've gotten into trouble in the past but am good enough as a commander to walk away relatively clean."

Loggar pursed her lips, "Sean, may we leave and walk back to my room . . . or would you like to go to your room?"

Sean's swallow made a soft audible sound. "Either one, but if you want "real" privacy, then we should go to mine."

"Yours then."

They both got up and walked out. The rumors would make the rounds again. All crew knew that a GRID ship didn't travel on power alone, it traveled on gossip. And tonight the Johnson would travel far – some lucky person won the pool.

Robin stared at the equations on her CRT. They were the

same equations that Dr. Loggar had worked on. Robin doubted Sean had anything to do with them. She looked at another page. Each page gave her a strange sensation. "Computer?"

"Yes, Captain Spaarin, How may I help you?"

"What do you know about the 'Most High Goddess' order?"

Robin tensed for the second or two it took the Computer to answer.

"The Most High Goddess was an organization that briefly had political influence in the then state of California on the planet Earth during the first quarter of the twenty-first century. Toward the middle half of the century the Most High, as it was popularly called, gained further political power. Most High controlled most of the Americas, the western hemisphere of the planet Earth. Even though the South Americas had mainly been stapled on Catholicism it still retained, underground and behind closed doors, a communistic culture steeped in some paganism. Ironically, Wicca was mainly a European product, but the Latin continent embraced Wicca and Paganism as a natural extension of the homegrown consolidated Catholicism. During official and highly visible celebration the usual parade of worshiped saints and idols made the rounds. But in the afterhours of normal life the real zealous forms of worship took place. Wicca was among the most popular – not in European style, but Wicca nonetheless."

"Stop." Robin said then slowly spoke; making sure her question was valid. "What is the current state of the Most High Goddess?"

"The Most High Goddess is practiced by an obscure minority of individuals still living on Earth. There is also data, which suppose some off world locations practicing . . ."

Wrong answer, Robin thought, definitely the wrong

answer.

Sean walked over to the tap and filled Loggar's glass and his with a red substance. "I hope you like this."

Loggar took the glass and sniffed at the edge. "Sangria, Earth, 2212, Poluv Brothers."

"Right! And I thought you were just a beer drinker."

Loggar sipped at the red liquid. "I am, but I find time to drink other things besides beer and ale."

Sean took a swallow from his glass and sat on the opposite side of the couch.

"May I." Loggar said kicking off her shoes and leaning back.

"By all means, get completely comfortable." He took another swallow.

Loggar looked around and noted Sean's taste in décor. Sean liked early 19th century Japan. It wasn't surprising. Most Men in GRID Command had this thing about early Japan. It had something to do with being a warrior and samurai she guessed. She noted the plain dark wood lines throughout the room, mostly vertical with a few horizontal beams placed in logically assumed places. Very pleasing to the eye, she told herself, very pleasing. She also noted the various swords on the wall and a collection of a handful of guns. Sean like weapons she decided. She wondered if he could use any of them but decided he had to. He seemed to be the type of man who would display what he was most comfortable with. She would ask him later about his collection. "Sean, why you?"

"Yes, I'm one of many in the GRID."

"What we discovered on the planet is one reason why you had been asked for." Loggar moved closer to Sean. "Why I asked for you." She inched closer.

Sean slipped off his shoes and inched toward the center of

the couch. "You know, I didn't know anything about you until Robin, I mean Captain Spaarin told me you asked for me . . ."

Loggar nodded, encouraging Sean to continue.

". . . You have a lot of clout, you're brilliant, which I just really found out, and you're different."

"Different." Loggar laughed out loud. She drained her glass. "May I?" She indicated toward Sean's near full glass.

He drained it and handed it to her.

Loggar walked both over to the tap. She walked like a woman trying to be sexy, but not drunk. The dress felt restrictive. She wanted to remove it. "Computer, more of that nice wine."

"Yes, Dr. Loggar."

Sean watched her with a growing arousal. He looked at the way the dress clung to her body, the way her calves were shaped, the way her hair flowed down her shoulders. Sean realized he was falling for the Doctor. The consequences were no doubt going to be severe.

"Here, Sean."

Sean took the glass and drank. He noted Loggar's chest rising and falling rapidly. He wondered what her breast really looked like. Her nipples pressed against the fabric. He shifted hoping that his arousal was not too revealing.

Loggar sat a hands breadth away. "Yes, I'm a lot of things and different is one of them."

"I believe you, Kathy."

She smiled.

Sean liked that.

"Sean, what we found on the planet was fantastic. It opens up another type of speculation about the origins of the Human species."

Sean leaned slightly toward her. "Not that we were placed here by Alien spin?"

"No, not exactly, but it will show that we have a common lineage and . . . "

Sean sat straight, "Lineage?"

Kathy looked wide-eyed and nodded. 'Damn the moment had been blown.' She looked at Sean to see how astute he was.

Sean's face played an interesting range of emotions and thoughts. "Kathy, I am not an Alien. Nor do I believe in 'em. I'll just have to see the proof. But that still doesn't answer my question."

Kathy laughed softly. "Such a bright man." She leaned into Sean's ear. "I want you to believe, I want you to see, I want you to know, trust me when I say you have to see for yourself."

Sean turned his head toward Kathy's voice and found her lips. He kissed them with a feeling he thought no other woman could draw out. She returned the kiss.

He didn't know what Kathy was feeling at this moment – he didn't care, but he knew one thing. A thing that was surely dangerous if not done right. Sean was falling in love.

Robin glanced into the CRT. It all came together. GRID Command placing her in charge, which she believed was orchestrated from another influential source, Dr. Loggar asking for Sean for unknown reasons, and Dr. Loggar's equation. Robin shuddered. This was the future she said. This is an advanced ship, with a collimation of Earth's technical genius. The Human species colonized hundreds of planets, soon to be thousands of planets, but this thing, this thing on the screen. Robin looked for the hundredth time. She knew what it meant. She herself was from the Most High Goddess, but the surprising part to learn was Dr. Loggar was also from the order. An order that has been able to maintain secrecy for a long time. Not overt secrecy, but able to maintain a very low profile in everyday walks of life. And that was hard in GRID society.

"Computer, display the planet we're going to."

The image replaced the equations and notes. "Computer, a close-up of the excavation site."

"That image has not yet been supplied, Captain Spaarin."

No matter, she thought, it just doesn't matter now. She read in the report of possible 'Wicca-like' symbols. She read the speculative answer that the civilization that once lived on the planet had possibly practiced a form of witchcraft, but that was only speculation. It's always speculation when you deal with the archaeological records of the past. But, Dr. Loggar is the Most High Goddess. Then she thought of Sean. He was going to get involved. My God! Oh, Sean I am so sorry, forgive me.

"Computer, where is Dr. Loggar?"

"Dr. Loggar is currently in Cmdr. Blakemore's quarters. Shall I call her?"

Oh dear no! "No, never mind." Oh Sean, forgive me. You are about to become something you thought I made you. You are about to become a pawn.

Good love is a mutual bond between two consenting individuals. The side looks and the quick smile speaks volumes oblivious to uninterested parties. Lovers dance in tune to the mutual drumbeat of each other's heart. Lovers abate the existence of a bland world restricted by the confines of plain regular familiarity of simple congeniality. Lovers make their own rules.

Chapter 9

Sean lay staring up at the ceiling. He glanced over and saw Kathy sleeping silently next to him. To his surprise Kathy was a reckless lover. She threw herself into a wild abandonment and let Sean's lust consume the both of them. He tasted, kissed, licked and loved every square inch of her body. She let him. In return she gave Sean as methodical a sensual pleasing. They both threw caution to the wind and made love as if they would never be able to make love again. It was a kind of passionate and consuming thing that lovers destined to be forever parted or forever changed would engage in.

He slowly got out of bed and walked into the bathroom. "Lights," he whispered. The door hissed closed behind him. He looked into the mirror. His stare was deep and intense. He looked side to side and frowned and said to the image before him. "I don't know how I feel about you now. I think you're still a bastard, and a fool, and . . . I don't know what, but watch yourself Sean, real closely." He used the bathroom and allowed his thoughts to drift.

Kathy woke up when she heard Sean utter 'Lights.' The door closed and she no longer heard him. Sean, she decided, was one hell of a lover. He had a type of aggressiveness the men in the High Order didn't have.   He was an outsider, an important outsider, but still an outsider. She rolled over and found his scent on the pillow. It was him alright. He was the one. She was certain. She realized, with relief, that Sean still didn't know why him. He had to see for himself that was all. He accepted that answer and it was good.

The door to the bathroom opened up and Sean walked out. He saw Kathy looking at him. "Did I wake you?"

She patted the covers, "No, I was just thinking of you."

He sat down and gave her a nice warm kiss and hug. "I hope my position as a Commander doesn't compromise your position?"

She kissed him back and ran her fingers down his thigh. "No, not at all, Sean. You are . . . good, and your position as a Commander doesn't change what I'm feeling for you. I'm civilian, and I can see anyone I want. Period."

Sean smiled not really knowing why. He kissed her again. "Feeling okay?"

She ran her fingers down the inside on his leg, "Feeling okay."

They made love again, even more aggressively than before.

Robin tossed and turned that night.   Her sleep was punctuated by a particularly bad dream. It was a dream where Sean was being dangled over a fire pit. She called out to him. Robin reached out but moved further away until he was just a spot. Oh Sean, forgive me. I didn't know.

"My enemy is not always the enemy of my friend." An enemy is not necessarily an adversary that pits one against a moral or ethical dilemma. Enemies come in many guises. Some are actually saints, survivors and saviors.

Chapter 10

Robin arose early, got dressed and headed for Top Deck. Sean was already there. A habit he developed early in his career.

Sean turned toward the sound of the elevator door opening, "Captain." He said smiling.

Smiling? Sean is smiling she told herself. Maybe the dream was only that, just a dream. Maybe Sean is not a pawn? She dismissed the idea. Sean didn't know the truth or was oblivious to the end result of the truth. Robin decided she would be extremely careful around Dr. Loggar, period.

Robin nodded to Sean, "Just making early rounds, Commander."

"Yes, ma'am." He said.

"How's your pupil, Dr. Loggar?"

"Fine, Captain, just fine. Dr. Loggar is currently sleeping at the moment, but we have another session scheduled at two bells."

Robin stared for a second at Sean, looking to see what he really meant.

"Very well, Commander. I'll stroll the decks then, continue the command until 10 minutes before two bells."

"Yes, ma'am." He said and redirected his attention to his CRT.

Robin backed out into the elevator. The elevator door closed. "Personnel deck," Robin said.

The elevator started.

Robin allowed her thoughts to wander about nothing in particular. She just let them flow into her. Some disturbing - Loggar as the Most High. Others worse - Sean a puppet, if not herself.

The elevator stopped. Robin walked out down the corridor. She stopped in front of the Commander's room. She touched the chime and waited. Several seconds later a voice came through.

"Yes?" Said the disembodied voice of Loggar.

Robin cleared her throat, "Doctor Loggar, this is Captain Spaarin, may I have a word with you?"

Loggar said, "One moment, please." She scrambled out of bed. Her dress lay crumpled on the floor. It had a spot on it. Loggar bit her lip and declared, "I can't wear this in public." She asked the computer, "Does Sean have anything I can wear suitable to receive a guest?"

The computer beeped and replied, "Dresser, top drawer, second layer, an old pull over shirt, length to your mid-thigh."

Loggar hurried to the dresser and followed the computers instructions. Yes, a tan pull over shirt that would fit perfectly. As Loggar put it on she realized that the pull over shirt was not meant for Sean. She walked over to the door and hit the open button. The moment the door opened and she saw the look on Robin's face she realized who the shirt's owner actually was.

Robin waited about three minutes before the door suddenly opened. Loggar stood in the doorway with a pained look on her face. Robin's face contorted, stunned for a second. Then recovered a stoic front.

Both women realized the shirt belonged to Robin. In the opened doorway both women stared into each other's eyes for a full two heartbeats. Loggar looked down, "Captain . . . please come in."

Robin stepped in. The situation was obviously awkward. "Doctor . . ."

"Captain . . ."

They both paused. The door slid shut.

A second ticked by, then another one. A full five seconds ticked along. Loggar was the first speak.

"Captain, I am sorry, I didn't realize the shirt belonged to you.

Robin swallowed. "No need to be sorry. It was something we didn't exactly advertise. I am surprised Sean kept the damn thing," then, "it does look good on you."

Loggar blushed and motioned Robin to the couch.

They both sat.

"Captain . . ."

Robin interrupted, "Might as well call me 'Robin', we have two things in common."

Loggar relaxed a bit and smiled slightly. "Okay, Robin. And, of course you may call me by my first name – private and public." She cleared her throat, "as you might have guessed Sean and I slept together."

Robin listened. Loggar admitting that she and Sean spent some time together stirred emotions she had thought buried long ago.

Loggar looked Robin in her eyes, "You still care for him? Don't you?"

Robin held her breath and counted to five before answering. "Maybe, our breakup was a bit awkward."

Loggar said, "Those following the court-martial had mixed feelings over it."

Robin shook herself at Loggar's statement. "Pardon me?"

Loggar repeated, "Those following the court-martial had mixed feelings over it."

"What do you mean?"

"Admiral Quail has family members in the Most High Goddess."

Robin thought a moment about that declaration. Quail had been disgraced by her and Sean disobeying orders. He was an old Admiral who should have retired a decade earlier. During the trial Quail talked to himself, slept and seemed to not be totally together. It was a tense and sometimes embarrassing scene. In the end it had puzzled her why she got the promotion and Sean didn't. He was senior to her by two years. It was Sean's watch that executed the rescue and open defiance. She felt uneasy during the entire proceedings. Sean's lawyers skillfully maneuvered the Prosecution in admitting that the Admiral had killed innocent personnel and endangered several more. It was strange that the judge dismissed the jury before the closing statements were made, but in GRID law a judge has the authority to excuse the jury if said judge thought the defendant may receive unfair sentencing. It was to everyone's astounding disbelief that the judge declared that justice had to be served and that a jury decision was not in the interest of justice. The judge went on about the sanctimony of duty and loyalty and trust and honor and responsibility. He went on that even though Robin had first disobeyed the order it was Sean's act that excused her from the ultimate responsibility of her actions. It was his watch. The courtroom exploded in shouts and exclamations. The judge warned that another outburst would bring a contempt of court to all people identified. The room fell silent. Then the judge went on about Robin and Sean saving lives, but they had also disobeyed an order. Justice had to be served. Because Sean had assumed full responsibility he had to be made the example. So the court ruled that Robin was innocent, under extraordinary circumstances and Sean was guilty, under the same extraordinary circumstances. The courtroom went wild and the contempt of court order fell on many heads. A week later, the judge quietly retired, the day before the Admiral retired. Robin was transferred and Sean was given a month suspension – no pay and that the decision would be a permanent part of his record.

Robin thought about what Loggar said. 'Admiral Quail has family members in the Most High Goddess.' That statement alone had more weight and depth than everything Robin could have fathomed in a lifetime. She was saved because she belonged to an Elite group. She was part of a conspiracy.

Several seconds ticked by. Robin's mind raced, 'My Goddess! I am part of this.' "

"Kathy," Robin started, "Sean hates me."

Loggar was taken aback. "Really?"

"Really." Robin's shoulders drooped. She nodded, "Yes, he hates me because I had distanced myself from him during the trials. And I did. My lawyer told me that it would be in my best interest to not associate myself with him."

Loggar cursed herself. 'What had I done?' It was on Loggar's word that Robin got away clean. To tell Robin or to shut up was the decision now. Her mind raced. 'If Sean ever found out I would lose him.' She cleared her throat. "Robin, you mustn't be too hard on yourself. The Most High Council agreed with the court. Unfortunately, I didn't know Sean; otherwise I would have tried my best to help him." And this was true, but during the proceedings Loggar was told that Robin was a Most High member and the other was not. Sean's name was never mentioned. The Most High takes care of their own; outsiders are left to fend for what they can.

After several seconds of silence Robin said, "I'm sorry to have disturbed you High Goddess . . . Kathy, I just wanted to know."

Loggar squeezed Robin in a strong embrace and whispered

in her ear, "I care for Sean, believe me, and from now on I will do what I can to make things right." She then kissed Robin on the cheek and briefly, if a bit firmly, on the lips, pulled away and stared her in the eyes. "Sean will be okay."

Robin nodded and her eyes welled with tears, but she held them from flowing and told herself that she was not gonna cry. She got up and straightened her uniform.

She said her goodbye and left.

Loggar sat on the couch for a moment, deep in thought. She got up and walked over to the desk. She sat down and pressed the Comm. button. "Is this . . . Top Deck?"

A disembodied voice replied, "Yes, ma'am, this is Mr. Devian speaking. How may I help you?"

Loggar smiled. She cleared her throat briefly, "Could you send a message, top priority, standard encryption, multiple addresses?"

"Yes, ma'am. Just type the message at your desk console, enter the addresses or names of the individuals to receive the message and tap on the Comm. Deck icon. I'll get it and give it immediate attention."

"How long will it take to reach Earth?"

"I'll have to tight beam it to the nearest beacon, one moment please."

Loggar held her breath and waited.

"About six hours. Any faster would possibly degrade the signal a bit."

"Thank you Mr. Devian. Expect my message in a few minutes."

"Yes, ma'am. Anything else I may be able to help you with?"

"Not at the moment. Thank you very much."

"You're welcome, ma'am." The channeled clicked off.

Loggar sat at the console and tapped the screen a few times. She entered a one-line message and tapped the Comm.

Deck icon.

She sat back pleased with herself. She told Robin 'Sean will be okay.' She meant it and this was part of it.

Loggar heard an audible beep on the console. She tapped the Comm. Receive button. "Yes?"

"Ma'am, it's me Mr. Devian. Message has been sent. Would you like me to signal you when a reply comes in?"

Loggar almost giggled, "Yes, please!"

"Very well, ma'am. I'll let you know a reply is waiting in *your* console Inbox as soon as it comes in. You'll have to enter you service number to read the message." He stressed 'your inbox.'

"Thank you so much, Mr. Devian. I wasn't quite thinking you know. Was it okay that I sent it from the Commander's desk?"

"Absolutely, ma'am. You're VIP. Trust me. I would know if it was not okay."

"Thank you again. Oh, one last question."

"Yes?"

"Do you know who Gaia is?"

There was a two second pause, then, "Yes, High Goddess, I do."

Loggar smiled and tears nearly welled up in her eyes. "Thank you Mr. Devian."

"You're welcome, ma'am." The channel closed.

Loggar walked to the couch and sat. "Computer? Do you have the transcript to the Admiral Quail, Blakemore, and Spaarin Trial?"

The computer beeped. "Replay of the entire trial or the condensed narrative form?"

"How long are they?"

"The entire trial recording is 17,283 minutes 37 seconds. The condensed form is 35 minutes."

"Dim the lights and play the condensed form."

The lights dimmed and Loggar relaxed on the couch.

The computer read and she listened to it. She smiled to herself thinking that what she did was going to, hopefully, set a few things right.

Within the half hour, the crew had two additional pools circulating.

Happenstance is the blending of circumstances – the occurrences of things happening outside one's control and happenings – things occurring with an unknown purpose. One word or phrase can set into motion a whole orchestra of events. On the inside of the tank, the fish know nothing except an inwardly bent horizon that is very short and that food appears from the surface.

Chapter 11

Robin sat watch on the bridge. She relaxed in so much as she dared. 'Necron', the planet, as it was named in the reports was coming within viewing range. "Forward viewer on, maximum magnification, please." Robin ordered.

"Aye, ma'am, maximum magnification." Mr. Foster said from helm's position.

'Necron' hung silently at the upper right edge of the screen. Mr. Foster adjusted the Johnson's position to place Necron dead center. It was featureless against a black background.

"Range, Mr. Foster?"

Foster typed briefly on his keypad, "Approximately 600,000,000 kilometers, Captain. Closing in at sub-light 7."

Dr. Loggar had placed herself in the observer's seat on the bridge. She held her breath as she witnessed Necron painfully and slowly grow larger.

Robin looked up to Loggar. "Well, Doctor. There it is."

Loggar nodded, "Yes, there it is." Then, "Are we in communication range?"

Kirkland spoke out, "Maybe a little too far. We could try

it, Captain. We might get a response if the excavation team has good comm. equipment."

Robin said, "Well, Doctor Loggar? We're about another 17 hours away travel time and about half an hour communication lag time?"

"Half-an-hour?"

Robin shrugged, "No GRID points to accelerate communication. We're on standard TF out here."

Loggar thought for a second, "Silly of me. I should have known. Could you send then a greeting telling them all is well?"

Robin nodded. "Mr. Kirkland, send my compliments to the Captain of the Lightstar with a greeting to both her and the excavation team. Add Doctor Loggar's 'All is well' please."

Kirkland nodded and started typing on his keypad. He looked up the Comm. officer of the Lightstar. It was a fellow class graduate. Kirkland keyed in a personal greeting as well.

> *Captain of the Johnson sends compliments to the Captain of the Lightstar. Dr. Loggar messages the Excav team all is well.*
>
> *Signed Comm. Kirkland.*
> **** Hey Davis, you on duty now? Kirkland****

"Done Captain."

Loggar smiled, "Thank you, Captain. I appreciate it." She got up and walked toward the lift and stopped. "Captain, could I see you some time later on, like after your shift?"

"Six hours fine, Doctor?"

"Yes, perfect" Loggar said as she stepped into lift and disappeared.

Robin thought with trepidation that Loggar was going to tell her something more about the mission, or worst yet, ask her for something that wasn't completely GRID duty. Robin sank deeper into her chair and looked at Necron. She thought how appropriate the name just might fit the planet. Earlier the Doctor had given her a data tape that revealed a little more information then GRID Command had. Loggar had said it was 'superfluous information that needs to be refined.' The data that Loggar had allowed Robin to view revealed a map of an area that was previously unknown. The Doctor herself had discovered it days before she left for GRID Command. This new location was a room that held a statue in its center. The statue was made of different types of layered metal. Its purpose was unknown at the time she left, but there was a connection between her request for Sean and the possible function of the statue. Necron, the dead, maybe most appropriate, indeed.

Freewill is but a phrase to those wishing to express a choice over an existence of happenstance. The truth is; life is but cause and effect. Freewill may play a role in being a participant in the situation as it unfolds, but when all cards are placed on the table there is only one truth: You are born and you die – where is the freewill in that?

Chapter 12

Ted Randals considered himself lucky. He had a great job, great benefits, great pay and it was something he enjoyed doing. Dr. Loggar was a brilliant archaeologist. And her theories about alien life developing in totally alien environments were absolutely stunning. She was high up in GRID Command, the High Goddess and very pretty. A rarity in a dirty field which aged people too rapidly. Ted had fantasized about her on numerous occasions. She embodied a kind of eroticism and sensuality that only a woman of her age can produce. She had power, money, influence, respect, and droves of young and old men clawing to be in her bed. She was his perfect wet dream incarnate. When she asked him to join the expedition to Necron he had almost fainted. He answered with. "Not yes, but hell yes!" 13 months later, he was still awed about all the things discovered on Necron. Just yesterday, Ted was thinking about the chamber found just before Loggar left for Earth. Everyone was excited about the find. It was amazing.

Herbert "Herb" Johnson, the team mathematician - magician to most, came storming in waving a hand full of papers. "God damn those fellows!" He shouted. Ted had been reviewing plans to open a new section the scopes had picked up. "Those fellows toy with me." Herb was dressed in an old olive drab military jumpsuit that was a size too small. It was his favorite choice of attire - secretly the rest of the team figured Herb wanted to be a soldier or something. Only Ted, possibly Dr. Loggar, knew that Herb had a weak heart, too weak for the military but strong enough not to be replaced.

Ted had said, "Herb, now what?"

Herb sat his 118 kilo frame down next to Ted's desk. "Those fellows! They give me simple things to tease me, then when I figured I got a handle on the math they drop a bomb."

Ted stared at Herb. He was waiting for the shoe to drop.

"Here, look at this and tell me what you think." Herb said, and walked away. Ted now sat looking at the papers Herb had given him. He saw a lot of equations - mostly meaningless to him, but he looked at it anyway. He knew Herb would ask did he read them. Ted would say 'of course.' at which Herb would say, 'what line contains the formula for such and such then?'

If Ted couldn't remember, Herb would lay a verbal assault as if his feelings had been deeply hurt and this outburst of vehement verbosity was the only way to ease his bruised feelings.

Ted was used to it now and played the game. Besides, Ted thought, 'Herb always teaches me something and I like that.'

On the last page of the papers was scribbled an equation which Ted recognized to be a GRID equation. Next to it was some strange symbols that were circled. Just next to that were the words. 'A modified equivalent.'

"Goddess." Ted whispered, "They had GRID travel!"

That day, Randals walked the halls on the excavated site. It was magnificent to be in the presence of such marvel.

Randals often walked the halls before he would go to bed. He wanted the images to be fresh in his mind when he finally closed his eyes. He wanted his subconscious mind to use recent images presented in front of him. He was awed.

That was Yesterday.

Ted sat himself down this day to consider all the things that developed. The Electronics team discovered a new power line last night. It was active. The report said that the line was feeding power to a new section that had been previously unknown. Goddess! Ted thought, so what is new? At that moment Herb stormed in with papers in hand. "Had time to think about what we talked about?"

Ted nodded.

"Good," Herb said dropping himself down in the chair. "Here's another thing to think about."

Ted took a single sheet of paper that was passed to him. He read it and looked up.

Herb smiled and said, "Yes."

Ted read it again "Are you sure?"

Herb chuckled, "You damn right I'm sure. They had time travel and I'm sure they visited us." Herb sat back and the chair creaked. "So with all this in mind boys and gins, we ask the ultimate question?"

Ted thought for a moment, asked, "What did the guys in chronology say about this area?"

"They think that the area has only been abandoned for fifty years. Count that! Only fifty short years. I was planned and your daddy just had his first wet dream."

Ted ignore that last remark. Herb had no way of knowing when his father had a wet dream, if ever! "Where are they? Is that the question you want me to ask?"

Herb pursed his lips, "You've played this game before?"

"Only with you."

"Ha-ha, you comedian you. Yes that was the question I

was thinking."

Ted smiled.   He got Herb this time.

"Ted, my good man, not only did these people have a grid system, they also had a form of GRIDless travel."

"What?"

"They had a warp drive like system.   Not only is it possible, it's fantastic." Herb leaned forward.   "With a little modification, we could have Warp capability too. That's how they traveled in time! Think of the possibilities. Time travel!"

Ted leaned further back in his chair. 'Time travel? Warp Drive?' He leaned forward. "What else did you discover?"

Herb chuckled, "A little behind on the reports are we?"

"Well, it is a lot, and I'm not Loggar, I still have to do her job and mine's. You aren't the only one who gives me reports, but you know this."

Herb chuckled louder, "Aren't we so lucky."

"Just tell me will ya."

"Okay, okay." Herb paused for all of three seconds. "They wanted us to find this place and learn as much as possible."

Ted blinked several times and puffed out, "Yeah right." He almost wanted to laugh in Herb face. 'What a silly idea' he thought. "How do you know that?"

"I was down talking to Milkens . . ."

"Milkens?"

"One of the lowly tech folks you people in admin tend to forget."

Ted scowled and cleared his throat. "I know who Milkens is."

Milkens told me he thought it interesting that all the computer and electronic equipment had multiple port configurations."

Ted frowned.

"They had different output and input connectors . . ."

"Ah!"

"Yes, each port is a duplicate with a different set of connecting criterion."

"Maybe, they used different devices for . . ." Ted began.

Herb interrupted, "Please, Mr. Administration, think about it. Each device had multiple port configurations, each one had a diagram showing voltage, well, their symbol for voltage, and each one was connected in parallel. They wanted us to figure out what was going on. And I'll tell you another thing. Most of the equations I've found were accompanied by more and more progressively simpler equations."

"What?"

"That's what I thought. I'd get an equation dealing with logarithms with five simpler, long-winded examples. At first I thought it was just scratch work. But I kept seeing it in one and two term formulas. When you see x raised to the 2nd in an equation, then you find $(x)(x)$ next to it you begin to wonder."

Ted sifted through the stack of papers.

Herb lean forward, "You know something, else?"

Ted stopped. "What?"

"This is only a feeling. But when you add up all the stuff about multi-port configuration, line power feeds, and simplified math equations you come to one conclusion."

"And that is?" Ted suddenly had enough of Herb and he wish he would get to the point.

"We were expected!"

The entities moved at a satisfactory rate, Agegi thought. It had been a mere 30 cycles since the Elders left, leaving him and the others in wait. Agegi saw the entities were smart, not intelligent but smart. They figured things out with some thinking.

He focused on two in particular; the other one he used to follow had left. The thin one remained. Agegi knew that the other was in charge and that this thin one was in charge until the other one returned. He listened to them talk. A tongue that was at first difficult to follow, but some words were surprisingly similar to the old language.

The funny shaped one leaned forward and said, "You know something, else?"

The thin one stopped touching the thin pieces of writing surface.

"What?"

"We were expected!"

The thin one held its breath.

And if Agegi could have laughed he would have.

Exchanges between two individuals can be both satisfying and rewarding. Habermas said that in order for involved parties to come away in a win-win situation, all parties must come to the table in good faith. They must be willing to acknowledge that everyone else has equal concerns and pressing issues. If not then they are just wasting one another's time.

Chapter 13

Sean approached the VIP room. He had a long thin box under his arm. "Kathy?" Sean said. He was about to turn and walk away when the door opened. Loggar was dressed casual attire: a t-shirt and Levi's.

Sean marveled at how the jeans clung to her legs and hips. "Are those Levi's? Real jeans?"

Loggar smiled. "Yes, they are? You like them?" Her voice took on a girlish hint.

Sean stepped closer, smiled. "I do." He moved closer. "They look . . . nice on you. Is that what Archaeologist wear on the dig?"

"This one does, and sometimes off." Loggar looked down and spotted the long thin box Sean had been holding.

"A box?"

Sean smiled and handed it to her. "Yeah, it's for you."

She took the box and peered deeply into Sean's eyes. She knew Sean felt something for her. She had hoped it was love, though lust would be enough for now. Then she felt guilty at what might happen to him. She really didn't know how all this was going to play out. She just wished, hoped really, that it would all work out in the end.

"Hey, what's the matter?" Sean asked moving closer. He placed a hand on her chin and kissed her on the cheek. "You don't want the gift?"

She opened it. A single blue rose filled the box. Loggar's eyes welled with tears. "Sean, a 'blue' rose. Isn't this rare?"

"Yes, it is. And unfortunately it'll die in a week. But unlike this rose, I hope that you and I will continue?" Then he quickly added. "I mean, I know we have jobs that take us far away, but if we're together, we could, you know . . . damn!"

"What?"

Sean sighed, "I'm sounding like some fool . . ."

"Sean, you're not."

"Kathy, I like you a lot. I mean, shit. I'm so worried that I'm not. . ." Sean tried again and Loggar waited patiently, "I love you! And I'm scared."

Loggar sat with a perplexed look on her face. She thought about the encounter her and Robin had earlier. It was good that they could talk, though Loggar felt that Robin had held back because she was talking to the High Goddess. Loggar got that a lot.

Sean saw the look and felt sick to his stomach. He blew it, plain and simple. He made such a damn fool of himself.

Loggar placed a hand on his cheek, "That was so sweet Sean, thank you for the Rose." She kissed him on the cheek. "And thank you for your honesty." She kissed him on the lips. "I love you, too." She kissed him again and this time it was passionate.

They made love that hour – passionate, reckless, uninhibited. Both were consumed by a thirst that neither alone could satisfy. It took both to fill their hunger's desire. Sean came twice. Kathy lost count after five.

Ted snapped out of the daze he was in., "Where did you get that idea? And if we were expected, by whom?"

Herb sat back in the chair. He took out a watch. It was connected to a long silver chain; it was a gift from the University. "I don't know, maybe the statue." He finally said.

Ted glared at him, "Herb, you like wasting my time don't you?"

"You don't believe me?"

"No. I don't."

Herb got up and started for the door. "You know, Ted?"

Ted had placed his head back in his paperwork. "What?" He said not looking up. "Is it something I don't know or need you to show me?"

"Probably both, you're a shit." Herb walked out leaving Ted to consider his words.

Agegi listened to the conversation with deep satisfaction. Ted was the one he would pick. He watched as Herb walked out. He wished that things would happen soon and that he would be free again. But then again, he had only been in wait for 30 cycles. No matter, freedom was near, and with freedom came the ability to control, conquer and destroy! This time around glory would be his.

Sometimes, goals get in the way of feelings and a person sometimes forgets what was originally important. It is a point of view whether it is true or not true. Paradigms come in all flavors. If you don't like one, pick another.

Chapter 14

Sean sat in the XO chair and waited. Robin sat in the Commander's chair, back straight, flush to the rest. She keyed in a command and looked up. Dr. Loggar sat in the observer chair that was over to the left corner of the bridge.

"Dr. Loggar" Robin said. "We're within real-time communication range. The Lightstar set up a GRID comm. line for communication. Shall we contact the base?"

Loggar thought for a bit, "Captain, we can try. What time is it down there?"

Robin glanced at Mr. Kirkland.

Kirkland keyed in a command to the Lightstar. "It is six bells first watch, 2300 hours base time, ma'am."

Robin looked toward Loggar.

"Let's see, Herb should be doing watch about now. Okay Captain, can we do voice?"

"Kirkland," Robin began, "Give me a tight beam to the Lightstar and relay it to the base. Voice to voice."

"Aye, ma'am."

After a second, Robin said, "Necron base, this is the GRID ship Johnson, Captain Spaarin speaking. We have Dr. Loggar with us. Requesting voice communication, over."

They waited.

Herb sat down at the main computer console. He had been trying to find proof about his hunch. Ted Randals he knew would always be a lap dog and an anal retentive mamma's boy. He had been Loggar's favorite from the start. He hadn't really figured out why. He knew they weren't 'doing' each other. Maybe it was this mother-son thing that Loggar was going through. He knew she would snap out of it eventually and see Randals for the dumb shit he really was. It was just a matter of time.

"Okay, Mr. Computer, let's see what you've found today?" Herb said out loud to himself. It was 2300 hours and he was basically alone in the main core. Most of the admin-types were asleep as well as the head staff members of each department. Occasionally a tech-type would find his way into the main core looking to query the computer about something. They would make small talk for a bit then they would leave, off to do their tech stuff. Herb only really liked two people. Loggar his boss, and Milkens in electronics, the only true genius beside himself. He typed in a command. The computer sat for a minute and responded with 'negative.'

"Shit." Herb exclaimed. "Goddamn piece of crap, give you a zettabyte of memory and what do you get? A system that forgets . . ."

Just then . . .

"Necron base, this is the GRID ship Johnson, Captain Spaarin speaking. We have Dr. Loggar with us. Requesting voice communication, over."

Different voice, Herb thought, He sat just for a moment. 'Let them think we're busy down here,' he thought. He sat back and entered a new command. This time it would not only trace the power feed into the new chamber, but it will send a carrier pulse on the signal enabling him to do a query on voltage spikes.

"Necron base, this is the GRID Ship Johnson, Captain

Spaarin speaking. We have Dr. Loggar with us. Requesting voice communication, over for the second time."

Herb waited three seconds. "Hello, GRID Ship Johnson, this is Necron base. Herb speaking. In a brief form of an old Earth greeting dating back to the 20th century, 'Howdy, Y'all!'

Robin listened to the, 'Howdy, Y'all' and turned to Loggar.

Loggar shrugged and said, "It's Herb, kind of a different personality, brilliant mind, but a loose stereotypical nerd. You'd have to get to know him to really like him. May I?"

Robin nodded at Kirkland.

Kirkland keyed in the command for channel opened and nodded back.

Robin silently worded 'okay' to Loggar.

"Herb, is that you?"

"Hey, Dr. Loggar, nice to hear from you. We got a lot of new things to show you. Your boy, I mean, Randals has been running things surprisingly smooth down here. When you arriving?"

Loggar looked at Robin who looked at Sean who looked at Foster.

Foster said, "Two hours ten minutes."

"Got that Herb?"

"Two hours ten minutes?"

"But I think an eleven o'clock arrival would be best. If you can, send all new information to us. Do it via the Lightstar."

The sound of clicking was heard. "Done, Doc. I think you ought to read paragraph five line twelve page four, first. I talked to Randals about it, but you know how that can be." Herb chuckled.

Loggar smiled. "Well, maybe. But do let him know and

give the rest a quick heads up on my arrival."

"Of course, Doc."

"Then I'll see you in 12 hours?"

"Twelve hours."

The communication line went dead.

There was an awkward silence for about a second.

"Well, Dr. Loggar. When we establish orbit in about two hours. Ten hours from then we'll shuttle down to the base. Would you like any specific personnel or equipment?"

Loggar thought, "Beside, Cmdr. Blakemore? You . . ."

"Me?"

"Yes, Captain. You're also required. It won't take too much of your time, maybe a few days, but I assure you, it'll be worth it."

"Okay, anything, or anyone else."

Loggar smiled, got up. "No, nothing I can think of at this particular moment. You're crew . . ."

Sean stiffened and the bridge chatter stopped.

Loggar caught her mistake. She cleared her throat, "The crew has been most helpful, thank you. I'll see you in . . . how long will it take to reach the surface by shuttle?"

Robin looked at Sean.

Sean, blank faced, said, "One hour."

Loggar continued, "I'll see you in ten hours then."

Robin nodded.

Loggar got up, gave a quick glance at Sean. He went military faced on her and it was unreadable. She entered the elevator. The doors closed and she was gone.

Robin got up. "Mr. Foster, take conn for a moment."

"Aye, ma'am."

She turned to Sean, "Commander, please accompany me into the ready room."

Sean nodded, got up and followed Robin.

Herb sat for a moment typing a global message to all personnel. Standard procedure was to log on every start shift and check messages, requests, and assignments. Herb knew that most of the staff would do just that. It was the other small percentile he was banking on that wouldn't. He typed in the last word and pressed the send button. Sitting back he grinned wide that Randals, the buffoon and office oaf that he was wouldn't get the word until the last hour. His grin turned into a laugh.

In the ready room, Sean stared at Robin.

"Commander . . . Sean, be careful . . ."

"Is the Captain asking me to be careful for a specific reason?"

Robin paused in thought. "Yes."

Several seconds went by.

"And?" Sean asked.

"Just be careful. Dr. Loggar believes you personally can help . . ."

"I don't see how, but is that why the concern?"

Robin pursed her lips and sighed. She definitely had feelings for Sean, and that was not in the program. "I . . . I just have a feeling Sean. Sometimes, goals get in the way of feelings and a person sometimes forgets what was originally important."

Sean stared at Robin for an intense second. He heard what she had said, but he wasn't sure what she had said. He opened his mouth then shut it. Opened it again and shut it for a second time. He sat and thought what Robin was trying to say. He had a softer feeling toward her since Kathy had entered his life. Maybe that was the thing that was needed, someone to enter his dismal existence and give it meaning. Kathy surely did. Sean visibly relaxed.

"Okay," then added, "Okay Robin, I will. But tell me

why the concern."

Robin leaned back into her chair and thought, Sean would ask that question. "Sean, do you know what Wicca is?"

"Wicca? You mean witchcraft? Witches?"

"Yes, I most certainly do."

Loggar sat in a dark room for several moments. She had a strange feeling in the pit of her stomach. She made the mistake of addressing the crew as Robin's and that made her feel bad. She hoped Sean could forgive the mistake and then cursed herself for such a stupid feeling. Sean was way above trivial things like a small mistake. Technically, it was Robin's ship. Unofficially it was Sean Blakemore's, commander of the Reginald Johnson for four years, up for a commendation, delayed because of personal problems and the bad mark against him. A mark she was indirectly responsible for. 'Damn!' She hated all this happenstance. She sat in the dark for at least an hour, uncertain.

The chime rang.

"Yes?" She asked.

"Kathy, it's me." The disembodied voice of Sean's came through.

"Enter, please." She spoke.

The door slide opened. Sean stepped through. It was dark in the room and Sean strained to see the figure sitting on the couch. "Kathy, are you okay?"

"Lights on." Kathy said.

Sean stood just inside the doorway. His brows furrowed. "I had a talk with Robin. She told me some things . . ." He let the pause hang in the air.

"Sean, what did she tell you?"

He stepped closer. "Are you a witch?"

Kathy held her breath. That was the one thing she thought Sean would never ask. She had it worked out, that she would show him the dig site, then the statue and then she would explain the symbols and what they found. After that she would breach the subject of witchcraft and Wicca. "She told you that?"

He nodded. She reached out and touched his cheek.

Sean almost jumped back, but caught himself. It didn't matter what Kathy did or what Robin told him, at least he told himself that. "Kathy, I'm confused. You tell me what a witch is."

Kathy guided Sean to the sofa, they sank in. "Sean, I have a religious preference that is different from most other humans. I practice a form of religion that was thought to have disappeared a century ago. People still remember it today because of movies, books, and old TV shows that never captured the true meaning of witchdom. Most of what you grew up with was fanciful tales."

"What is a witch then?"

Kathy sighed deeply and said, "I'll tell you what a witch is not. A witch is not some wrinkled, long nosed crank stooped over some huge pot boiling disgusting ingredients to perform some non-realistic wish."

Sean chuckled.

"A witch, male or female, is someone with a belief in the Goddess. Not just a God, but a Goddess as well. It's not too different from Hinduism if you really want to split hairs. We see things differently from most other religions. We're nature based, and most importantly, we're old. We were before Christ, or Judas. The Greeks and Romans borrowed extensively from us. In a way, we were the first true well thought out religion."

Sean stared,

"I had hoped that I would slowly introduce you to the notion of Wicca, backed with the findings on Necron."

"Necron? You mean that planet has something to do with

witchcraft?"

"Well, yes and no. We found a lot of Wicca symbols and a lot of procedures for doing certain tasks ritual like in nature. A small percentage of us think that Earthlings long witnessed the rituals of an advanced species and tried to copy them. Wicca may have formed from this copying."

Sean thought.

"You see, this planet gives validations to a religion that was crowded in a lot of wrong perceptions. This planet is vindication."

Sean looked up. "What's my part?"

Kathy moved close to Sean and placed her arms around him.

Sean didn't resist. "Am I some type of puppet?"

"Absolutely not! You are the most important thing, person, needed for us and you're the most important thing in my life. I love you, Sean. Those are not just words I mean it. I need you as well as all of Wicca. Trust me please."

Sean leaned into Kathy and gave her a hug. At this point in his life he didn't care if his life was in danger. Sometime during one's lifetime a person loses hope. Sean lost hope years ago. Consciously he blamed Robin for the situation, subconsciously, he knew the truth. He was not the person he had wished, should have been. He was flawed and that hurt. Ultimately, he just wanted to be loved, if not by himself then by someone else. Kathy gave it to him and all was okay.

It was six bells morning watch. Dawn was in the mess hall drinking a cup of coffee. She stared out the view port. Johnson sported two mess halls, Officer's watch and Starboard's Bow. The Officer's watch, of course, catered to warrant and commissioned officers. Starboard's Bow to everyone else. Thing was, the Commander and Dawn enjoyed visiting the Bow every now and then. It was a way to get a feel for the crew. A way to know what Johnson was thinking. Dawn sat by the view port and just let her thoughts wander. She had another hour before her shift began. She was going to take the Forenoon watch. Captain would be there, no doubt. She didn't think that bitch, Spaarin ever slept. She sipped a mouthful of Cookie's coffee and felt someone sit next to her.

Sean walked into Starboard's Bow looking for Dawn. He knew her routine and was pretty sure she hadn't changed it. They had been through a lot and he hoped they would be through many more. He saw her there, sitting, staring out the port. He walked up and sat next to her.

Dawn looked over her shoulder. "Hey Commander, how's it going?"

Sean smiled, "Okay I guess. The company I'm keeping is pretty cool. Any interesting scuttlebutt?"

Dawn laughed. "Interesting? And How!"

"Really?"

She nodded and took a swallow of coffee. "Yep, some damn good stuff, too. You want to hear it?"

Sean raised an eyebrow, "You know I always like a good spin of the yarn. Give me the big juicy stuff. Skip the small stuff."

She took another sip of coffee. "You're whipped three sides to Sunday."

Sean laughed out loud. He caught himself after a second, cleared his throat, and said, "Really? Took the crew long enough to see it."

Dawn smiled. "Two hours after Doctor Loggar came aboard the ship started a pool."

Sean smiled, "Who won?"

"Mason in Engineering, I got second. I'll buy you a dinner the next time we get leave. Damn good second place, two weeks' pay."

Sean whistled out loud. "That was a good pool."

Dawn nodded and smiled.

Sean pressed his lips together. "You're gonna have to tell me when and what the next big pool is about."

She turned to him and looked Sean straight in the eyes. "It's when you'll kick Captain Spaarin off Top Deck."

Jealously is a combination of several emotions: Fear, Love, and Shame. Fear, because our self-interest in the thing that we desire is in danger of being taken. Love, because we have a very strong physical and emotional attachment to our desire. And Shame, because we are embarrassed that our object of jealously has that much control over us. Jealousy is thus a very inefficient and wasteful emotion, unless one does not care.

Chapter 15

Randals watched as the shuttlecraft landed gently on the north-landing pad. It was the only pad close to the new chamber site. He figured Loggar would like to see it first. She had traveled a long distance and he figured she would like to see anything new immediately. Trying to make everything run smoothly almost taxed his capabilities. But he got through fairly well and he hoped she would realize that, maybe even appreciate it. He had only gotten word of her arrival about an hour ago. Damn that Herb for delaying the message. He acted like it had slipped his mind. The fat fool should be fired. That is if it were up to Randals, Herb would be bounced off Necron. But Loggar liked Herb, thus Herb was tolerated.

Sean piloted the shuttlecraft down to the surface. He would pilot a craft every chance he got, even if it was just a regular milk run from supply station to ship. It gave him a chance to show off a bit he supposed. Robin couldn't fly a shuttlecraft if her life depended on it – she made her way through the ranks by way of administration and security. He started as security and moved over to pilot school. He was damn good too. Rated top point zero, zero, zero one percent in all of GRID. Nine other pilots rated better than he.

Just before release Sean asked if anyone got motion sickness. Robin sat in the co-pilot seat, as worthless as she would have been and Loggar sat behind her on the wall bench seat. Both said no. Sean checked to see that his passengers had their seat belts on and said 'good.' He switched off the gravity compensator and let the shuttlecraft free fall to the planet. It was one hell of a ride and Sean enjoyed every second, including the screams from both Robin and Kathy – especially the scream from Robin. He had the vid recorder on the whole time. The crew had started a pool on the landing. They knew the Commander would drop the compensator and give his passengers one hell of a joy ride. The vid recorded who screamed the loudest and longest and at what microsecond it would begin and end. Sean got fifth place. Not bad for his first pool.

The shuttlecraft cycled through the landing procedures. The landing light flashed green. Randals approached it as the side door opened. Loggar stepped out first. A young woman with GRID military insignia followed her. A man followed behind her he also had GRID military insignia. Randals stared at the man for a moment. The man looked familiar, but Randals knew he never met this person before in his life. Then it dawned on him. Loggar had retrieved him for the statue. He was going to perform the rites. That revelation alone made Randals dislike and hate Sean. Loggar caught Randals approaching them. "Ted, glad you can meet us."

Randals nodded. He was staring at Sean.

"Ted." Loggar said, "This is Commander Sean Blakemore."

Sean reached a hand out. "Hello."

Randals continued to stare. After several seconds ticked

by, Randals extended his hand as well. "Nice to meet you, Commander." Randals said slowly.

Sean shook his hand, but felt uneasy. If Sean trusted his instincts and gut feeling he would swear that this Randals didn't like him. Sean always believed that if someone didn't like you from first impression screw them. They got it wrong and wasn't worth the effort to change their minds.

Robin stepped up.

Loggar said, "And this is Captain Spaarin."

Randals tore his stare away from Sean. Robin shone with a light he had never before seen in a woman, save for Loggar.

"Please to meet you, Captain." Then slowly turning to Loggar, but damn was the Captain beautiful, "We found another chamber. This one is the greatest find of all."

Loggar raised an eyebrow.

Randals asked quite pointedly, "Are they cleared?"

Loggar nodded, "With everything, Ted. Do you understand? Do not hold anything back from either of them."

Randals slowly, reluctantly nodded. "Well, several records pointed us to this area. The dig team broke through only a few days ago."

The group started walking to the main building.

Loggar nodded impatiently for Randals to finish.

"The chamber is larger than the first."

Loggar asked, "Larger than the chamber with the stature?"

Randals' eyes flicked to Robin then to Sean. "Yes, much bigger."

"Well?" Loggar asked.

"The chamber has twelve more statues like the first."

Loggar stopped, "What?"

Randals continued, "Yes, totally like the first, in every aspect."

"Machine?"

Randals nodded. "Yes."

"Good Goddess, man. Show me now, please."

Sean listened to the exchange. He thought how funny one man could sense the jealousy of another. Did women have this same sense? Sean asked himself. They must. As they walked toward a large tented area Sean would catch Randals looking at him.

The thing Sean would have liked to say to Randals was not be mad. Loggar liked him and he liked her. It wasn't his fault she had no intimate feelings for Randals. Sean stopped in mid-thought; maybe she did have feelings for Randals. Maybe she was even sweet to him now and then. Oh well, too bad I'm getting it now, and I don't want to share.

The chamber was large, about 100 meters in diameter. Sean noted a podium of sorts in the center of the chamber. It was empty, raised about two feet off the floor. Along the wall in twelve niches were twelve statues. All of which looked like bronze. The chamber was lit by arc lamps angled toward the ceiling. The light from the lamps gave the chamber an eerie orange glow.

Loggar stepped in first and muttered, "Fantastic. Robin, you first, step through the doorway. Sean you stay there for a bit."

Robin nodded and stepped through. The chamber seemed to briefly come alive. Robin sensed, if not felt, a flash of energy. The chamber brightened to a green color then faded to the orange glow from the arc lamps.

Robin frowned, "What the?"

"Ted, you next, hurry." Loggar said.

Randals stepped in. Nothing happened. He was disappointed.

He thought that Loggar felt disappointed as well.

Loggar looked at Sean.

"I suppose it's my turn?"

Loggar nodded. Her glaze was glassy and unfocused. She

had the look of a frightened little girl mixed with the look of a determined woman.

Sean stepped into the chamber . . .

There was a deep rumbling sound from some unknown place in the chamber. The orange glow was replaced by a dull, yellow glow. The walls seemed to pulsate and radiate with a sound and color unheard or unseen by humans. Robin felt it, Loggar felt it, Randals felt it, and above all, Sean felt it.

"Holy shit!" Sean muttered.

Loggar clasped her hands together and danced a little dance like a small girl, "I knew it. I knew it. Thank the Goddess I knew it." She spread her hands out wide trying to absorb the energy emanating from the walls and within the chamber.

Randals thought he heard a deep moan from one of the statues. He froze and nearly soiled his pants. He heard several more statues moan, or at least he thought he did. "Can we leave now?" His voice raised two octaves higher at his near panic.

Loggar opened her eyes and smiled. Sean was the one. Robin was the one also. She nodded and promptly walked out. The rest nearly stumbled over each other trying to walk out but not looking as if they were in a hurry. The yellow glow subsided to the orange glow from the arc lamps.

Loggar smiled. "Tomorrow Ted, we'll assembly the group at the office. We have much to plan." She started walking toward the main building. Sean and Robin followed.

Sean stepped up next to Loggar. "Umm, what the hell was that?"

Randals held up his hands parallel to the floor. He watched them shake visibly. He was scared. He looked over to Sean who had just stepped up next to Loggar. Randals decided that Sean was the enemy. He took the last hope of him being with Kathy. He shattered his illusion. Randals' hands still shook. Things were going to get fuckin' spooky from this point forward.

Loggar smiled, "Let me think on it Sean and I'll tell you later. I gotta think through this. Okay?"

He slowly nodded once and said, "Okay."

Agegi watched in earnest as the one in charge had returned. This time she had others with her, a female and a male. A ray of hope shone on his plans as he saw the female had given the room a spark. 'She is a distant relation to an Elder.' He thought, 'Fascinating.' It was only when Sean had stepped through the doorway did Agegi's excitement peak. This is the one. The one-in-charge had gone to get this one!' Agegi set upon his task to "help" the little ones "awaken" him. This was the third time he wished he could laugh.

Decisions are born out of necessity. When comfortably situated one may take all the time to make a decision. There is never a reason to hurry; we have all the time in the world.

Chapter 16

Sean had stayed with Loggar that night. It felt strange to be making love to her on planet side. Sean had been exhausted and all he wanted was sleep. Kathy kissed and touched and teased him into arousal. She had a different feel about her on Necron. Sean couldn't pinpoint it, but their lovemaking was a little different. Loggar had screamed twice and loud before Sean collapsed on top of her. It was a bit bizarre but Sean welcomed the orgasm. They slept soundly.

In the office now, Sean listened to the reports of the various departments. He found himself strangely drawn to Herb, the mathematician. Herb looked somewhat silly in his one-size too small jumpsuit, but he spoke with a voice that sounded brilliant.

"Milkens and I concur that this place was meant to be found." Herb continued, "All the equipment ports, the redundant equations, all that stuff indicates someone wanting all this stuff to be studied."

Loggar listened carefully. She read all the reports. "Phillip, what about the statutes and do you have a possible reason for Sean . . . Commander Blakemore apparently starting a reaction in the north chamber?"

Phillip Grebfine stood up and cleared his throat. He was a wired looking man who had a habit of stressing most of his words. "The statues are robotic in nature. We think that by applying heat of unknown calories may be enough to activate most if not all the effigies."

"Heat?" Loggar asked.

Phillip nodded rapidly.

Sean thought Phillip had too much caffeine in his diet.

"Yes," Phillip continued, "the material of the center android — best, in the first chamber, words to describe it, is mixed with plastic-like polymers. The material is hard now, but with an interior temperature of 150 degrees we believe that it will become soft, almost like skin"

"And the Commander's presence?"

He shrugged. "Don't know. We think that most of the chambers are controlled be gene response. Kurp could tell you more on that."

Loggar turned to an old man who looked as if he were asleep.

"Kurp?"

He slowly raised his head. Big bushy eyebrows hung over small black eyes. He grunted once. "Commander Blakemore's DNA matches 79 of the test DNA we found in the med. area of this facility. Blakemore should be able to enter most of the chambers we had to force open. Whomever designed this place may not have thought that someone as close to Blakemore's DNA would walk these corridors. This man may be the closest thing we have to a Necronian."

"Excuse me?" Sean blurted out. "I'm not a whatcha called me.

I'm human, Earth human . . ."

"I know that young man, don't get upset over a label. Your DNA pattern is close enough for government classification. Besides, haven't you ever wondered if some other species had seeded Earth?"

"No."

"What was that young man? Did you say no?"

"Yes, I said no." Sean snapped.

Kurp chuckled softly. "Sorry, Commander, but sometimes an old man likes to have fun. But don't feel bad. The good Captain here is 77.5 percent close."

Robin looked over to Kurp. She had momentarily daydreamed of distant aliens seeding Earth some distant reality ago. "Mr. Kurp. 77.5?"

He nodded.

"You mean, the Commander and myself are related? Like brother and sister?" Robin had a morbid thought and paled.

"No, you and I have a common gene structure 99.0159693 compatibility. As much as 1 would like to hope, you are not my daughter."

Robin blushed.

Kurp continued, "It just means that you and the Commander have more of a desirable gene structure this place wants. Now whether you two have alien blood . . ."

Sean coughed.

". . . is purely speculation. It could be just total accident."

Loggar sat back in her chair. "How is it this place knows?"

Tim Shepard spoke up. "It takes a sample of air containing molecules exhaled by everyone. It doesn't exactly read your genes; it analyzes the chemical combination that you breathe out and makes a statistical calculation. If you match within its perimeters, which you've shown you do, it'll do something."

Sean asked, "Do something? Like magic?"

The room went silent and all heads turned to Loggar.

She leaned forward. "Something like that Sean. But we figure it's all technology."

"What?"

"Think of it this way. A group of people land on Earth way in the past. The locals see the new people doing and saying things. Things happen. They think it's magic. It's not magic, just technology."

"And the seventy-seven something percent?"

Kurp said, "If they have the technology they have the medical know-how to gene slice and re-engineer them. We know it for a fact. I got a zettabyte worth of data to prove it. Give me an hour and I'll explain at what point in our history where it occurred."

Loggar turned to Herb. "In your report Herb, you said that we were being watched. By whom?"

Herb scratched the top of his stomach. It protruded out a bit. "The guys in the electronic department noted that when certain rooms were occupied energy sparks would develop and travel to the first chamber. Possibly into the statue." Herb caught the eye of one of the technicians. Both smiled at each other.

The tech took out a small device and turned it on. He watched the readout.

Loggar leaned closer toward Herb. "Have all the rooms been noted?"

Herb's grin turned to a smirk. He nodded. "All the rooms that have been identified have a large red E on the inside and outside near the door jam."

Loggar let her eyes glide across the room from Herb to the door jam. "Good Goddess, Herb! There's an E at the door."

All heads turned to the E.

Randals shouted, "Shit. Herb. Why didn't you tell us? "

Herb held up a hand, "Quite please."

Everyone listened.

Herb looked over to the Tech. "Got something Milk?

Milkens nodded. "Hell yeah. The thing peaked just before you told Dr. Loggar about the E and suddenly dropped off. No spikes now."

Loggar looked at Herb. "A test?"

Herb nodded. "Yeah, the thing may be 'alive' or working. It has been listening and probably looking all this time. Remember I mentioned the formulas?"

Loggar nodded.

"I went back to an old backup file on some equations. The redundancy was not there. This thing I think has been guiding us along. Helping us to understand this facility and itself.

Randals shot out, "Dr. Loggar, I can't believe Herb would do such . . ."

Loggar raised a hand up to silence Randals.

His mouth hung open for a second then it shut tight.

Sean felt his embarrassment.

Loggar said, "Herb, give."

"Everything we had found four months ago was not due to accident. I went back and checked on all new findings, the new chamber, the questions, the library, all the stuff was conveniently placed so we would 'stumble' on them. I think that the statue or something close to it wants us to learn as much as we can."

Loggar leaned back and closed her eyes. "I want everyone, I mean everyone, to submit what they know or think they know. Herb, you set up the next meeting place that is secure."

Randals started to say something but was silenced again by Loggar's hand. He shut up.

"It should be big enough for all the department heads to sit comfortably."

Herb grabbed a piece of paper and started writing. "I can think of only one place. I won't say it out loud. Read this." He slid it over to her face down. "It may have been able to read this but it doesn't matter. If you think it's a good idea then you can set up a time now."

Loggar read the paper. 'JOHNSON.' She thought a bit and then nodded "Good thinking. Great choice. Does anyone have something to say before we adjure to the next meeting.

Randals stared Loggar in the face. "Yes, I do."

Loggar sighed. She had an idea what it was going to be about but she did ask. "Yes?"

"Are we going to breach the existence of the order and her secrets to strangers?"

All heads turned to Loggar.

Kurp spoke up. "I know that Captain Spaarin is in the Most High, but the Commander?"

Loggar pursed her lips. She knew this was going to happen.

"Sean Blakemore is not."

Murmur rose in the room.

Kurp continued. "How far are we going to go?"

The room fell silent.

After a second Loggar turned to Sean. "Sean. I didn't want to put you on the spot just yet. I wanted to ask you in private first, but it seems best to ask you now." She gave Randals a particularly piercing look.

Sean felt queasy and sick to his stomach. He hadn't eaten for too many hours. Most of this talk was starting to bother him. He had also noticed the others giving him strange looks. He nodded a go ahead.

Loggar said, "We are all members of the Most-High Goddess."

Sean nodded.

"We are all doing this for the Most-High Goddess."

He nodded again.

"We are going to need your help. For the research part, our technology is good enough to record and possibly understand most of Necron. But there are a few things that technology alone will never be able to answer. There is a room, the library that contains hard copy books. These books were used, we believe by the elite. You and Robin are possibly descendants from these elite."

Sean opened his mouth, Loggar interrupted.

"I know, Sean, you are not an Alien, but the fact remains that you are the only person who can activate most of the rooms - you did one room earlier." Loggar waited to see if Sean would response.

He didn't.

"We, of the Most-High Goddess want to go beyond what technology has to offer. We want to do Wicca."

Sean's mind raced through all the events that happened to him in the past two weeks. He remembered how sad he had been and at his wits end before this assignment came up. He thought about how much he loved Kathy and what she had given him. She loved him he knew that. He didn't care why, it was just so. Sean sat and thought for a long time. Loggar and the rest waited patiently. Sean looked over to Robin. She had no hatred in her. Her face was soft, her eyes inviting. She was stunning. He looked at Kathy, the woman he now loved. Her lips were pursed and her brows furrowed. She was concerned. Finally after Sean decided what he wanted to say he had to figure how to say it. After a moment or two Sean cleared his throat.

All members listened intently.

Sean said the only thing that made perfect and utter sense for him. He took a deep breath and let it out slowly. He said, "I want to join the Most-High Goddess."

Agegi wished he could laugh.

There is a very old saying. It's based off millennia of experience and situations, yet it is the least listened to and followed of all wise sayings: Be careful what you wish for, it may happen.

Chapter 17

Sean sat opposite Loggar at a small table in a room that didn't have an E stenciled near the door. Kathy Loggar felt "safe." Sean did not. "Privacy" was a word that didn't really exist. It didn't exist on board the Johnson, or throughout GRID system. "Safe" and "Privacy," in Sean's mind, were words used to give a false sense of security. He let Loggar continue on. If she felt "safe" in this room then he wouldn't be the one to spoil the atmosphere.

"Sean," she said, "Wicca is a nature-based religion. Witches know that, as men and women, we are part of the central nervous system of Gaia, which is in turn a part of the kingdom of Ka . . ."

"Gaia? Ka?"

Loggar nodded. "Yes, Gaia is the Earth organism. Ka is the main entity where Gaia exists. Before space-travel, we thought Gaia was it. It wasn't until a hundred years ago or so did the Most High accept the fact that Gaia was part of a bigger picture. We had to rethink our entire concept of the "universe." She stressed the word universe. We based all our ideas and concepts on the motion of the stars, the Sun, and of Earth. We structured our lives around planetary motions. In a way, we were probably the first astronomers. To do a ritual, one has to know the right celestial settings.

Sean sat motionless and absorbed what he was listening to. Sean's notion and concept over the all God thing was scant. He didn't believe in a God, or a Goddess. But what Loggar was telling him somehow drew him further in. It was as if her words were some type of magical drug that would allow him to transcend all his problems. Wicca to him was rapidly becoming something to believe in. It was a long time sense he allowed himself the luxury of believing in something besides GRID. Loggar got up and walked over to a shelf of books. She ran her fingers alone to length of the shelf and stopped at a small black book. She pulled it out. "Here, Sean." She gave it to him. "Read this. It will answer a few questions."

Sean looked at the cover. It said, 'Wicca: The Myth. The Truth.'

Loggar gave him a big smile and kissed him on the cheek. She looked at her watch. "I have a meeting with several of the departmental heads. Sometime in a few days, we're going to do a gate ritual."

Sean looked up. "Gate ritual?"

Loggar nodded. "Yeah. We're . . . actually you're going to perform a rite of passage so to speak. You're going to awaken Agegi."

"Awaken? Agegi?"

Loggar nodded, "The single statue in the first chamber. Since it seems to be watching us and guiding us it seems logical to help animate it."

Sean listened to her words with a bit of uneasiness. He thought the whole thing a bad idea, but who was he to question the validity of . . . well . . . Kathy, the Most High Goddess? He turned his military gut feeling down several notches. He continued to listen.

"Herb and Milkens 'found' a file that contains the words to activate the statue fully. It's not too different from a passage we've used in one of our rituals. It seems that the

Necronians used words to perform various tasks. Some of the tech and theory lads think that this entire complex had two modes of operation. They worked at a computer terminal not too different from ours or they simple spoke the commands. The lads in tech, bless their hearts, recovered older versions of the same software. The phrases used were less complex and easier to remember. They think that as time went on the Necronians made just about everything they did into a ritual."

Sean listened and nodded. But the one thought that haunted him was, 'is it safe to activate Agegi? With trepidation in his voice Sean asked. "Is it wise to activate the statue?"

Loggar's smile dropped. Sean wished he had somehow rephrased his question differently. "I mean, this is Alien technology and didn't Herb think that it was kind of strange that the group started "finding" things?"

Loggar said, "He used the word 'stumbled'." Her words came out curt, sharp, and had an ugly undertone.

Sean chose to ignore the way she answered him. He told himself that this was her project. She and all these scientist type were the experts. They understood, more than he could Wicca in its entirety. Loggar continued, "I've talked it over with most of the others. We're going to set up a level 9 force field just outside the doorway . . ."

"And me?"

"We'll set the shield to allow organic matter to pass in and out."

Sean moved the book around in his hands.

"You okay Sean?"

Sean signed. "Maybe, maybe not. I just don't know if I'll fit." He stopped and considered his words. "What if all this doesn't work?"

Loggar shrugged, "Then it doesn't. If you're concerned about what the' others think, don't worry. I get a general sense that they like you."

Sean looked at the book again. He opened it to the beginning.

He chuckled at his choice. Usually he opened a book in the middle and read a few lines just to see if he would like it.

"You chuckled Sean?"

Sean nodded and gave Loggar a slanted grin. "Yeah I did." He began reading and walked off.

Loggar watched him and smiled inwardly. Sean was going to work out just fine. A little naive to the ways of the Goddess but he was going to work out.

Randals stared into the monitor. He read with wide-eye fear. Cold sweat formed on his forehead. He heard a sound and nearly jumped out of his seat.

A tech came in, got a tool, and walked out.

Randals continued to read the text scroll before him. At one point he began to smile. His smile turned into a chuckle then turned into a hysterical fit of laughter. After a moment he shut down the terminal, got up from his chair and leisurely walked out of the room and down the hall. Randals was deep in thought when he stepped through the doorway. It was his office and on the door jamb was a large E painted near it.

"No, no, no. Not there. Backup, Milk."

Milkens, the tech from Electronics, followed Herb's instructions. He stepped forward several paces, paused then backed up. He held a TF emitter of some sort.

"Right there! That's it."

Milkens stopped.

Herb walked over to the tech. He wrote a big X just in front of Milkens' feet. "I think this is it."

Milkens nodded. Herb had his flashes of brilliance, but this one surely out did them all. The problem had been how to null out the building's gene sampling ability. Herb figured that if they couldn't null the ability out then they could somehow trick it. Make it accept all DNA.

Herb placed a medium sized box on top of the X. He turned it on.

Milkens and he stepped back.

Herb said, "I feel tingly all over. You feel it Milk?"

Milkens nodded. "The TF field is damping the air."

Herb reached into his pocket and pulled a small spurt bottle.

"Ready, Milk?"

Milkens nodded.

Herb took a deep breath and squeezed. A misty poof of air whispered away from the little bottle. The lights and the machinery fizzed, bleeped, and popped, "Hot damn." Herb shouted. "We is friggin' geniuses."

Milkens patted him on the back, took out a notebook and started writing feverishly. He mumbled to himself. Herb knew to leave Milkens alone when he was in this state. Herb watched as the man poured his thoughts into his journal. Milkens looked up after a minute and proudly said, "I can miniaturize the box."

"What about the sample?" Herb asked.

"We could encode it onto our clothes. The field would be strong enough to pull the sample off our clothes and deliver it to the sampler."

Herb nodded. "Do you think you could make three by the time of the rite?"

"Yeah. I can do it."

Herb looked around for a terminal. It was in the corner. Herb walked over to it. The markings on this one were different from the standard ones. For one thing, they had to trick the complex into turning it on, so it had to be special. He ran his fingers across the symbol. It looked familiar. "Hey Milk, what does this look like to you."

Milkens peered over Herb's shoulder. "Well, I been damned."

"Huh."

"That's the symbol for Marduk."

"*The* Marduk?" Herb's stomach sank.

Milkens backed up. "Yeah, that's exactly it. Necron was more than a good name for this place, it's perfect. I think we should tell Dr. Loggar about this one."

Herb turned and let out a loud sigh. A mystery is about to unravel.

"Again, Sean, repeat it again."

Sean sat in the middle of the floor and recited the piece again. Loggar listened with eyes closed. Sean said the passage with feeling this time. Loggar's skin tingled. She shuddered. After Sean finished she said, "Very good Sean. That was very good. Now do the Imbolg. Recite the passage before you deliver the Charge in its entirety.

Sean closed his eyes and dredged up the words:

"Behold the Three-Formed Goddess;
She who is ever Three - Maid, Mother and Crone;
Yet is she ever One.
For without Spring there can be no Summer,
Without Summer, no Winter.
Without Winter, no new Spring."

Sean opened his eyes. "Well?"

Loggar smiled and touched Sean on the shoulder. She nodded.

"Excellent Sean. In one day you memorized a fourth of our basic knowledge."

Sean shrugged. "I'm good with certain things."

Loggar moved closer and rubbed herself along Sean's side.

She whispered in his ear, "I know."

Someone coughed.

Loggar and Sean turned.

Herb and Milkens stood just outside the doorway. "Sorry to disturb you two, but Milkens and I have something to show Dr. Loggar. It'll only take a minute. Afterwards you guys can pick up where you left off."

Sean turned a bright red.

Class for now was adjourned.

Loggar entered the room first.

Herb pointed to the screen and indicated where the symbol was.

Loggar stepped up tentatively and glanced down at the strange characters. She touched it and nodded. "This is *The* Marduk symbol. Fantastic! The files indicated we might find something like this, but to actually stumble on . . ." She stopped and turned to Herb and Milkens.

Milkens was writing in his journal when he suddenly stopped.

He looked up and swallowed hard.

Loggar said, "You two. What were you two doing in here?"

Herb replied, "Just checking on the rooms. You know, looking for things."

"Things?" Loggar raised an eyebrow.

Herb and Milkens looked at each other. Both nodded rapidly.

"Yeah, Doc. Things. This section hasn't been thoroughly explored."

She scanned the room with her eyes, walls, ceiling and the floor. "Herb, what's that X doing on the floor?"

Herb remained silent.

Loggar stood on top of it and looked around. "Herb,

would this be something you and Milkens are doing without departmental approval?"

"Dr. Loggar, please, I'm head of the . . ."

"Now I know something is wrong. Give."

Sean had stayed just outside the doorway. Earlier he found that just by crossing a threshold a room would erupt with activity. The first four times made him jump. The next four intrigued him. The last four pissed him off. He couldn't just walk into a room with equipment without it suddenly coming on.

Loggar walked over to the terminal and touched it. It was warm toward the end. "How?"

Herb started to fidget.

"Herb!"

"Okay, okay. Doc we'll talk."

"Well?" Loggar said after Herb had paused a second too long.

"We turned the room on."

"Turned the room on? How? Impossible! Show me."

Herb glanced at Milkens.

Milkens jotted down some notes.

"Okay watch." In an overly dramatic way Herb took the black box tucked in a corner of the room and placed it on the X. "Ladies and gentlemen, for your amusement, the great Herb and Milk will dazzle your eyes and tantalize your senses." He threw the switch on.

The air in the room felt tingly against their skins. Even at the doorway. Sean felt it.

Herb pulled out the spurt bottle. "As you can see ladies and gentlemen, this innocent looking squirt bottle has amazing properties. Observe."

A wisp of vapor escaped from the bottle.

A second later the room popped and beeped, the terminal came on and dozens of suspended display images filled the room. Corner to corner the room was touched by symbols of color and light. Readouts of some unknown source hovered in front of them. It meant nothing to those ignorant of the incomprehensible.

"Amazing!" Loggar exclaimed. "How?"

"We took a sample of the commander's DNA and cultured it. The box ionizes the air. When the sample hits the air it spreads out so the Necronian sniffer picks it up." Herb swept his hand around the room slowly. "The results."

"You were going to keep this from me?" Loggar said with a tight jaw.

"No, no. Milk and I were planning to make three miniaturized versions of the dampener. We just wanted to get the fundamentals down first. That's all."

Loggar relaxed her face and smiled. "You know you could have told me."

Herb nodded. "Yeah, and you would have mentioned it to Mr. Administer, too."

"Well, yes. He is my proxy when I'm gone. He should know some of the things I know. Just in case."

"Yeah, but not this time. He would've tried to control our procedures."

"Oh, Herb, Randals isn't like that, he's . . . well . . ."

Herb uttered, "He's well, what?"

Loggar closed her mouth. "Okay maybe you're right, but you still . . ."

Suddenly the room powered down.

"Sean," Loggar asked, "could you step in here please?"

Sean paused a bit. He was lost in thought about what had just transpired. Did Herb and Milkens find a way to not use him? He felt strange, almost bad, at not being needed but hurt that he could be useless. He stepped into the room.

The room came to life.

Randals typed feverishly on his terminal. He had to get his thoughts down on file. This was important. He was going to do something he hadn't dreamt before. But before he never had the means or the 'know how'. Soon would be different. He felt it and it was good. His life was going to be forever changed.

Words are but sounds to the ear, wave fronts that make a passage through the ether. But thoughts, they are different. Thoughts may travel or stand still. Even thoughts as old as time may be just that, as old as time and thus mean nothing at all. Be careful what you invoke. Tread lightly into a dark room you've never been in before – something may bite you and you can't remember were the door is.

Chapter 18

The group had assembled at the entryway to the chamber. All were clothed except for Loggar and Sean.

Sean's face was beet-red from embarrassment. Earlier, most of the men slapped him on the shoulder and said, "not to worry, you'll get used to it. Nice body though. I looked like that once – three decades ago. You'll be fine." With all their words of encouragement and praises, Sean felt uneasy. He just couldn't put his finger on it. Was it because he was naked? Or was it because too much depended on him? Loggar told him that he and she would be 'drawing down the Moon.' She would then charge the Circle, and drawing down the Sun would proceed.'

Loggar stepped up behind Sean and whispered lovely in his ear. "Sean, my beloved. I am ready. Are you?"

Sean turned and looked at all the faces staring at him. He caught Robin's eyes. She stayed somewhere toward the back. Her role in this would be very minor. Herb had a robe on, as all the rest, but his was a size too small.

Loggar kissed Sean on the ear, then the side of his forehead.

Sean looked into her eyes. He saw the same eyes he fell in love with, what several weeks ago? But these eyes were somehow a little different. Still her eyes and yet not her eyes. He stared into the chamber. The statue stood motionless in the middle of the room. It seemed to taunt him into awakening it, almost daring him too. 'This,' Sean thought, 'is not such a good idea.' He was not going to turn them down. He had disappointed a lot of folks in the last few years. Maybe this was his chance to make up for it. The statue stood there, with its blank bland face. He turned back to Loggar and the group. Randals was off to right. He had a particularly determined expression on his face. "I'm ready." Sean said out loud.

The group collectively took a deep breath and relaxed.

"Then let us begin."

Two men, dressed in brown robes, walked up with an altar. It was waist high and had a large bowl sunken halfway into the altar table. Several athames, they all looked hand-made, were on it. Sean was to pick the athame that had a deer's foot for the handle and a long narrow iron blade. They lit the candles and walked away. Loggar drew an imaginary circle around the receiving room to the main chamber. She stood in front of the table with her backside exposed to the main room. Sean knelt in front of her and gave Loggar the five-fold Kiss.

Sean said, "Blessed be thy feet, that have brought thee in these ways." He kissed her on the right foot and then the left. Loggar spread her arms and stood with feet apart. She held the scourge and her athame.

"Blessed be thy knees, that shall kneel at the sacred altar." He kissed her right knee, then her left. "Blessed be thy womb, without which we would not be." He kissed just above her pubic hair. He was too nervous to enjoy his position. "Blessed be thy breasts, formed in beauty." He kissed the right breast, then the left. They quivered slightly from each kiss. "Blessed be thy lip, that shall utter the Sacred Names." Sean stood up and embraced her, kissing her lips in the process. He knelt again and using his right forefinger touched Loggar on her right breast, then her left breast, then just at the baseline of her pubic hair.

He did this twice finishing with a touch to her right breast.

Loggar spoke, "I invoke thee and call upon thee Mighty Mother of us all bringer of all fruitfulness; by seed and root, by stem and bud, by leaf and flower and fruit do I invoke thee to descend upon the body of this thy servant and priestess."

Sean spread his arms outward and then downward "Hail I say! From the past Horn pour forth thy supply of love, I lowly bend before thee, I adore thee to the end, with loving sacrifice thy shrine adorn, thy foot is to my lip," he kissed Loggar's foot, "my prayer up borne upon the rising incense-smoke; then spend thine ancient love, O Mighty One descend to aid me, who without the aid am forlorn." Sean stood up and took a step backwards.

Loggar drew the invoking Pentagram of Earth in the air in front of Sean and said, "Of the Mother and divine mine the scourge, and mine the kiss; the five-point star of love and bliss here I charge you, in this sign."

Sean and Loggar faced each other.

Sean swallowed hard. Little sweat beads ran down his forehead.

Loggar's face was blank and still.

Sean said, "Listen to the words of the Great Mother; she who of the old was also called among men."

Loggar still facing Sean with a look that began to unnerve him, said, "Whenever ye have need of anything, once in the month, and better it be when the moon is full, then shall ye assemble in some secret place and adore the spirit of me who am Queen of all witches. . ." she went on several minutes and finished with ". . . I am the gracious Goddess, who gives the gift of joy unto the heart of man. Upon earth, I give the knowledge of the spirit eternal and beyond death. I give peace and freedom, and reunion with those who have gone before. Nor do I demand sacrifice, for behold. I am the Mother of all living, and my love is poured out upon the earth."

Sean took a breath and said, "Hear ye the words of the Star Goddess; she in the dust of whose feet are the hosts of heaven, and whose body encircles the universe."

"I who am the beauty of the green earth." Loggar said, "and the white Moon among the Stars, and the mystery of the waters, and desire of the heart of man, call unto thy soul. Arise."

The assembled group stood up.

Randals rocked back and forth on his heels. He seemed to be swept up in some dream-like vision and feeling.

Loggar continued, "Come unto me, for I am the soul of nature, who gives life to the universe. From me all things proceed, and unto me all things must return; and before my face, beloved of Gods and of men, let thine innermost divine self be enfolded in the rapture of the infinite. . ."

Sean raised his arms wide; he was swept up in the moment. He felt alive and young and new and energized. He spoke with confidence and half believed he had power. He started in a low tone and finished loud and with energy behind his voice. "Bagahi laca bachahe'. Lamac cahi achabahe', Karrelyos, lamac lamac bachalyos. Cabahgi sabalyos, baryolas, lagozatha cabyolas, samahac et famyolas, harrahya!"

Loggar and the group responded with, "Harrahya!" The sound resonated around the entryway.

Sean and Loggar faced the altar with their arms raised in the Homed God salute, fists clenched with palms forward and first and little finger fingers pointing upward.

Sean said, "Great God, return to earth again! Come at my call and show thyself to men. Shepherd of Goats, upon the wild hill's way, Lead thy lost flock from darkness unto day. Forgotten are the ways of sleep and night - Men seek for them whose eyes have lost the light. Open the door, the door that hath no key, the door of dreams, whereby men come to thee Shepherd of Goats, O answer unto me!"

Loggar's heartbeat increased. Sean recited the passage with more passion than any male member of decades with Most High ever did. She chanced a glimpse at the assembled members. She saw on some of them that this was it that Sean was going to do it. It alarmed her but she drank in his energy and it was wonderful.

Sean and Loggar moved closer to each other, rubbing shoulders. In unison they shouted over the humming sound of the group. "Akhera goiti!" They lowered their hands. "Akhera beitji!" They shouted.

The group formed a circle, facing each other, with man and woman alternating as far as possible, and linked hands.

They chanted the Witches - Rune together. Sean was swept into a delusional sense of reality. He felt light headed and started panting. The hum started out softly and increased to a sound that seemed to shake the walls with its illusionary energy.

"Eko, Eko, Azarak, Eko, Eko. Zomelak!" They shouted. "Eko, Eko, Cernunnos, Eko, Eko, Aradia!" They shouted louder.

Time seemed to blur as they chanted over and over again. And when they reached a point that Sean believed they could yell no further Loggar shouted, "Down!"

They all sat still facing inward.

Sean was covered in sweat. His eyes stung. He blinked hard several times in an attempt to produce tears. He wiped his eyes with the back of this hand. 'Bedamn the group if they thought ill of him for lacking the discipline to endure the stinging.' He thought.

Loggar stood up and offered a hand to Sean.

He grabbed it and hoisted himself up. He stood with his back to the Altar and clenched his deer-footed athame. He placed it in his right hand and lifted it up to his left breast. The point was upward.

Loggar faced him and gave Sean the five-fold kiss. Afterward, she knelt and invoked, "Deep calls on height, the Goddess on the God, on him who is the flame that quickens her; that he and she may seize the silver reins and ride as one the twin-horsed chariot. Let the hammer strike the anvil, let the lightning touch the earth, let the lance ensoul the Grail-let the magic come to birth." She touched her right forefinger to Sean's throat, left hip, and right breast, left breast, right hip, and then the throat again.

Sean followed her touch and remembered she was 'Invoking the Pentagram of Fire' Loggar spread her hands outward, palms forward and said, "In her name do I invoke thee. Mighty Father of us all, come in answer to my call! Descend, I pray thee, in thy servant and priest." She stepped back.

The group rose.

Sean made the Invoking Pentagram of Fire towards Loggar with his athame. He turned to face the chamber. With sweating palms he grasped the athame with both hands and invoked the "Pentagram of Fire" at the statue. He took a step into the chamber and yelled, "Let there be Light!"

It is an age-old belief that wishing, wanting and having should never come to pass. In wishing you set into motion a desire of wanting and in wanting you begin the process of having. But the trick is to have a healthy balance between the three. One can wish for the Moon, but without the where alls and resources the Moon is forever minus a minute away. As the Greeks put it, there has to be a balance between Theoria (thought) and Praxis (action). If the balance is not struck, then the result is that one is either silly looking or just plain completely stupid. Theoria and Praxis – think carefully.

Chapter 19

Agegi witnessed the entire preceding and was appalled. The elders would never have subjected him and the ancient ones to such barbaric rhetoric. There was nothing he could do but let them do their silly little ritual. Then it happened. The one called 'Sean' stepped into the chamber. The room came alive with heat and light. He felt his skin softened as the temperature climbed higher and higher. These creatures indeed meant to awaken him and that was good.

Sean stepped into the chamber. The room seemed to pulsate with light and heat.

The group walked in and assembled themselves along the wall. Loggar stood to his right.

Sean was thankful for not having any clothing. The temperature began to climb. One of the techs had told the group that the temperature would have to reach 136 degrees for about ten seconds if the Statue was to be activated. Sean counted to twenty.

The statue moved, the heat vanished, and the room fell silent.

The sound of air rushing into long unused lungs resonated throughout the chamber. An eerie sound on someone who had drowned years ago and suddenly their lungs were able to expand and draw in something that had desperately been missed and needed. The statue took a deep breath for the first time in a long time.

It let it out slowly and enjoyed the once again ability to breathe air.

Sean's first impulse, as it was for the others, was to run. But the fascination of watching the statue come to life mesmerized him. It was because of him that the statue awakened. Sean took a step forward and looked into the blank eyeless face of the statue. Agegi looked down at Sean. "Who has awakened me?" His voice echoed throughout the chamber. In the far corner, someone pissed on himself. Two people fainted, and one of the oldest members suffered heart failure. She died silently.

Sean looked into the face and said, "1 am a remnant of an Elder. I am Sean. Who have I awakened?"

Agegi breathed again, inhaling air for a long time then exhaling it in an equally long time. Damn it felt good to breath. The process of inhaling and exhaling was worth being subjected to the silly rituals of these curious people. He stepped off the platform and looked at Sean.

Loggar and the group took a collective step backward. Sean stood fast, damned if he was gonna back down from something he brought to life.

Agegi looked at the group, then back at Sean. "I am Agegi, an Ancient one."

Loggar whispered. "Oh shit."

"You speak our language?" Sean asked.

"I do many things. I am Agegi, Sean. Why have you awaken me?" Agegi said, playing the game and going through a poorly scripted play.

Loggar took a tentative step forward. "To learn from you."

Agegi turned his blank face to Loggar.

Loggar almost cringed but kept her composure, if Sean could do it, she could do it.

"What is it you would learn from me?"

"We have a religion based on the Elders and the Ancient Ones. We . . . we are awed by you."

Agegi spoke, "Are you worthy of my inspiring awe?"

Loggar stepped forward, placing herself in front of Sean. "We as a people have tried to hold the ideas and concepts of what we learned generations ago. We mimicked what we saw and thus created a belief. You are part of that belief and we are prepared to take a step forward in our understanding of that belief. We would only like to further our understanding from a being that was part of its origins."

Agegi took another step forward. "And what do you have to say remnant of the Elder Ones?" Agegi moved its smooth featured face toward Sean. Agegi liked this one. He was different.

Sean cleared his throat. "I want to know what my purpose is." There, he said it. Something he had buried deep inside for too many years. And with saying it Sean realized that maybe the Most-High Goddess was not a thing for him. "I want to understand why I am here. Hasn't there been a time when you asked yourself that very question?"

For a second time in Agegi's existence he was moved by a question. Sean struck a nerve. Agegi would forever remember that. "Yes, remnant Sean, long ago, but now things are different," Agegi breathed. His breathing was measured in massive inhaling and exhaling of tens of seconds. "I am different. I know my purpose."

From somewhere in the back Randals shouted, "And what is your purpose?"

Loggar gave Randals a hateful stare as he walked up front.

Randals had committed a breach in protocol. Loggar cursed herself. Herb had been right, Tony was a wildcard and today he was going to grandstand.

Agegi stared into Randals direction. "Come here." Agegi commanded more than requested.

Randals stepped forward.

"You ask a question. Are you prepared for the answer?"

Randals responded with an answer he had been prepped for.

He nodded. "Yes. I am."

"Then step closer."

Randals walked to within arm's reach of Agegi.

Agegi looked down. He was a full two and a half meters taller. He reached out and placed his hand on the top of Randals head. Sean stared with jealous fascination at the scene. Randals made first touch.

"What are you called?"

"Tony Randals." His voice quivered slightly.

"Then Tony Randals, this is my purpose." And with that Agegi's hand tightened on Randals' head. Long thin probes extended from his fingers. They inserted themselves into Randals brain, seeking out vital information about this strange species that was willing to worship the likes of him. And finally, after all this time, which seemed like forever, Agegi finally laughed.

Destiny is a funny thing. One never knows when it is truly destiny or a deep seeded desire to fulfill a long- standing fantasy. Do we just toss our reservations to the wind and take charge or back away and rethink our decisions. Either way, who is to say that destiny is not being fulfilled? Destined to step forward, destined to step back. Both are points of views from the same vantage point.

Chapter 20

Agegi let go of Randals' head. He dropped to the floor like a ragdoll – lifeless. Agegi waved his massive arm in the air and recited, "Itahl, toghan, moghan. Behold!"

Randals jumped up looking like he was in a daze.

"Who is your master, one called Randals?"

His head jerked a bit. He said, "You are my Master. You are Agegi, an Ancient one, giver of new found powers, giver of immortality and new strength." Randals, jerked walked toward Sean and Loggar. Those of the group left standing retreated to the entranceway. One of the robed fellows had his hand placed on the button to turn the force shield on.

Agegi turned his attention to the group and said, "Follow me and I will grant you power beyond your wildest dreams." He lifted an arm and Randals lifted several feet off the ground with his arms outstretched and his feet crossed. Agegi toyed with them by displaying Randals in this crucifixion pose. Agegi said, "Who am I?"

Randals coughed.

"Who am I?" Agegi said again, his voice echoing in the chamber and another one of the older members collapse from heart failure.

Randals said, "You are the one who controls my life and if I fail you my life is yours to end."

"Again!"

Randals shouted, "You are the one who controls my life and if I fail you my life is yours to end."

"Again!"

"You are the one who controls my life and if I fail you my life is yours to end."

"Never forget it," and he closed his fist and Randals collapsed to the ground like a puppet with severed strings.

The group looked on at the scene terrified. The robed fellow hit the power on button and the entranceway sparked into a frosty blue film.

Agegi laughed and opened his fist. "This is how I reward my minions. One called Randals, turn that device off."

The limp body of Randals jerked several times and he inhaled a deep breath of air. He jerked up and walked toward the field. At first he seemed to be some sort of Frankensteinian monster, movements stiff and jerky, but by the time he reached the field his walk was normal, almost graceful.

Herb was on the other side of the field. When Agegi grabbed Randals head and seemed to have killed him, Herb whispered to himself, 'thank you for killing that ass.' But when he saw Randals get up he nearly soiled himself. He took an involuntary step back as Agegi's new follower approached the field. The force field was a level 9 barrier. At the last minute Loggar decided to disable the organic safe mode. Now, anything moving through it would be disintegrated.

Randals felt like a new man. His eyesight sharpened and he felt like he could do anything. He understood that Agegi could cut his existence off by his will, but Randals was thinking that maybe this was indeed a blessing. He stepped toward the force field. His new body wasn't quite working. It took a few steps. He stared at the barrier and through the frosty film he saw Herb. A burning desire to finally shut the fat fucker up drove him toward the field. He knew that Agegi was all- powerful and would allow him to walk through the field and live. So, Randals placed his hand through the barrier and he felt searing pain but he continued to move forward.

The others watched in absolute horror that someone would willingly walk through a level 9 field. They heard Randals' scream. It was loud, unnerving, an absolute horror. It was the screams of souls being skinned alive. It resonated throughout the chamber and down the entranceway, deep in their bodies and bones. Randals screamed louder but continued to walk through the field.

Sean looked with a morbid fascination. He saw Randals' fingers and then hand, wrist and arm boil up in a pink cloud of smoke. His sleeve curled up in a kind of black flake. Pieces broke off and fell to the ground. Randals screamed louder and continued walking and walking and walking. Sean stared closely, then he saw that Randals' fingers, hand then wrist was forming on the other side of the field. The appendage was a black semblance of an arm but turned pink then pale yellow. Randals walked through the field, clothes, skin, flesh, bone being burned and boiled off on one side only to be reformed into a smooth new layer of bone, flesh and skin on the other side.

What seemed like forever, Randals emerged from the barrier anew feeling like never before. He stood naked, breathing heavily, reached out his hand. The robed fellow dropped his hood and stepped aside. The power switch turned off and the barrier sparked, flashed off.

Agegi laughed and enjoyed this game. He had their attention now. He simply said, "Who wishes immortality?"

There was a moment of silence. It hung in the air for a

bit. Then the robed fellow stepped into the chamber. Five others followed. Randals took his place next to his master and watched him turn his fellow scientists and Most High Goddess worshipers into Ancient minions.

Loggar watched in absolute and total disbelief. 'What have I done?' she asked herself. 'I have unwittingly awakened an Ancient one.' She gasped as Randals walked through the barrier and survived and nearly cried as six members stepped up to become Agegi slaves!

Sean caught Robin's stare and nodded. He grabbed Loggar and moved her away from Agegi and the group. No one seemed to notice. They made it to the doorway. Two more members stepped in line. Herb, Milkens, Robin, Kurp, Loggar and Sean stepped away and ran. Sean didn't care where just as long as it was away from the chamber.

This bears saying, "Be careful what you wish for." This bears re-iterating. "Be careful what you wish for." And this bears summarizing. "Knucklehead, think about what in the world you are trying to do here!"

Chapter 21

After a minute of blindly running through Necron, Sean stopped and asked, "What the fuck was that all about?"

No one answered.

He said, "Someone must know! We just unleashed some fucking thing I do not know what in the name of Most High Goddess and no one can answer me?" He squeezed his eyes tight in frustration.

Still no one answered.

He stood naked in the hallway and turned his back on them.

Loggar said, "Sean . . ."

He did a sideway glance.

"I didn't think this was going to happen. You must understand our knowledge going into this was limited. This was beyond the facts presented." She cleared her throat. "I didn't know Agegi was an Ancient one."

Sean turned around. He face twisted up in disbelief, bewilderment and contempt all at once. "Didn't know? Didn't know? And what in God's . . ." He corrected himself, " . . . in Goddess' name is an Ancient one?"

Loggar was hurt and ashamed. She had been the conductor of this train and it wrecked incredibly before her eyes. All her teachings told her that anything was possible and that setbacks were someone else's problem. But this one, this one problem was of her doing, of her making. No one could assume the burden of this mistake, this train wreck, this disaster. She sighed, "In the belief system of Wicca, there were but two major factions, the Elders and the Ancient ones. The Elders were the architects of this magnificent world of technology. They are the good guys. The Ancients were made to serve the Elders, but like most servants they wished to be the masters. We have plenty of stories of Ancients trying to master humans on Earth and occasionally the Elders intervening and eliminating the Ancients or reigning in the runaway maverick ways of control. Agegi is an Ancient and his behavior seems logical." Loggar slipped in social scientist mode and she saw half a book out of this experience.

Sean said in disgust, "And you made me a pasty in awakening that thing!" He jabbed his finger in the Chamber's general direction.

Loggar was hurt. "No Sean, I made you a part of this because I care deeply about you, I love you, and I wanted you to be a part of this."

Robin silently gasped and held her breath for a second.

The air seemed to thicken and Sean stood there with his jaw clamped tight.

"Sean, you must believe me." Loggar pleaded.

Herb coughed, "As touching as this moment is I think we need a plan. Everyone got an idea? Yes?"

Milkens stared at his feet and Kurp sank to the floor. Loggar, with teary eyes, turned away.

"Look you two, you're the military minds here. Do something!"

Sean sighed and looked at Robin. "Well, Captain you got any bright ideas?"

Robin just stared.

Sean turned to Herb and asked, "First we need to get the

hell off this planet. How far down are we from the surface?"

Herb said, "Ten levels. We passed the elevator."

They backtracked and saw that the elevator was blocked by one of Agegi's new minions. No doubt the standing orders were to keep them from getting off the planet, catching them or killing them. Not necessarily in that order.

"Herb," Sean asked sneaking back around the corner, "Are there any other ways out of here?"

"All in front of us . . .wait; there are those huge doors at the end of one of the branched hallways."

"Why so . . ." Sean froze and went pale. He heard talking voices coming toward them. "They're coming. Go!"

The group ran as fast as Herb could run. Herb clinched at his chest but kept going. His breathing was getting ragged and it hurt to take in air. He broke out in a sweat. Robin and Sean hadn't even started sweating. This run was more like a quick pace to them. Kurp, Milkens, and Loggar barely fared better then Herb. Years of Archaeological digs never taxed them physically only mentally. The group turned one corner and then a second. Herb stopped in front of a door and placed his hand on a small square next to the door. It had a symbol that looked like a cross between a flying saucer and a twentieth century jet plane. Sean wondered as the door slide open. The room was empty save for what looked like chairs along the wall. It reminded Sean of a briefing room. They entered one more room and it came alive. Sean swore and almost jumped out of his skin. An alarm of some sort went off.

"Damn I hate this magic shit."

The room was a narrow passageway, a 100 meters in length that lead to very tall double doors. The doors seemed to be a solid mass of steel, and meters thick.

"Okay Herb, how do we open these doors?"

Herb shrugged and said, "I don't know. I was hoping that it operated on "Magick" or something."

Sean stepped toward Herb, who took a step back, "What do you mean "Magick" or something?"

Loggar spoke up, "We think that behind here is another ceremonial chamber connecting to three other passage ways. The doors are made of a material that blocks most T-wave scans. We've seen several, we think, passages."

"Great, just great!" Sean said. Then he heard someone yell, 'We've found them!'

"Herb!" Sean shouted.

"Okay, okay, stand there."

Sean did so.

"And touch the door."

Sean did so but the doors remained closed, however, the group heard some sort of mechanical click. Sean looked back and saw about five minions at the far end of the chamber. They started walking toward them.

"Damn you Herb! Think man."

"Okay, okay, okay. I remember in the text that there was something about speaking some words to open the door."

"What?"

Loggar said, "Sean, this place is full of technology that allowed the Elders to perform "Magick." That's how they lived their lives."

Sean bit his bottom lip. Damn these foolish people and their equally foolish ways. "Okay, what do I say?"

Herb and Loggar shrugged.

"What?" Sean gasped.

Robin stared at them in disbelief. "You guys are the local scientist here and the expert witches, you've got to know the words!"

Herb shook his head. So did Milkens and Loggar.

Kurp grunted, walked over to Sean and whispered in his

ear.

Sean said, "You've got to be kidding?"

The minions were about half way there when they heard Sean yell out, "Abracadabra!"

The doors started to open. They started running toward the group.

Sean had his arms outstretched when he said the Magick word, but dropped them as he started to run. The doors slammed shut. "What the?"

Kurp said, "Young man, you have to keep your arms outstretched as you walk through."

Seam swept his arms open and the doors opened. He dropped them slightly and the doors closed slightly. He looked back as he ran through the now open doors – nearly 10 meters thick. He could only surmise what the doors hid. He turned around with his arms still open and faced the minions. They were about 10 meters away when he heard Robin shout, "Sean, shut the door! Now!"

Sean waited until the first two minions crossed the threshold and he dropped his arms. The doors slammed shut with a sickening wet slap. It caught one minion almost beyond the threshold and a second just entering it. Sean turned and dropped his jaw.

The chamber was a cathedral. "What the . . .?"

Sean stood witness to row after row after row of glass coffins. Coffins were the best word he could come up with. Loggar, Robin and the rest stood about several meters in front of him. Dazed, mesmerized and stunned at the magnitude and expanse of the number of these things. Sean stopped counting, in one direction, after one hundred, the chamber went on forever minus a foot. Off in the distance Sean saw a bright blue-white light pulsate in the distance. It looked maybe half a mile away. He walked up to Loggar and said, "What is going on?"

Loggar stood in awe of the expanse of coffins. She walked up to one and saw the face of a middle-age woman. Her hair was brown and she looked very very human. She went to another coffin and stared at an old man for about several seconds. This was beyond her wildest dreams! This was the discovery of a lifetime! She hurried to another coffin and then another, giggling in the process. She was bursting at the seams.

"Sean," She began, "You wanted proof of Alien life?" She impatiently shook her hand at a coffin. "Meet the Necronians!"

There are two types of salvation: Salvation through asking for forgiveness and Salvation through forgiveness. Each type has its own price to pay. One is paid by loss of dignity, control, power and influence. The second is paid by loss of influence, control, power and dignity. The difference between the two types is the order of what is important.

Chapter 22

Sean walked up to a coffin and stared deeply into it. It was absolutely unbelievable. His inner core being screamed that it was all a lie. It had to be a lie. And that this was a dream and that he would wake up in just a little bit because this place was just a construct of his subconsciousness. But he looked deeper in the face behind the glass cover. It was not a dream and this was a person. Damn! Reality could be a hard slap to the face. He looked up to Loggar.

"Now what?"

"W-W-What do you mean?" She stammered.

He stared at Robin and the others and simply added, "What do we do from here?" Sean wheeled around looking at the door. His anger building up, In one surge he turned back around and let it all come out. "I trusted you! I let you come into my life. I let you use me. I let you blindfold me into this Wicca thing and where has it gotten me! Where!" He screamed. "We got monsters behinds us and dead folk before us. Now I'm just asking you for a simply solution to all this. You people with all the answers." And in a flash his anger was gone.

Milkens cleared his throat. "Umm, Commander, they are not dead."

Sean shot him a look.

Milkens visibly cringed, but recovered fast enough to restore some bit of dignity.

"Come again?" Sean said.

Milkens cleared his throat. Herb had known Milkens for more than a decade and he knew he was a very withdrawn and shy guy. In a conversation, Milkens admitted to be very intimidated by the man. Randals he laughed at, Loggar he respected, like all the other high officials in the Most High, though Robin was a captain in the service and commanded a GRID ship she was Most High and very beautiful. But Blakemore, he said, was a true honest to goodness Battlecruiser commander, he was a hero who rescued people and fought the SI war. This man commanded loyalty and respect and authority and the glamorous and not so glamorous things in the Service. This man frightened him. Milkens told a deep breath. "The Necronians are alive."

Sean blinked. "I thought that's what you said."

Milkens nodded and continued. "They are in suspended animation, just waiting for something or someone to awaken them."

This was madness Sean thought. "What kind of people would purposely put themselves asleep for who knows how long, just to be awaken at the 'right' time?"

Kurp stepped up and said, "Because they were probably bored. Think about it. You can do anything you what just by waving your arms and uttering a few words and presto! Something happens. That kind of ability can get old. These people lived it from birth and they probably lived decades, maybe centuries before they started to age. Living in a place where one's ability to utter the right words probably got very and understandably trite."

Sean looked around and saw the others nodding.

"But you guys try and practice it all the time."

Loggar chanced a touch on Sean's shoulder. "Yes we do, but we never get there. We, mainly, speak the words and go through the rituals to bring the group into a sense of purpose. We really do want to do Magick, but we know we can't. Rituals just basically heighten our sense of our surroundings and focus us as a group. Our philosophy gets us through the day. We are Witches."

Kurp grabbed the moment and said, "And if we were Necronians we would probably be here, lying in wait for something to happen."

Sean suddenly looked tired. He shook his head several times and pressed his lips tight. He looked for a place to sit but found none, so he decided he was going to sit on a 'coffin.' The thought made him ill to the stomach. Milkens said these folks were alive, but still, they looked too still for his liking. Maybe they weren't dead. Maybe these people could help them. Maybe not. "How long have they been here?"

Milkens spoke, "Maybe several decades, maybe several centuries, maybe even longer, hard to tell really. We do know that Necron was abandoned maybe a hundred years ago."

Sean paced amongst several coffins. One older male in his sixties, a child in their teens, a woman in her forties. He peered in a 'coffin,' the person was a young woman about 30 something. Sean smiled at his attempt to guess her age. She was probably 300, maybe 3,000 or 30,000! Good Goddess this was bizarre. She had light brown skin and long black hair. Beautiful was an understatement. He touched the glass and suddenly felt dizzy. He had to sit down so he placed himself at the edge of the 'coffin.'

"Okay, my question still stands. Now what?" Sean said.

He suddenly had this feeling that something was

happening. He couldn't place his finger on it, but something was happening. He looked over to the light in the distance. "Any idea what that is?" He asked no one in particular.

Herb said, "Good question. Since I think we are safe in here I was going to suggest we walk there . . . umm, did you lock the doors?"

Sean shot him a look, "I don't know, did I?"

"Maybe we should make sure. I think you should touch the door again."

Sean shrugged, "Whatever, I'm just a resident tool here."

He didn't look at Loggar but he knew she had a pained look on her face.

The group walked over to the door and stood there.

Sean, just to see if he was still connected with the doors spread his arms wide. The door opened and he saw Randals, Agegi and a handful of minions. Two of them broke from the group and raced toward the opening. Sean waited until they were dead center then he closed his arms. The doors slammed shut crushing the minions. He walked over to one of the doors and touched it. The group heard internal mechanisms clicking, then silence. Sean stepped back and swept his arms open. The door remained closed. That was the best thing that has happened thus far he thought.

Agegi stepped toward the door. It opened and he saw Sean with his arms open wide. He told two of his slaves to stop him, but as they crossed the threshold Sean dropped his arms and effectively killed that plan. Then Agegi heard the doors lock. Randals was next to him when Agegi turned around. He looked down and said, "We have to find a way to wake the others."

Randals bowed his head once and said, "Yes, Master. Might I suggest these?" And he held out his hand. Randals had two prototype sniffer maskers that Milkens and Herb had been working on.

"Do they work?" Agegi demanded.

Randals smiled, "Perfectly, Master."

Sean turned around and dropped to his knees. The others rushed to his side.

Robin was the first to reach him. "Sean, are you okay?"

Sean, for a split second had this feeling that life was being drained from him. His head throbbed and he felt like his heart was about to burst. His muscles in his legs and arms didn't seem like they wanted to work. So he dropped to his knees and started to shake violently. After a few seconds he said, "Damn that was strange. I felt like I was dying for a moment."

Loggar reached Sean a second after Robin and she muscled her way between the both of them. She said, "Oh, Sean, I am so sorry. Please forgive me. I didn't know. This is all my fault and I don't know how to solve this one. I'm scared and I'm afraid this is not going to turn out okay for any of us! I just wanted all this to work out. It would hurt me forever to know that you hate me, but I would understand. I just want to tell you that I love you and I am so, so, sorry. And I ask only for your forgiveness."

Sean stared into her eyes for a moment. He really didn't have a reason to be mad at her, at least none he could think of, and she really seemed to be sincere about her feelings and he did have strong feelings for her and she was asking for his forgiveness. Here was this prominent scientist, the leader of a religious group, and a strong power within GRID asking him for forgiveness, and asking it in front of Robin. That had to mean something, really. Kathy came to Sean when he was at his worst and she helped him to get out of his hole. He was used, but it didn't matter. The GRID has and will continue to use all for its purpose, so what was Loggar's crime? She included him into a secret world that was very powerful. Sean hugged her and whispered in her ear, "Don't worry, I love you and we'll talk when this is over and done with, okay?"

She looked at Sean and wiped away her tears. She was very embarrassed to be crying in front of the others. She couldn't help it. She loved Sean and terribly needed his forgiveness. This whole mess was her fault. No amount of justifying would alter the fact that she played into Agegi's agenda. It was her fault that Sean had to kill four good men. It was her fault that Randals and others were turned into monsters. And if they died tonight or were turned into those horrible abominations it was again her fault. She cried a little bit more. Red eyed she looked at the others. Damn them for thinking she was weak, but when she looked at Herb and Milkens and Kurp, all three had tears welled up in their eyes as well. They smiled at her and walked over and hugged her. They understood because they too claimed some responsibility over this whole thing.

Robin, however, was stone faced with military discipline. She resented Loggar for pushing her away from Sean. And when Loggar started crying, that dropped her a dozen notches in her book. Robin resented the fact that Loggar played her like some background instrument in a full orchestra.

They all heard a noise behind them and looked up.

Every single one of them paled with surprise, shock and fear.

Sean was the first to recognize her. He sat on her coffin moments again. She was the beautiful woman with the long dark hair and the light brown skin. Now she stood in front of them, standing, breathing, alive and naked! Sean blinked several times. Was this a dream? A nightmare? Was he dying and this was the angel coming down to help him cross over?

She said, "I think I can help you out of this."

There is a penalty for Arrogance. Not one of imprisonment, but one of transformation. To be transcended to levels never imagined nor dared reached by those who dare to take that one step beyond the normalcy of mediocrity. To be arrogant, one must have knowledge, to have knowledge one must be privy to information. To assume arrogance when all data, all information has not been collected is cause for punishment. May the punishment fit the crime.

Chapter 23

Agegi stood in front of the entrance to the second chamber, the one that had 12 other statues. It was several hours since they left behind Sean and the others. When the doors opened Agegi glanced inside. It was the chamber. The chamber that housed all the Elders left on the planet. And he was going to get his revenge after all. Awake, they could best him, but asleep, he could crush every single one of them. This human was going to be the instrument for getting back what had been lost: his power. Long ago the Necronians turned him and all those that followed him into these abominations. He was flesh, bone and blood transformed into polymers, metals and exotic fluids.

Once long ago he had been alive and lived like any organic creation. He was not different from any other Necronian. The reason he was the way he was lay in the reason that he questioned the Council on their decision in their deep sleep endeavor. He advocated they abandon this absurd plan to split the population into two distinct groups: Sleepers and

Time Travelers. And just be explorers and creators. They had been the third oldest verifiable creation in the galaxy. The other two had vanished a million years before them in an epic war that destroyed thousands of star systems. Both had been races that lived for a hundred million years and wasted it all for dominance of the entire galaxy. Each foolishly vied to reign over the visible Universe. In the end neither won. Both succeeded in bringing about the ultimate tragedy. They utterly wiped themselves from the visible existence of the known Universe. It was a fight that either dared to risk it all. No one won; both lost. The Necronians had been able to develop on their own and become the superior species in the whole of the Galaxy. And within a million years they had become the oldest living active species and had visited millions of worlds. They had touched thousands of them with their seed and only a few had responded with positive growth and potential. Agegi himself had been one of the first to visit Earth.

In three-quarters of a million years the Necronians conquered mortality and decided that they would be travelers and explorers. It was over half a million years ago and he remembered the first time he saw the beast hiding in trees and huddled in caves. They had a rudimentary understanding of fire, tools and language. He had a choice of half a dozen humanoid species to work with. So he changed them all! He pushed and pulled and prodded all the groups to converge into three distinct groups. One short, stout and muscular. One tall, gentle and powerful. The other slender and intelligent with much promise. He merged two and gave them fear and religion all in one visit. The third he let die out. He believed that the Council should continue developing new species in their image and that the Necronians had an obligation to the Universe to seed the entire galaxy and ever galaxy henceforth. But the Council ruled him down and dismissed him from the Chamber of Decisions. It had been ugly. Later, he and his followers vowed to break away from the Council, take others with them to the planets they developed and live out their days ruling over these shaped worlds.

One of the rules the Council established long ago was that no one person or persons, without Council approval may influence another world. Doing so resulted in a harsh penalty. For Agegi to affect his plan he had to know entirely what the Council decided for all of Necronian. But his recent nature toward the Council had effectively barred him from the final plans and the in-between details. Agegi remembered the moment the Council police entered his home and searched his files. He had placed a seal over the files, but Marduk, the head of the Council, overrode it at the time. A few of his followers escaped, some even made it to Earth. He didn't. He and twelve others were detained and jailed. The proceedings were swift. Under penalty, he was to live his days out as an Ancient – a fallen Elder. Ancient in the old tongue meant: Altered Sentient.

The irony was not lost on Agegi. The very creatures he started and his followers influenced were here to both help and hinder him in his plans for revenge.

Randals smiled at himself to be servicing Agegi like this and was able to help bring the others alive. The maskers were taped to his chest. Agegi told him that clothing would never be needed again. Randals meant to ask him why, but he could feel his body changing. After he walked through that force field and came out alive and whole. He noticed that his body was becoming tighter, his muscles harder. He was changing and he could only guess into what. He looked back at the others, six of them left and nodded. Agegi had corrected him on the proper invocations needed to start the process. Randals swallowed hard and 'Invoked the Pentagram of Fire.' He spread his hands outward, palms forward and said, "In his name do I invoke thee. Mighty Father of us all - Lagh, Pen, Balen, Hernar. Cernunas - Come in answer to my call! Descend, I pray thee, in thy servant and priest." He stepped back.

The group rose.

Randals made the Invoking Pentagram of Fire toward Agegi with his athame. He turned to face the chamber. With sweating palms he grasped the athame with both hands and 'Invoke the Pentagram of Fire' at the statues. He took a step into the chamber, a group member came up behind him and started squirting Sean's DNA into the room. Randals yelled, "Let there be Light!"

Intense heat and light set the room aglow. Randals counted to twenty and he could feel the mist from the squirt bottle flow over his shoulders and around his neck. It was working. It was working. Then in one bright flash and a burst of light the chamber went dark. The first second nothing, no light no sound, everything was still, then Randals heard something take in a deep breath, then he heard another and another. He counted twelve distinct breaths in all and the lights came on. All twelve statues stepped away from the wall and walked toward them. Agegi turned his bland face to them and said, "Revenge is at hand. They will pay for what they did to us."

They all started to laugh.

Adruqu looked at the assortment of humans with curiosity. It was one thing to see them in her mind and another thing to see them with her eyes. They were huddled together going through some sort of bonding. Before that, the one named Sean sat on her container. He had enough of the DNA to start the activation and thus she stood before them.

The travelers foretold of the humans and that Adruqu would have a hand in saving them. She knew their dilemma and offered her assistance.

Sean, she saw, recovered from the initial shock of seeing her. The Relations Council said they would be immobilized for a time, until their brains could assimilate what was transpiring. They said that Sean might recover first. He did.

Sean stepped forward. He had his head angled awkwardly and asked, "Who are you? Are you real?"

Adruqu laughed cutely and walked to Sean. He took a step back but stopped and let her touch him. "I can give you vocal words and explain or I can just give you the information."

"How?" Sean asked.

Adruqu got closer and touched Sean's bare chest with hers and she kissed him deeply. The kiss was passionate and long. After a moment she broke the kiss and moved over to Loggar. "You are Kathy Loggar, Most High Goddess." And smiled.

Loggar stammered, "Y-Y-Es, I-I am. How did you know?"

Adruqu looked to Sean and said, "We have been watching. Would you like me to pass the knowledge on to you?"

The group stared at Sean. He licked his lips as if savoring the best substance in the entire Universe. He turned to them and nodded. He chuckled at nothing in particular. "Do it Kathy. Do it for me, please."

Loggar turned and looked into Adruqu's eyes. Her pupils were not that much different than humans, maybe more oval. In fact, they were a lot of similarities save for some internal organ difference. Maybe even some physiological differences. She let Adruqu draw close to her. Loggar was about the same height and she was warm. She could smell her sweet breath as her lips got closer and then their lips touched and Adruqu embraced Loggar tightly. Loggar was swept up in nothing she had ever encountered. She loved the way Sean kissed her, his passive aggressive, give and take way of kissing. Sean seemed to magically know how to kiss her, but Adruqu's kiss was beyond anything she had experienced. Energy seemed to flow from her like sweet tasting water from a glass dipped in the magical waters of the Fountain of Youth. Their tongues touched, flickered back and forth against one another. Then Loggar heard words in her mind and saw pictures and images and scenes. Adruqu was giving her information and she understood all at once what was going on and what needed to be done next. Then the kiss ended and Loggar almost cried out 'No!' Once she and Adruqu withdrew she looked over to Sean. He reached out and grabbed her hand. He nodded and smiled. He heard Milkens raised voice, "My turn!"

Robin was the only one to refuse. Adruqu explained that the kiss was her way of exchanging data. She was giving each person special nanobots, which was how each person understood certain things. Adruqu explained that their brains were not that much different because the human species had been shaped. She said that each person would now be able to understand her native tongue and in time would understand a great deal more.

Robin rocked back and forth as she listened. In the end she snapped that she didn't like the way the information was given. Sean shrugged, turned his back and asked Adruqu, "What I don't understand is why you guys settled on this plan?"

Adruqu chuckled sweetly and said, "It was the only logical and sanity saving thing we could do. I am over 100,000 years old and . . ."

Herb interrupted. "100,000 years old? But what about that old man we saw next to you and the older woman and the child? If I was 100,000 years old, I would rather look like I was 20!"

Kurp cut in, "Yes, young . . . " he caught himself and

chuckled, ". . . looking lady, with your technology I would not want to be this old looking, and the child? Is the child as old?"

Adruqu smiled. She was enjoying this encounter immensely. Before she slept, the others told her Aliens would awaken her. She was frightened at first, but she was told it would be by descendants from one of their developing worlds and that they would need her help. She gladly accepted the task. "Drepha is my son, the 'old' looking one, and he went into sleep before it was his time to rejuvenate. Andurio is my mother, as she too has to wait. The child," she chuckled, "is our father, Maniluso."

Sean listened and waited patiently.

Adruqu said, "But Sean's question is still unanswered. Our civilization had been around for a million years.   Our prehistory goes back maybe another 2 million years.   We achieved space flight within 40,000 years and immortality soon after that. We traveled the entire galaxy in 500,000 years and started projects a little after we achieved faster than light travel. In all the other half-million years of our existence we lived, traveled, explored, created and soon became bored. We as a species had nothing else to do. In my 100,000 years I have been to the galactic center and back, I know several thousand languages and just as many sciences, I've given birth a thousand times. I've visited just as many worlds. My main disciplines are astronomy, biology, music, exobiology, physics, and chemistry. You would rate my IQ in the three hundreds and I am but average. I've died tens of times and made first contact as many times. I've built empires as well as destroyed them and I am but one single individual. Think of the millions of others lying asleep behind me. We utter words and make gestures and things appear and magically happen." She closed her eyes for a second and uttered softly, "tolas, kolas, yuhonki, ye ohtgi dukufa." And a cross between a honeydew and peach appeared in her outstretched open hand. "Tock, tock, tock." And three more appeared. She handed everyone a fruit except Robin.

Sean touched the fruit in his hand. The skin was smooth and had a gray-orange color with a texture like honeydew.

Adruqu said, "The dukufa is a very juicy and sweet fruit. It has been engineered to respond to the touch of someone with nanobots in their system."

"Come again," Sean said.

"Look at the fruit and tell it to open, but use the tongue." Adruqu urged them.

Sean cleared his throat and said, "Dukufa lup aba ca na dabra."

The fruit split into a half dozen pieces. He almost dropped a few.

Loggar and the rest tried and laughed and walloped on their new talents.

Robin stayed some feet from them. She just stared at them feeling hurt, alone and betrayed all in one. Maybe a little bit angry. Sean was willing to forgive Loggar, but Robin was not ready yet. Sean seemed happy with her and that bit of information seemed to bug her. She nearly jumped when she saw Sean looking down at her.

He had his arm outstretched. "Robin, join us."

She looked up into his eyes, not knowing what to do. In the moments after Agegi wakened and everything got shot to hell she froze on them. She was Captain, she was supposed to be in charge, but she hesitated. She never hesitated, never! She commanded a Battlecruiser into war and came out victorious. She fought alongside her crew when the SIs boarded Gallant. But she froze back there and they all saw it. She saw it in their eyes. Sean asking "Now what?" Loggar and the rest waiting. Then Sean ran and they followed. They all followed him blindly through the corridors, passed the elevators that would have taken them to the shuttles, into this place. Then Sean yelled at them for all being fools and not being able to do a damn thing. It hurt Robin, but he was right! Then Loggar pleaded for his forgiveness. She dropped to her knees and apologized! The Most High Goddess reduced to groveling at the foot of a male, Robin's ex-lover and former-friend. At the moment Loggar begged, she figured Sean was getting a hard-on, but when she looked she saw that he hadn't. He was not getting off on some power trip. She continued to look into Sean's eyes. His hand was still outstretched. Robin summed up her entire situation. She failed herself and she was ashamed and Sean was not gloating. She reached up and grabbed his arm and pulled herself up. Then both walked over to Adruqu.

Adruqu asked, "Are you uneasy about the method of exchange?"

Robin said, "I don't know if I'm worthy of it." And she suddenly looked down at her feet. Adruqu stepped closer to Robin; Sean backed away. Adruqu touched her on the hand. Robin nearly jumped. Adruqu lifted Robin's chin, said, "and am I not worthy to give it to you?" And kissed Robin deeply.

Robin's eyes widened in shock and fear, but she relaxed after a bit and let the kiss take her away. Adruqu stepped away. Robin's hands trembled.

Kurp coughed and everyone turned to face him. "I am puzzled by one thing, Adruqu."

Adruqu smiled and said, "Yes?"

"How did you know our names and how did you know you would be awakened by Sean?"

"We have all been aware of your presence from the very beginning."

"From the beginning?"

She nodded, "Yes, we are asleep but aware and we are all connected to one another. The project allowed us to create a paradox on Necronian. I am not the only one who uses the container. Other self is on another world, exploring. And while we have been talking someone else on the other side of the Gate has returned and exchanged places with their other self. Before we placed ourselves in sleep we made our rooms and machines with redundancies. We knew that one day a descendant would return to us and would unlock our secrets . . ."

Herb yelled, "I knew it, knew it, knew! Five bucks, Milk."

Adruqu continued, "It was I who gave you information Herb. We built into our plans that one day someone would open the Great Doors and that someday someone would touch my container."

Sean said, "What else do you know that you haven't told us."

"Many things, but since I have given you the nanobots, you will know. But for now the two main things I have not yet told you are that I am different; I am the third self and will make my stand with you."

"Stand?"

"Different?"

"Third self?"

Adruqu nodded, "We are still living our lives in two different ways. One we travel through time to different places and the other we sleep here. Once every 694 days our self returns, and for 60 minutes we exchange data, and talk about the next 694 days. If we decide to make it longer then we do so. But each person has the opportunity to explore."

Kurp asked, "How long have you been asleep?"

Adruqu said, "Only 6 months."

Kurp shoot out, "Good Goddess! You guys have been exchanging all this time and we didn't know?"

Adruqu nodded, "How and why would you know? We've been doing this for over a hundred years and there hasn't been a reason for us to directly contact you. All that has been required is for you to continue to do what you do until you had been able to open the Great Doors. The rest now has been played out. The doors will open and you will make a stand."

Sean said, "What do you mean, 'the doors will open and you will make a stand? We can't fight those things out there!"

Adruqu smiled and said, "You didn't know Magick then. Now you do. And you know our language. What more is needed?"

Sean blinked at that statement and faced the door. He closed his eyes for a moment and said, "Ruogka!"

He was clothed in a white caftan. He giggled and turned to face the others. "And who said there was no such thing as Magic?" Sean walked up to Loggar and said, "My Most High Goddess should not always be nude, behold, the finest cloth in all the galaxy." He closed his eyes again, visualizing a silk-like flowing simple gown. He opened his eyes and said, "Ruogka!"

And Loggar was clothed. She shrilled like a little girl and yelled in delight, "Sean, it is so beautiful!"

Herb discarded his robe and closed his eyes. He saw himself in a caftan like Sean's but with gold trim and he pronounced, "Ruogka!" And he was clothed.

Milkens and Kurp did the same thing. And they all jumped up and down like giddy school kids.

Robin slowly took off her clothes and imaged her uniform. She then said, "Ruogka!" Nothing happened. She closed her eyes again, straining to make the uniform appear. "Ruogka!" Nothing happened. She turned to Adruqu who was looking at her. The others stopped their kid playing and looked at Robin.

Sean said, "Adruqu, it didn't work for Robin, how come?"

Adruqu sighed, "She has separated herself from the group and no longer believes in herself."

Robin almost wanted to cry. Her eyes puffy and full of

tears and her bottom lip started to tremble.

Sean thought for a moment then walked to Robin. "Robin, for years I hated you. I hated you for walking away from the trial with a promotion and me with my teeth kicked in. During the trial you broke all communications with me and I waited for you to contact me."

Robin looked away ashamed and horrified. She knew that one day she and Sean would have this conversation but she didn't think it would be now.

Sean continued, "When you took command of the Johnson I was just furious. It was like, how could GRID Command do this to me? I commanded the Johnson throughout the war. I hated you even more, but after a time it slipped away. Robin, I never accepted responsibility."

Robin said, "But you did Sean, you rescued them, I didn't. You executed the rescue. I just watched. I should have talked to you during the trial, but I was told to stay away." Then she stopped.

"I know," He said, "You were part of Most High and Most High takes care of their own." He looked at Loggar.

Loggar nearly crumbled and Herb, Milkens and Kurp stared at the floor in guilt and shame. Loggar felt like her heart was ripped out of her chest. Sean had to have guessed her secret and therefore hated her.

"Robin, it doesn't matter, none of it matters. I should have been adult about the whole thing. I wasn't. Forgive me for hating you. Okay?"

Robin sniffled and pouted for a second. Sean apologized.

Sean walked over to Loggar passed the others, who still had their heads down. Loggar wanted to die on the spot. Sean smiled at her and said, "I've already forgiven you, please forgive me now."

Loggar blinked several times. "Forgive you about what?"

Sean's smile broadened, "For not believing you."

"W-What?"

"For not believing in Aliens and Magick and the whole process of capturing what you believe in. You let me into your world and helped open my eyes. I believe in Aliens. And I believe in Magick." And he hugged her and they both cried.

Betrayal is such that it may be subtle or blatant. When it is subtle it rips and tears at your heart and your dignity and all that you stand for. When it is blatant you see it coming and can mount an adequate defense. Confronting this type of betrayal takes all the energies and all the feelings one can squeeze out at a moments notice- that's easy. The other can never be fully confronted. The assault is too devastating, too deep, and too thorough to confront in one battle.

Chapter 24

Randals looked up at the laughing Statues. They were like Agegi but not like him. He had a gold sheen. They were dull brushed silver. After a moment they stopped. One of the other Ancients spoke.

It looked down at Randals and said, "Our new front line troops?"

"Greruti, yes. This one is Randals, a most helpful one indeed. Without him and his fellows you would still be frozen. But we most hurry. The Elders are asleep in their folly of a plan. We but have to open the Great Doors and slaughter them as they sleep. Then we may take the other's flying crafts and make claim to other systems."

Greruti nodded.

As Randals followed them down the chamber he could not help but think that the Ancient ones all had history together. He and the other humans were the babes in the woods, the new hired hand. 'New front line troops' particularly didn't sit well with him. He was not going to be any ones red shirt. He decided that once this was over he would take a shuttle of his own and find his own place in history. The hell with them all.

Adruqu frowned and said, "It is almost time."

Sean turned to her, "What do you mean, it is almost time?"

"Agegi has awakened the other Ancient ones. He has others with him. The other Ancient ones being awakened was not foreseen."

Herb said, "Our fault. I created a device that would fool your DNA sniffer thing."

Adruqu thought for a moment and smiled, "Of course, that should have been foreseen. I suppose that is the price to pay for arrogance. Being as old as we are, we think we have all the answers." She laughed out loud. Almost scaring the group. "No matter," She said, "we will still make our stand. Agegi and his minions wish to destroy us in our sleep. He would kill or transform you. I hope we are in agreement that this must not happen."

Sean thought for a second. "Wait a moment here. You knew all this was going to happen. Why didn't you stop us before awakening Agegi? You could have prevented all this in the very beginning. You'd be asleep and safe."

Adruqu looked at him inquisitively.

Sean tried again, "We didn't have to go through all this." Then it dawned on him. "You wanted all this to happen. You wanted to put yourself in danger; you wanted Agegi to be revived. This is all some sick game you wanted played out."

Adruqu turned to Sean. She stepped toward him and he took a step toward her – stopping her from moving any closer on her own choice.

He starred deeply into her eyes. He was mad as hell, yet another arrogant shit manipulating him. Playing him like some pawn in a twisted game of chess. "I'm getting tired of having my fucking chain jerked around."

Loggar stiffened, but Sean reached back and touched her on the shoulder to reassure her it was all right.

Adruqu thought and said, "Sean, I am sorry for all this, but at this moment it is something that can't be changed. . ."

"Yes it can! We can run through that time machine of yours!"

"It is not that simple," Adruqu said, "The events have been put into motion. Yes it true that we could have stopped you, but that would have defeated our purpose."

Sean hissed, "And what purpose is that?"

Adruqu blinked as if the answer was simple and very plain. "For you to be able to earn the right to do Magick."

Sean stood still and looked at his hands. Some how he knew things he didn't know before. He scowled and thought of a fireball and threw his hands at the corner of the door. A ball of fire whipped and whirled in front of him and roared toward the door and exploded in licks of flames and heat knocking everyone to their feet except Adruqu.

"Sean!" Adruqu yelled. "Think defense" and she fired a light ball at him.

Sean hesitated for a second but thought the word 'defense' and the energy ball engulfed him and a second later passed behind him.

Everyone stood silent.

Herb spoke first, "We can all do that?"

Adruqu said, "Yes. You just have to believe, think it, give the word and it will happen."

The natural ambient silence of the chamber was broken by the sound of the Great Doors' mechanism. The Great Doors' were unlocking.

Herb said, "Oh shit. This is not the time to just learn how to do this! You guys are sick for throwing us into the fire like this. I'll never forgive you!"

Sean faced the door and realized this is exactly how they

meant this to happen. Adruqu said that the Necronians were aware of everything that was happening and that they all were watching this. It was something like a vid program to them. Look, behold, the Monkeys learned Magick and now they are going to show us some tricks. Sean shot Adruqu a dirty look. She nodded that she understood him perfectly well. Sean turned back to the door. "Okay, if this is how you want this played out then so be it. Let's have our showdown and give you guys millennia to talk about the Hu-muns and how they fought the Ancient ones."

Loggar understood, so did Herb, Milkens and Kurp. Robin stood in the background, uncertain.

Herb closed his eyes and yelled, "Ruogka!" And he was dressed in a purple long tunic covered with Griffin motif. It was something out of the 12th century, animal skin boots and a thick leather belt. He wore a tall pointed hat complimented by a purple long cape and in his hand was a large wooden walking stick.

Not to be out done, Milkens imagined himself as some white sorcerer, a fine white linen gown with a white rope belt around his waist with a heavy cotton mid-waist cape. He saw a heavy oak wood staff six feet tall in his mind's eye and uttered, "Ruogka!"

Be careful of the words you say.   Someone may get pissed off!
Also, be worried of a woman scorned and all that.

Chapter 25

Randals stood in front of the door. Davis and Martin stood on both his sides. They were all that was left of the turned Most High. After he touched the Door to unlock it Agegi had the other Ancient ones fell behind him. Agegi stood directly at Randals back and said, "Now my faithful Randals open the door."

Sean stood facing the door. Loggar and Herb to his right. Milkens and Kurp to his left. Adruqu was directly behind him kneeling. Robin was somewhere in the background. He didn't think that she would be of any use to them or herself. She still had her own internal battle to win.

Randals faced the door and said, "Aba ca na dabra!" and the door started to open.

Sean heard the door open before he saw it. He looked and saw Randals with his arms outstretched. Then he saw Davis, Martin, Agegi and twelve other things like Agegi.

Agegi looked down at the spectacle and laughed. The remnant of the Elders and his companions were taking a stand against him. He spoke, "Sean, remnant of the Elders, join me, move aside, or die. It is now my destiny . . ."

Sean thought about what he was going to say. He wanted to say something witty and maybe provoking. In the end, only two words would probably give him the effect he wanted from this arrogant SOB. Sean summed up all the anger he was feeling and dumped it all at Agegi. He screamed, "Shut up!"

Agegi hesitated for a moment. Sean told him to 'Shut up!' How extraordinary. That was the last thing he'd imagine anyone to say to him. "Move out the . . . "

"Shuddup!"

Agegi paused again. "And you are going to make me?"

Adruqu stepped from behind Sean smiling. "I will do that, Agegi."

Agegi searched his mind to remember the face of this Necronian. "Adruqu. I am surprised . . ."

Adruqu interrupted him and said, "Shut up!"

Agegi stepped back as if he had been slapped. Anger boiled up inside him and he roared. The sound carried energy throughout the chambers. "How dare you . . ."

Sean, Adruqu and the rest just simply yelled, "Shuddup!"

Agegi clenched his fist and shoved Randals aside.

Randals slammed against the wall and dropped his arms and the doors slammed shut.

Agegi stumped toward Randals and demanded the doors be opened.

Randals slowly got out. "Yes, Master." As he was about to take his place the doors opened and Adruqu, Milkens, Kurp, Loggar and Sean ran through the open doors. Milkens, Kurp and Herb ran through with glowing hands and fired bright white light balls at one of the Ancient Ones. It got hit by all three balls, screamed, hollered and disappeared in a bright flash of light. Sean and Loggar cleared the door. Sean dropped his arms and the door slammed shut locking them outside the cathedral. Loggar volleyed a huge red flame ball at an ancient. It was enveloped and it screamed and yelled and vanished in a flash of light. Sean hit two Ancients at once.

He tossed two large balls of fire at them, both Ancients poofed in flashes.

Agegi roared his anger and ran toward Sean. Adruqu stepped in front of him and surrounded Agegi with an energy field. He screamed and roared and screamed and roared.

Randals and the others stood stunned. They saw the others doing Magick! That meant that the chamber held the secret all Wicca had been looking for. It had to hold it. How else could they do the things they did. And this woman, who was she? An Elder?

An Ancient one stepped forward and swung at Kurp. A split second before Kurp remembered to think defense. The blow swept him up into the air and shattered his arm. He landed against the back wall but had enough sense to hurl an energy bolt at the Ancient. It flashed out of existence and he fainted.

Herb and Milkens ran further right and each took out an Ancient. Then they saw two Ancients rush them. They both thought the word 'Defense' and it felt like a freight train hit them. They slammed against the wall and blacked out.

Loggar imagined an intense fireball and hurled it at the two Ancients. They flashed out of existence.

Sean crossed left, ducked a swing from an Ancient and fireballed it to the hinterlands.

An Ancient covered the distance toward Sean, raised its arms and flashed in a bright light. Sean looked back and saw that Loggar had saved him.

Randals witnessed the carnage. It had happened no less than seconds. He moved up quick on Loggar and slammed her into the wall. She crumbled like a ragdoll. Then he and the others lunged for Sean. Sean sidestepped one, but caught a fist in the stomach and dropped to his knees. Then he felt hands grab both his arms and squeeze hard. The radius and ulna bone from each arm shattered and he fainted from the pain.

Adruqu yelled, "Stop or I'll destroy your Master."

Randals grabbed Sean and moved his limp body to the door. He touched his hand to it and the Great Doors unlocked.

Adruqu repeated, "Stop or I'll destroy your Master."

He dragged Sean's body back a bit and yelled out, "aba ca na dabra!"

And the Great Doors opened.

Randals yelled back, "Destroy him then. I'm busy."

All three ran the distance to the other side, dragging Sean with them. They dropped Sean's unconscious body on the ground with his arms still outstretched.

Randals saw the rows and rows of containers. Then he saw the bright column of light. "That must be how they learned Magick."

Robin kicked herself for not following the others through the door. She did the ultimate act of cowardliness. She let her friends and comrades go into battle alone. But just as soon as the doors closed they opened and she saw Agegi suspended by Adruqu. She heard Randals say 'Destroy him then. I'm busy.' And watched as he dragged Sean through the door. Randals dropped him. He and the others looked around and Robin knew what she had to do. She saw in her mind's eye that she had power. She believed she could do it. She had to, and deep down inside she knew the reason she could do it. She still loved Sean and he needed her at this very moment.

Randals took a step and Robin stood in front of them.

"You're not going to go any further."

Randals looked at her and laughed. "Your friends are defeated. Move out of the way . . . stupid bitch!"

Robin clenched her fists tight and thought for a second. Her anger was building up and up. She hissed, "How dare you call me that."

Randals laughed and said, "They left you here because you are the weakest. Yeah, I know the whole story. You let Blakemore hang to dry. You are a coward. Screw you, you Bitch! Move out of my way." And he ran toward her.

Randals outraged Robin! How dare he call her such things? Damn him and the others. She was not a coward, not stupid and certainly not a bitch. In a split second she thought the word 'Stop' and in that moment everything seemed to crawl. She saw Randals and the others slowly come at her. She saw Sean raise his head to see her. She saw Loggar, Herb, Milkens and Kurp open their eyes – all on her. And she saw Adruqu smile as she held Agegi within a barrier. A second seemed to take forever, everything, time, perception dragged on for eternity minus a minute . . . then . . . in a flash Randals, Davis, and Martin stood frozen inches before her. They were solid metal.

Epilogue 1

Sean and Robin stood at the entryway to the shuttle. Adruqu was back asleep waiting for her other self to return in another 514 days. Sean cursed her and all the Necronians for all this. Their little group played out like some vid show for the common masses and Sean hated that. But that was a memory now. After Robin froze Randals, Davis, and Martin, Adruqu did the same to Agegi. She said she could only do so after all the superfluous stuff had been dealt with, meaning the other Ancient Ones and Agegi's minions. Sean doubted it and believed she could have taken them all out at once. Adruqu also fixed their wounds. She said that the nanobots would always be with them until their natural death, but that they could only perform Magick on Necron.

That night Sean and Loggar slept together. They made love but were much more subdued and tender toward one another. Afterward they cried and made up and cried some more. And they both apologized and cried more still. Loggar was going to stay for a bit to collect more data. She wanted to find the other species the Elders developed, guided, changed or whatever the term of non-guilt was. She told Sean that when she got what she needed she would contact GRID Command and have Johnson pick them up – if they weren't too busy and if it was okay with him. She told him that night that she loved him very much and asked him, in between love making, if he would consider being by her side – forever. Sean surprised himself and said yes, but he wanted to command the Johnson for a while. She understood and said that he dare never worry about asking for favors. He smiled and said he didn't want to abuse her privileges and they made love again.

Robin called the Webster to rendezvous with the Johnson and pick her up.

Herb, Milkens and Kurp were the only ones left of the original staff. Loggar had requested new members to the team. The Webster, who was bringing them in, was waiting for Robin to authorize the transfer. Loggar also sent a detailed report to GRID Command. Some things she left in, some things she left out, but the report was a masterpiece, though she claimed total responsibility over the accidental deaths of her staff. Herb knew that GRID Command would look at the deaths as just another cause for the service. Why not, Loggar proved the existence of Aliens and that there are possibly brethren out there amongst the stars. That meant more to all of GRID than a handful of lives lost.

Epilogue 2

Just before going to the Johnson, Sean read a message sent to him from Kirkland. It said "eyes only to Commander Blakemore."

Kirkland knew what it was and he had leaked some of the contents out to the command staff. The common crew didn't know yet. There were three messages. One to Loggar, one to the Commander, and the third addressed to Captain Robin Spaarin.

Now Sean held a hardcopy addressed to him in his jacket pocket. He and Robin entered the shuttle and he flew it to the Johnson. He was amused by the contents, but considered it just one more thing to affirm that it was okay to like himself.

Dawn met them at the shuttle dock. She had this lopsided smile on her face. He knew that she knew. He figured Kirkland decoded the message and informed the entire command staff.

That evening Robin, Dawn, Sean, Kirkland and Foster were having mess in the Captain's dining room. The conversation was light. No one really said anything of importance. Dawn was going to wait until Sean was alone before she asked him the actual specifics and not the damned cover-up report. Then Top Deck called.

Sean said, "Yes."

The computer said, "Captain Spaarin, the Webster is here. They are ready to receive you."

Sean reached under the table and pulled out a hard copy

printout and handed it to Robin.

Kirkland watched with anticipation. He read all three messages. The message sent to Loggar read: Situation rectified. More messages to follow.

The message sent to Sean read: To one Sean Blakemore. After revisiting past issues it has been decided that past decisions were not in the interest of GRID Command. The Quail family has made a public apology and admits that a mistake had been made. The Quail family gives you its deepest regrets for the entire misunderstanding. GRID Command message follows - GRID Command has reviewed past decisions and has hereby made changes to the status of Sean Blakemore. Sean Blakemore is now promoted to Captain, status and back pay are retroactive to five years 23 days.

The message to be given to Robin read: Commander Blakemore, under review has been promoted to Captain, retroactive five years 23 days. The Johnson is under Captain Blakemore's command. Nothing follows.

Robin read the message more than once. She looked up at Sean.

He nodded and took a sip from his soup. "I want you off my ship, Captain."

Riker in security won the pool. Three months' pay!

She nodded, wiped her mouth, and said, "Computer, get me the Webster."

The computer beeped, then, "This is the Webster, Commander Rogers speaking."

Robin said, "William, send a shuttle to pick me up ASAP."

The voice said, "Captain Spaarin. Of Course, immediately." And the connection broke. The Webster received the same message that Robin read. The shuttle was seconds away from docking. Captain Spaarin's promotion was set at five years two days ago. Sean was now her senior.

At the end of the day Sean felt pretty good. He got his Captaincy – damn time, was bonded to a very beautiful, intelligent and influential woman and escaped death, all in less than 24 hours. He smiled at the "gift" he left the Necronians. It was something small and he hoped it would make them think about it for many years after he was long gone and dead. They left Randals, Davis and Martin in the main chamber with Agegi, motionless, still statues. Sean had a box placed just at Agegi's feet. Within the box was an invoice. It read:

For a waste of time: 3,000,000,000,000 credits
For human life lost: Unpayable
For starting this entire mess: Unforgiveable

Terms to be negotiated: Upon arrival in the known here and now space-time continuum or until the Human species decides to occupy Necron in mass.

Have a nice epoch!

ACT II:
Alien Shores

Stay! Stay! You saucy sailor boy, Do not sail afar; I love you and will marry you, you silly Jack tar. 'Twas but to tease I answered so, I thought you could guess that when a maiden answers no she always means yes.

(From Saucy Sailor Boy. Circa. 18th century, Earth.)

Chapter 1

Sean Blakemore sat at a table in Starboard's Bow – the enlisted officer's mess hall. He sat by a view port eating Cookie's latest creation of Skilly. It was a little bit of everything. Some meats, vegetables, different splashes of sauces – red, green, hot, sweet, herbs, spices, anything and everything in the galley. Sean marveled at the delicious combination of flavors and tastes. Cookie out did himself, he always did. Sean would never admit it in open public, of course. Mr. Grant, the Officer's Watch main cook, would be highly offended. For the officers on board Johnson, they had to endure Grant's slightly above mediocre abilities. GRID rules specifically prohibited enlisted officers from cooking meals for commissioned officers in a sanctioned Officer Mess facility. Sean toyed with the idea of making Cookie a Warrant Officer and transferring him to Officer's Watch, but he was certain Johnson's crew would riot. So he and some of the other officer's satisfied their cravings for good cooking with the occasional visit to Starboard's Bow – under the guise of "getting" a feel for how the Johnson was running.

It was on an occasion not too different than this moment Sean remembered talking to Dawn. He saw her, his first officer, looking out a view port. It was just before the 'crazy-

time.' A term Sean accepted for his time spent on Necron –
the planet of aliens, fantastic technology and Magick! He
looked out and saw a star streak by. He used a large spoon to
sip juice from his Skilly and chuckled to himself. All hands in
the mess hall knew to ignore the Captain's bursts, as they
called it. Suddenly out of nowhere the Captain would laugh
and those around him would get swept up in the infectious act
and laugh too. Of course, only the Captain would know the
reason for his bursts. Sean asked Dawn about gossip on the
ship and Dawn told him she had a juicy one. Straight face she
said that he was "whipped three sides to Sunday." Meaning
that Dr. Loggar had effectively gained control of his little
head, which controlled his thinking head. Sean had a burst.

The last time Dawn caught him off guard was when she
told him that she was a Most High follower and that close to a
third of the ship's complement were as well. The Johnson held
three thousand personnel and one thousand followed Wicca!
Sean took a mouthful of Skilly and swallowed. He continued
to look out the view port and marveled at the turn of events
that got him his long withheld captaincy, the discovery of the
'sleeping' Necronians, the living statues, and his . . .

His thoughts were interrupted by the intercom. "Captain
to Top Deck, emergency message from GRID Command.
Decryption is imminent.

Sean hurried through four more mouthfuls of Skilly and
rushed to Top Deck. He thanked Cookie for another good
meal. Cookie beamed brightly and hummed 'The Saucy Sailor
Boy' and went about his business.

Sean entered Top Deck. He listened to the chatter of
beeps, hushed talk, keyboard clicking, background hums and
the like. He walked over to the Command chair and sat down.
Dawn was in the XO chair. Sean asked "Well, Dawn,

anything good?"

Dawn looked up from her CRT and said, message from GRID Command is 93% decoded. We have vid and text."

"Who's it from?"

Dawn tapped on her CRT and after a second replied, "Dr. Loggar."

Sean frowned. He had just spoken with Kathy a few hours before. She said that the research on Necron had taken an exponential leap. Adruqu was communicating with them on a regular basis via terminal and that she had provided years' worth of data, particularly locations of seeded planets, charts, medical data, everything and anything. It was beyond fantastic. So, why had she sent him a special communiqué byway of GRID Command? "Dawn?"

"Yes, sir?"

"Authenticate upon full decryption."

"Already in progress, Captain."

"How long will it take?"

"About 30 minutes, give or take a dozen seconds."

"I'll be in the conference room, continue with the conn."

"Aye, Sir."

Sean got up and walked through the sliding conference room door. He walked over to the table and sat in the main chair. He swiveled around to watch the stars streak by. The conference room desk was made of pressed Oak wood. All of GRID Command used Oak wood for what they considered tables of importance. It was vanity, but no one stopped to question why Oak and not some other wood. It was something established over three centuries ago.

Then, "Captain?" It was Dawn's voice.

"Yes, Dawn?"

"Dr. Loggar on channel six, standard encryption."

"Thanks." Sean said, and pushed a button marked 'channel six.'

Loggar's image pixilated to a full picture. Her brown hair was tied back into a ponytail. A small strand of hair was loose between both eyes. Her eyes brightened when she saw Sean.

Sean smiled and said, "Hey Kathy, two calls in one day?"

Loggar blew Sean a kiss and said, "This one is more business than pleasure. You get my gift?"

Sean nodded. "Yeah, received it not too long ago. I haven't had a chance to open it yet. I promise I'll look at it very soon. It got me curious, though." He left it at that and let the silence hang in the air a moment.

Loggar slowly nodded, she frowned. "You should have received it a few hours ago. Probably nothing wrong." She thought for a second. "I know you will love it, but the main reason I called is that I need you to come pick me up. It's been cleared through the proper channels – you should be getting a new set of orders soon."

Sean's smile broadened. Any chance to see his beloved was always welcomed. "Good, anything you can tell me now?"

Loggar giggled, "That's what the gift is for, Sean. I'll leave you to look at it, okay?"

Sean nodded, "Okay. I'll get back to you when I have a time of arrival."

Loggar leaned closer to the screen and she placed her hands as if she were holding Sean's face. She kissed the screen.

Sean smiled and touched the screen as if he were touching her cheek. It was their custom for good-bye.

The screen went blank.

Sean got up from the table and walked out to Top Deck.

Dawn got up from the XO chair and handed Sean a hardcopy. "GRID Command, Sir."

Sean took the hardcopy and read it. Sure enough, it was new orders. The Johnson was going to Necron – and so was the Webster. Sean sighed heavily. "Dawn?"

"Yes, sir?"

"Course laid in? ETA?"

"Twenty-four hours, ten minutes. The Webster is already en route. Webster will be there a good eight hours ahead of us."

Sean thought for a moment. The Webster already en route! That spoke volumes. That would mean that Robin got orders before he received his or GC delayed his orders, which could mean political jockeying – some folks still had a bad taste in their mouths from his quick promotion and the Quail apology, or Loggar requested Robin first and then as a second thought requested Sean. Sean tossed that last thought out. It had to be some sort of in-house posturing. He would talk to Kathy about it later. When they were alone.

Dawn watched the play of emotions on Sean's face. She, too, thought much like Sean did. GRID Command was playing games or Loggar was. She weighted both as fifty-fifty.

"Dawn, what would it take to get us there in twelve hours?"

Dawn smiled. She had anticipated Sean's question. "Running the engines hot at one-one-zero percent, bypassing GRID points and making some scary long jumps."

Sean walked over to his chair and sat. He tapped on his CRT. "Engineering?"

Mr. Curtis "Pulse" Landtrap had been head engineer of the Johnson for two decades. It was whispered that if Pulse said it couldn't happen then God himself had to acknowledge it and move on. Pulse got the word from the XO that Captain was going to run the Johnson hot, real hot – twelve hours hot. Damn it was good to finally have a "Captain" sitting in the chair. Pulse had nothing against Blakemore; it was just a real mean slap in the face to a fine ship like Johnson to be commanded by rank less than "Captain." Pulse broke out the drinks when he heard about the promotion.

Blakemore was a fine leader. He deserved nothing less than Commodore, really. Pulse had time and Goddess wishing, he and the Johnson would see it.

Top Deck was calling; it broke him out of a wondering trance. Pulse walked over to his desk and tapped on his CRT. "Yes, Captain." Damn that felt good!

Sean's image appeared in the tiny view screen. "Pulse, the Johnson is going to be running hot for about twelve hours."

Pulse nodded, "Engines prepped Sir. We got the call earlier; the Johnson is ready to go. Just give the word."

Sean smiled, "Very good, Top Deck out."

Pulse smiled to himself. The Captain was pleased. He looked up from his desk. Engineer was divided into five sections: Main part – dead center of the Johnson surrounded by ten meters solid alloy and three layers of shield screens, Port and Starboard Bow sections, Port and Starboard stern. His desk placed him in the center of Main part. He could see all bow and stern areas from his location. He tapped on his CRT to open up Engineering comm. "Now hear this, Johnson is gonna run hot. Man stations and look lively. Repeat, we are gonna run hot. Engines at one-one-zero percent." He clicked off.

Doctor Karen Collins, Chief Medical Officer, had received word from Dawn. The Captain was going to do War jumps and to expect incoming. Foster alerted her staff and gave them their instructions. She had thirty doctors, ten per eight-hour shift. Though the ship ran on old six four-hour shifts, she kept her staff on the three eight-hour schedules. She called the entire medical staff to duty. Collins was expecting the worst. War jumps meant nothing less.

Sean tapped on his CRT. "All hands, this is the Captain. Prepare for War jump, prepare for War jump. All personnel not called to duty station stay in quarters and Trank deeply. This is not a drill. Johnson will be driving for twelve hours. I repeat the Johnson will be running hot. One bell to jump. Captain out." Sean tapped on his CRT again. He typed out a quick message to Loggar and told her to expect him in twelve hours. He typed out a general reply message to GRID Command and told them he would reach Necron in the expected twenty-four hours planned. He had a hunch that GRID Command was going through some sort of positioning change. Robin, of course, would get the information about the Johnson arriving eight hours after Webster and would proceed normally. His gut feeling told him Robin could be playing both sides. Though they departed on neutral terms, there were a few moments for embarrassment. Robin froze during a crisis and Sean was pretty sure it nagged at her ego. He couldn't possibly know what she was thinking these days. After he asked, actually told her to leave his ship, communication was spotted – and only from text communique.

Top Deck, Engineering and Medical were abuzz with activity. The Last time Johnson had done War Jumps was during the SI wars – officially ended, but unofficially still on. Though the Johnson is one of the oldest ships in GRID Command she is one of the fastest. The newer ships jumped on shorter GRID waves – higher frequency, thus using less energy to travel further. Johnson was almost all raw-power. It was meant to be a multi-purpose ship with four different main batteries – newer ships, like the Webster had either one or maybe two types of main firepower, and its missions were for a vessel that was good at quick strikes, escort, stealth, and absolute defense. Johnson, being one of a few left, was the last of the "all-weather" ships. Its main engines are from the era that GRID waves are best traveled on long sinuous waves. The disadvantage of traveling on long GRID waves was its effect on the crew. The shorter, higher frequency waves of the newer ships allowed personnel to function as if under almost normal conditions. GRID travel sometimes affected the human nervous system. Sometimes crew had to be placed under sedation during prolonged travel. The Johnson was going to use a war maneuver that basically made the entire crew nauseous, in short useless.

Sean waited in his chair and counted off the minutes. Top Deck was in overdrive. He checked the time, a minute to go. He tapped on his CRT and said, "Johnson, do you hear me?"

A male voice answered. "Yes Captain Blakemore, I do."

"You know what we are about to do?"

"Yes, Captain, I do. We are going to do a War jump for twelve hours, seven minutes and 36 seconds."

"Yes Johnson. You have the coordinates?"

"Yes, Captain."

"You have any questions?"

"No Captain. I understand what I am supposed to do. War jump will start in twenty seconds."

"Very good Johnson, you are a good ship."

Sean took a hypo-spray from his shirt pocket and pressed the head to his deltoid muscle. He felt the rush of sedative spread from his shoulder to the rest of his body. He placed the spent hypo back in his pocket and tapped on his CRT. "All hands, all hands. Ten seconds to jump. Repeat, ten seconds to jump. Johnson is aware and in control. Trank up now, Captain out." He looked over to Dawn. "Just like old times, huh?"

Dawn placed her spent hypo in her shirt pocket. "Yeah, old-times. Did I ever tell you I hated War jumps?"

Sean replied, "Did I ever disagree with you?"

And the Long jump began. Sean winked out of consciousness and dreamt – nothing.

Then his messmates drew him up, But on the deck he died, And they stitched him in his hammock Which was so fair and wide, And they lowered him overboard And he drifted with the tide, And he sank in the Lowland, Lowland, low And he sank in the Lowland sea.

(The Golden Vanity, 1685, Earth.)

Chapter 2

Sean's vision blurred. He was slowly coming out of Trank. His temples throbbed but he wasn't in pain – too used to War jumps he supposed. He fumbled in his pocket and pulled out a hypo of STIM – it was a stimulant and pain response blocker. He pressed the hypo against his arm and felt a cold-rushed-jolt hit him. His eyes snapped wide open and his vision was crystal clear. For ten seconds he could read the small text on the Nav-console, twenty feet away. STIM gave him 20/5 vision for a brief burst. He looked around and saw Top Deck coming to from the walking dead. Zombie like movements were replaced by the eye snap open wide reaction from STIM. He tapped on his CRT. "Johnson, do you hear me?"

The deep voice replied, "Yes, Captain Blakemore, how are you feeling?"

Since the Johnson responded with a question all was well. Had the Johnson been in trouble it would have immediately replied with a status report.

"I'm fine, thanks." Sean had to reply in an exact word code. "The Jump went well?"

"Yes it did," Johnson said, "while en route I realized I could save us some time. Mr. Landtrap has done a wonderful job in maintaining my engines. I was able to push them at 120% with no danger to crew or mission. We are two hours ahead of schedule."

Sean smiled. "Has Necron noticed our arrival?"

"Not that I am aware of. Comm. channels are silent and I am running in external stealth mode."

"You're a good ship Johnson. Back to normal mode."

"Yes, Captain. Returning to normal mode."

Sean tapped out a command from the keyboard and touched his CRT. All lights inside Johnson switched from the normal bright yellow-white fluorescent to an amber glow. The ship was officially on stealth mode.

Sean sat in the amber light thinking about the Johnson. Out of all the things that bugged Sean, having the Johnson toggled to "normal" mode bugged him the most. Sean fought GRID Command tooth and nail on their decision. During the first half of the SI War, old ships like Johnson were being compromised. Instead of finding ways to secure the ships, GRID Command moth-balled half of them, and gave the rest "Toggled" modes – the crew called it "dumb" mode. The moment Sean punched in the command to switch Johnson to "dumb" mode Top Deck fell silent for nearly a minute. Sean missed the Johnson's AI. Flipping the switch was like cold-cocking an old friend because a stranger said 'do it, or else.' And so, he watched the main screen in silence. Necron floated in the center and grew bigger with each second. "Scan for activity. Anything yet?"

Dawn tapped on the CRT. "Nothing, Sir. No, belay that. Signal on a tight beam."

"Can we pull in residue data?"

Mr. Kirkland was at his Comm. Station. "Captain, recording residue data now. Beam is encoded with a variation of Level 9 protocols. It'll take a while to decode."

Sean ran through different scenarios, Loggar contacting Robin, someone contacting Robin, someone secretly contacting Robin. "Mr. Kirkland, how long to decode?"

Kirkland ran the procedures in his head. He figured out the variant and concluded it would be about 30 minutes. "Maybe three hours, Sir."

Sean nodded, "You got one."

Kirkland nodded, "Yes, sir."

Loggar checked the time. The Johnson wouldn't be in orbit for another hour or so. She had one of the new techs run scans, but nothing turned up. After their little adventure with Agegi she had the two main chambers sealed. She also placed several layers of Level 7 shields at each entrance. She was the only one to know the remote codes to deactivate each shield. That day still haunted her. She would wake up in a cold sweat clawing the sheets. It was a day she never hoped to repeat.

Robin sat in the command chair sipping tea. She played what happened to her on Necron. The more she thought the angrier she got. It didn't bug her so much that GRID Command made Sean a captain, he deserved it. She was bugged that they made him her senior! She was promoted first, she earned it. It was a slap to her face. But maybe things were going to right themselves again. She had an ally now and things were going to get interesting. Word was that Loggar was a bit too reckless. First, Robin was reluctant to tell the whole truth. But once she saw the hypocrisy of the Most High she talked. Several senior Officers had their suspicions but couldn't prove anything. Loggar was highly respected and listened too. And, that was the problem. GRID Command was a military branch, not civilian. Something had to be done and it had to be done soon. So, Robin was 'picked' for this delicate mission. Webster had another five hours before it reached Necron and as the minutes ticked by Robin fumed and got angrier still. She felt more than heard the pop. All hands turned to look at the sound. Her cup of tea had vanished in a pop of light. Astounded, Robin looked at her hands. She looked up and told Command Deck as they were; all was well, nothing wrong, or something to the effect. She remembered Adruqu telling her that she could only do Magick on Necron. But, they were at least 1500 light-years still out from Necron. It started as a quick jerk tightening of her gut, then a warm fuzzy feeling and last a realization – the proverbial "light bulb" blinking on.

"Mr. Dansel, prepare for War jump."

Mr. Dansel, the Webster's main navigator said, "Yes, ma'am. Preparing for War jump."

Robin tapped at her chair screen. "All hands, all hands, this is the Captain. Prepare for War jump. Ten minutes. Ten minutes mark!" She tapped out a few more times. "Engineering."

A tiny voice came out from tiny speakers. "Yes, Captain?"

"You heard the preparation. Make it so. Ten minutes."

The tiny voice came back. "Ten minutes, ma'am."

Mr. De La Cruz, Comm. Officer, said, "Captain, message coming in from Necron. Level 9 protocol with variant."

Robin smiled. Today was going to be a good day after all. She couldn't wait to see Sean's face when he landed on Necron. He told her, "I want you off my Ship, Captain." That was fine. She probably would have done the exact same thing. Wait until he hears the words, "I want you off this planet, Captain." She amused herself for a few minutes replaying the pending encounter over and over in her head. Revenge is so sweet tasting when delivered cold.

"Captain, Webster is ready for War jumps." Mr. Rogers, the Webster's XO said.

Robin tapped out a command. "All hands, all hands, War jump in 10 seconds. Mark!" She tapped a few times and then spoke to Mr. Dansel. "Ten seconds to War jump, Mr. Dansel. Make it a public countdown."

"Aye, ma'am." Mr. Dansel opened up the public channel, "Ten, nine, eight . . . "

Robin sat back against her chair. The Webster was a newer ship and thus didn't require the crew to Trank-up like on the Johnson. The crew would come away with a mild headache, some nausea, maybe even dizziness . . . "

"Seven, six, five, four . . . "

But that was a small price for progress. "I want you off my ship, Captain." Robin curled her lips in a mean-spirited smile. "I want you off my ship, Captain." 'Fine then you shit. I'll get off your ship, but revenge is a bitch.' She never said that, of course. But does it matter? Revenge is revenge, however it is served.

"Three, two, one . . . jump!"

What will we do with the drunken sailor? Earlye in the morning? Put him in the scuppers with the hose pipe on him. Hoist him aboard with a running bowline. Put him in the brig until he's sober. Make him turn to at shining bright work. Put him in a boat and row him over. Hoist him up to the topsail yardarm. Make him clean out all the spit-kids. That's what you do with a drunken sailor. Amen.

Chapter 3

Sean sat at the head of the conference table. Around the table seated Commander Dawn, Lieutenant Junior Grade James Kirkland, Dr. Karen Collins, Chief Warrant Officer Curtis Landtrap, Lieutenant Junior Grade Julian Foster, Lieutenant Senior Grade Nikki Quock – from Security and Lieutenant Commander William Molino – Chief pilot of Johnson's Fighter Wing Group. Sean looked around the table. Only Mr. Landtrap and Ms. Quock were not of the Most High. After his talk with Dawn, he went back through ship's records and wanted to know, personally, who was Most High and who wasn't. It surprised him. Cookie was, but Grant wasn't. Half of Top Deck staff was – all six shifts. All of Medical was not, except for Collins. Almost all of Security was except for Quock. It was an interesting mesh-mash of talent and beliefs sitting at the table. He wasn't exactly sure what he was going to tell them. Loggar's gift was a vid message set to transmit to Loggar and himself the moment her files had been compromised. Someone in GRID Command broke into her office and rifled through her hardcopy and computer data. Also, the tight beam from the base to the Webster was a tip off that Loggar had a spy on staff. He cleared his throat. "We have a situation."

Mostly everyone nodded. Dr. Collins and Ms. Quock were the only ones not up to speed.

Sean continued, "Ms. Quock and Dr. Collins, after this meeting I have a vid I need you both to see."

Both nodded.

"Mr. Kirkland, can you give us a condensed summary on that message sent to Webster."

Mr. Kirkland sat toward the far end of the table. He had been in the Most High for nearly his adult life. The day Loggar came abroad the Johnson he knew things were going to change. It delighted him to see the Captain and the Most High take an interest in each other. It was like a fantasy. The leader of his belief and the leader of his life coalesce. One couldn't have it any better. So, being part of the Command Staff was one big friggin' wet dream. He cleared his throat. "Yes, sir. I was able to make sense of about 95% of the message. The other 5% is made up of terms and words not in our language banks – I haven't deciphered them yet. The joist of the message reads that samples of some advanced alien technology have been acquired and duplicated and ready for pickup. Also, that certain individuals – tight clothes, eyebrows, cereal, and legs, no doubt code names, have been observed to "continue' to perform unexplained abilities." Kirkland finished.

Sean sat and waited a bit. "Thank you Mr. Kirkland." He thought long and hard on this, but decided he had to let his staff in on it. "Computer, play Most High Goddess one. Please."

Sean had discussed this earlier with Dawn. She agreed that the Command Staff must know but she didn't know how to breach the subject. Dawn was elated that Sean decided to become a follower of Wicca. It even delighted her more that Sean was a descendant of the Elders. She was totally loyal to Sean and would follow him to the ends of Heaven and Earth, which on more than one occasion she did. She loved Sean but wasn't in love with him, oh, she would have been his lover if he had ever asked, but he never did. She was happy to be his friend and first officer. Sean told her things that his Parents would suicide from and she made sure that he could trust her. They did have a brief sexual moment during the SI wars – secretly Dawn wished they continued, but she knew she needed to be his foundation and friend, not his whore. And one day Sean needed someone to talk to and he was grateful they just talked and not fucked. Personally, Dawn mainly preferred females to males and she kept her affairs and flings very discreet and quiet. Only a handful of crew knew that she was bisexual. It was something she didn't feel she had to keep quiet, she just wanted to keep her options open, and being mysterious did make for better sex.

The Computer played the vid. Everyone sat in silence.

"The Most High Goddess was an organization that briefly had political influence in the then state of California on the planet Earth during the first quarter of the twenty-first century. Toward the middle half of the century the Most High, as it was popularly called, gained political power. Most High controlled most of the Americas, the western hemisphere of the planet Earth. Even though the South Americas had mainly been stapled on Catholicism it still retained, underground and behind closed doors, a communistic culture steeped in some paganism. Ironically, Wicca was mainly a European product, but the Latin continent embraced Wicca and Paganism as a natural extension of the homegrown consolidated Catholicism. During official and highly visible celebration the usual parade of worshiped saints and idols made the rounds. But in the after-hours of normal life the real zealous forms of worship took place. Wicca was among the most popular – not in European style, but Wicca nonetheless." Then the screen flashed to Sean and Loggar and the others awakening Agegi. They watched as Agegi grasped Randals' head and turned him into his minion. Then it flashed to Sean, Kurp, Milkens, Loggar, Herb and Adruqu fighting Agegi and the Ancient ones.

Then the vid flashed off. The room was silent. Several seconds ticked by in awkwardness which Sean never felt before. He waited another ten seconds.

"Any questions?"

Nikki Quock faced Sean. "You can do all that?"

Sean passed out hardcopy notebooks to each person. "Read through the data and yes, on Necron I can do that stuff."

Each person took a book and leafed through it. Collins he expected to have questions – she was medical. Quock would be concerned with defending the ship. Pulse would try and figure out a way to make the Johnson better and Kirkland and Foster would just what to play around with the fireballs.

Sean waited.

"Captain?" It was Collins. "I'd like to run some tests."

Sean nodded.

"How much does Control know?" That was from Quock.

"About a third. They know the planet is inhabited by the Necronians, and that Agegi was awakened – by unknown reasons, and Adruqu defeated the Ancient ones and Agegi, and that is about all. Dr. Loggar wished that non-Most High followers not be told all the details. I'm telling you all this because I know I can trust you with this. And . . . " Sean waited a heartbeat. He looked over to Dawn. She smiled and nodded. " . . . I have to confess something. After becoming a Most High follower I learned that a third of the Crew also follows Most High." Sean took a deep breath. "Folks, followers of Most High or not, you are my Command Staff. There has never been and will never be any prejudice. That goes for ship wide. Everyone has to be treated equally and fairly – in discipline and reward. Am I understood?"

All nodded in agreement.

"Now there is one last thing. There is no need for any of this to leave this room. Crew doesn't have to know and I certainly don't want to see any pools as to what was said today." Sean stared at Kirkland.

Kirkland blushed and nodded.

Sean said, "Adjourned."

Everyone, but Quock and Collins, got up and walked out.

Sean said, "Computer, play Loggar message 78."

"Sean, my files have been compromised. We should be getting this vid at the same time. Now that we know that my computer system has been broken into, we have to act quickly. Hopefully, you are on your way here. Once I receive this message I'll request you pick me up. I'll tell GRID Command that I need to get back to Earth. These are times too fantastic to tell you. I'll have to show you.

The vid flashed off.

Sean looked at both of them. "Any questions."

Quock spoke up. "How powerful is the Most High?"

"Seemingly very powerful. I didn't know how deeply entrenched it was until I met Dr. Loggar. I had some bitterness with them, but I've worked through my duhkha and moved on. Ms. Quock, you and Mr. Landtrap are not members of Most High . . . " Sean stopped.

Quock thought through the ramifications of what Sean just said. That must mean that everyone else on the

Command Staff is Most High. She wasn't sure how she should receive that. She nodded.

"Up until six month ago I was not a member. I am still a follower of Buddha-Dharma. Remember that. Even though I let myself lean in a direction that put me at odds with my duhkha, I still thought about my path. I tell you this because I don't want you to feel any pressure in becoming a Most High. As far as I am concerned, you need never join. You will be privy to any and all information. Period."

"Thank you, Captain. I hadn't felt any pressure. And thank you for letting me know there is none."

Sean smiled. He liked Nikki Quock. She was fresh out of the Academy when he met her. She had just "learned" some guy at The Badlands – a bar joint for the locals. Sean liked the place because it served a nice chicken combo meal. Real chicken. The guy sassed her about the uniform. She said 'whatever' and continued talking to one of her fellow classmates. Knucklehead, as Sean secretly called him, snatched her drink from her hand and upended it. He wiped his mouth with his sleeve and said, 'buy me another, sweet cheeks.' She wheeled on him so fast he couldn't stop the surprised look on his face. She placed him in an Aikido hold and dropped his head – hard, on the table. She banged it several times. She then casually called to the Barkeep and said 'this gentleman is going to buy a round of drinks and food for everyone in the bar.' He tried to protest, of course. The Barkeep smiled and asked him personally. He started to say no, but a slight squeeze and a sudden 'slam!' had him groaning out 'yes.' She let him go and stepped out to the dance floor – a small ten by ten dark wood square. Knucklehead shook himself and walked up to her. He was a full half-meter taller. Music was playing in the background, Sean couldn't place the music but it was a local rock fusion ragga-jazz band. Quock closed her eyes and started dancing. Knucklehead grabbed for her arm, but only got air. He dropped to his knees with Quock holding the other hand in a bend-squeeze maneuver. She whispered something in his ear and Sean could see tears welling up. He nodded. She let go. He walked over and collected a handful of drinks and started passing them out. Sean had two servings of Chicken and a bottle of wine – expensive wine, that night. After he passed out the food and drinks he sat quietly by her side for the rest of the evening. She allowed him in the conversation between him serving drinks all night. He even tipped the cook and hostesses. When GC handed Sean the Johnson he needed to fill some ranks quickly. He hunted Quock down and offered her the position of Head of Security. She said yes. Then Sean asked her what she had whispered into that guy's ear. She laughed and told Sean she said that well-behaved good boys got her attention and if he impressed her enough and followed directions she would think about giving him some that night. Sean laughed and gave her the highest rank he was allowed to – Lieutenant, Junior Grade.

Quock got up. She checked with her staff, excused herself off Top Deck, found herself stepping across her quarter's threshold, found her bed, curled up and shook for a few minutes. She was glad the Captain told her she need not worry about being Most High – she was sure that was what he meant. It was the end of her watch anyway. She walked over to her desk. A picture of a happy couple was on it. It was her and the guy she met in a Bar called The Badlands. They had been together for about five years. Just recently, a year to the day, Tom decided to join GRID Command. He had a talent for fixing engines: turbines, electric, induction, quantum, he just could. He was finishing his second semester and she was proud of him. They had been lying in bed a year ago. He reached under the pillow and pulled out a hardcopy of his acceptance letter. He made the grade and GC accepted him. She never told him that she found his application a month before and followed the 'paper' trail. When it looked like it stalled she asked the Captain to help out. He was a Commander then, but he still had some friends in GC. Within a week the process continued and Tom was accepted. He took her out on the town to celebrate. A week after that, her shore leave ended and he was called to the Academy.

Collins sat and stared at Sean.

He smiled. "Yes, Doctor. You have a question or two."

She had a question or two. Sean sat in front of her different. Six months ago he was in a very sorry state, excessive drinking, sleeping disorder, moody, near manic depression, almost anti-social. Then he turned himself around. She wondered what really happened on Necron, but all she got was 'read the report.' Six months later the truth came out. Sean experienced the dream of a lifetime. Interacted with the Most High Goddess, understatement – she got in on the pool as well and got second to last place, met alien life, learned an alien language and could do Magick! What Most High follower wouldn't want that? Now, she would be included in everything. "Will I be able to learn Magick?"

Sean and Loggar talked about this one evening. Sean synced his watch with the Planet Necron. The planet rotated every thirty-eight Universal Hours, but Loggar and the Team worked in twelve and one half hour shifts. One evening Sean tight beamed Necron to see if she was up. He couldn't sleep. She was up and they talked the "night" away. She told him that she was afraid to make Necron public – public to all of Wicca. It would be like playing God, she giggled, Goddess. All Most High followers and even all of humanity would want to know how to do real Magick. It was a huge responsibility and she dreaded even the most positive of outcomes. It was simply something humans aren't ready yet. Sean agreed, but he harbored a secret perverted wish to populate Necron with

"Monkeys" running up and down the corridors flashing fireballs left and right. It'd serve the Necronians right. He'd like them to wonder if a remnant of an Elder would open the 'Great Doors' and dance on the containers. "Oops, sorry, I woke you up. Anyway, what's your name? Can you do Magick? Do you want to kiss me and give me nanobots? Teach me please!" Sean answered Collins. "Probably not. Adruqu gave us that ability because of special circumstances. If Agegi hadn't been awakened I doubt we would have known about the main chamber. We'd still be trying to guess what was behind the Great Doors."

Collins nodded. She understood but was still disappointed. Of course, who would not want to do Magick!

Sean said, "However, Kathy did specifically ask for my Chief Medical Officer, so I guess you are going to see some things you may not have guessed at.

That made Dr. Collins feel better. Maybe there was something to get out of this. And Sean called The Most High by her first name. She wondered if Sean would consider being Most High God? She was several feet away from the would-be second most powerful individual in Most High. Today had to be something special.

Sean walked out of the conference room. Dr. Collins stepped into the lift and headed to Medical. She had a lot to think about. Sean walked over to the command chair and sat. He tapped at his CRT. Johnson was no longer in stealth mode. "Mr. Kirkland, get me Necron base, please. They are expecting a call."

Haul away the bowline; the Yankee ship's a rollin'. Once I had a Yankee girl, and she was such a daisy. Once I had a Scotch girl, and she was fat and lazy. Then I had an English girl, and she was tall and crazy, Haul away! Haul away! Haul away, Joe!
(Tack and Sheet shanty, before 1812)

Chapter 4

Loggar, Kurp, Milkens and Herb stood just inside an overhang that overlooked the landing pad. Sean said he would meet them in ten minutes. Loggar remembered the first time she was with Sean when he piloted a shuttle to the surface. Robin was in the co-pilot seat and screamed just as loudly as she had. Sean flew that craft by the seat of his pants. He asked if either of them got motion sickness. Both said no and he dropped the shuttle into the atmosphere, came in hot and glided the shuttle in dead stick. Once on the surface he laughed and said he wanted to do it again. So, when Sean said ten minutes, she was sure he meant ten minutes.

Quock and Collins accompanied Sean to the surface. He asked if either got motion sickness. They looked at each other and laughed. Sean dropped the shuttle into the atmosphere. He came in hot and glided the shuttle, dead stick, near the landing pad. About a kilometer from the pad he hit the retros, increased shield strength, barrel-rolled several times and stood the shuttle of its rear before he dropped the nose and came in for a soft landing. Quock and Collins heard of the Captain's piloting skill but this was the first time they witnessed it personally. Sean blushed when both women laughed and spontaneously applauded.

Loggar held her breath when she saw the shuttle barrel roll in, stand up and suddenly drop to a landing. She felt sorry for whomever was in the craft with Sean. She and the others walked to the shuttle as its doors opened. Loggar saw her darling Sean, in his uniform with Captain's insignia, with two very pretty women. She guessed one was a civilian and the other some sort of combat, maybe security, personal. She ran the last few steps and embraced Sean in a long lovely hug. Then she turned her attention to his companions.

Sean said, "Kathy, this is Dr. Karen Collins, Johnson's Senior Medical Officer, and Lieutenant Nikki Quock, Head of Johnson's Security.

Loggar shook hands with them.

Sean said his hellos to Kurp, Milkens and Herb. He noticed that Herb was, maybe, a size smaller. "Herb, did you lose some weight?"

Herb beamed and said, "Yep, fifty pounds and I feel great, down to a Large now.

Loggar shook both their hands. "Sean, we have learned so much since you left. Tonight we have planned a celebration dinner."

Sean frowned, "I'm not sure we'll be able to do any celebrating. Did you know the Webster has been ordered here as well?"

"The Webster? Robin?"

He nodded.

"Interesting."

"Also, we intercepted a message sent to the Webster. It was on a very tight beam and encrypted with a Level 9 protocol."

Loggar stood still for a moment. She had to catch her breath. A second ticked by, then two, then the realization kicked in. "Someone in GRID Command wants what we have."

Sean slowly nodded, "Possibly. It may also be a power move as well. I have to get you on the Johnson. You four have one hour to get ready."

Kurp spoke up, "Now young man, do you think it necessary that we make such a hasty move? I was going to run a sim on the latest data . . . "

Sean shook his head. "If I'm wrong we'll be back in time for that celebration. The Webster is due here in another three hours, but I got a gut feeling we don't have that much time. How many personnel do you have?"

Loggar said, "Ten, including us four."

Quock spoke up, "Captain, if you trust them then one of the other six or all six are spies. I think we should leave the others."

Sean thought over the ramifications of that action. Leave the others sounded sane enough, but what if the spy wasn't a spy per say. GC had invested a great deal of time and expense in this dig. Maybe they wanted a more accurate account on the goings on here. Someone knew, had to know, that Loggar's reports were not completely truthful. And then there was Robin's involvement. They hadn't parted on the best of terms. He kicked her off his ship and that had to leave a stinging mark on her ego. Sean sighed. There could have been half a dozen what ifs, maybes, probably could've-would've-should've been. "Who do you trust, Kathy?"

"Well, you and whoever you tell me to trust, Herb, Milkens and Kurp, of course. I thought I could trust Robin."

"And the other six?"

"They're all highly competent. I trust Marie, Dennis, and Tony. Gordon reminds me of Randals . . . "

Herb laughed.

" . . . and Myra and Ashley are a bit too quiet."

"Your call, but we need to move now."

Loggar thought for a moment. "We need to take Maria — she's in charge of the Nanobot project. And Tony is her assistant. Gordon is the language expert . . . oh Sean, I can't make that decision."

He nodded, "Okay, assemble everyone but tell them nothing. Herb, Kurp and Milkens can get started on a quick pack." He looked at them. "Stuff the shuttle with what you can. We leave in five-zero minutes."

Lay aft, is the cry, to the break of the Poop to my way haye, blow the man down, or I'll help you along with the toe of my boot! Give me some time to blow the man down!
(Blow the Man Down, After 1818 maybe derived from an African-American Song, Knock a Man Down)

Chapter 5

Tony Desella, Maria Albright, Gordon Ross, Myra Lincoln, Dennis Hinckley and Ashley Bush sat in chairs around a large table. They stared at Sean for a few moments.

Sean hadn't really decided what to do, but he figured if he had the six unknowns in one place they couldn't send off a message to Robin.

"Why are we here again?" This was from Gordon.

Sean said nothing. He sat and stared back. Collins was on his right and Quock stood at the doorway. She had unsnapped her holster. Her gun was now free.

Gordon said to no one in particular, "I see no reason to hold us hostage."

Sean looked at his timepiece. Twenty minutes to go. He pulled out a CSD and turned it on. It was about the size of his palm. A tiny screen flicked on. He typed in a code of numbers from the tiny keyboard.

Dawn's face appeared and she said though tiny speakers. "Yes, Captain."

"Dawn, have the Johnson moved to the opposite side of Necron and send out some scout ships. I want to know when the Webster enters 'Now' space. I got a gut feeling we have to cut this visit short."

Dawn repeated the orders.

"Dawn?"

"Yes, sir?" She replied.

"What pools are circulating?"

Dawn smiled, "Well, the one who would scream first and loudest was a surprise. Who really knew Quock and Collins as thrill junkies? Only Clinton in Armory guessed that Collins and Quock would enjoy the ride. That was a good one. A month's pay! The latest one is whether the Webster will catch us with our pants down. Oh, and there is a small one about us getting into a fire fight with the Webster."

"Hmmm, can you put me in the fire-fight one, you know, give me a random spot . . . it's on when we fight not if, correct?

Dawn's attention was diverted for a moment. "You're in, sir. You want to know your spot?"

Sean shook his head, "Nope, can't have the crew thinking their Captain is a cheat."

Dawn's tiny image smiled. She nodded approvingly. "Captain, scout ships deployed and Johnson is moving to the far side of Necron."

"Thanks, Dawn. We'll be coming aboard in about three-zero minutes. I'm gonna run the shuttle hot. Captain out." Sean cut the connection. He wondered what type of pool his statement 'running the shuttle hot' would generate.

Collins and Quock smiled.

Quock said from the doorway, "Captain, there is a way to automatically place you in a pool."

Sean looked up, "Really?"

Quock nodded, "When we get to the ship I'll ask Mr. Kirkland to set you up with an account. He's got some really sophisticated programming and some nice AI algorithm . . . "

Gordon took the opportunity to ask, "Why are we here,

again?"

Sean stared at him for a second. "Continue Quock."

"He's got it worked out that you can input specific parameters and the system will only place you in the pools you want or think you'd be interested in. You can even set aside your max pay in for each pool."

Sean smiled, "Nice."

Gordon frowned and said, "Look you. I don't know what is going on here, but I'd like some answers."

Sean yawned, but said nothing. He was, however, feeling a bit hungry. "Are you two hungry?"

Collins and Quock nodded.

Gordon slammed his fist down on the table.

Some of the others started to speak up.

Sean wondered if he really could still do Magick. He thought of the dukufa fruit Adruqu had produced months before. Then he uttered, "Tolas, kolas, yuhonki, ye ohtgi dukufa. Tock, Tock." Three dukufas appeared. Sean tossed one to Collins and Quock each. Everyone stared slack jaw at Sean. He sat back and said, "Dukufa lup aba ca na dabra." The fruit split in a half dozen pieces. "Collins and Quock, you'll have to peel yours the old fashion way." He put a slice in his mouth and savored the taste. "Mr. Ross, is it?"

"No, it's Doctor Ross."

Sean laughed and placed another slice in his mouth. "What do you do here?"

"I don't have to answer you." Gordon huffed, "I'm the one asking you for answers."

Sean thought for a second and pointed his hand at Gordon. He then lifted his arm upward and Gordon floated up out of his chair. "And I don't have to gently put you back on the ground . . . what do you do here?"

Gordon looked down and broke out in a sweat. He was afraid of heights but never told anyone. "I'm a linguist."

Sean smiled, "Na ficha ponija ka?"

Gordon stammered, "I didn't understand you?"

Sean raised his arm higher and said, "You're not a very good linguist."

"Okay, okay, I didn't send the message. It was Tony!"

Tony jumped to his feet and yelled out, "That is a lie. You bastard!"

Sean closed his eyes and said "Ruogka!"

Tony had a gag around his mouth and his hands were tied by rope. He jumped and slammed into the table. He nearly panicked but caught himself."

"Shut up and let him finish." Sean said at Tony.

Tony sat.

Sean looked up to Gordon and raised him higher. He dropped him a foot and shook him a bit. "You have more to tell me."

Gordon's heart pounded. He wished this were not happening. He swallowed hard. "We are working for GRID Command. As investigators."

Sean lowered him to a chair. "Ruogka!" He said and Gordon was gagged and bound in thick rope. Sean's CSD went off. He touched the screen and Dawn's face appeared.

"Captain, Webster has entered normal space. It's about four-zero minutes away."

"Thanks Dawn."

"You want a fighter escort?"

"Have one waiting in launch tubes just in case."

"Aye, aye. Fighter escort in tubes on the ready."

"Thanks. Captain out." Sean closed his eyes again. "Ruogka!" Maria, Ashley, Dennis, and Myra were bound and gagged. He placed Gordon back in his chair bound and gagged. Sean finished his fruit, got up and walked toward the door. Quock and Collins finished their fruit as well.

Collins said, "Wish I could do that." And smiled.

Quock nodded.
Sean smiled back, "Maybe one day you will."

A hundred shall serve - the best of the brave, and the chief of a thousand shall kneel as thy slave, and thou shalt reign queen, and thy empire shall last Till the black flag by inches, is torn from the mast. So wake, lady wake, I am waiting for thee, oh, this night or never my bride thou shalt be, so wake, lady wake, I am waiting for thee, oh, this night or never my bride thou shalt be.

(A pirate Song, circa. unknown)

Chapter 6

Sean hunted Loggar and the rest down. He asked Loggar to pick one person essential from the six. She picked Maria. When Sean and Maria got to the shuttle he stopped dead in his tracks. It was grossly overfilled. "Um, Kathy, you really need all this stuff?"

She nodded, "You only gave us an hour!"

"Okay. Pile in." Sean hoped the shuttle could lift. With the eight of them and a silly amount of books, equipment, boxes and stuff he wondered. He juiced the engines to one zero five percent. The shuttle rose slowly. They needed escape velocity. He pushed the engines to one two zero percent and prayed. The shuttle increased speed and zipped toward the upper atmosphere. He tapped on the shuttle CRT. "Johnson, we are coming in."

The shuttle vibrated from over taxing the engines. Sean punched them out of the atmosphere at the shuttle's top speed. He knew the inertia was going to be the make or break of them.

Quock sat co-pilot. She tapped out a few commands on the shuttle's CRT. "Captain, Webster scanned us."

Sean nodded. He tapped on the Comm. keypad. "Johnson, we need some company." He left the comm. channel open.

Molino came through on the speakers. "Captain, en route now. ETA ten minutes."

"Captain!" Quock called out. "Webster is ETA ten minutes. Detecting fighters. ETA six minutes."

"Molino," Sean said, "did you hear that?"

"Roger that, shuttle. Picking up the pace. Running engines hot."

Molino left the comm. channel open. He thumbed the fighter-to-fighter channel on. "Wing Group. We got the Captain to save. Run engines hot – one three zero percent. Repeat. Run engines hot. I want a defensive 3d ring around that shuttle. Viper, Puma and Snail – run back guard. The rest will form the ring. Ice maiden, and myself will run loose cannon. Execute."

Johnson's Fighter Wing Group leapt forward. In the distance the Webster was dead reckoning toward the shuttle. A half dozen fighter crafts were half way between the Webster and the tiny shuttle.

Behind the Wing Group Johnson was coming up fast.

Quock said, "Captain, ship-to-ship message. Coming from the lead fighter."

Sean pushed the shuttle engines to one four zero percent. He knew at this rate the main coils and circuitry would burn out in minutes. He sighed. "Put it on the speakers."

Quock tapped on her CRT.

"Shuttlecraft, this is the Webster's Fighter Wing Group. Advise you shut engines down and allow to be towed in. Under the GC Rules of engagement, and by Order of Captain Robin Spaarin, you are ordered to hand over materials from

Necron."

Sean tapped the Comm. Reply on the CRT. "This is Captain Sean Blakemore, of the Reginald L. Johnson; said material is en route to Earth via the Johnson. I order you to stand down. Return to Webster and I'll forget about you and your captain threatening a senior officer." Sean knew what the answer would be.

The reply came back definite, no leeway. "Begging pardon, Captain Blakemore, we cannot stand down. Shut down the engines or we will shut them down, by order . . . "

Sean clicked him off. "Johnson, what is your ETA?"

Dawn replied, "Five minutes, shuttle. Opening landing bays to receive you hot. Relative-speed is going to be light two."

'Good Goddess!' Collins thought. Johnson was going to try and capture us head on. She looked over to Loggar, who must have seen the reaction on her face, because she looked worried.

"Dr. Collins, what's going to happen, exactly?"

Collins cleared her throat and tried to speak in an even tone. "The Johnson has special equipment that can capture and slow down a runaway craft. It should be okay; the Captain is an excellent pilot. And we've done this many times." She neglected to tell Loggar that all the captures happened at less than light one.

Loggar remembered Sean liked Han. He sure did have his piloting skills. That thought made her feel a little better.

Johnson's Wing Group was seconds from the shuttle. Molino thumbed his comm. channel to broadcast ship-to-ship wide spectrum. The Johnson, the shuttle, the Webster's Wing Group and the Webster would hear the broadcast. "Webster's Wing Group, this is Lieutenant Commander Molino Chief Pilot, please stand down. The shuttle is coming aboard the

Johnson. Nothing is going to prevent that. Am I understood?"

A few seconds later. "Your position is understood. I am asking you to reconsider. My orders are clear. All materials must be taken aboard the Webster."

Johnson's Wing Group reached the shuttle and took up defensive position. Molino tracked the shuttle's heat signature. He knew the Captain pushed the engines to redline. He thumbed the comm. channel. "Element and Perfect, shuttle's engines are about to fail. Tracker beam to capture." He thumbed the comm. channel again. "Wing Group, brace for enemy contact. Engagement in imminent, repeat, engagement is imminent. Make the Johnson proud." Molino had the comm. channel to wide spectrum.

Robin sat still as she saw the tiny shuttle grow larger. Her fighters fell in behind the Johnson's Wing Group. She clicked on the channel to the Webster's fighters. "Engage the enemy. Engage the enemy." She clicked off

Dawn followed the exchange between the two fighter groups. Then she heard, "Engagement is imminent, repeat, engagement is imminent." She tapped comm. to landing bay control. "Bay Control. Are you ready? Shuttle and two fighters are coming in hot."

A voice in the distance said, "Yes, Bay Control ready."

She tapped ship wide broadcast. "All hands, all hands, Capture maneuver in progress. Damage Control take your position. All guns prepare for enemy contact. Enemy contact. This is not a drill. Repeat this is not a drill. Engagement is imminent."

Sean saw two fighters pull ahead and in front of the shuttle. He saw the pale blue-white light from their tracker beams touch the shuttle nose. He smelled the shuttle engine coils burn out before he heard the "Slam! Boom!" The engines died. Everyone was pushed back hard in their chairs as the two fighter ships controlled the shuttle now. He tapped on the ship-to-ship comm. channel. He recognized the call sign markings on both fighters. "Element, Perfect. Thanks for the tow."

A female voice came back. "No problem, Captain. We just wanted to see if towing a shuttle in for capture maneuver was as easy as the text book said."

A male voice came through, "Not like it's gonna be hard or anything . . . This is your pilot speaking, ETA in ten seconds. Please sit back and admire the ridiculously fast streaking stars to either side. In the event of an emergency . . . "

If the Universe had been able to compose music for events pivotal in nature then this would be a moment. Johnson's remaining Wing Group dropped behind the Webster's fighters. It was a split second and a push of the button. They flared their forward retros and flashed behind the surprised fighter group. Molino and his team engaged the enemy. By any standards of a battle, gunfight, fist-i-cuffs, dirty bar room brawling, whatever, the one that strikes first and hardest with the most deadly intent comes out victorious. It took seconds. Like two seasoned samurai warriors squared off from a long stance, it took a moment of blazing flash, cross and slashes of swords for one to remain standing. Within seconds the Webster's main Wing Group had been reduced to none.

Robin saw two things happen. The shuttle, in tow by two fighters, entered Johnson's mid-body landing bay at a speed that would produce no survivors. The second was that the Webster's Wing Group was gone. Winked out in so much of a flash and pop that it left her and the entire Command deck silent. For nearly five seconds no one moved. Then a proximity alert sounded. A computer voice in the background said, "Collision alert. Collision alert." Robin blinked several times and snapped. "Hard to starboard!" The view screen banked sharply and the Johnson's Port Engine cluster shields sparkled static light in all directions as it slid across Webster's port side shields. The display was like a symphony of dazzling and shimmering webs and fingers of colored lights arcing out into open space. Both the Johnson and the Webster lost some momentum as the energy from both ships bleed out into the ether.

The last thing Sean remembered was, "In the event of an emergency . . . " He felt a pressure on his head from all sides. His vision tunneled into a narrow point of light and it felt as if his heart stopped. He couldn't breathe and he heard this deep tune in both ears. The shuttle passed through the stasis field, the first field of a hundred that was used to stop runaway crafts. The Johnson used this maneuver dozens of times and everyone walked anyway fit. This was the first time it was used in terrifying speeds passed light one, but lately things seemed to be a first anyway. Everything seemed to have stopped, indeed it had. The stasis field placed all atoms in an almost zero state of motion. The ninety-nine other fields were used to siphon off the inertia and potential kinetic energy from forward velocity. All crafts made a complete stop by the last five fields. The pressure from Sean's head lifted, his vision returned and he could breathe again. He heard over wide broadcast that the 'shuttle was safe in Landing Bay and that Wing Group was approaching Starboard Side Bay opening. All hands prepare for hot approach.' Sean surveyed the compartment. He mostly saw scared faces from his passengers. "Everyone okay?"

He got hesitant nods, but concluded everyone was all

right. He walked over to the side door and keyed in the open code. Seals released and the door whooshed out and up.

One of the Landing Bay's Ensigns approached. Deck apes as they were called. "Captain, everything okay?"

Sean replied, "Yes, Ensign thanks. Please take our passengers and secure them in Quarter's on deck two. Make it one of the community rooms. Get someone to secure the equipment. We'll sort out who sleeps where later."

The Ensign saluted, stepped into the shuttle. "Please follow me. Your belongings will be safe. I will escort you to temporary quarters. Once the situation is over we will place you in appropriate locations. Please follow me."

Sean said, "Quock, Collins, you have duties to perform."

They nodded and left.

"Kathy, accompany me to the bridge." He reached out a hand.

Loggar grabbed it. And followed Sean through the beehive of activity. He saw Element and Perfect, Lieutenant Dallas and Lieutenant Fifth, step out of their fighters. He approached. They both snapped to attention.

"As you were." Sean said. "After all this is over, Wing Group is getting shore leave of choice." He walked away with Loggar in tow. He headed into a lift. The door hissed closed. "Top Deck." He said and then, "Stop lift."

He crushed Loggar into his chest and passionately kissed her. He whispered into her ears after the kiss broke. "Goddess, how I missed you."

She blushed and whispered, "My warrior, how I missed you."

Sean smiled, "Resume."

When Loggar first met Sean, he was a lonely man. He was vulnerable and she played on this. Admittedly, she took advantage of his weakened state and used it to manipulate him into becoming a Most High follower. But while on Necron he showed her that he was a very strong individual. He easily made others like him; he had a presence that one felt comfortable with. He said little but did a lot. He led by example.

In the Most High she never really experienced someone that was a true leader. Most in the High Council were handed the titles by way of political maneuvering – usually short of bribery. Sean was a Hero, a leader and he had integrity. And today, she witnessed individuals willing to die for him. They placed their very existence ahead of his. There was something to be said for the military, a lot really, but today she decided it was 'bravery,' 'courage,' and 'duty.' To follow orders and perform in a professional way that saved their very lives today was beyond anything she had ever experienced. Ever! And this made her rethink many things about GRID Command. She had no idea how this was going to play out, but she felt she was on the right side of the fence and that gave her the strength to believe she was doing the right thing.

The lift door opened and the air felt thick with words and sounds. Sean called it 'Deck chatter' Loggar remembered. He once told her that GC was a very superstitious lot. Quiet a Top Deck for over a minute and the ship would suffocate and die. She laughed, but he only smiled at her. He kissed her on the forehead and said, "Who wants to tempt those odds?" She remembered nodding. Sean led her over to the Observer's seat. He walked over to his chair and sat down.

"Dawn, the fighters aboard, yet? The scout ships?"

"Last one hit landing bay. All is secure."

He nodded and said loudly, "I have the conn."

Dawn nodded, "Very good, sir. You have the conn."

The ship shook violently.

Sean said, "Mr. Foster, for each impact, you owe me a credit."

Foster said, "Aye, sir" and was damned determined to pay the Captain as little as possible.

Sean tapped at his keyboard. "Pulse, I'm gonna need one-three-zero percent."

Pulse was at his desk when the Captain piped in with the request. He shook his head and thought, 'What a mad man.' And chuckled softly. He punched the Comm. Button. "Captain, I'll give you what I can, that last pass took out some packs. We had to shut down several decks."

Sean's voice came through the speakers. "One-three-zero, Pulse. It's not a suggestion. The Webster is not going to let us walk away from this."

Pulse frowned, but nodded. "Yes, Captain. Engineering out." He clicked off. "Hey!" He yelled. "Smithy! Give me one three zero percentage on the engines. No back talk. The Captain is gonna try one of those impossible maneuvers that made him famous! Ten seconds Man, ten seconds!"

Robin tapped into Engineering. "Chief, I'm gonna need more power to the shields. Johnson may be making a stand." She called out to her Tact Officer. "Target Johnson's weapons. I need that ship defenseless." She tapped out a message to Sean via her Command Screen.

The Johnson shook from an impact.

Sean said, "Two credits, Mr. Foster!" He closed his eyes and listened to Top Deck chatter. It was a splendid thing. The Johnson was running like a fine tuned instrument soloing for all it was worth. He moved his head to tactical. The weapon's chief, Mr. Kelley, had just instructed Weapon's control to target the Webster's Main weapons. He heard him say, 'The Captain is going to do it. Be ready.' Sean turned his head slightly right and heard Kirkland on the Comm. Channels. He was instructing Damage Control to prepare for situations on aft and bottom decks. Sean turned his head to the left. He heard a whisper from two crewman, 'Cap'n's gonna do it. Bet the bitch gets surprised.' Then he heard Dawn. 'Medical, prepare for possible incoming. This is make or break.' Sean opened his eyes and smiled. He loved his crew. He could wish for none finer. He looked over to Loggar. She was in the Observer's chair watching him. He winked at her and turned his attention to the main view screen. "Mr. Foster."

"Yes, sir?"

The ship shook from a phase torpedo impact.

"Three credits. How far is the Webster?"

Foster tapped out a command on his terminal. "Webster is one-zero-zero kilometers, mean distance."

Sean tapped on his keyboard. Calculations streamed on his CRT. He punched in a few more commands. Nodded at the results. "Mr. Foster, change shield harmonics. Data is on your CRT.

Mr. Foster tapped at his CRT. "Changing shield harmonics to 1.23 attoseconds."

"On my mark, let the Webster close to within five-nine kilometers and decrease shields to one-third power to radius 5.8."

The Johnson shook again.

"Sir, four credits, on your mark let the Webster close to within five-nine kilometers and decrease shields to one-third power then increase shield diameter to radius 5.8, understood."

"Once shields surround both ships, pivot and come about across the Webster's forward weather deck and surge to light seven."

Foster repeated the command.

Sean saw an incoming message on his CRT. It was an urgent ship to ship from the Webster. The message read,

"Sean, please stop. We don't have to fight. You are leaving me no choice." He typed in a reply and sent it.

Sean called out to Gunnery, "Gunnery! Stern guns, fire!"

Robin sent her message and waited a few seconds. She knew Sean well enough that he wouldn't surrender. She had to try; she owed that much to him. Then a reply came back. It read, "Sorry, Robin, you also leave me with no choice. Remember the Way of the Warrior – Bushido." She looked up to see the Johnson's stern guns open up with full force. Her helmsperson said, "Shields at eight-seven percent, Captain! Johnson is pivoting and distance dropped to five-eight point seven kilometers."

Even as Robin shouted out the words she knew it was pointless. "Increase distance and shields!"

The Johnson accelerated across the Webster's forward weather deck electrostatically snatching the Webster's shield emitters. Nearly every emitter from bow top to stern port and starboard gone. Then the Johnson banked hard starboard and fired hull guns on the Webster's weapons. After it passed the Johnson pivoted rear and took out Webster's main engines – crippling the ship. The Johnson pivoted forward and streaked off leaving the Webster near dead in space.

Sean sat back and watched the Webster list. He checked his Inbox and saw a message from Robin. He clicked on it and read it. "Damn you! Damn you to hell!" He laughed – the Captain's burst. "Mr. Foster, get us away from here. Random setting."

"Aye, aye, sir. Heading is coordinates 10, 22, 100."

"Execute." Sean said. He then got up and walked over to Loggar. "Care for a snack? I'm hungry."

Loggar was dumbfounded. Sean had just made space debris of a far more superior ship. He had an outburst of the tickles and was now hungry. When she first sat in the observation chair Robin had been in command. She knew Sean was originally the "Captain" of the Johnson but she never saw him perform. Personally she had never "seen" real combat - just the vid files tight beamed to GC. Of course, she had that dichotic state of wanting and not wanting to see combat. When the search for a compatible DNA to the Necronians was found, she was surprised the match was an Officer in GRID Command. She actually had two surprises. Robin was also a descendant. She retrieved his bio and studied it. It read like Sean was a Heinleinian character – he just had so much knowledge. Now she witnessed him first hand and was simply awed. He piloted a shuttle like a pro. He so much as shrugged off a near death situation like it happened every day. He sat in that chair and calmly formulated a plan that took out one of GC's best ships with an experienced Captain behind it. And now the man was hungry. Incredible! She understood why he was the only commander in GRID Command who could command a Battlecruiser. "Yes, please, and tell me what in the world just happened. I must've blinked and missed an entire moment in time."

Sean laughed lightly, smiling. "You didn't miss anything, Johnson has a good crew." He helped Loggar out of the chair and they walked to the lift.

Dawn said over her shoulder, "Dr. Loggar, don't let the Captain off lightly. Make him explain everything!"

"You have the conn, Dawn." The elevator door opened.

"I have the conn, sir, but begging the Captain's pardon, are we really headed to Earth?"

"Nope. I just want some distance between the Webster and us. She'll be ineffectual for at least twelve hours. That'll buy us some time." The lift door closed.

Dawn tapped on her CRT. She checked the pools results. McCoy in Medical got first for when the Webster would be disabled. Landers got first for the Landing Bay approach. Delvin got first on when and who would win the fighter battle and Rico, in Damage Control, got first for when the Captain decided to go to Mess. She was so close on all of them!

*'Twas eight o'clock in the morning when they began to fight,
and so they did continue there till nine o'clock at night; fight on,
fight on, says Captain Ward this sport well pleases me, for if you
fight this month or more, your master I will be.*

*O then the gallant Rainbow, she fired she fired in vain. Till
six and thirty of her men*

*All on the deck were slain; go home, go home, says Captain
Ward and tell your king for me, if he reigns king all on the land
Ward will reign king on the sea.*

(Ward the Pirate, circa 1680 by W. Onley in London)

Chapter 7

Loggar and Sean sat at a table in Starboard's Bow. They
were lucky. A table overlooking the forward most view port
was available. Sean loved this spot but he would never declare
'Rank hath its privilege' so he was happy that the spot was
open. Cookie made a victory meal. It was a sort of chicken
breast cooked in some sort of sauce. It lay on a bed of flat
noodle pasta covered in a white sauce. It was absolutely
delicious. Cookie himself served Sean and Loggar.

Sean said, "Cookie, you ever think about becoming a
warrant? Maybe run two mess halls?"

Cookie laughed and simply said, "maybe, maybe not.
Can I have a quarters facing immediate bow? Maybe one large
view port?" And he walked away.

Sean made a mental note to ask Pulse if his team could
convert one of the forward rooms to a quarter with a view.
Cookie gave him an opening and Sean was determined to take
advantage.

"Okay, Sean, explain to me how you easily defeated one of GRID Commands finest?"

Sean had forked a piece of chicken and swirled some pasta. He took a bite and savored the taste. He nodded, "Easily . . . that is a pretty misleading word. The Johnson could have easily been destroyed."

Loggar thought a second and said, "Easily destroyed? Really?"

Sean forked and twirled another bite. Damn, Cookie was good. This settled it, he thought, Pulse's team was going to make Cookie's new quarters. He was going to discuss it with Dawn and get her input. He was sure Mr. Grant would be highly pissed, but, hell, if the man knew how to cook and or either knew how to supervise other cooks he would never have contemplated replacing him. The main question was, of course, how to get rid of him. He couldn't space the man. Sean took another bite and thought he had died and gone to 'food critic' heaven.

"Sean?"

"Sorry, this dish is just too delicious. Yes . . . hmmm . . . I guess I could start with how the Webster was defeated. Or would you like the mechanics? It wasn't anything Robin did wrong; it was what Robin didn't do right."

Loggar, for the first time, took a bite of her chicken meal. It was tasty. "Hmmm, what she didn't do right?"

Sean nodded. "What she should have done was drop her shields and then immediately raised them. Basically, the Johnson merged shields. And since we had the greater inertia the electrostatic force and inverse square law were on our side. We had the greater potential of attractive force. Webster tried to strengthen her shields . . . "

"And in strengthening the shields, Webster created a more positive potential toward the Johnson! The shield emitters would either burn out or be ripped from the Webster's hull. Something like a tractor beam for emitters?"

Sean nodded. "The Johnson had forward momentum, the reason for getting the engines at one three zero percent. There would be some bleed off of forward speed. But we had the momentum advantage. And in initially dropping the Johnson's shields strength to a third and increasing the diameter by almost six we guaranteed that both shields would merge."

Loggar said, "Ahh, you fired upon the Webster to weaken her shields and when you expanded the Johnson's shield, at a certain shield harmonics, it became one large shield!"

Sean grinned. His lover was very smart. "Yep, and when the Johnson cut across the Webster's top bow we shrank the shields. The Webster was going one way, the Johnson, with the more positive potential, was going the other way had the greatest attraction. We stripped off, in a few cases literally, the Webster's shield emitters. It's a very risky tactic."

Loggar took a bit. "How so?"

"Well, for a moment the Webster was within the Johnson's shields. The Johnson would have been completely unprotected from any firepower from the Webster. A few good torpedo shots and we would not be having this conversation."

Loggar shuddered. "Really?"

"Really. Fortunately, Robin has an ego issue. She feels that Johnson and its fighter squad are an old and antiquated lot. Most of the newer captains think that way. Some of them think they follow the Way of the Warrior but they don't, not really. They think massive guns and a new ship can win any war."

Loggar sat and listened. They had finished the main meal. Earlier she ordered a red wine, Sean did the same. Now she was listening to him. It delighted her that Sean finally opened up and started talking about himself and how he did things.

"It's tactics and understanding the enemy." He sipped his wine and gazed out.

An Ensign walked over to them. "Ma'am, Captain, May I get you anything?"

Sean smiled; the rumors were going to fly tonight. "Yeah, another bottle and some cheese and crackers." He looked over to Loggar, "Kathy?"

She thought for a moment, "Do you have any grapes? Red?"

The Ensign nodded, "Yes, ma'am."

Loggar beamed, "I've had this craving for grapes for six months now."

The Ensign nodded and stepped away.

"Sean," She began, "You know something has to happen."

He nodded. His back was against the edge of the table with his elbows on top. He crossed his legs. "Yeah, I know. Six pilots died today. That is never good. GC seems to be split, maybe." He waited for her to say something. She didn't. "One or two things happened today. Robin is working inside GRID Command and her orders are real, or I'm operating outside GC and my orders are not real."

He let that sink in.

"However, Webster had been deployed to Necron hours before Johnson. Your message to me had apparently been delayed." He stopped to consider something and looked at Loggar.

She had an alarmed and distressed look on her face.

"Kathy, don't worry, I'm thinking out loud. It helps me sort through things, even the most obvious. My orders are legitimate. They went from you through the proper channels. That tells me that someone went behind your back – is going behind your back."

The Ensign brought the items, set them on the table, and

left.

Sean looked back out the view port. "How many enemies do you have within GRID Command?"

Loggar said nothing for a long time. "May we take these things to your room?"

Sean smiled and nodded. He got up and walked to the Ensign. He said something to him. The Ensign nodded. "Okay, Kathy, let's take a walk first. We should get your staff situated and your equipment secured."

She nodded and followed Sean out.

They parried and thrust, they side-stepped and cussed, of blood they spilled a great part; the philologist blokes, who seldom crack jokes, say that hash was first made on the spot.

They fought all that night neath the pale yellow moon; the din, it was heard from afar,

And huge multitudes came, so great was the fame, of Abdul and Ivan Skavar.

(Abdul Abulbul Amir, 1877 by Perecy French)

Chapter 8

Things were not going well. The Webster's main Fighter Group Wing had been erased from existence. She shook her head over that one, six fighters gone in a wink of light. During the SI war Webster had defeated numerous SI controlled squads. Webster's pilots performed flawlessly – they always had. They flew in, flashed phasers and spent torpedoes and came back home. This was the first time Wing Group Alpha didn't return. What made it hard was it took less than three seconds. Robin couldn't believe it. Johnson was an old ship – 146 years old. It ran on a disabled AI and traveled on long GRID waves. The crew had to be heavily sedated for War Jumps – not the kind of ship she would want to command. The fighter ships were at least sixty years old. So, the first main question was, how did the Johnson's Wing Group defeat Webster's. The second main question was, how did the Johnson so easily incapacitate the Webster so completely?

She sat in her quarters and thought. She had sent out security to Necron base. The team reported five individuals.

Robin had them transfer all remaining equipment back to the Webster. She hoped that, at least, something of importance could be retrieved. One good thing was that one of GC's insiders was on the Johnson and at first chance she would, hopefully, send out some information. So, Robin sat and thought of the past. She remembered Sean loved to talk about the Way of the Warrior. Sometimes he said something worth remembering, other times she heard the words but didn't listen. Sean truly believed in this Way. To Robin it was a dead belief that should have been put to rest hundreds of years ago. But Sean believed and practiced it. He decorated his quarters in Feudal Japan and had samurai and Ninja weapons displayed in many corners of the room. His room was fashioned in an old Japanese-like style. Cut linear wood and pale colors on the walls, with brown wood furniture. Sean said his room followed Feng Shui. 'You walk in and it feels right.' Now she looked at her own room. Funny how a major defeat can make you rethink a few things. She bit down on her bottom lip. Robin's thoughts carried her off. 'Sean can't be a better captain. Johnson can't be a better ship. Old fighters can't be better fighters.' Maybe he is. Maybe it is. Maybe they are.

"Computer?" Robin said, "Playback mission vid and 3d sim from the moment we entered Necron space. Show it on wall screen facing me."

The Computer beeped. The vid started playing.

"Turn the lights down."

The lights dimmed.

Robin watched twenty minutes of vid and simulations of a battle she didn't win. It repeated eight hours straight – Robin hardly blinked through all eight hours.

Now when we're out a-sailing and you are far behind. Fine letters will I write to you with the secrets of my mind, the secrets of my mind, my girl, you're the girl that I adore, and still I live in hope to see the Holy Ground once more.

Chorus: You're the girl that I adore, And still I live in hope to see the Holy Ground once more.

(The Cobh Shanty, possibly about Queenstown (Cork), Swansea Dockland, or NY Harbor)

Chapter 9

Sean sat at the head of an octangular table in one of the bigger conference rooms. His side and the far side were wide enough for one chair. The other sides could share two chairs each. Loggar sat to his left, Dawn to his right. His Command Staff, Herb, Kurp, Milkens and Maria sat alternately with the others. Sean said, "Okay Kathy, the floor is yours."

Loggar nodded and looked anyone in the eyes. She did this to ease her nerves. She called it the first forty-sec jitters. "I'll assume Sean has briefed you on what really happened on Necron." She got nods. "I'll also assume you know of The Most High Goddess." She got nods again. She smiled. "Sean has told me that his Command Staff must not be excluded from any information, members or not. If I hadn't witnessed how this ship operates under extreme conditions I would have objected to a request like that. But after witnessing first hand, I have no objections to telling you any and everything.

For many years, the Most High has had to operate in extreme secrecy. We are a shadow group within GRID Command as well as many other major institutions throughout GRID Space. We are not a group seeking power.

We have that. We actually have about two-thirds of the seats. We are seeking knowledge. Our main drive has always been to find our origins as to what made Wicca. Necron gave us that information. However, we stumbled upon the very thing that gave Wicca its life. Magick. The Necronians never used 'magic' in the sense of illusions and parlor tricks; they used actual technology to power their 'magick': nanytes and nanobots. Sean, Herb, Kurp, Milkens, Captain Spaarin and myself can do Magick on Necron. And after much research found out, we can do Magick on other planets with Necronian technology. Also, Sean and Robin may be able to do Magick anywhere."

Sean froze on that statement. "What?"

Loggar nodded. "Adruqu told us that anyone with 63% DNA compatibility could perform Magick outside of Necron proper."

Sean thought of a dukufa and said, "Ruogka!"

Nothing.

"Okay, so why didn't that work?"

Kurp spoke up this time. "Adruqu told us that in theory it was possible, what would be the trigger depended on the person." He shrugged. "One day you'll be pissed as hell and poof, or maybe even laughing your ass off and then poof, maybe you'll be grieving and then poof. She either didn't know or wouldn't tell us. Maybe more of that manipulation on their part."

Sean sat for a moment deep in thought, Magick without Necronian strings. "Okay, sorry, continue Kathy."

"Well," Loggar began, "We found ten more Necron-like planets and ten thousand three hundred twenty seven worlds influenced by the Necronians. The influence spans about three million years and 0.58 percent could have reached space faring technology – that's about 60 species with space traveling capabilities. It would have been a matter of time before we ran into them. Up to now we have only explored about a percent of space within the Milky Way. We had planned to do more research, but my computer system on Earth had been compromised. One of the projects we had been working on was migrating Necronian nanobots over to Humans by In Vitro. It seems that our nanobots had to be introduced orally. We suspected that as the nanobots traveled from one oral environment to another they, first, activate, and second, imprinted themselves with the new host DNA. Adruqu could deliver the nanobots. We cannot. Once inside the new host they multiply and split into different types. They grow dormant once passed outside and away from our bodies.

My reports to GRID Command only showed the barest of a hint of success. Someone may know more than they should or figured the Nanobot Project had been more fruitful."

Collins asked, "More fruitful?"

Loggar nodded. "We can introduce nanobots, orally, into the host using a glucose-based solution. The nanobots only allow the host to produce limited magick, and nothing more. In a sense, we created stupinans."

The group chuckled.

Quock asked, "What exactly can these stupinans do?"

"I'll let Maria explain that." Loggar leaned back in her chair.

Maria Albright cleared her throat. "We learned that the Necronian atmosphere is full of nanytes – the nanobots' helpers, so to speak. We may be talking a googolplex."

Someone whistled.

"They all communicate on two distinct channels, we think there is a third, but haven't been able to verify. One is very low infrasonic, the other is subspace low wave harmonic. In both causes the waves can travel a greater distance using less energy. The disadvantage is that information is limited to only a few bytes of data at a time. One big advantage is that all the nanytes and nanobots communicate continuously. The host thinks and says a command and all the local nans do whatever they do. We've identified about a half dozen different types so far. However, we've only been able to successfully replicate the simplest of the half dozen, thus the moniker 'stupinans.' Now, as to, what the stupinans can do. When a command is given, say, a fireball, the surrounding nans create a potential energy difference. In the case of the fireball, it is a temperature difference. Numerous layers of nans absorbing and transferring the energy difference to the nans producing the differences protect the surrounding tissue. The stupinans are perfect for doing just that. When a threshold has been reached energy is pushed away from the host." She shrugged. "A fireball is created."

Sean said out loud. "A perfect military application."

Loggar nodded.

"You had spies in your midst. GC found the information interesting and sent Robin to retrieve project notes and data. She has to be operating on rogue orders. Otherwise GC would not have sent the Johnson upon your request."

Loggar said, "My thinking too. Will the Webster be able to follow us?"

Sean nodded, "Yeah. It took some heavy damage, but it is very much a possibility. Robin's first priority should be to get the engines back online, the weapons then the shields. We didn't take out sensors so she has an idea as to the direction we traveled in. The best thing to do is decide on a final destination."

During the whole time Milkens had been writing in his notebook. He and Herb were assigned the task of converting Necron map coordinates to GRID coordinates. They had over ten thousand such coordinates. All were cataloged by the first time the Necronians "touched" the world to the last instant of visitation. Milkens looked over to Herb, who seemed to not notice him. This moment seemed like an opportunity of sorts, but Milkens was struck with an attack of shyness. His heart started beating rapidly and his breathing became shallow. He felt like he might faint. But he took several deep and rapid breathes like Herb showed him and said, "I have several that might be of interest."

Everyone turned to look at him.

Herb smiled. His buddy was starting to step out of that shell.

Loggar spoke, "Milkens and Herb had been in charge of recording all the locations of Necron-worlds and influenced planets and translating them to GRID coordinates."

Several seconds timed by.

Herb elbowed Milkens.

Milkens looked at his notes. He wrote out the start of what he was going to say. "Yes, we, Herb and myself, converted thousands on coordinates . . . umm . . . we think we are . . . have been able to get within several thousand kilometers of . . . umm . . . of the actual . . . Necron coordinates . . . that is the system that Necronians used and what we use now. Did that make sense?"

He got encouraging nods.

Milkens heart settled a bit and his breathing slowed down some. He took another deep breath and said, "The Necronians, it seemed to us, divided their planet's population into ten groups. Each group . . . nine of them . . . left to establish bases on nine other places. I . . .we," He motioned to Herb, "have the GRID coordinates."

Sean smiled, "Any special planet we should visit?"

Milkens felt a bit more relaxed shook his head. "None. Adruqu wouldn't tell us and we hadn't been able to extract that data from the computers. It's really kind of a flip of the coin."

Sean sat back and thought for a second. He looked over to Loggar. "It's your call. You are basically in charge of this mission. My orders read, 'To assist and follow your direction'. A wide latitude of interpretation on my part, but it seems logical for you to tell us which way to go."

Loggar turned to Herb and Milkens. "Well, what would be a good choice?"

Herb leaned forward, "Good question. Four are pretty much like Necron Prime. They sleep and time travel. Two strictly time travel, two are interdimensional travel and one seems to be a backup of the other nine."

Pulse said, "Backup? I don't get that?"

"Yeah," Herb started, "A backup. We aren't actually sure what that means either. From the data we could gather it seems that this planet is a redundancy of all the other planets. The sleeper chamber seems to be able to house a billion individuals, though the entire population of all of Necrondom seems to be in to the tens of million. That might be a good place to start?"

Sean nodded. "Kathy?"

"Okay, let's go there."

"Herb," Sean said, "Give the coordinates to Mr. Foster." He gestured toward Foster.

Foster nodded.

Herb handed Foster a hardcopy.

Foster frowned.

Sean asked, "A problem, Mr. Foster?"

"No, Sir. The coordinates will take us into unexplored territory."

Sean answered, "And?"

"And, it is nearly lateral to the Galactic arm from our position. I'll have to calculate the amount of time it will take to get there, but at a glance it looks like we are talking three days under War jumps or two weeks safe travel."

"That indeed is something to consider. Okay, work out the details. You have eight hours."

Foster nodded.

"Okay," Sean said, "if there is nothing else, I think we should meet again in that time."

Everyone got up and left the room.

Loggar stayed close to Sean. He whispered in her ear. "Your quarters or mine?"

She giggled and said his.

When the two entered his room they both were surprised to see a table with an assortment of cheese on it. Also, red and white grapes bunched up on a plate waiting to be eaten. A bottle of red wine sat next to it. A note was attached to the bottle. It was from McCoy and Delvin. It read. 'Thanks, Captain. Enjoy.' Sean smiled and popped the top off. On a ship like Johnson the price of items generally meant nothing. The bottle was old; no doubt from Cookie, but the gesture was worth something. Sean poured two glasses of Wine. He said, "Glad you are here."

Loggar answered after sipping the glass of wine. "Glad I am here."

Come, messmates, pass the bottle 'round our time is short, remember, for our grog must stop, and our spirits drop, on the first day of September. For tonight we'll merry, merry be, for tonight we'll merry, merry be, for tonight we'll merry, merry be, tomorrow we'll be sober.

(Farewell to Grog, sung August 31st, 1862 on the U.S.S. Portsmouth)

Chapter 10

Robin said, "Computer stop AV. Turn the lights on."

The vid stopped and the lights brightened. Robin got up and stretched. She had sat there for eight hours straight. No doubt about it. Sean's ship and crew were good. Robin watched in detail the Wing Group exchange. Commander Molino had signaled his team to execute a simple little maneuver. He said, 'Make the Johnson proud' and all the fighters save the two using tractor beams to assist the shuttle fired forward thrusters. It was a simple plan. Hit the thrusters, slow down and the enemy flies forward. Then engage them immediately. Robin wondered if the Wing Group practiced in Sims or real-time. Probably both. The Johnson was definitely a tough ship. Robin mused over the fact that two fighter crafts and a shuttle entered the landing bay at near light two. She ran the calculations in her head. Close to a hundred thousand kilometers per second! The Johnson's stasis field had to have been beefed up. Maybe there was something to be said for the older ships. Triple redundancy, reinforced everything, pure overkill on many things. Today, she saw pure overkill systems in action, the capture maneuver and the trick with stripping

Webster's shield emitters. Only an insane and desperate Captain would do such a thing. But hadn't Sean been desperate? The Webster is a far more advanced ship. That should mean something. Then she remembered Sean once telling her that advanced technology didn't always win battles, the War maybe, but not always the battles. Knowing the enemy and understanding tactics won more battles then mere brute force. He said, 'treat the enemy as if it were ten thousand individuals, and treat a ten-thousand individual army as if it were one person.' Her wing group was treated as one individual. The Webster was treated as many individuals. Robin smiled as if she gleamed some hidden piece of truth. "Damned smart of you Sean." She said to no one. 'Know your enemy.' She walked over to her desk and tapped her Command Screen. "Engineering. How are my engines doing?"

A tiny voice came back. "Fine, ma'am, testing main engine feed now. Hold please."

Robin waited several seconds. "Well?"

"Engines at eight-zero percent, ma'am. To get them to one-zero-zero percent will require dry deck."

Robin let that sink in. Eight-zero percent. Damn! "It'll have to do. ETR on shields and weapons?"

"We can jury-rig the shields. We lost seven-six percent of top and mid weather deck, along with port and starboard bow to stern shields. We can get shields to seven-zero percent effective in ten hours. Bow guns three through six are ineffectual. They will require dry-deck repair. Guns one and two are up and operational. Torpedo tubes are ineffectual. Dry-deck repair as well."

"Very well. Carry on. Captain out." Robin straightened out her uniform and walked out her quarters. A most devastating attack the Johnson made. It won't happen again, really. Webster will get its revenge. Robin didn't quite believe that 100%.

Foster sat in Starboard's Bow looking at his CSD. He had Cookie's staff fix him a strong pot of coffee. Foster wasn't sure what the ingredients were, after taking a sip he was sure he didn't want to know, but the stuff was almost like STIM. The 'eye snap open' effect snuck up on you. He had just finished his second cup when Dr. Albright walked in. She was a looker. Nice long legs that stopped at her chin, breast that jiggled stiffly when she made quick movements. Pouting lips, small jaw, and lovely brown eyes. He wondered why she was in Starboard's Bow, most guest usually wander over to Officer's Watch for 'okay' food and heartburn, when she stepped up to his table.

"This seat taken?" She asked.

He was hit with an 'eye snap open' moment. He stared at nipples stiff under the tight sweater hiding them. He gulped and pried his eyes off her chest eyes and looked her in the face.

She smiled and said, "Well?"

He blurted out, "Sit, sit, the seat is yours."

She sat and looked Mr. Foster in the eyes. She noted the crooked nose on a long face with small eyebrows over almond shaped eyes. Medium lips that occasionally spread wide and thin in a smile. She liked his face and decided he would be the one. Her choice of healthy sex partners had been narrowed down to one; her assistant, Tony, and she couldn't have that. "I was wandering if you could give me a tour of the ship. I got lost twice trying to find this place. And when I saw a familiar face I knew this would be my lucky day." She smiled sweetly and brushed some hair behind her ear with her hand.

Foster smiled, a lucky day indeed. Then, he remembered he had to finish his calculation for the Captain. He had another five hours to go. "I'd love too, but I gotta finish this up for the Captain."

Maria pouted.

Foster's heart sank to his testicles. "Um, maybe I can work as I give you a tour, Dr. Albright?"

Maria bounced in her seat and her breast jiggled. "Call me Maria, Mr. Foster."

"Call me, Julian . . . Maria." He smiled.

"I am a bit hungry. I got an idea. We can take something to eat to your quarters and while I eat you can finish the calculations. We can take a break, relax a bit, and you can continue with the calculations . . . if you haven't finished after our break."

Foster already came up with three different sets of calculations. He smiled, called one of the ensigns over and said, "Sounds like a plan to me."

Sean and the others were seated around the conference table. Mr. Foster passed out a hardcopy of his plan. He had several. Mr. Foster had been thorough enough to include diagrams, equations and possible scenarios. Sean had encouraged his staff to produce such material when time permitted. Collins loved too. Quock and Pulse produced the least. Surprisingly Foster and Molino were the most prolific in hardcopy reports. Molino loved to explain how and what of Johnson's Fighter Wing Group and Foster loved to show the how and what of Johnson period.

I've outlined three solutions." Foster said. "Each is risky."

Sean leafed through the hardcopy. Dawn had a better understanding of the overall mechanics of the Johnson. Like Sean, she was a line officer. That is, she learned all aspects of a ship - bow to stern, weather deck to below, engineering to medical, boatswain to midshipman, nothing was overlooked. "Dawn?"

She jotted down some notes on the hardcopy. She noted that Foster's most ambition plan was to run the Johnson near redline for three-five hours. She knew Pulse, might object to that one. "Are we in a hurry?"

Sean thought about that. Were they indeed in a hurry? Robin didn't know where they were going. So, maybe being in a hurry was not a good thing. GC had no ETA on getting Kathy back to Earth. His gut feeling told him that taking the slowest route would not be the best decision. "Not really, but we can't take our time either."

"Then my recommendation would be one-one-zero percent for six-zero hours." Dawn declared.

"Two and one-half days. That means we'll have to Trank up two times. Damn, I hate midflight Tranking. Pulse? Is the Johnson up to it?"

Pulse put down the report. "Yes, sir. The Johnson is running in tiptop shape. It can do it. Johnson could easily make the run in thirty-five hours – I think. I'd hate to run the engines that close to redline for that long."

Sean, for a brief moment, thought about asking the Johnson. Who else would know if pushing the engines that hard were possible but the engines themselves? GC gave no mercy for breaking orders, so Sean decided to wait until just before the jump. "Can anyone think of a reason to not jump in the next three-zero minutes?"

Loggar said, "Umm, this jump is nothing like the last time?"

Sean was amused with himself. He forgot. The last time Loggar was aboard ship the Johnson took several days to get to Necron. She's never experienced War Jumps. "Make it four-five minutes. Everyone dismissed except Dr. Collins, Kathy, Herb, Milkens, Kurp and Maria."

The rest of the group got up and left.

"Collins, I'll leave them to you."

She nodded.

Sean turned to Loggar, "After Dr. Collins finishes I'd like you on Top Deck with me."

Loggar nearly blushed and said, "Of course."

Sean got up and walked out.

Collins watched Sean walk out of the conference room – she wondered if he ever would become Most High God. She saw the look in Loggar's eyes when he walked away and knew that Loggar herself may have asked him. She cleared her throat and asked, "Anyone get motion sickness?"

Two hands went up. "Herb's and Milkens'."

They both looked at one another and laughed.

Collins nodded to herself. "Looks like you two will be staying with me in Medical."

Two more hands went up.

If you should want to know my name, My name it is young Johnson. I've got permission from the king To court young girls and handsome. I said: My dear, what will you do? Here's ale and wine and brandy too; Besides a pair of new silk shoes, To travel with a rambling sailor.

(The Rambling Sailor, variation of The Rambling Suiler, a song about James V of Scotland's travels)

Chapter 11

Loggar sat in the observer's chair. She looked around the room and noted how busy everyone was. She was getting use to the constant chatter surrounding her. She was beginning to make sense of the whole thing and she liked that. Loggar took the hypo-spray marked "1" on it. Collins had instructed her and the others on what to do. Loggar pressed the head of the hypo against her arm. She shivered as the sedative washed over her entire body. She felt a sloppy sleepiness start to take hold. She relaxed and let it happen. She looked over to Sean and blew him a kiss.

Sean looked over and saw Loggar. She had the hooded eye look of a junkie about to take a journey. 'Kathy's first trip.' He smiled at her and she blew him a kiss. He grinned, but not too broadly. The crew can't have the Captain blowing kisses across Top Deck. He said, "Dawn, you have the conn. Let's get started." He took his hypo-spray and pressed it into his left arm. He relaxed and just let it all happen. He heard Dawn in his peripheral consciousness.

Dawn had just placed her spent hypo back in her pocket. She tapped on her CRT. "All hands, all hands ten seconds to jump, repeat, ten seconds to jump. Johnson is aware and in control. Trank up now, First Officer out." Dawn looked over to Sean. "Just like old times, huh?"

Sean laughed lightly, "Yeah, old-times. Did I ever tell you I hated War jumps?"

Dawn laughed herself. She and Sean played this game each time the Johnson War jumped. In a small superstitious sense, it was their way to make sure each jump was a success. She never denied that GRID Command was a very superstitious lot and had many strange quirks and rituals. The first and last time they didn't go through their skit, the Johnson overshot its destination due to a freaky encounter with a class twelve string and just missed emerging into a Red Giant by ten thousand kilometers. That was one scary situation. "Did I ever disagree with you?"

And the jump began. Loggar winked out of consciousness and dreamt – something. Dr. Collins told her that not everyone had the same experience. Some dreamed others didn't. She explained that ship's like the Johnson traveled on long GRID waves, which played havoc with the human central nervous system and inner ear. Untranked individuals would suffer from violent motion sickness lasting days, if not weeks. What Loggar realized is that she was having lucid dreams. She decided to dream of her and Sean together and alone – no care in all the Universe. This was her special place and she would often visit it. Now she would have two days to spend there. What more could a Goddess ask for?

Robin received a message from Command deck. The insider had transmitted coordinates using normal communications but with the Level 9 code piggy backing. It was aimed at Earth. The Webster's Communications Officer picked it up as a routine backup transmission relay. Robin straightened her uniform as she stood up. She walked out of her quarters and headed for Command Deck. She was determined that the Johnson would pay, It and the Captain. 'Get off my ship,' she thought. 'Get off my ship.' She laughed. She entered Command Deck and sat in her chair and said, "Navigation?"

Ensign Lenior spoke up. "Yes, ma'am?"

"Calculate minimum time to these coordinates." She tapped on her Command screen.

Lenior retrieved the data and typed on her keypad. After a minute she said, "two-four hours at eight-zero percent engine capacity."

She tapped on the Command Screen. "Engineering?"

A voice came through, "Yes, ma'am?"

"Give me everything you got on those engines. We are going to War Jump for at least two-four hours. I need nine-zero percent mister, understand?"

There was several seconds of silence. Then, "Yes, ma'am. Nine-zero percent."

Robin tapped on her Screen. "All hands, all hands, prepare for War jump. Repeat, prepare for War jump." She sat back. 'Get off my ship.'

She flew into a passion and turned away from me, resolved within herself she would be revenged on me; her gold ring from her finger, as she was passing by, she slipped it in my pocket, and for it I must die.

(The Sheffield Apprentice, circa 1800s)

Chapter 12

The Johnson emerged into 'Now' space some distance from Necron-ten. Loggar fumbled for the STIM. She could barely make out the large 'STIM' markings on the hypo. She took another hypo out, didn't see 'STIM' on it and decided that the first hypo she picked was the correct one. She pressed it to her arm. Her eyes snapped open and she could read the small text to a CRT thirty feet away. The tiny writing read, 'Destination reached, AI in off mode. Normal operations resume.' She looked over to Sean. He was already standing up and walking toward her.

"How are you feeling?"

Her heart raced for a moment. "Okay, I guess. So, that was a War jump?"

Sean nodded, "Probably the worst you'll experience."

"And only on the older ships the crew has to be sedated?"

Sean nodded again.

"What happens if you reentered into a fire-fight, or a star of something?"

"Johnson keeps us safe. During the jump, Johnson's AI is switched to semi-aware mode. Unfortunately, the SI war left GC paranoid. All ships of Johnson's class have to keep the AI toggle off during normal operations."

Loggar saw the sadness in his eyes and heard it in his voice. She dropped the matter to talk about another time. "Anything yet on Necron-ten?"

Sean turned his head thankful Kathy changed the subject. He walked over to one of the many stations on Top Deck. "Miller?"

A young woman, about twenty-two turned around. She was the Sensors Officer. "Yes, sir?"

"Anything? Activity?" Sean asked.

Miller shook her head. "Nothing. Sir. I had the recorders running. I just finished looking at the records from entering 'Now' space to one-zero seconds ago. The planet seems to be completely absent of most energy."

"Thanks, Miller." Sean walked away and back to Loggar. "Nothing. We'll head for the surface in a few hours. Care to accompany me to Mess?"

She smiled and nodded.

The Webster entered 'Now' space. It was a billion kilometers from the coordinates. Robin wanted the Webster out on Johnson's sensor range. Webster's Sensors Officer picked up the Johnson on Visible Light spectrum. It had just entered orbit and a small transport shuttle headed toward the surface. Robin calculated that it would take about five-five minutes before the Johnson's normal sensors would detect the Webster. She wasn't sure if its Sensors Officer would be looking for a GRID wave signature. She hoped for a lucky break.

"Navigation!" She snapped. "Full power in. Get me to that ship."

"Aye, aye, Ma'am."

Robin sat back. She tapped on her Command Screen. "All hands, all hands, Battle stations. Repeat, Battle stations, enemy contact in two hours. Prepare for battle."

Quock stepped out the transport first. She had her hand on her pistol. She motioned for two of her security team members to guard the transport. The others she sent forward into the building. Sean, Loggar, Collins and Maria stepped out. Sean and Collins both wore sidearm. After several minutes, one of Quock's staff returned.

"Ma'am, all clear for the first one-zero-zero meters."

"Thanks, Kent. Setup a defense perimeter around the building opening. Send in a forward scout."

Kent saluted and Quock returned it.

"Okay, Captain, so far nothing."

Sean nodded, "Okay, let's see what's here. Collins, you have anything on Sensors?"

Collins had her Medical CSD out. She tapped on the tiny keyboard. "No life forms except us."

"Dr. Albright, anything?"

Maria tapped on her CSD. "Nothing Captain. And I mean nothing. No nanobots. This place is absolutely dead of Necronian Magick."

Sean uttered, "tolas, kolas, yuhonki, ye ohtgi dukufa."

Nothing.

He said, "Strange. No Magick at all."

Loggar had been thinking for a moment. "Sean, I'd like to see if this Necron has an Inner Chamber."

"Okay. Quock?" He called out.

"Yes, sir?"

"I got a gut feeling about this place. Something isn't right. Secure the area and bring two personnel."

She nodded, "Young, Andersen, with me and the Captain."

Loggar had a CSD supplied to her from Sean. Herb, Milkens, and Kurp had wanted to join them on the surface, but she told them to stay. Just in case. She turned the CSD on and tapped at the tiny keypad. A map popped up on the tiny screen. It was a most probable route to the Inner Chamber. "Okay, I got a path. Hopefully it's a right one."

They followed her in. Necron-ten, a place devoid of Magick.

Webster was within a million kilometers when her alarms went off. Johnson had launched fighters and positioned itself to attack the Webster.

Robin tapped on her CS. "Engineering, how are my shields?"

A reply came back. "Ma'am, you have one-zero-zero percent."

"And weapons?"

"Only guns one and two are functional. One zero zero percent. Tubes are ineffectual."

"Very well, Captain out." She cut the connection. She tapped on her CS again. "Fighter squadrons, launch!"

Fighters streamed from the Webster out into space. Robin ordered all eighty crafts out. She was going for broke.

Dawn was reading some obscure material when the alert came in.

The Sensors Officer said, "GRID ship has been detected in the area. Ship is about a million kilometers away. Coming in at Light Two. It's the Webster."

Dawn said, "Damn! How did they know?" She tapped on her CRT. "All hands, all hands, Red Alert, Red Alert. This is not a drill. Enemy engagement is imminent." She tapped on the CRT again. "All fighters launch ASAP." She closed the connection. "Mr. Foster. Take us out of orbit. Shields at full strength."

Foster said, "Aye, aye, Ma'am. Breaking orbit, shields at

full strength."

Dawn tapped out security. "Security, I want a platoon sent to the planet immediately." She tapped on her CRT again and waited a few seconds. Sean's voice came out.

"Dawn, yes?"

"Captain, the Webster has entered 'Now' space. It will be here in less than a minute. I'm sending a platoon of security to the surface and launched all fighters. Do you want to belay that order and try and come aboard the Johnson?"

Sean said, "No, We'll stay here. It'll take at least ten minutes to reach the Johnson. I'm sure Captain Spaarin is not going to let me reach the Johnson safely. Take the Webster out, Dawn. Cripple that ship beyond Dry Dock repair."

Dawn replied, "Aye, aye, sir." She tapped the connection closed. "Gunnery! Prepare to take out the Webster's weapons. I want gun ports and tubes X'ed out. Understand?"

Gunnery Control Ensign Milksovlic replied, "Ma'am, taking the Webster's weaponry out."

Robin tapped on her CS. "Security, Send a squad to launch bay." She turned to her first officer, Commander Rogers. "I'm going to the surface. Take the Johnson out." She got up and left Command Deck.

Sean, Maria, Loggar, Collins, and Quock had walked through the main corridor. Quock left Young and Andersen at the elevator doors. The Base had some power but no nanobots. The group took an elevator to the lower levels and walked to the Great Doors. The doors were opened. They walked past the doors and into the chamber. It was eerie to walk the ten-meter width of the Great Doors. Sean had an urge to keep his hands stretched out, lest the doors come crashing in on them.

The group stopped just inside the chamber.

"Sean," Loggar said, "This chamber looks to be 10 times bigger than the one back on Necron-one."

Sean looked around. The place was enormous. He walked over to a container. It was empty. He walked past several. All empty. "Kathy? What do you think? They're all empty."

Loggar walked passed a dozen containers. Then she looked in the direction of were the Pillar of Light should be. The base projector that created the light was further away on this Necron adding to the effect that this chamber was much larger. "I think this is just what we thought it was. A backup planet, ready to accept the entire population of all on Necron."

"All?" Sean asked.

"All. Every single last one of them. Time and interdimensional doubles as well."

Collins, Maria and Quock walked passed a dozen containers. Mesmerized by the sheer volume of space and the myriad of containers.

Sean's CSD chirped. He pulled it out. Dawn's face appeared on the tiny screen. "Captain, you have company. A transport is headed your way. Sending backup security." Dawn looked up and yelled, "Fire tubes one, three, five!" Then she looked to her right. "Molino, intercept that transport." Then she looked back at Sean. "Having fun on the surface? Anything exciting?"

Sean thought, 'Only Dawn could multitask and keep a cool head like that.' "Nothing exciting. Literally. This place is dead. It's empty. Just waiting to be filled."

Dawn looked right. Frowned. Then back at Sean. "Sorry, Captain, Webster's transport ship got through. You are going to have company in a few minutes."

Sean nodded. "Thanks, Dawn, we will handle on this end. Out." He tapped the connection off. "Quock? You heard?"

Quock had just closed the connection on her CSD. She nodded. "Already have security on alert."

Sean collected the group and they hurried to the upper levels. The elevator doors opened and the group was caught in a crossfire. Sean stuck his head out and saw, to the left, the Johnson's security team and to the right, saw Webster's security team. Robin was behind them firing a sidearm. When she saw Sean she holstered her sidearm and closed her eyes. Her hands seemed to glow a dull red. Then she threw an arm forward and a red fireball rushed from her hand. The fireball sizzled in the air and crashed just short of the elevator. Sean was thrown back. Everyone stopped shooting and stared at Robin. Stunned and unbelieving. She pointed a finger at Johnson's security team. A half dozen on them were tossed aside like toy soldiers in a child's room. Webster's security team stared dumbfounded.

Robin looked at them. "I'll explain later. Arrest them while I take care of the others." Robin flung her hand vaguely in the direction of Johnson's security team and those standing flew through the air and into the wall. Robin walked toward the elevator. The doors closed before she got there but she knew where they were going.

The doors closed before Robin reached it. Sean picked himself up. "Kathy, you saw that?"

She nodded. "She shouldn't be able to do Magick. No nanobots in the air." She turned to Maria and said, "Maria, how?"

Maria thought for a few seconds. "Captain Spaarin has enough of the Necronian DNA to control the nanobots."

Collins said, "If that's the case, why hasn't the Captain been able to do Magick?"

Maria shrugged, "The Captain hasn't gone through an emotional state that would trigger his ability."

The elevator door opened. The group ran out and passed the Great Doors. Sean turned around and touched one of the doors. Nothing. He spread his arms out wide and then closed them. Nothing. Then it sank in. Robin was going to get them. He turned to the others and shook his head. "Not this time." Then, "Quock, Collins, that side of the door. Kathy, Maria, with me on this side. Shoot on my command."

Everyone took their places and waited.

Robin stepped out the elevator and walked toward the Inner Chamber. She figured Sean would set up an ambush, but he had a surprise waiting for him.

Sean could hear Robin approaching. Her footsteps echoed loudly. When he was about to give the signal the footsteps stopped. Maria ran out, "They are here."

Robin knew they were close. She stopped and listened. Then she heard Albright. Maria ran out into the open. "They are here." She pointed to either side on the Great Doors. Robin smiled and nodded. "Get back to the surface. Tell my team I'll be with them shortly. I just have some things to take care of."

Sean listened with dread. Robin was going to murder them. He gave the signal. Quock and Collins stepped out and started shooting.

Robin had anticipated something of the sort and imagined a force shield around her and Maria. The pulse shots bounced harmlessly away. Robin flung her hand to the right. Collins and Quock crashed into a wall, both blacked out. She flung her hand to the left. Sean and Loggar flew backwards into a wall. Maria raced away while Robin stood in front of Sean and Loggar. Her hands aglow in red light and she had a scowl that would give the Devil pause. "You hypocritical bitch! I hate you and all that you stand for. The best thing I could do is rid this world of the likes of you."

Sean moved Loggar behind him. "Robin, please. You don't want to do this."

"Shut up!" She yelled. Years of pain rushed to the surface and exploded. "You were always the better between us. The better pilot, the better leader, people liked you; you were GC's poster boy. You were on the fast track because you were a line officer and I wasn't. Then we had the Quail incident and you fell and I didn't. I bested you! I got promoted first. I got the better ship. I was first!" She hit her chest with a closed fist. "I should have been able to do Magick first. Then she . . . " Robin spit the word out like it burned the inside of her mouth. " . . . got you involved and I was a second player again." She sliced the air with her right arm. Sean and Loggar felt an intense rush of heat pass over and around them. "Not anymore. I will take the nanobots back to Earth and I will be promoted to the board, then I will take over the Most High. And there will be nothing you can do to stop me." She flashed her hand at Sean and he flew back, knocking Loggar to the ground. Sean hit the wall hard and landed heavily on the floor.

Loggar got up slowly. "Robin, I never did anything to hurt you."

Robin stepped closer and raised her hand, pointing a finger at Loggar. "You did everything to hurt me. You took Sean." And a fibrous surge of electricity leaped from her finger and struck Loggar.

Loggar's body was engulfed in a luminous discharge of fractured light. She screamed.

Robin's lips curled up into a smile as she discharged another bolt.

Loggar screamed louder and thrashed on the floor. Then she stopped. Smoke rose from her clothes as she laid there looking so much like a heap of burnt clothing. She seemed lifeless.

Robin walked over and kicked at the body with a foot. Loggar remained motionless. Robin walked away laughing to herself. The words, 'the witch is dead, the witch is dead Ding-dong the wicked witch is dead' danced in her head.

One night I dreamed I was walking along the beach with the Lord. Many scenes from my life flushed across the sky. In each scene I noticed footprints in the sand. Sometimes there were two sets of footprints. Other times there were one set of footprints. This bothered me because I noticed that during the low periods of my life when I was suffering from anguish, sorrow, or defeat, I could see only one set of footprints, so I said to the Lord, "You promised me, Lord, that if I followed You, You would walk with me always. But I noticed that during the most trying periods of my life there have only been one set of prints in the sand. Why, when I have needed You most, You have not been there for me?" The Lord replied, "The times when you have seen only one set of footprints is when I carried you."

(FOOTPRINTS IN THE SAND, By Mary Stevenson, written in 1936)

Chapter 13

Sean shook himself awake and rose. He saw Loggar's body, motionless, on the floor in front of him. He ran over to it. He knelt beside it and lifted a lifeless hand. He reached out and cradled her head in his lap and a flood of grieving emotions washed threw him. He couldn't stop the tears. They just kept coming.

Robin stopped laughing when she heard Sean sobbing. She turned. "I didn't kill you? Pity. Well, anyway, you like what I've done?"

Sean sobbed harder. He never had to face death like this. The death he faced was in the line of duty. You had your orders, did your duty and you died. That was easy to cope with. This was different. There was no war, no mission stamped with 'enemy contact.' The hurt was beyond anything he'd ever felt. "Oh Goddess." He said. "You can't be dead. No you can't. We have a life together. Goddess, please, wake up. Kathy, don't leave me!" The tears flowed harder. "No! No you can't be dead. I love you! This can't be happening. Please, come back to me! Wake up!" He continued to cry. This was the first time in his life he could not stop the tears, the pain or hurt. Wave after wave after wave of despair washed over him. Kathy, the one who gave him a reason to live was lifeless, in his arms. If only he had Magick he could have stopped Robin. Tears flowed down his cheek and he kissed Loggar on the forehead. The nanobots failed. She is dead. Sean lifted his head up and looked at Robin. She killed her. He gently placed Loggar's head down and got up. She is dead. He faced Robin and began to feel an intense rage burn within him. It was a small fire at first, but with each heartbeat it grew hotter. She is dead. "Why?" He said.

Robin stood staring at him. "Because I hate both of you."

She is dead. "You didn't have to kill her!" He was getting warm. He could feel his temperature rise. He wiped his eyes with a sleeve, drying the last of despair and grief away. "You didn't have to kill her!" He shouted again. He took a step toward Robin.

Robin lifted a hand and he crashed into the wall again.

She is dead. Sean got up, a rage so intense and hot that he felt his skin burning. "You didn't have to kill her, you silly stupid ass bitch! You didn't have to kill her!"

Robin laughed and said, "What are you going to do about it? Fool!" And she flung him into the wall again.

Sean felt it. It was hot and intense. It was like a pop deep inside him. The sleeper had awakened. He got up slowly and stood straight. He clenched his fist tightly, said with a closed jaw, "This, you fucking psycho!" And pushed a sizzling red fireball at Robin.

Robin put her arms up to protect her face. The fireball exploded around her. She slid about three meters from the impact. Her uniform sleeves were blackened and flaked to the floor. She saw Sean standing over Loggar's body breathing deeply. He so much as growled at her. He took a step forward. A blue light pulsated around each tightly closed fist and a light seemed to shine behind Sean. Under other circumstances, Robin would have enjoyed the scene. Sean was lit in divine light.

Robin pointed a finger at Sean. A string of thick electrical branches sprung from it.

Sean's surrounding light brightened as the electrical bolts approached within inches. Sean stepped closer as the bolts sizzled and popped off and away from him. She is dead. Sean's eyes seemed to glow white.

Robin shot another electric bolt at Sean. It crackled and fizzled into nothing.

Sean stepped closer. "I stand as your Judge, Jury, and Executioner. As your Jury I hereby find you guilty of treason and betrayal. Kathy trusted you and you repaid her by going behind her back." She is dead. Sean lifted his hand and slammed Robin against the far wall.

Robin hit hard and felt her shoulder dislocate.

He lifted his hand high in the air. Robin rose. "As your Judge I sentence you to death." She is dead. He slapped his hand down hard.

Robin hit the floor with an impact that snapped femurs, tibias, and fibulas.

Sean stood over her. His eyes still glowing white. Intensely burning with hatred and anger. Robin looked up at him, in pain. Her pride told her to not let him see it, but she must have shown something. Sean looked down upon Robin Spaarin, his once friend, lover and now enemy. "As your

Executioner . . . as your Executioner, I fulfill the sentence of this court." Sean smiled, "May Goddess have mercy on your soul." And he sliced his hand sideways across Robin's chest. Her back snapped in several places. Robin heard several audible loud cracks. She screamed for several seconds and fell silent. Sean looked down on the now lifeless body of Robin. Now she is dead. He dropped to his knees and tears started flowing down his cheek. It was almost like grieving for Kathy. Despair covered him like a wet blanket. The anger and hatred drained away. Then he felt a hand on his shoulder. It was Adruqu. "How?" He said between sobs.

Adruqu lifted him up. He looked over to his right and noticed the Pillar of Light in the distance. Necron-ten was no longer a dead world. "Sean, my descendant, why do you cry for your enemy?"

He looked into her eyes. "My enemy was once my friend. Robin deserves that I mourn her death. She was a comrade in arms. We may have disagreed on some things, but she was still a comrade. I cry for many reasons. Friend and love lost, a fellow warrior lost, and in having been the one to exact revenge, a bit of myself and soul lost. Killing in anger is not honorable. And I don't feel any joy in having to do this one. But it came down to 'kill or be killed.' And the one thing that hurts most is that I killed out of anger and hatred, not out of principle, duty or bushido." Sean's eyes still wet from tears. "I should have been more controlled." He dropped his head in shame.

Adruqu considered what Sean told her. Though she had over ninety-nine thousand years over him, she knew it amounted to no more than a hundred years of pure empirical thought. Sean spoke from his heart and that was what mattered most. "Sean, I understand Bushido." She smiled and grabbed his hand. "Follow me. We are going to make things right."

Sean followed her to two containers. Both were luminescent. He stepped up and saw Robin in one container and Kathy in the other. He spun around and looked into the distance for Kathy or Robin's body. Both gone. He turned around and looked at the two, peacefully sleeping. He shook his head. How it occurred was beyond him. Adruqu probably wouldn't tell him.

Adruqu smiled. She guessed at his thoughts and said, "Ask me and maybe I will tell you."

Sean turned to her. "Am I to choose which one lives and which one dies?"

This stuck Adruqu as funny. She laughed. "No, you just choose. The body you see of Robin now is not the body you killed. This is a body that has been here for six of your months. The body of Kathy you see now is the body that was killed today. Robin has been with us for a time and has witnessed all that has transpired. She saw her death and understood why she died. Now she understands. Kathy wants to be with you."

Sean's eyes welled with tears again. "What must I do?"

"Believe Sean, you just have to believe; only a pure soul will awaken both." Then she vanished. Not a trace.

Sean looked around but didn't see her. He then looked at both containers. Sean stood between them and relaxed. He inhaled deeply, held it and exhaled deeply. He let his mind find the middle way and thought of . . . nothing. He counted each inhalation and breathed smoothly and evenly. His mind was in the middle state he was in standing meditation. Then he saw his Truth. The Here and Now were as profound as anything he had ever felt. He said out loud, "All the evil karma ever committed by me since of old, on account of greed, anger, and folly, which have no beginning, born of my body, mouth, and thought -- I now make full open confession of my deeds and wish to find forgiveness. I pledge not to commit evils, but to do all that is good, and to keep one's thought pure -- This is the teaching of all the Buddhas. However innumerable beings are, I vow to save them; however inexhaustible the passions are, I vow to extinguish them; however immeasurable the Dharmas are, I vow to master them; however incomparable the Buddha-truth is, I vow to attain it." He opened his eyes. He saw a soft blue glow around him. He reached out to the two containers. He closed his eyes again and spoke, "Thus." And touched them. He felt energy flow from his body into the containers. Then he blacked out.

Epilogue 1

Sean woke up in Medical. He was dehydrated – the inside of his mouth felt dry and it hurt to swallow.

"Sean?"

He looked and saw Kathy sitting next to his bed. She reached out and touched him on the cheek.

"We were worried about you." She said.

He swallowed. "How long was I out?"

"About two days. How are you feeling?"

"Like crap. I'm thirsty and my head hurts."

Collins walked over. "Morning Captain. Here, drink this." She handed him a small bottle. The substance inside it was green.

Sean took it and nearly drained it in one swallow.

Collins then gave him a hypo-spray in the arm. "That should take care of the headache."

"What happened after I blacked out?"

Loggar said, "Well, it was quite amazing. After Robin killed me I found myself looking at the entire fight. You were magnificent. I was sitting in a room with Necronians! It was amazing. Some of them were watching the fight on a huge vid screen. Adruqu sat next to me. She asked me if I wanted to go back. I told her 'of course!' Then Robin appeared next to me. She sat watching you kill her. Then Robin and I woke up in the containers and you were on the floor collapsed. Ms. Quock and Dr. Collins were over you. From what I was told. The platoon of security landed and took over. Robin contacted the Webster and halted the fighting."

Sean laid there absorbing everything. The headache finally

went away.

Loggar continued, "Maria exposed the entire conspiracy. Some of my rivals wanted the nanobots for immediate application. They had promised Robin a seat on the Board if she could get the nanobots. Then later I would be involved in some accident. My allies on the Board identified the conspirators and justice was swift."

Sean tried to sit up. He was too weak so he just continued to lay there. "Do I still have the nanobots?"

Loggar nodded. "Adruqu told me you earned the right to keep them. Sean, my love, it looks to me like you are the only human in all of GRID who can do Magick anytime you please."

Sean wanted to test it out but he was too exhausted. He thought, 'Magick any damned time I please? I'll be damned!' He laughed.

Murphy in Supplies won the pool.

Epilogue 2

Sean sat in his chair on Top Deck. He had just talked to Robin. She was doing fine and apologized for the entire mess; she also wanted to tell Sean that her new cook was safely on board. Sean smiled and told her to not eat his omelet. She laughed and clicked off. Their friendship hadn't been mended, but killing and near death experiences had a way to start the healing process.

Apparently, Adruqu saw fit to duplicate Robin back on Necron-one. Loggar intervened on Robin's behalf and had all charges of treason dropped – reason sealed confidential. This Robin was not the Robin who ordered six pilots to their death, or the others who died during the fight with the Johnson. Officially, the records would show that CG deferred judgment to Loggar. Unofficially, Loggar acted as Most High and absolved Robin of all charges. The conclusion was that Sean dealt with the other Robin. The Board realized, after much debate and bickering, that punishment had been carried out. The question, now, was why super beings, which had mastered time and interdimensional travel, would take an interest in a few individuals. The frightening thought was that maybe they were all duplicated – just waiting to die and be resurrected again. It was a terrifying thought, indeed. The Necronians were sick individuals toying with them. It was good GRID Command decided not to respond with Military action. Succinctly, that would have been a dumb move. The only good thing that came out of this whole mess – it depended on what side of the fence you stood on, was that GC was more firmly controlled by The Most High, the conspirators had either been pushed into retirement, or reassigned to duty locations the likes of God would be afraid to be in. Hundreds of individuals "taken care of" by the swift actions of Most High followers or sympathizers. But Sean considered that notion for a moment. Was it a good thing to have that much power centralized in one person? Sean didn't know which was scarier. The Necronians and their seemingly inexhaustible ability to do anything, anywhere, anytime, anywhen, or sleeping with the most influential individual in all of GRID Command!

Currently, Loggar would be staying aboard the Johnson as resident expert exobiologist. Johnson's new standing orders read: visit, explore, and make first contact with worlds the Necronians seeded. Herb, Milkens and Kurp were also assigned to the Johnson and part of the Command Staff as well. By a military standpoint, this made sense. Find out what you are up against, know your enemy, and see if there are any allies out there.

GC wanted to transfer Sean and his crew to a newer vessel. Top of the line they said. Fastest and most powerful in the fleet. Sean laughed and said the Johnson was 'Top of the line' and had proved it by besting a more 'advanced and powerful' vessel. Loggar said that the Johnson would suit her just fine. The matter was dropped. Of course, Sean didn't let the opportunity for a few upgrades go by. Johnson was in Dry Dock for a month, his GRID engines upgraded to Short Wavers. Wing Group got the shore leave of their choice; actually the team was torn on three locations. Sean gave them all three.

Cookie opened the door to his new quarters. He dropped his duffle when he saw the room. It was twice as wide as his old room and 40% deeper. He stepped inside and walked over to the view port. It was half the size of this new room and went from ceiling to floor. 'Damn, Captain.' He thought. 'All this for a better omelet.' And as Cookie unpacked he sang a Shanty.

> *"I am a sailor stout and bold, long time I've plowed the ocean; I've fought for king and country too, won honor and promotion. I said: My brother sailor I bid you adieu, no more to sea will I go with you; I'll travel the country through and through, and I'll be a rambling sailor.*
>
> *If you should want to know my name, my name it is young Johnson. I've got permission from the king to court young girls and handsome. I said: My dear, what will you do? Here's ale and wine and brandy too; besides a pair of new silk shoes, to travel with a rambling sailor.*
>
> *The king's permission granted me to range the country over; from Bristol Town to Liverpool, from Plymouth Sound to Dover. And in whatever town I went, To court young maidens I was bent; and marry none was my intent, but live a rambling sailor."*

ACT III:
Lines Crossed

Chapter 1

The Johnson had been in Space Dock for the last four weeks getting her engines upgraded to the newer GRID drives. Sean and crew were looking forward to finally ditching Trank and STIM. It was during the last week when Collins requested to run some test on Sean to further understand the Necronian nanobots. He agreed and figured she'd ask him to turn his face to the left and cough along with other questionable tests. She did that, too, but went further. This latest test had him standing in a Decompression/Compression Thermal chamber - DeCom. He could only think of being crushed to death, expanded like a balloon, broiled alive or all of the above, in different orders. Collins asked him to relax, again. He was wired up to a dozen beeping blinking machines and could see Kathy seating next to Collins. The Doctor's staff was abuzz just outside the large chamber windows. The chamber was one of a dozen large chambers, located in Med Mid Deck, used for a variety of reasons. This chamber was a favorite for temperature experiments and rapid decompressing.

"Okay." Sean said.

Several seconds passed, then, "Captain . . ."

"Yes?"

"You are not relaxing." Collins said over the chamber speakers.

Several more seconds passed.

"Captain . . . "

"Yes?"

"You're still not relaxed."

Sean laughed. "Doc, it's a bit of a challenge when I got dozen of wires protruding from me."

He heard Collins' chuckle. "Well, yeah, but I still need you to relax. Thank about something you'd rather be doing right now."

Sean said, "Okay," and closed his eyes. He started thinking about bedding Loggar, but figured that wasn't going to relax him.

"Captain . . ."

"Yes?"

"Think about a nice pleasant walk on a beach somewhere nice."

Sean concentrated. A walk on a beach. What type of beach? Is the sand devoid of life? Will something jump out and eat me. Is the water too close? Where's the next exit Ville? What am I breathing? Would I be able to drink the water? Can I . . .

"Captain?"

Sean still had his eyes closed, "I'm relaxed."

"No, Captain. Open your eyes please."

Sean did so . . . and nearly startled himself. "What the . . . ?"

Collins watched a dozen monitors as they recorded the unbelievable. She had slowly spiked the chamber temperature to 500 degrees C. The wall radiators glowed a dull orange. What air was left created small drifting wispy semi translucent waves across Sean.

"How do you feel?"

Sean looked around. He saw a dirty brown haze surrounding him. He knew what the glowing radiators meant, but felt absolutely nothing. "Doc? Kathy?"

A Staffer said, "Doctor, the Captain's heart rate is

increasing. Blood pressure at 150 over 95."

"Captain," Collins began, "Take a deep breathe. You seem to be unharmed."

Sean's voice came over small speakers in front of Collins. "Ummmm, you're not the one inside hell."

Loggar leaned over Collins' shoulder and said, "Sean, my love. The nanobots are protecting you. Your backside should feel warmer than your front."

Sean nodded. His back felt about ten degrees warmer.

Loggar continued, "The nanobots are actively redirecting surrounding heat behind you. It's quite remarkable, really. You ought to see the infrared scans."

Sean nodded and thought, "If you say so." He lifted a hand up and looked at it. Brown fog surrounded it. "Amazing."

"Sean," Collins started, "I'm bringing the temperature back to normal. Let me know if you feel uncomfortable."

The chamber radiators' orange glow slowly dimmed to matte grey. A minute later Sean felt a rush of cool air.

Another minute passed. "Captain, take a deep breathe please."

Sean did so. The air smelt burnt. A hint of metal hung just inside his nostrils.

"How do you feel?"

Sean had been on an adrenaline rush. Now, coming off it, he felt suddenly drained. "Tired."

The chamber door opened and Sean slowly walked toward the entrance. His knees buckled but he caught hold of the doorway. Several staffers reached Sean and helped him to a chair. Collins walked over and placed a small disk on his forehead. She then stepped back, with a MedScanner in her hand, guided it up and down Sean's body.

Collins said, "Captain, you lost three kilograms. You're

dehydrated and . . . wait." Collins frowned and rescanned Sean. "You just gained a kilogram and electrolytes are back to normal."

Sean nodded. He was feeling better. "There's a question in there."

Loggar looked over Collins' shoulder and read the scans.

She nodded to herself.

Sean looked at Loggar, "Kathy?"

"Your nanobots, Sean. They are actively collecting material from around us."

"Collecting?"

Collins walked into Chamber one and ran her hand along one of the walls. Interesting she thought. She walked over to the opposite wall and slowly moved her hand along the surface. It felt "off." She walked over to the observation window and touched it. Her eyes snapped open. It felt rough.

Loggar said, "The nanobots are infinite in their abilities. Even though it looks like we can perform magic or we have special powers, it's all technology-based. The studies we conducted on Necron showed that the nanobots are as good as their environment."

Sean frowned.

Loggar continued, "The reason you felt tired earlier was because the nanobots were drawing energy from you. A large amount of energy. . ."

Sean replied, "But, what about me feeling better in seconds?"

"The nanobots replenished your body's sugar supply, salts, water."

"How?" Sean pushed.

Collins walked out of the chamber. "By cannibalizing whatever material is nearby."

Sean snapped, "It's eating the Johnson?"

Loggar replied, "Yes and no." And left it at that.

Collins stepped up close to Loggar. She looked her straight in the eyes. "The no part means we are the other source."

Loggar returned the stare. She wondered if this had been a challenge. "Under certain circumstances . . ."

"And they are?"

"The nanobots will, of course, use Sean as a resource. They are highly intelligent and work to keep the host alive . . ."

"The host being me," Sean spoke.

Loggar broke eye contact with Collins. "Yes, Sean. Anyone or anything near you is fair game when you can't supply the nanobots with what they need."

Sean paused in thought. Then said, "I'm not sure I'm comfortable with this."

Loggar nodded. She wanted to tell Sean he was missing the big picture. He had power. "On Necron there's an abundance of resources to fuel the nanobots."

Sean said, "I need to be certain."

Loggar thought for a moment. She guided Sean to an unoccupied desk. She turned to Collins and asked, "Do you have any sugar? Maybe carbon, too? A small piece of both."

Collins walked to one of the many cabinets along the office wall. She opened one and pulled out two boxes. One box was marked "SynSkin" and the other STIM tablets. She walked back to Loggar and Sean. She handed both to Loggar.

Loggar smiled, "I think this is perfect." She pulled out a wrap of SynSkin and two STIM tablets. She turned to Sean and handed the items to him. "Sean, can you make some sort of fire from one hand?"

Sean replied, "I don't know." He thought for several seconds and extended his middle finger. He chuckled as he thought "finger fire."

A second or two later his middle finger ignited in a bluish flame.

Collins scanned Sean. She turned to an assistant, "Paul,

record this on monitor two."

Paul nodded and grabbed a nearby MedScanner. He tapped in a few codes on the tiny screen and pointed the device at Sean.

Collins asked, "How are you feeling, Captain? Heat? Anything?"

Sean said, "Both hands are tingling, but other than that, fine."

"Open your other hand, Sean."

He did so. Half the SynSkin was gone and only one STIM tablet was left. Sean increased the flame.

Everyone watched as the rest of the SynSkin and tablet crumbled, then faded into his palm.

Loggar broke the silence, "Collectively, the nanobots are intelligent enough to know a proper food source. We'd have to conduct a few experiments, to know for certain, if the nanobots would use the nearest living organism as a resource, if nothing else existed."

"Is there a way to turn them off? Like before?"

Loggar shrugged impatiently.

Collins and Sean caught the gestures true meaning.

"Kathy, I really can't in all good consciousness feel comfortable knowing that I'm feeding off my crew. My Goddess, that's pretty creepy."

Loggar's mood turned dark. "Sean, the nanobots should always use you first . . ."

"Or whatever I'm touching?"

She stopped and remembered the SynSkin and STIM tablets. Sean had a point, but this was science. This was something bigger than all of them. This was magick. This was why The Most High was out here. Humanity, on its own, would never have reached out as far so fast. It had always been The Most High that worked behind the scene. It was The Most High that now had the means. Loggar sighed. "Sean, there are so many questions about the nanobots. But, we shouldn't be too overly cautious in finding out the answers.

Sean stared into his lover's eyes and was gripped by a slew of emotions. "The Johnson is in dock for a few more days. I'd like to be certain I can decide who and what gets eaten; if not then we need to turn these things off." He stood up and turned to Collins, "Give me a full report at the next Staff meeting. I'm hungry. I'll be in Starboard's Bow." Without another word he walked out leaving Loggar and Collins alone.

Loggar was about to follow, but stopped.

Collins watched Loggar hesitant.

Loggar faced Collins with a blank expression. "Doctor, I need you to be with me on this. We are about to leap forward in human existence. The Necronians handed us a gift and we have to understand it."

Collins leaned in close. "I can't jeopardize the Johnson or its crew. I'd love to do magick, but not at a potential price of soul."

Loggar pursed her lips together and mentally counted to ten. Technically, she could order Collins to cooperate by way of The Most High. She could also make her go away. It would take one communique to GRID Command and Collins would be transferred off the Johnson. But what exactly would that accomplish? Loggar thought, 'I have power, but to abuse it is not the end game.' "Doctor, I agree."

"You do?"

"I've been chasing magick my whole life. Now that I've tasted it and know it is within reach again I sometimes miss the immediate picture. I'm looking at everything from a distance."

Collins nodded. "You do have to understand the Johnson is not just a ship to us. We've been through hell and back during the SI wars. Johnson is our friend."

Loggar nodded and smiled though she really thought

Collins was foolishly being sentimental over a vessel. She thought the same of Sean. "The next round of tests should be Sean's control over the nanobots.

Collins nodded. "Agreed. Let me go over this last test. I'll give you a copy of the report."

Loggar said, "Thank you, Doctor." Then she moved closer. "May I ask you a personal question?"

Collins nodded, "Certainly."

"What are your feelings toward Sean?"

"The Captain?" Collins laughed.

Loggar frowned.

Collins responded, "Loyalty, Goddess. Nothing more, nothing less. He's lead us through the worst of the SI war. The Johnson is the only ship in GRID to have 100% mission accomplished. But if you're wondering what I feel on a more personal level, relax. Everyone knows the Captain is in love with you . . ."

"That's not exactly what I was getting to. I just . . ."

"Just wanted to know if you had any challengers?"

Loggar stared for a moment.

Collins waited a few seconds. She had to lean in close to hear Loggar.

"I wasn't worried about that. I just wanted to know if you liked Sean."

Collins searched Loggar's face for tales. "Yes, I like him. I respect him. I don't think anyone else on board feels differently."

"May I call you Karen?"

Collins nodded.

"Please call me Kathy."

Collins thought this was an interesting turn of events. "Okay . . . Kathy. A bit strange calling the Goddess by her first name."

Loggar smiled. "I need a new circle. I'd like you to join it."

An extremely interesting turn of events Collins thought. Asked to be part of The Most High Goddess' inner circle. Dawn is gonna spit bricks when she finds out.

"Think it over, Karen. I see I need general counsel from intelligent like-minded thinkers."

Collins nodded and watched as Loggar turned and leave the labs. She watched Loggar disappear down the long corridor. "Never become friends with Heroes unless you're not worried of being disappointed." she said to no one.

Chapter 2

Sean sat in Starboard's Bow. Cookie greeted him and served up a new batch of Skilly. Sean always knew the last batch would be the best, but Cookie just kept making superior comfort food. Even though Johnson was at Space dock, most of the crew had at least one meal on board the Johnson. Some had all three. And that made Cookie very happy. Today was no exception.

"Captain," Cookie began, "we got a batch of lobster tails from Earth . . ."

"Lobster? Cookie! You're going to spoil us."

Cookie laughed, "I aim too, Cap'n, I aim too. I was thinking of making a Lobster Bisque for the crew and Lobster Thermidor for the officers."

Sean licked his lips, "Goddess Cookie, you got me salivating already. How many days to eat we get?"

"The Officers two meals. The crew I can stretch to six meals. Leftovers will make it to Skilly."

Sean smiled, "Sounds good to me. When can the crew be treated?"

Cookie's smiled broadly, "Tonight for both messes."

"Thanks, Cookie. I'll dine at the Officer's mess tonight."

"Very good, Cap'n. Dr. Loggar will be with you?"

Sean pursed his lips.

Cookie thought, 'Oh no, Goddess and the Cap'n had a spat.'

"Not sure, Cookie."

Cookie nodded, "Very well, sir. Is there anything I can get

you? More Skilly? Maybe I can drop some lobster meat just for you?"

Sean smiled, "And have the crew riot because I bumped the line? I'll wait my turn like everyone else."

Cookie nodded, "Sir. By your leave, then."

Sean nodded, "Carry on, Cookie."

Loggar found Sean in Starboard's Bow talking to Cookie. She waited until they finished. She slowly walked up next to Sean and sat down.

Loggar cleared her throat. "Sean, may we talk?"

He slowly turned his head toward her. "Depends."

Loggar chanced a smile. Sean did not return it. "Sorry."

"About?"

"Sounding like a mad scientist."

Sean nodded, "Very."

"Please understand, Sean. I've been pursuing Magick all my life. I . . . we are so close to understanding what the Necronians have. We are on the verge of an evolutionary leap with this new technology . . ."

"Kathy, the SI war. Lest we forget."

"No, I haven't forgotten, it's just that . . ."

"Just that technology turned on us. We lost millions of lives because we figured out how to make that same evolutionary leap." He stared into her eyes. His expression turned dark. "We were so close to understanding the technology. We were so close, oh so close."

Loggar remained silent. Sean's words bit deep, but she had to keep her eyes on the prize.

Sean continued, "Kathy, I lost friends because of technology. I suffered for years . . ."

"But, Sean, this is different."

"How so? Agegi different? Randals different?"

"No, that was a mistake . . ."

"That I'd rather not repeat. How can you be sure this won't be redux?"

"I can't," Loggar finally said. "I can't okay?" Tears were starting to form. "I can't . . ." She trailed off.

Sean's heart was pained. He wanted to hold his love and comfort her and tell her it was okay. It wasn't. He wouldn't. Not this time. He couldn't. Not yet. "Kathy . . . My Goddess . . . I have to be certain." And he leaned over and kissed her on the forehead. Sean couldn't walk away without doing that much.

Cookie stood in the shadows with tears in his eyes. Goddess is crying, but Cap'n must be hurting more. He must.

Chapter 3

Sean made his way to Top Deck. What he needed was to keep his mind busy. The next staff meeting was hours away and Sean had nothing to do but wait. Time. Not his only enemy, but up there. "Top Deck," Sean said as he entered the lift. He had several seconds of thought to himself before he reached the bridge, then, Deck chatter hit as the doors opened. Sean felt better as he always did when he heard Deck chatter. Top Deck was his sanctuary, his escape. He spent way more hours here than anywhere else. He stepped out and walked over to the command section.

Dawn was in her seat. She looked up. "Captain, bored?"

He smiled, "Yeah, something like that."

"Well, since you're here, I have the list of transfers. One you might be interested in is a brilliant Ensign for Engineer. She's gonna be Pulse wet dream for sure."

Sean sat in the command chair and tapped out a command on his CRT. He slowly scrolled through the entire list of transfers. About half-way down he came across an Adriana Newton.

Dawn watched as Sean scanned down the list. She knew when he reached Newton.

He looked up. "Seriously?"

"Scores are off the chart. Number one in class."

"Really?"

"She transferred from the Barack."

"The Barack is top of the line."

"First week she increased engine efficiency by 8%, read her

bio. Very interesting."

He did. Father's name, Sean. Mother's name, Adrunia. She read like a Mary Sue with too many coincidences.

Sean looked up. "When do we get the transfers?"

Dawn answered, "Sometime tomorrow. Gonna be an interesting mission this time around."

"The least." Indeed Sean thought. First Loggar and this fixation on magic, then Adruqu showing up as an Ensign. Coincidence? Hardly. The Necronians mastered time travel epochs ago. Nothing was a coincidence to them. They created their own circumstances. But this begged the question. What is about to happen?

"Captain?" Kirkland, the Chief Comm Officer said. "Message coming in from GC."

"Coding?"

"Standard, but marked for Captain's eyes first."

"I'll take it in the ready room."

Kirkland nodded and tapped out a few commands on his CRT.

"Code is Charlie Echo Zero One Zero, sir."

Sean nodded as he walked into the main ready room. He sat at the main console and typed in the command code to play message.

The CRT displayed the familiar GRID logo. A moment later Command General Whithaven appeared. His face was service weathered and his voice was raspy. Sean hoped GRID service would be kinder to him in his later advanced years.

"Captain Blakemore," the General began, "All is well I hope. News of your recent activity have not gone unnoticed and we appreciate your service and loyalty to GRID Com. Upon receipt on this message GRID Ship Reginald L Johnson will be re-designated as Explorer Cruiser. You are the commanding officer. Counsel is Dr. Kathy Loggar. Your missions will be defined by mentioned counsel, but you are the ultimate authority backed by unanimous consent of GRID Command."

Interesting, Sean thought.

The Commanding General leaned forward. "Sean, unanimous consent." He leaned back. "May the wind remain steady at your back. CG out."

And that was it. Extraordinary. CG and GC gave Sean a blank check. The CG so much as told Sean that he had official backing from GRID Command as well as unofficial backing from the Most High Council. Sean reminded himself that this "new" council had been loyal to Kathy – could still be, but to give a nod and wink to him meant support was only as good as the next wink and nod. Sean tapped out the Ship Intercom on his CRT. "Dr. Katherine Loggar, please report to Top Deck at earliest convenience. Repeat. Dr. Katherine Loggar report to Top Deck at earliest convenience." He signed off and smiled. That would make her and everyone else wonder. Normally he would have tracked her down like a puppy. Things change. For better or worse time would tell.

Loggar was in her quarters, misty eyed and full of pity, when Sean's voice came over the Intercom. His voice was neutral but something changed. She had cycled through a list of woes when her message light on her desk blinked rapidly. She walked over and keyed in the 'read message' command on her CRT. The GRID Command logo appeared on the main screen. Command General Whithaven's face appeared. He smiled slightly, which let her know things were still in her favor. "Dr. Loggar. The Council approves and grants you full access to the Johnson. The Johnson has been re-designated as an Explorer Cruiser. Captain Blakemore will remain ultimate authority of the Johnson but has been ordered to follow your counsel. Captain Blakemore has unanimous support of GRID Command. I hope all is well with you. CG Whithaven, out."

Loggar realized she had been holding her breathe during the message. But there it was. The Johnson was her's through Sean. She bit her bottom lip as she dissected the message. 'Ultimate authority, her counsel, unanimous support." All very powerful. Of course Sean would have ultimate authority. This was a military craft. But unanimous support? She supposed she should have been happy, but she wasn't. Not entirely. Unanimous support. From the full council. Sean had the confidence of The Most High Council. Her council. The one loyal to her. Then she remembered Sean asked her to report . . . report to Top Deck. Usually he asked if she would meet him on Top Deck. No doubt it was related. She walked into the bathroom and prepared herself. After eyes dried, hair re-combed and skirt adjusted she was ready. She was still hurt and worried but she was also The Most High Goddess.

Collins considered Loggar's offer. She hadn't accepted, nor did she reject it. The Most High allowed the Goddess to have up to ten individuals as part of her immediate circle. She could also have more than one circle provided the circles never met or didn't have easy access to one another. This way she could separate commune and covenant without risk of cross prejudice. She could maintain Inner circles within circles, of course. She could take on more than one lover within the circle. It was understood that one, two, more or everyone was a potential lover to the Goddess. It was her choice and by joining her circle you acknowledged that. It was also understood that anyone who was Goddess' lover could become sexual partners with anyone within the circle. Collins wondered if the Captain was aware of that clause. Probably not, which got Collins thinking of the Captain in a way she hadn't before. Like Dawn, Collins was bisexual with strong leanings toward women, but potential sex with the Captain?

Just by the Goddess making the offer she's forever changed the way how she sees him. Just then she heard over the Intercom, "Dr. Katherine Loggar, please report to Top Deck at earliest convenience. Repeat. Dr. Katherine Loggar report to Top Deck at earliest convenience." The lack of emotion did not escape her professional ear. The Captain was upset and mad and Loggar would have to just deal with the Captain's mood.

Collins walked over to a shelf of hard-copy books. She pulled out, "Goddess' Way." It was The Most High rules and regulations guide book disguised and written as a fantasy romance novel. The first edition was printed in the 21st century. Each Goddess had the option of revising the book. Loggar's edition was the 25th, but Collins preferred the 6th edition, which she held in her hands. Loggar's edition was next to a book on horticulture. There was nothing wrong with the Loggar Print. It read well. It was neither overly exciting, like the 2nd edition, or overly boring, like the 16th edition. But the 6th edition was the best. It covered everything. Sex, drugs, governance, punishments, rewards, hiding in plain sight, interacting with outsiders, and dealing with threats from within and without. Collins turned to the chapter dealing with circles. Goddess Fey stressed that circle members must be lovers of each other – male or female. They had to regularly engage in promiscuity with one another to satiate their individual urges. When it came time to please the Goddess they could be selfless and give in totally to her thirst, whims, and pleasures. The Loggar edition had circles more for counsel, guidance, and communing, which wasn't bad actually. Collins flipped through a few more pages and decided she should re-familiarize herself with The Loggar print. She pulled the edition off the shelf and turned to circles. The first paragraph read,

"It was in the evening hours when the Goddess reached the inner chamber. Her circle was waiting for her. She chose her counsels carefully. Some lovers, some close friends, some challengers. All would have to satisfy her needs on this night. She was the focus and her appetite for carnal consumption was especially heightened."

Collins closed the book and decided she needed to talk to Sean. She walked out and headed for the nearest lift.

Sean couldn't actually say he was in a bad mood. It's been worse, but it's also been better. He only had to wait about ten minutes before Loggar emerged from the lift. He stood up and met Loggar half way. She reached him and stopped. Both stared at one another for several seconds. Deck Chatter stopped. Another handful of seconds went by. Sean said, "As you were people." He turned toward the main conference room. "Kathy, please follow me."

Loggar nodded and followed.

Once the door closed Sean resisted the urge to embrace Loggar and passionately kiss her. This rift was killing him. He motioned for Loggar to sit at the table. He had Cookie make them a salad lunch with strawberry truffles on the side.

Loggar sat and waited for Sean to sit.

He did but remained silent. He placed his napkin across his lap and began eating. She followed. During lunch he poured her a glass of wine. After both had finished he pushed the tray of truffles toward her. His eyes never strayed. During the entire time he never smiled. After Loggar bit into her second truffle he cleared his throat. "Goddess."

All her doubts faded away. Sean was mad at her, but he stilled loved her and that was alright. This strange man sitting before her, she thought, guards his thoughts well. He does not shout or scream but what he does, his actions and gestures, speaks loudly with high volume. She knew her mistake and Sean was letting her know he knew. He drew a line in the sand and would not cross it.

"Sean . . . my Sean, I . . . I . . . we need to find a solution to how the nanobots behave or we will find a way to turn them off."

Sean exhaled, then smiled.

Collins stepped on to Top Deck. Dawn was sitting at the Captain's station. She looked up and greeted Collins. "Doc, what's up?"

"Is the Captain alone in his ready room?"

"Dr. Loggar is in there with him. Cookie sent up lunch earlier."

Collins frowned.

"Karen, what's wrong?"

"What makes you think something is wrong?"

"Because I know you, that's what."

Collins thought for moment. "Dr. Loggar is forming a circle and . . . "

"Really? I hope she asks me to join, I'd love to fu . . . "

"Dawn!"

"What? Being part of a circle is great, even if it's a local covenant."

"So, why hasn't there been many on the Johnson?"

Dawn laughed, "There are lots of small deck circles. The one I'm waiting for hasn't been started yet. It'll have a certain Doctor as the center . . ."

Collins paused. "Me? I'm no . . . Goddess?" Her mind raced. She knew everyone on board, follower or not, looked to her for advice. She was the Ship's Doctor, of course. Everyone had to see her eventually. Including the Captain. "Am I?"

Dawn smiled and nodded. "That's why we love you.

Everyone has always thought of you as our Goddess."

"How come I didn't know?"

"Can we say, oblivious? Which in itself is good. We figured eventually you'd realize it and form your own."

"Wow. How come you never suggested it?"

"Let's see. War, Crisis after crisis, Captain's depression, then his depression, and oh yeah, his depression. Then our faithful trip to Necron. And here we are."

Collins smiled. She'd kiss Dawn if they hadn't been on Top Deck.

"Did Loggar invite you?"

Collins nodded.

"Are you going to accept is the big question?"

"I don't know. I was going to talk to Captain, first. There are so many things he may or may not know. I . . ."

"You're scared."

"What?"

Dawn chuckled, "You're scared and you think the Captain is this innocent young boy who won't be able to handle sharing his woman with others."

"Nonsense . . . I am just . . ."

"Frightened." Dawn laughed softly. "The Captain is still a man with two brains. The term Horned God is not referring to something above his eyes."

"Would he be willing to share her with another man?"

Dawn nearly laughed out loud. "She's calculating, but not stupid. The circle will be made up of women. If we had been planet side, then yeah, there'd be a few men. But on a battle cruiser, with a bad ass Captain? I'd see transfer imminent in the poor sap's future."

Collins nodded.

"The other question is, would you be able to share him with other women?"

"What?!?"

"You heard me. Would you be able to share the Captain? Once you crossed that line how far are you willing to go?"

Collins blinked rapidly.

"We all know you like him, which is why we wondered why you never formed your own circle."

"But . . ."

"Karen, I know. The Captain and I have history, but that never stopped me from being loyal."

Collins stopped mid thought. "I thought it was all rumor."

Dawn leaned in close. "Imminent danger and threat of dying the next hour can bring people closer. Sure I love the Captain, but I also like him. I was sad the day we stopped but it never changed my feelings or a wish to have some more. If Loggar invites me into her circle, please oh please suggest it, I'll enjoy every second again."

Despite herself Collins laughed. "You're wicked."

Dawn smiled and licked her lips. "All this talk has gotten me heated up. What are you doing tonight?"

Collins smiled. "Depends on what happens after that door opens. I'll be dining out or in."

Loggar finished the last Truffle when she said, "Sean, you read the Goddess' Way?"

"A few months ago. I never mentioned it?"

Loggar shook her head.

"It was very interesting. Disguising the manual as a fantasy novel. Brilliant."

Loggar nodded again. "As you know, the Most High Goddess has an option to form a circle. Actually, Local and Regional Goddesses have that option as well" She paused.

Sean counted to five, "And you are worried?"

"A circle has never been formed on the Johnson."

Sean nodded. "At least none I know, but then again I had no idea about the Most High before we first met. In fact, a

Commander rarely knows the intricate details on board ship. The First Officer knows that."

"Dawn?"

Sean nodded. "Yeah, if she doesn't know what's going on board then it's not happening."

Loggar considered that. Later she'd ask Dawn to join her circle as well as recommendations.

"What are your feelings toward Dawn?"

"Kathy, what gives? Are you wondering if I'm sleeping with other women?"

"If I form a circle, you'll be expected to sleep with at least one other."

Now that blew Sean's mind. Expected to have extra-relational sex?

"And so will I. That includes men too."

Now that was a sobering thought. Would he be willing to share his love with another man? Or more than one as he understood the concept of circles? Would he also be willing to sleep with another man? "Kathy, the Most High never had the military in mind, as far as I know. I'm not sure if I can put myself in that position."

"Sean, I have a circle within GRID Command.

Sean frowned.

Loggar placed a hand over his. "Though it's been years since I convened a gathering, it's something that was and is necessary."

Sean remained silent.

Loggar placed a hand on his cheek. "My lover and friend. Never worry. I have chosen you as the Horned God. If you ever accept you'd be number two within the Most High."

Sean gathered her hand into his and kissed it. "Kathy, I know."

"Then why are you holding back?"

"As being the Horned God?"

She nodded.

"Not sure exactly. Fear maybe. Is it necessary I be one?'

She shook her head.

"Then no rush, right?"

She nodded. "And you don't have to take on another lover, though I would feel better if you did."

"Kathy . . ."

She leaned over and kissed him passionately. "The Most High ways are different, Sean. Selflessly they cater to the Goddess, local, regional, The Most High. The Goddesses of our Order are the center of what we hold sacred. We bring life into the Universe. Gaia and Ka, and now whomever we run across ties and binds us as one. That is our way. And I hope you will give yourself totally to that way. "

"If I became the Horned God, then what?

"You'd be invited to join GRID Command. We now control two-thirds voting rights. . ."

"Two-thirds! Control!"

She nodded and continued, "You could pick your own assignments, your own missions, anything Sean. Anything within reason and that could be easily justified. You'd be promoted to Commodore, then eventually Admiral. . ."

"But Kathy, would I have earned the promotions?"

"Sean, GRID Command thinks you have. Everyone on the council said you would have been Commodore years ago if not for the Quail incident."

Sean felt sick to his stomach.

"They also think you're the best Captain GRID has produced and you belong out here. At least for another tour or two."

Sean admitted to himself the Johnson was his place though he would fancy being called Commodore Blakemore. Now that would wad up Robin's panties for sure.

" . . . we are still a secret society. We hide well in plain sight . . ."

Sean nodded.

" . . . and we've learned to be patient."

A very sobering statement, Sean thought, but not quite true if recent events are factored in.

"GRID Command unanimously supports you, Sean. Unanimously. Followers and non-followers. So, in a way you are already considered the Horned God by followers and greatly respected by others."

"Let's get back to the circle."

"Okay." Loggar replied smiling.

"Who would be in it and exactly what would you use it for?"

"Counsel, Sean. I asked Karen . . ."

"Collins?"

She nodded, "To be the first in my circle. I need clinical objective minded individuals in this circle. I'm colored by being too close to Magick. This morning proved that. I need someone not part of the equation."

Sean nodded in agreement. Then, unexpectedly his imagination went wild. In his mind's eye he saw Collins' lovely red hair flowing across his stomach and thighs.

Chapter 4

Collins was about to leave Top Deck when the door to the ready room finally opened. Loggar was in good spirits until she saw Collins.

Collins looked up. It was too late to retreat. She hadn't really figured out what she was going to say or do. She cleared her throat. "Doctor, Captain."

Sean stopped mid step. "Doctor? A visit to Top Deck?"

Collins nodded. "I have that report you requested earlier." Sean knew it was a lie. He was certain Loggar saw through her lie, too. "Okay, you can give it to me in the Ready Room." He turned to Loggar and forced a smile. "Tonight? Dinner?"

Loggar eyed Collins, then Sean. She smiled and tried to sound relaxed, "Certainly Sean. I'll be with Herb and the others if you need to talk." She turned and faced the Doctor. "Karen. All is well?"

Collins nodded, her smile still forced, "It is, Kathy. We can talk later at your convenience."

Loggar nodded and made her way to the Lift. Everyone stood fast until the Lift doors closed.

"Captain, we do need to talk."

Sean nodded, "Okay Doctor. Follow me."

And the two disappeared behind the door.

Sean moved aside the empty dishes. He sat.

Collins waited for Sean to get comfortable before she sat down.

They stared at one another for a moment.

"She mentioned circles," Collins broke the silence.

Sean nodded. He pursed his lips. "A lot to take in."

Collins nodded.

"Kathy mentioned local and regional Goddesses. The Johnson doesn't have one?"

"I would be the one."

"How come?"

Collins shrugged, "Oblivious, sir."

"Me, too."

Silence stood awkwardly between them.

"Now what?" Sean asked.

"Do you like me?"

"Pardon?"

"Do you like me Captain?"

"A bit more than I should admit."

That was a relief to Collins. Dawn had hit the nail on the head. She had always liked the Captain, but tried to keep everything professional. There were nights, when she was alone, she would dream of the two of them. She would have just reached an orgasm, thighs still trembling when the dream would end. She leaned in slightly.

Sean noticed. His only other ship board relationship had been with Dawn. But that was years ago and at the height of the War. He promised himself not to get physically involved with another shipmate. He leaned in slightly.

"You understand once we cross the line . . ."

He nodded and leaned in closer. "I understand. Are you prepared?"

And before she knew it they kissed. It was like a flood. She explored his mouth with her's. His lips were amazingly soft and his tongue matched her's. The texture was wonderful she told herself and kissed him harder. Sean slid over the table and sat next to her. He embraced her as a lover back from a long absence. His arms surrounded her in an embrace that conveyed . . . fulfillment. He held her as they kissed with finality of a thirst finally quenched. Her hand slipped into his lap and she felt how hard he was becoming. She grabbed and stroked him up and down enjoying how she was able to make him so hard. He kissed her neck and moved a hand over a breast. She reached into his pants and felt how soft his skin was. The tip was moist. She played her finger across it as he caressed her breast. She withdrew her hand and licked her fingers. She reveled at how sweet he tasted. He rubbed his other hand across her cheeks. He became further aroused at how toned and firm she felt. He lifted her up onto his lap. She had already pulled him out and feverishly stroked him into rock hard. His hand reached down and felt that she was moist. His fingers moved her panties aside and he found her recently shaved. He played his fingers over her. She was swollen with arousal and her aroma was intoxicating. He grabbed her hand and began rubbing himself along her folds until he gently slipped in. She inhaled as he entered and kissed him again. She worked her hips, stroking back and forth. He used both hands on her cheeks and kept her in rhythm. She frantically thrusted her hips until a thick wave of ecstasy washed over her, then one intense wave after another. In moments she was spent, her thighs spasmodic and her mind racing. Sean just held her. He was in no rush now that the line had been crossed. There would be time enough for him.

"Sean," she whispered, "what have we done?"

"Something we should have done long ago."

Collins wiped tears from her eyes. She nodded. "Now what?"

"Tonight we have dinner and work out all the details."

Collins straightened her dress and slipped her panties back in place.

Sean tucked himself back in place.

Minutes later both were composed and ready to face Top

Deck. Both exited the door at the same time.

"Thank you Doctor. I will take everything you've told me under consideration."

Collins faced Sean and nodded. "You'll have the rest of my report this evening." She turned and left, but not before giving Dawn a sideward glance.

Dawn smiled and knew what just happened. She turned to Kirkland. "Mr. Kirkland, cancel that last pool and delete it from record."

He laughed, "Yes, ma'am, but how should I classify it?"

Dawn replied, "First Officer Decree. Results too ambiguous.

Chapter 5

Sean was back in Chamber one. This time there was a table in with him. Everyone agreed priority one was for Sean to able to control how the nanobots acquired fuel. He looked over the various items: Cooked steak, bowl of STIM tablets, Glass of water, Glass of Adult beverage, Glass of Juice, slab of raw beef, and a cube of bread. Sensor scans were placed around each item.

Collins leaned into the console mike, "Captain, ready?"

Sean nodded and said, "Yes."

"First test, please."

Sean concentrated and his fist ignited into a pale blue ball of fire.

A monitor blipped. Collins glanced at the readout. "Se . . . Captain, concentrate on the STIM, please."

Loggar looked sideways to Collins. During the entire prep time Collins avoided eye contact. Something was off. Loggar leaned toward the monitor and said, "Sean, I'd like you to concentrate on the raw meat first."

Collins frowned and switched off the mike. She turned on Loggar. "May I ask why the raw meat first?"

Loggar stared into Collins' eyes. "That's what I wanted to start with."

"I thought we had a plan and tha . . ."

"I changed my mind. I think we should go through organics first."

Collins counted to ten. Even though Loggar was head

scientist and the Most High Goddess didn't give her the right to hijack her tests. She switched on the mike, "Sean, there's been a mistake. Start with the STIM, please. The instruments and computer are programmed specifically for STIM as the first test." She clicked the mike off.

Loggar stared back.

Collins said, "Goddess. My lab, my rules."

"I see," Loggar replied.

"Not sure you do. We already agreed on how the tests would proceed." Collins spotted another Doctor. "Joyce, please take over and follow the test procedures. Thanks." Collins walked over to the door, "We need to talk."

Loggar nodded, not quite knowing whether to be afraid or angry.

The two walked down a hallway to Collins' office. Once inside Collins offered Loggar the visitor chair opposite her desk chair.

Loggar sat.

"May I get you something, Goddess?'

"Why not Kathy?" Loggar said.

"Seems to me we just had a power play a moment ago and I need you to still see I understand our positions."

Loggar took that in and processed it. "Okay, point. So, what did you tell Sean after I left?"

Collins ignored the question and asked again, "May I get you something, Goddess? Water, coffee, tea?"

"I asked you a question, Karen."

Collins dug in further. "And I asked you a question first. You want something or not?"

"I want an answer. Screw the pleasantries."

Collins walked over to a small fridge and pulled out a juice carton. She took her time to her desk all the while ignoring the evil glare from Loggar. She hadn't really decided what to say. She sat down, opened the juice and took a drink. Maybe more than what she should have.

Loggar notice and realized Collins was struggling with what to say. "Whenever you are ready then."

Collins wiped her lips. "I asked Sean if he understood circles."

"And?"

"That was it. We talked about his role and what could be expected of him."

"And nothing else? You did nothing else?"

Collins played cool as much as she could. She knew Loggar studied people for a living.

Loggar looked for tales and Collins wasn't going to give her one. So she told a half-truth.

"I was scared, so I wanted to know how the Captain would feel if . . . if we crossed the line."

"You like him?"

"I had never allowed it passed being professional."

Loggar studied Collins face for a long moment. "How come you never formed your own circle aboard the Johnson? Everyone I've asked tells me you're the ship's Goddess."

Collins welcomed the break and happy to discuss something she didn't have to lie about. "I didn't know I was thought of as the ship's Goddess until a few hours ago."

"Excuse me?"

"I didn't know."

Loggar frowned.

"Circles are not very common on board a battle cruiser. Yes, there are a few ship deck ones, and the Most High members are pretty good at keeping things on the down-low. So, no, I didn't know I was the ship's Goddess, so therefore I never formed my own circle, and I never saw a reason to join any of the lower rank circles, either. Having done so would have changed the dynamics as well as my role as the Ship's Doctor and Counselor. Besides, being part of yours would have immediately made mine irrelevant."

Loggar nodded. "Tea, please."

Collins smiled. "Sugar or plain?"

Loggar leaned forward, "Sugar, please. Very sweet."

Collins got up and made Earl Gray. She dropped in several sweet pellets. She poured herself a cup of Zen Calm, walked back to her desk and handed Loggar the tea.

Loggar sipped, "Very nice."

Collins sat back and relaxed. "I accept by the way."

"My circle?"

Collins nodded.

Loggar smiled and took another sip. On her third sip of tea Loggar asked, "Any thought on who else may join, should join?"

"Dawn."

"I like the Commander. She's got spirit. I was thinking of keeping the Circle small. I'm not sure adding men would be a good idea . . ."

Collins nodded, "There can only be one big cock in the hen house."

" . . . Sean said he experimented in his youth, but I think he's wholly heterosexual." Loggar giggled, "You're right about that. Sean is strong, but not terribly tough when it may come to sharing. I don't want to take the chance, but if we were to have men, who?"

"Part of the Command Staff. Kirkland and Foster. Kirkland's a cunt hound, Foster is a gentleman. I'd add Cookie. He's pan sexual, but also a gentleman. No one from Engineering."

Loggar listened. She loved Cookie's recipes and was surprised to know he was pan sexual, but it made sense. He had that kind of spirit. She could see it. Kirkland she knew was a hunter. He was competitive and hyper-sexual. She got that the first day on board the Johnson. Foster was introspective. That would add greatly to the circle, she thought.

"What about your staff?"

Loggar laughed. "What about them?"

"None are worthy of your circle?"

Loggar ignored the underlining tone, "Not for the Johnson. They'll stay my command staff as Sean has you and the others as his." She rubbed the back of her neck, "Don't get me wrong. Herb and Milkens are brilliant, but a little too immature and undisciplined. They both hyper-focus on function, not execution. And, I'm not physically attracted to them."

Collins nodded. "And, me? Or Dawn?"

Loggar placed the cup of tea down and walked over to Collins. "You're very lovely, Karen. Wish I had your natural color hair."

Collins leaned back in her chair. She thought, 'Kathy is going to be aggressive by leaning down and kissing me or she'll drop down on her knees and kiss me.'

Loggar reached down offering her hands. She thought, 'Either she'll take my hands and pull me down or she'll let me help her up.'

Collins thought control. 'She's seeing how I handle control.' Collins accepted Loggar's outstretched hands and lifted herself up.

Loggar moved in close, her chest touching Collins'. "You're not afraid of what would happen between you and I, are you?"

Collins shook her head slowly. She answered by lightly brushing her lips against Loggar's. "Are you afraid?"

Loggar answered back by returning the kiss. She pressed firmly and slightly parted her lips inviting Collins to enter.

Collins felt Loggar's soft lips against hers. There was the hint of Loggar inviting Collins to cross the line. She did and thrust her tongue deep into Loggar's mouth. The kiss grew intense and their embrace more carnal and lascivious.

Collins nearly popped Loggar's shirt buttons as she undid them. She grabbed one breast and kissed its nipple.

Loggar reached down and slipped her hands between Collins' legs. She played her middle finger between her folds until her panties became wet.

Collins inhaled and held back a moan. She kissed and licked at the other nipple.

Loggar's other hand bunched up a fist of Collins' hair. She lifted her head up and kissed her intensely. She grabbed her jaw and fiercely played her tongue against Collins'. Loggar gyrated her hips against her leg while she ran her tongue back and forth along her jaw line. Then with a raspy whisper into Collins' ear she said, "You are mine. I so wanted you the first time I saw you." She ran her tongue along the side of Collins' neck.

Collins quivered after hearing Loggar's declaration. She slipped her hand between Loggar's legs and felt soaked panties. She slipped the panties aside and inserted one finger.

Loggar continued her tongue along Collins neck and jaw. She then pulled Collins away and pushed her toward the desk face down and bent over. She reached down and snatched Collins' panties down to her ankles. Loggar rubbed her hand across Collins' cheeks giving her a quick and sharp slap ever few seconds.

Collins felt an acute pleasure with each slap. She moaned involuntarily as Loggar dropped to her knees and worked her tongue between her cheeks.

Loggar used her hands to spread Collins' legs and cheeks. Then she worked her tongue from top to bottom, occasionally slipping her tongue deep.

Then, without warning, Collins orgasmed spasmodically. She dropped to her knees, turned and looked Loggar in the eyes. "Goddess," she uttered.

"Goddess," Loggar replied back.

Sean was becoming worried. Collins and Loggar disappeared some time ago. Fear started to creep up on hi . . .

"Captain, relax please. Your heart rate has increased."

Sean snapped back to the tests. He nodded and took in a deep breathe. "Relaxed."

Joyce said through the speakers, "Thanks Captain. You're doing excellent. Let's move on to the glass of water.

Sean nodded and concentrated. His hand flame turned pale blue. He supposed the flame was the hottest yet with STIM and Adult beverage the next hottest. The raw meat produced an orange flame and the juice produced something pinkish.

"Okay, Captain. Last test. There's a pressure plate mounted on the door. Can you produce some sort of projectile at the door?"

Sean smiled. Of course he could. That was the original reason he received the nanobots.

Collins and Loggar entered the Lab just as Sean finished the water test. Both stepped in the test area and stood behind Joyce. Sean looked up and the two of them side by side relaxed. His heart rate soared. The monitors reacted setting off alarms.

Sean felt great. His heart raced at the sight of Collins and Loggar. He concentrated on the pressure plate and sent out a fire ball. It was bright blue with wispy electrical tentacles grasping at air. It collided with the door in seconds. The force, tremendous, blew the door off its hinges and warped the surrounding door frame. The two ton door landed several meters away in a smothering smoky mess of twisted metal. The entire area was silent. Sean stepped out and looked around. All eyes were on him. A bit of stage fright gripped him. He could only say the first thing that came to mind, "Oops."

Chapter 6

Loggar lite several ylang ylang patchouli scented candles spread across the room. It was the VIP quarters that Sean had converted to her personal room. She had it decorated in plain polished dark wood panels. The carpet was tan and spread from wall to wall. The room came with a kitchen, walk-in closet, dressing room, bedroom, full sided bathroom with a walk-in shower next to a 5-person tub. Its water supply was separate from the common ship wide water system with advance filtration so as not to deplete crew's supply. A large 254 centimeter vid screen took up a small part of one large wall. The Johnson had four such rooms. This one was stationed port side amidships lower deck.

Loggar thought, 'It's been six months since I've invoked a group circle. After learning true magick circles don't seem the same.'

Sean, Collins, Dawn, and Loggar stood in front of one another wearing soft cotton caftans. Sean also wore underwear. He had an erection that was much too uncomfortable.

All the women noticed, but suppressed giggles.

Loggar walked to the center of a large mat in the middle of the floor. She spread her arms wide. "Computer dim lights to point seven, please." The candle lights glow increased. Their fragrance wafted through the air heightening the anticipated invocation. A heavy slightly nectar scent drifted through the room. The patchouli scent emerged and lingered lightly underneath the ylang ylang's aroma. Its earthly crisp wet soil fragrance wasn't strong enough to overpower the ylang ylang but just strong enough to transport one's mind away from technology and steel too deep in the forest. The way Loggar liked it.

"To the directions of east, south, west, then north, the Mother Earth, to our birth place Necron, to the Infinite and beyond. You can see me in your eyes, when they are mirrored by a friend. You can hear me in your voice and feel me in each breath you breathe; you can feel me in your heart and with each beat. There is no end to the circle. You are here to give me guidance and direction when I may become lost. You are to assist me in finding direction and guidance when darkness falls. I am here to give you love, comfort, safe haven.

Welcome all to my circle.

You are my counsel, which will help me find the light through the darkness of uncertainty. You are my council when a direction is set and the light has been located. I hold great honor and trust in each of you and therefore ask you to come unto me the one thing I cherish and hold sacred . . . My flesh."

Collins stepped into the circle.

"Most High Goddess, I accept your welcome and release my own counsel to find their own guidance. I shall give you counsel when you are lost and give you council when light is found."

She removed her caftan.
Dawn stepped into the circle.

"Most High Goddess, I accept your welcome unto you and freely give you my counsel when you are lost and give you council when light is found."

She removed her caftan.

Sean swallowed hard and tried to clear his throat with soft grunts. He failed and the embarrassment was all the more pronounced. He stepped into the circle.

"Most High Goddess, I accept your welcome unto you and freely give my counsel when you are lost. And I give council when light is found."

He removed his caftan and slipped off his underwear. His cheeks turned red when popped out. He looked up and tried to think of something other than the three women in front of him. The irony was not lost on that he's bedded all three at some point during his command on the Johnson.

Loggar walked over to Collins and kissed her briefly. She did the same to Dawn and Sean. She turned around and out stretched her arms. Collins kissed the back of her neck. Dawn stepped in and kissed the other side of her neck. Sean knelt down and kissed her left cheek, then her right. Loggar turned around and Sean kissed just above her fold. He took in her fragrance and let it soothe his insides. Dawn and Collins joined him. They both kissed her folds, then one another. Sean started licking. As he rested his upper lip against Loggar he worked his tongue up and down. She moaned and grabbed the back of his head and pressed firmly. Tonight was her night and she was going to get as much of it as she could.

Sean licked harder, lapping up her juices and drinking to his fill of intoxication. Loggar shuddered violently and used two hands to hold Sean's head in place. Her knees nearly buckled when Sean pulled himself away. He stood up and Loggar embraced him tightly. Dawn grabbed Sean. Her grip was strong and she stroked him long and hard. Collins helped Dawn stroking while she placed her lips on Sean. He moaned as Collins inhale him entirely. Her mouth was warm and moist. He felt her tongue drag underneath. She did that several times getting him slick, then both Dawn and Collins eased him slowly into Loggar. She shivered as he went passed her lips and slide deep inside. He started working his hips. Sean was slow but Loggar grabbed both cheeks and guided him to her rhythm. Within minutes she orgasmed coating Sean slick with herself. He pulled out and Dawn pulled him into her mouth. She sucked hard and long deep throating him. Loggar lay on her back and guided Collins over her face. She played her lips across Collins making her moan. Collins worked her hips in circular motions making sure she covered every inch of Loggar's face. Within a minute she climaxed over Loggar. Sean had dropped to his knees. Dawn backed into him and pushed hard. Sean grabbed her hips and pounded hard rapidly. After a minute both yelled out in orgasmic chorus. Loggar reached for Sean's face and kissed him. She whispered in his ear, "My Love." He kissed her on the lips and smiled. Moments later everyone was asleep.

Chapter 7

Sean and Dawn watched the steady stream of new recruits and transfers, all one hundred fifty two pass through the main hangar bay doors. Stations were set up just inside to receive everyone, a nice neat row of tables with the sets of letters above them, last names beginning with A-Da to the first table, De-F on another. So on until W-Z on the last.

Loggar was in the lab with Collins looking over the last batch of data. Sean had learned how to direct the nanobots effectively enough. He felt better and accepted the nanobots as his now. As he was watching the stream of bodies he felt a smart pinch just inside his right ear. "What the?"

Dawn looked over, "Something wrong?"

"Yeah I just felt this sharp pain in my ear. Strange," then he looked out to the mass of bodies and saw her. At least he thought it was her. "Dawn, there!"

Dawn spotted the young woman. She looked younger than her vid still.

The two watched from the mid deck platform as a particular recruit made her way to the table marked Ne – P. It took several minutes for the young transfer to get logged into the ship, assigned quarters, and given a meal card. She was given a map of the Johnson and pointed to a Lift. She fell into place with a dozen other transfers. They all walked in a lift and were gone.

Sean turned to Dawn. "When's orientation scheduled?"

"Four bells afternoon watch. You want to give the welcome orientation?"

Sean smiled, "I do. It's been a long time, but I think I can manage without embarrassing myself."

Dawn nodded, "I'll have Kirkland start several pools."

Sean laughed out loud.

Thompson in Maintenance won a week's pay.

Adriana sat in the first row. She finally made it and now she would see The Sean. The man she was destined to meet. Her entire life had been worked up for this moment and she was prepared. Her Mom told her that Sean Blakemore would need special counsel. This day would mark the beginning of Sean's new life. Her Mom even told her the exact time she would see him. Adriana, of course, would laugh and thought her Mom foolish sometimes, but more often than not she was spot on. She worked hard and applied herself. Top of her class, she had the pick of any GRID ship. Johnson was not the ship she chose first. Her Mom told her that she would have to crew two other ships before the Johnson. She stressed that it had to be so. Everything depended on her following her advice to the letter. So she did. And now here she was, waiting for Captain Blakemore to give the orientation speech.

Sean had Kirkland conduct a background check of Adriana. Everything in her files could be all a coincidence. But, it could also be the doings of the Necronians. What can't you do when you control space and time? He walked into the auditorium and immediately spotted Adriana. She was seated in the front row. She had the issued female mid skirt with Engineering Blue colors along the side. Her hair was short and she was cute young. Her skin was light brown and looked soft and smooth from his vantage point. She looked very much like Adruqu, but more human of course.

Someone yelled, "Captain on deck!"

All attendees stood at attention.

Sean walked to the podium, "As you were, people." He toggled on Ship wide intercom. The orientation would be heard throughout the Johnson.

Everyone in the auditorium sat.

Sean cleared his throat. "I don't normally do orientation but since we are no longer at war or rushing off to right some wrong I have some me time."

The entire room erupted into laughter.

"I'd like to personally welcome everyone here. Some of you have taken a long journey to reach this destination. Some of you had doors opened for you. And yet, still others, probably just rolled out of bed this morning and decided to find the lunch line. And here you are."

More laughter.

"What I'd like to stress is that The Reginald L. Johnson is not just any ship of the line. The Johnson is of the old guard. A semi-aware vessel that had the misfortune of being a semi-aware vessel. During the SI war many Johnson class ships, yes – The Johnson was the first, were compromised. That's why all vessels built afterward are dumbed down. Most of you, if not all, already know this. As a result of the compromise all Johnson class ships have to toggle the semi-aware off during normal runs and toggle semi-aware back on during extreme long and war jumps. Fortunately for you the Johnson has been upgraded to the newer class of engines not requiring Tranking. Unfortunately for the Johnson, and all that have served aboard for so long, will not be needed as often. Probably not ever. That is as long as the SI are still out there. I say this to you so that when you walk the halls of the Johnson, when you travel the lifts or enter into a room, to remember that the Johnson is a good ship. It has served us very well as we will return the favor. We have too. It's important."

Sean stepped away from the podium and started walking down the aisles. He felt relaxed and alive. Today he would announce their new mission. "Today marks another important event. The Johnson has been reclassified as an Explorer Cruiser, hence our mission is no longer to seek and destroy or seek and protect. It's seek and find. It's seek and gain. It's seek and discover. In the past half year things have occurred that has told us Humans are not alone in the galaxy. We really are part of a greater picture and as such we are now going to contact others into the far unknown and beyond. We are going to do extremely long jumps going forward, but with the new upgrades we'll remain sane. I have no idea what new things we'll find or discover, but as some of you have heard through scuttlebutt it is amazing and absolutely true the things we have found or discovered so far. A lot of it will remain classified for security reasons, but some things just can't be kept secret." Sean paused, now he had their attention.

There was murmur throughout the room.

Cookie sat at his desk and listened. His eye's moist with happiness. He was also frightened like most of the crew. ". . . into the far unknown and beyond" the Captain said. Cookie shivered from excitement.

Pulse had his back to the monitor when the Captain said, ". . . it is amazing and absolutely true . . ." God man, Pulse thought, this is for real. He looked at his console. 'Alien tech,' he thought, 'with some tweaking we could really make the Johnson something to envy.'

Loggar and Collins stopped working as did the Med Staff. Everyone listened. " . . . In the past half year things have occurred that has told us Humans are not alone in the galaxy. We really are part of a greater picture and as such we are now going to contact others into the far unknown and beyond . . . " They both looked at one another and smiled.

Sean continued, "GRID Command has redefined our mission as completely and utterly scientific. We are an explorer vessel now. We are explorers. Dr. Katherine Loggar, has been charged with guiding us along our new path. Our mission, with her counsel, is to search for new intelligent life-forms. We are to find our lost cousins and establish a new alliance. I'm certain we will be met with questions and suspicion. We may even meet with aggression and hostility, but no matter, we will push forward and learn more about ourselves through discovering others. I am extremely confident that we will meet this mission, as we have with others, with professionalism, honor, and integrity. I hereby welcome each and every one of you to the Explorer Cruiser Reginald L. Johnson."

Dawn yelled, "On your feet!"

Everyone stood up.

"Dismissed!" And the room emptied out quickly.

Cookie smiled. He heard the scuttle about Cap'n having special abilities he got from their last mission. Kelley from Engineering said that Mason told him Barnes saw the Cap'n blow the doors off one of the DeCom chambers. He said it was like real magick but with Alien technology. Word was that the Goddess and some of her staff could do it too but only on that strange planet and maybe certain worlds, which seemed to make sense now. Cookie decided he had to make something special for the Cap'n. Maybe a Cali cut with his Lobster Thermidor. He also had been saving a bottle of Louis XIII cognac. The substance was practically priceless. His grandfather saved three bottles during the Purge and gave two to his father. Cookie left the unopened bottle on Earth in a safe deposit box. The other bottle was in his quarters. It survived a war and the run in with the Webster. He figured he had 250 ml left, which was more than enough.

As Adriana filed out with the others she finally understood. Her Mom knew this day would come and thus prepared her as best she could. This was the day the Johnson would go into the beyond. Today the Johnson transformed from War vessel to Explorer. Today, the Johnson crossed the line.

Chapter 8

Adriana was unpacking when she heard the chime. She was sharing a four bunk bed room with three other transfers. Chris was assigned to Medical. Her first impression of him was good. His quick-wit came out minutes after meeting and he had an immediate way of setting those around him at ease. She'd probably like him the most, maybe. Latasha was from Navigation. She was tall with rich black hair. Her skin was smooth and she had an accent that just couldn't be tied down easily. She was intense but not intimidating. Karolina was from Medical. She had pretty grey eyes that stood out against her dark skin. Adriana thought her exquisite. She loved her melodic voice.

The chime again. Adriana walked to the door and opened it. The Sean stood there in front of her. He was an imposing figure in her eyes. "Captain!" she fumbled, "please enter. How may I help you?"

Sean stepped in and looked around. "Adriana, is it?"

She nodded.

"Quarters to your liking? Met your bunkmates yet?"

She nodded, "Yes, sir . . . and yes sir."

He turned and faced her.

She nearly lost her breathe. Not quite swooning.

"You look very familiar; perchance I've met your parents?"

"Maybe. My father disappeared during the SI wars. My Mother did a lot of traveling before I was born. They met at the Faulkner Colonies."

Sean smiled. Amazing he thought. She really did look like

Adruqu. He could come out and just ask if she knew her. He could also ask if she knew magick, but that would make him sound like a nut. He suddenly doubted his reasoning for intruding. "I really didn't want to intrude . . ."

"Not at all Captain!"

". . . but you reminded me of someone I know. Don't think your Captain crazy . . ."

"Of course, not!"

Sean thought himself crazy. "Ensign, walk with me, please."

She paused. There was something she had to remember, something very important. Seconds ticked by as she thought hard.

Sean turned around, "Is there something wrong Ensign?"

Panic was creeping to the edge awareness. "Ummm, no, sir. There's something I just need to find." She quickly looked around.

Sean started to step back into the room.

Just as panic was about to cross over to full consciousness she remembered. "Sorry, sir! I remember." She quickly went through her flight bag and found it. A letter her Mother gave her. "Ready, sir." She hastily left the room.

Sean eyed the young ensign. She was cute, maybe a bit airy. From her files he would be hard pressed to do better. He nodded and took Adriana to Starboard's Bow. His usual table was empty. He personally hoped it was not because Rank Doth Have Its Privileges, but knew exactly it was the case.

Cookie greeted the two, Cap'n, Ensign Newton."

Sean turned to Cookie, you know the Ensign?"

Cookie smiled, "I have a good memory Cap'n. The Commander lets me read the transfer list and bios so I know who's allergic to what foods. Luckily, we got good stock this time around. I don't have to do any scolding or mother henning." He laughed.

Sean thought maybe he should talk to Dawn about Cookie. Apparently there were things about the man he didn't know about.

"So, what would you like, sir and Ensign Miss?"

"Coffee for me, Cookie."

He nodded.

"Cranberry Juice?" She waited to be disappointed.

Cookie smiled wide. "Stocked up yesterday. You'll be pretty much the only one drinking it."

Adriana beamed.

Cookie stepped away.

"I read you Bios, Ensign. Very interesting. Your Mother drove you pretty hard academically."

Adriana nodded, "Yes, sir., she did. Most days I hated it. Don't get me wrong, but you know, as a kid I wanted to do kid things . . ."

Sean listened and became fascinated. Adriana really lived a human life or she was a pathological liar.

" . . . I did most of my college years . . . "

Sean interrupted, "Amazing . . ."

"Pardon sir?"

"College by ten and not just easy subjects."

Adriana blushed. She knew where this was going. Mother, education, the religion, but she was prepared. Mother made sure of that. The Captain asked the right questions and she hit the right marks every time.

A few minutes later Cookie came back with a tall frosted glass of Cranberry juice. He placed it in front of Adriana. Sean's coffee was on a small tray. A cut lemon, small containers of sugar and cream were next to the cup. Cookie placed it carefully in front of Sean. A nice wisp of steam rose from the cup. Then Sean noticed the letter. "Ensign, I have to ask. Have you ever heard of The Most High?"

She smiled slightly. Her Mother was right again. Adriana

nodded, "Yes, sir. The best known secret in all of GRID."

Sean laughed.

"I'm not a follower per se. My Mother was a local Goddess, but she had incredible influence over regional matters."

"I see." Sean's eyed the letter.

Adriana held it out for Sean to accept.

"And this Ensign?"

"This was passed down to family members from my Great-grandmother. The envelope has never been opened but it is addressed to you, sir."

Sean exclaimed "I knew it!"

Adriana was startled. "Excuse me, sir?"

Sean eyed the young girl. "This is from Adruqu?"

Adriana went wide-eyed. "You know of my Great-grandmother?"

"Know of her? I've met her!"

"Impossible, sir!" Adriana said, "She's been dead over a hundred years. She . . ."

"Not impossible, Ensign. Why are you here? Adruqu sent you, didn't she?" Sean's temperature rose. He was angry now. "What's her plan?"

Adriana thought things had horribly gone wrong. The Captain was angry and saying things that made no sense to her. She remained silent.

Sean's first thought was to tear the envelope to shreds. "Ensign," he said between clenched teeth, "why are you here?"

"S-sir?"

"Again, why are you here?"

Adriana's mind raced. Mother said nothing of this. She was wholly not prepared for an angry Captain. "T – t - to . . . to. . . serve, sir." Adriana was appalled. It sounded so pathetic. She cleared her throat. "To serve." She repeated.

Sean considered ordering her off the Johnson. She was part

of some Necronian scheme. What pissed him off more was the thought of Adruqu thinking she could manipulate the situation. Then Sean remembered the letter. He held the now crushed envelope in his hand. It wasn't heavy, just felt different. The feel of paper was strange to him. This particular piece felt smoother than what he remembered old paper felt like. He turned the envelope over and looked at the red wax seal. The imprint of a three quarter view of the Johnson was unmistakable. Sean broke the seal and pulled a letter out. The paper was parchment-like. The linen threads were tightly woven of which Sean was certain not of Earth product. The first line took him off guard.

Adriana watched as Sean read the letter. His expression changed from anger and disgust to disbelief to doubt to surprise to acceptance. He looked directly into her eyes and smiled.

"I think you should read this and I am sorry, Adriana. Seems you are just as much a pawn in this as I am."

She took the letter and read it.:

To my dearest Sean Blakemore,

Please don't be mad at our great grand-daughter Adriana. She is innocent and knows nothing that has transpired between us. My main purpose has been to help you in any way I can. You've touched my heart in ways I've forgotten existed, so in return I give you Adriana, our great grand-daughter. She, of course, may choose her life as she sees fit, but she is a part of you — our product of union.

Sean, my love, guide her, help her, she is her own person, but now she is your family. In the future days of your new destiny she will help you through great adversity and odds no other Human would be able to overcome. Accept her as your own.

With eternal and infinite love from your absent concomitant,

Adruqu

Adriana looked up. "Sir? Grandfather?"
"Of which you will never call me." Sean said sternly.
"How? When?"
"It's a long story, Ensign. Not many people are privy to it, but it looks like you'll be one more added."

Chapter 9

Collins and Loggar had been reviewing Sean's last set of tests. Toward the end of the test Sean had been able to control the nanobots with expert precision. He was able to direct legions of them to multiple energy sources simultaneously.

"Fascinating." Collins said. She was looking at a nanobot under an electronic microscope. "The nanobot's body structure is like that of a living creature. If I didn't know better I'd say these things were alive."

Loggar nodded. "Precisely. I hate to admit this, but we don't have the technology to create anything near as complex and capable."

"The Stupinans?" Collins answered.

"Exactly, and that is probably as far as we'll get in the next few decades. We can't even identify memory. How do they store data?"

Collins nodded.

"Damn! I so hate this. So close. Just so close and not fair." Loggar turned away from Collins and bit her bottom lip. 'It's not fair,' she thought, 'not fair at all. He wouldn't even know about magick if it weren't for me.'

Collins knew what was going through Loggar's mind. It was obvious she was upset and disappointed. She just wasn't sure if it was toward her not doing on-demand magick or Sean was conceivably the only Human in known space who could.

Loggar counted to ten. She was devastated. The only time she would ever be able to do magick would be any Necron world active with nanobots. She turned to face Collins. "I'm okay, really. This is just a bit hard to accept."

"Kathy, maybe the big picture is the wrong one."

Loggar frowned, "What do you mean?"

"Maybe we should focus on one or two things?"

"Like?"

"We can make nanobots, yes. But these nanobots can only repair or remove tissue. Maybe that is something we should concentrate on."

Loggar shook her head, "I'm not getting it."

"Healing, near instant healing!"

"Hmmm . . ."

"Or communications. Can you imagine doing circles with just thought? No words, just images, sounds, feelings, all transmitted and received using nanobots."

Loggar's mind started to race. She was starting to see a different picture.

"Not sure we'll ever be able to push fire bolts or levitate things, but we can produce a good show with other abilities."

Loggar looked around to make sure no one was looking as she leaned in close to Collins. She gave Collins a quick passionate kiss. "Karen, thank you."

Collins licked her lips and smiled. Loggar's lipstick was citrus flavored. "Goddess. You going to spend time alone with the Captain tonight or can I find my way into your room?"

"Lately, I've been wearing Sean out. I need to give the poor dear a break." She then smiled, "Maybe he could just watch?"

"I don't think watching would be on his mind after a few minutes. Dawn?"

Loggar felt a twinge between her legs. "Definitely. I can ask Sean to select something from his collection of entertainment. He is a very naughty young man." She giggled.

Collins heard about the Captain's horde but thought it a rumor. "It's been years since I've seen a good flick. Any good plots in his collection?"

"Lots. He is into storyline and plot. Most refreshing. See if the Commander is available, but from what I can tell, she probably has a bigger collection than Sean . . ."

Collins laughed and nodded.

". . . She just comes across that way."

Collins forgot about Dawn's collection. Extremely impressive. Some of it leaked out to the common crew. Her embarrassment was spared that none of her self POVs were included. Dawn suspected Kirkland was behind the distribution. She had a brief encounter with one of the Department heads, which Dawn assumed leaked the codes and location. After Dawn dropped the relationship and changed all her codes Vids stopped appearing on decks. A week later the Department head unceremoniously transferred off the Johnson onto a slow moving waste collection barge.

"Speaking of Sean," Loggar mused, "I wonder if he's available for a snack? Computer, locate Captain Blakemore."

"Captain Blakemore is in Starboard's Bow."

"Is Commander Dawn with him?"

"No, Captain Blakemore is with Ensign Newton, she is a transfer from the Mega Cruiser Barack. She is assigned to Engineering."

Loggar's heart skipped a beat. She thought, 'Probably nothing really. Just something innocent.'

Collins said, "Goddess, he's not like that."

Loggar's mind raced. "No, of course not. He has us now, doesn't he?" Self-doubt crept in. "We're all he needs."

Collins became amused. Loggar was jealous. It was alright for her to take on lovers, but if Sean himself decided to hunt then something was wrong.

"Maybe he's offering advice?"

Collins said nothing.

"I'll make my way there. If he's still there then good, if not then no big deal." And she walked off at a subdued quick pace.

Cookie had just delivered Sean's third cup of coffee when he nearly collided with Loggar. "Pardon, Goddess."

Loggar craned her neck over toward Sean's table.

Cookie said, "He's doing okay Ma'am. Would you like me to bring you something?"

"Glass of red wine," she said in the distance. She was already halfway across the room.

Sean laughed, "Seriously?" His manner was relaxed and the expression on his face showed he was thoroughly enjoying his company.

Loggar caught the expression and hurried up to Sean. Her features were dark and ugly. 'How dare he enjoy himself with another woman I hadn't selected.'

Sean spotted Loggar. His smile faded when he saw her expression.

"Sean, there you are!" Loggar said a little too loud. "I was hoping to find you here."

Sean stood up, "Kathy, I'd like . . ."

Loggar spun on Adriana, "And who do we have here . . . ?"

Adriana stood up, "Dr. Loggar, it's a pleasure to finally met you . . . is everything alright?"

Loggar stood stunned.

Sean leaned over and whispered in her ear, "It's not Adruqu."

Loggar slowly turned her head to Sean, "Not Adruqu?"

Adriana said, "That's right, Goddess. Adruqu is my Great grandmother."

"Seriously?!?"

Adriana nodded.

"And the kicker," Sean began, "guess who is Great

granddaddy?"

For some reason Loggar welcomed the news. Sean taking on another woman? Guilt hit hard. She felt guiltier still in thinking how very beautiful Adriana was with impure thoughts.

"Adriana, don't be offended but I'd like Dr. Collins to run some DNA tests?"

"Of course, Captain." Then Adriana felt dizzy. She quickly sat down. Her vision blurred and she started to sweat.

"Ensign, Adriana, are you okay." She heard Sean ask. At some point she nodded because he stopped asking but the room tilted, then she saw the ceiling. Everything was a collage of confusing images. She faded in and out of consciousness.

"Captain, what happened?" Collins asked.

Sean looked visibly upset. His eyes were moist, but he remained composed. "One second the Ensign was fine, the next she looked like half the blood in her head had drained to her feet."

Collins ran a scanner over Adriana's body and checked a reading on a nearby CRT. "Everything seems to be okay. Nothing to worry about. Looks like her blood pressure dropped rapidly. It's normal now."

Sean felt better. "Maybe it was something I said."

"And that was?"

"Doctor, a request that needs to be off-record."

Collins raised an eyebrow. "Intrigue? Do tell, sir."

Loggar stayed close to Sean. Her lips were tightly pressed together and she looked sad.

"A DNA test."

"Of whom?"

"The Ensign here."

"Against?"

Sean cleared his throat, "me."

Collins smiled, "I see."

Sean nodded.

"And, I'm to run the test myself?"

Sean nodded.

Collins snatched a strand of hair from Sean's head.

"Ouch! You could have warned me."

"And take out all the fun." She slipped the hair into a small opening on top her hand-held scanner. She walked over to a workstation and picked up a small tumbler scanner. Walking over to a sleeping Adriana she pressed one end to her right antecubital. A little led light on top of the tumbler turned from red to blue. Collins tapped out a command on the hand-held scanner. She then walked over to a CRT. A few seconds later she looked up. "Captain? How?"

Sean's expression went from stressed to acceptance. "The Necronians, Adruqu to be precise."

Collins checked again. "Her Grandfather . . . no, wait. Her Great-grandfather!? Extraordinary." Then she laughed. "And for a moment I thought our Captain had skeletons in his closet."

Sean said, "This changes things." A worried look on his face appeared. "I have immediate family?"

Loggar placed a hand on his shoulder, "Sean, this is wonderful. Haven't you always wanted family again?"

"Kathy, the pain. I lost too much during the war. I'm just now getting over it."

"But, Sean, the Necronians have command over Space and time. Adruqu saw something in your past and possibly your future to give you a granddaughter."

His expression turned ugly, "She has no right to interfere. Playing God. This is all a game to her. . . "

"How can you be sure?"

He looked at Loggar and frowned, "Are you kidding me? She's bored. Must be. And now I'm an object to be studied and fucked with? I'm not liking this one bit."

"Captain, if I may," Collins interrupted.

Loggar and Sean looked over.

"Maybe you're going about this the wrong way, sir."

"What do you mean?"

"I wondered why Adruqu gave you the ability to use magick off Necron proper. Think about it. Kathy, Herb, Milkens and the others may only do magick on one of nine Necron worlds, maybe others. But, you Captain, can do it anytime."

"I think it's to torture me. I swear if we hadn't worked out my nanobot feeding problem I'd have you find a way to turn these things off."

Collins nodded, "And there you are."

"Come again?"

"Captain, you have compassion. You have the power to pretty much destroy a great deal many things, yet you would gladly give it up if it harmed those around you. You can make certain things appear out of thin air. You can levitate things. I bet you can also heal certain types of injuries."

Sean reflected on that.

Collins continued, "I can see you're concerned still. Captain, if the Necronians can travel into the past they can travel into the future."

Sean said, "Adruqu passed a letter through Adriana's mother to give to me. The letter said Adriana would assist me in the future. The letter said Adriana was family, but her own person to decide her own life."

"Makes sense. Adruqu saw something in the future, went back in the past and started a family."

"The last time I saw her was over six months ago and we did not have sex . . ."

"Not in the normal sense. . . "

"Normal?"

Loggar said, "Clones Sean, they can clone anyone and transfer total life experiences to the clone."

Collins said, "For you Captain, maybe just your DNA." She walked over to a CRT and tapped out a few commands. Information flowed across the screen. "Something else to consider."

Sean moaned. "Yes?"

"You have a great granddaughter now."

Sean nodded at the obvious.

"Who has a mother . . ."

"Oh, dear Goddess . . ." Sean uttered.

***

Sean sat in the Command chair thinking. Dawn sat next to him. "Captain, you know there is a pool about you and Adriana?"

"Already?" He turned toward Kirkland.

Kirkland concentrated on his board and looked like important info was streaming over his CRT.

Sean turned back to Dawn. "Give me the cats."

"Lover, daughter, niece, lost friend's daughter, cousin, prey . . ."

"Prey?"

Dawn nodded, "Funny, I know, and victim."

Sean had a twinge of exasperation, "Victim? Some of the crew see me as a predator?"

"The rumors, sir. The rumors."

Sean cleared his throat. "Mr. Kirkland!"

Kirkland startled, "Yes, sir!"

"Niece."

"Pardon, sir?"

Sean glared, "Niece."

Kirkland smiled and tapped out several codes on his CRT.

Midshipman Stark won with closest time and pick.

"And, Mr. Kirkland, you may spread the word."

"Sir?"

"Hands off. Understood?"

Kirkland coughed and gave an audible swallow. "Understood, sir." He typed out a few commands on his CRT. "The word is spreading."

Sean smiled. Adriana would certainly hate him, at some point, for making her off limits, but that was the price to pay for being family – his family on his ship.

Chapter 10

Adriana sat up as Collins motioned a scanner across her forehead. "Doctor, I feel fine."

"Then answer me this, why faint?"

"The information the Captain gave me was a tad overwhelming. I just had a lot to take in. So, I fainted."

Collins nodded. "And, lack of consistent sleep and food for several days. When was the last time you had a glass of water?"

"I had been very nervous in transferring to the Johnson, meeting The Most High Goddess, and finally seeing the Captain."

"Who turns out to be your Great grandfather."

Adriana nodded, "That, too. It was the one thing I didn't see coming."

Collins nodded.

Adriana continued, "And when the Captain told me about my Great grandmother . . . well, it was just too much. I tried to be calm about it."

Loggar stepped forward, "In knowing your legacy is non-terrestrial? I'd faint too."

Adriana heard the words but somehow didn't believe in their sincerity. Her Mother often said 'Power given by position is different than position gained from power.' Loggar's power was as solid as the allegiances around her, her Great grandfather's power was tangible. She read the history books and tactical manuals. The Captain's battle notes were required reading.

"I'll release you, but I need you to eat a full meal. I'll call down to Cookie and tell him to expect you. Understand, Ensign?"

Adriana smiled, "Yes, ma'am. Understood."

***

Adriana took the lift to Starboard's Bow. As she walked in Cookie was there with a big smile on his face. "Well, Miss Ensign. The Doc tells me you like starving yourself."

Adriana retorted, "Not true! I've just been nervous. That's all. I can't eat when that happens."

"Are you nervous now?"

Adriana thought about it, "No."

Cookie replied, "Then good. Sit at the Cap'n's table."

Adriana, "Oh no, sir. I couldn't do that."

"Call me, Cookie, young miss. Everyone does."

"Cookie, that's the Captain's ta . . . "

"Which makes it yours, too."

"But, but . . ."

"Sit, now, or I first tan your hide, then I tell the Cap'n why I tanned your hide. He can agree or bring me up on charges."

Adriana stared at the table.

Cookie stood over her and looked down. He was a tall man with very broad shoulders. He looked more like Security than a Cook."

Adriana sat finally.

Cookie grinned and said, "I would ask what you want, but I know what you need. Relax, I have just the thing for you."

Adriana sat looking at the retreating Cookie. She became acutely aware everyone was staring at her. They knew something and that bothered her. Minutes later Cookie walked into the area with a tray. It had a large bowl of steaming hot chicken noodle soup on it. The vegetables came from Cookie's personal garden. Only the best for the Cap'n's niece he told himself as he prepared the dish with his two hands. He placed the bowl in front of Adriana.

"Eat." He said.

The soup's aroma was heavenly divine to Adriana. She picked up a spoon and scooped up soup. She blew on the liquid and sucked the spoon dry. She never had soup as delicious as this.

Cookie was looking at her when she finally placed a spoonful in her mouth. Her expressions was all he needed. His eyes suddenly moistened.

"Cookie," Adriana started, "My Goddess, this is good." Then she rapidly finished the bowl. "Another please, but in a smaller bowl? I don't want to waste any."

Cookie, pleased, collected the bowl and left humming the sea shanty "Sally."

***

Adriana entered her shared room with a tight belly. She walked over to her bed and collapsed. The entire day finally started to catch-up. She was spent. Adriana's other three room mates were no doubt elsewhere, which was fine by her. Her travel bag was tucked firmly under her bunk but she was too tired to retrieve her personal hygiene bag. She wanted some time alone to gather her thoughts. In less than four hours she went from a destiny of meeting the Captain to being his Great granddaughter. She wandered why her Mother never told her, then she understood why. All of this, on the surface impossible, but underneath the top soil the truth germinated. And it all made sense. She was here to help the Captain out. Having him family made it all the more imperative to be there, here for him. She started to drift into sleep when she realized she hadn't officially reported to Engineering. She forced herself up, pulled her travel bag from underneath the bed and retrieved her hygiene kit. After a quick wash at the small room sink she brushed her hair, checked her make-up and teeth and walked out of the room. The nearest lift was seconds away and she took it to Engineering.

***

Engineering was a busy place. Adriana had memorized Johnson's floor plans months ago. She knew the layout almost to the rivet. The Chief of Engineering's station was dead center of the room with branches leading to different parts of Johnson's massive engines and complex plumbing and electrical system. Adriana spotted Commander Landtrap and walked toward him. He looked up when she was near enough. He was holding a TAB. A wide smile appeared when he recognized the Ensign.

"Ensign Newton! Glad to have you aboard." He held out his hand.

Adriana shook his hand three times. "Thank you, sir. Any special assignment or duty station you want me on?"

"Are you familiar with the new engine upgrades?"

"I am, sir. They're a generation ahead of the Barack's, but I've studied the system in earnest."

"Good, I'm gonna need someone to help us through." He swiveled his CRT toward Adriana. "I'm having a hard time calibrating this section here. The book says I have to compensate . . ."

Adriana listened politely. She already figured out the problem. The Commander was still in old tech mode. The harmonics math was wildly more complex and didn't like being short-cutted. He was a victim of averaging the average of averages, thus pulling his numbers off by small percentage points, but enough to make someone scratch their eyes out.

" . . . I'm thinking it's the math but I'm an old dog and I think I'm trapped in shortcutting. I'll give you the rest of the day . . ."

Adriana reached over and tapped out some commands. The Commander's voice trailed off in silence as he realized she was working the problem. Adriana knew this one in her sleep. The Academy drilled the procedure in her head and the Chief Engineer on board the Barack made the same mistake. She finished in less than a minute.

"Holy starbursts . . ." Pulse stared at the results and the equations. He cycled through her math and after a moment laughed. His eyes moistened and tears started streaming down his cheek. "Smithy!" He yelled out. "Get Roberts, Gupta, and Ga Ka! Pronto!"

Adriana was startled. She hadn't expected this reaction.

Moments later Pulse's work area was surrounded by Engineers. Two of them laughed out loud, another danced an old Irish jig and said, "bet paid."

After a while everything and everyone settled down. Pulse's area was once again normal. "So, Ensign, what else are you a surprise about?"

"Pardon, sir?"

"Engine harmonics? So easily done? You're cutting edge and we like that. Oh, don't mind them, they get a little excited with an epiphany or two."

All Adriana could do was nod. It really was easy she thought. Really.

Pulse eyed her, "Ensign, how fast can you read?"

Adriana thought a moment. The last time she tested she went too fast and had a 1% error rating. "If I don't push it and want 0% error, then 285 words per second."

"Thought so. There are times I have to be at the Captain's staff meetings. Not that I don't like them, it's just that most of the time I have nothing to contribute. But being you're the FNG I think we need to have you earn some wings. The next meeting you'll represent Engineering . . ."

"But . . ." Adriana started to protest.

"Don't even worry. The Captain uses free area rule. Anyone may answer any question in any field. The thing is, I really only know engines, older engines at that and I need to focus and catch up."

Adriana nodded, "okay, sir."

Pulse smiled. Today, the Goddess sent him mana from heaven. He was going to exploit it any way he could.

Chapter 11

Herb's CRT streamed data at a fast clip. He was looking for an anomaly. The Necronians "handed" them exabytes of data pertaining to planet coordinates and developmental on influenced worlds. Luckily, the Johnson had at least several zettabytes of free space available for him to use. The amount of data was staggering. He and Milkens worked pretty much twenty hours a day farming through the data. So far they identified about three hundred worlds that should be post bronze age era. Twenty were within a month travel at long jump. Three worlds equal to GRID technology at eight months. And three whose technology surpassed GRID thousands of years ago.

Milkens handed Herb a TAB. This one was about twice his palm size. He liked it for the small size and high core processing power. The screen was bright and could be seen from almost any angle.

Herb rotated to portrait view and saw what Milk was referring too. There, a Gaian Continental Subdivision type planet less than ten days at long jumps. It matched up with data from the Johnson's optics. He thought Loggar would be pleased. "Milk, it's time for the meeting."

Milkens gathered up his charts and TABs and followed Herb out the now sliding door.

***

Everyone sat round the main conference table. Sean

walked in with Loggar and Adriana. All eyes turned to Adriana as she found an empty spot at the table

Dawn replied, "Herb, that's SI territory."

Herb frowned. "That would be a bad thing, but most of Necron worlds are in that direction."

Sean asked, "Would it be worth the risk?"

Loggar said, "I think so."

Sean knew Loggar was biased. Of course she would say yes.

Collins agreed, "I'd say yes. At least to check out what is there."

Sean said, "It would give us a reason to see if SI conquered this area or is merely licking electronic wounds for a comeback. Ensign Newton, what are your thoughts?"

He caught her off-guard. "Captain, I thought I would answer only Engineering questions?"

"Not on this deck. My Command Staff may bring anything up regardless of department."

Adriana felt the focus of eyes on her. She took a deep breathe, exhaled and began, "The light that would show us signs of SI activity won't reach us for another 50 years. The same goes for standard broadcast. Since there is a lack of any intelligent signal from the planet as of 50 years ago I would say per-industrial at best, if there is sentient life. We'll either come upon a planet stripped of natural resources or void of SI activity entirely. One or the other but not in between."

Sean smiled.

The others remained silent.

"Ensign, what was your other major at the academy?"

"I had a few Science disciplines, sir. Quantum, macro physics, astronomy and GRID Technology Medical and Anthropology were my minors."

Collins looked up.

Sean looked over to his Chief Engineer, "Sorry Pulse. The

Johnson has never had a need for a science officer until now. Ensign Newton just became the Johnson's first Chief of Science."

"I knew it was too good to be true, Captain, but can you spare her in between adventures?"

Sean laughed, "Of course. The Johnson launches in 18 hours. I'll want the Ensign glued to your hip during the first shakedown."

That made Pulse happy.

Sean turned to face Quock. "Lieutenant? Thoughts?"

Quock replied, "How far out will we hit now-space?"

Foster answered, "About one month optics when we first re-enter, then we'll move the Johnson in with four more short jumps that will get us within three days optics. From there we drive in under ion."

Collins lifted a hand, "Captain, this is the first time we'll encounter Alien life other than the Necronians. I was thinking we should stay at one month optics and send in a scout. I'm worried about possible panicking if the natives spot us too close too soon. I mean, My Goddess, we would be the aliens."

Sean turned to Loggar, "Kathy, this is your call."

Loggar considered every scenario, including scaring the natives. "I had talked to Mr. Foster earlier about our approach and the three day optics seemed reasonable. Particularly if the planet is per-industrial . . ."

Adriana said, "But Ma'am, we had telescopes about four hundred years before space flight."

Loggar paused, ". . . very true. Ensign," and chewed her bottom lip. "There really isn't a reason to rush into this, is there?"

Sean grabbed the opportunity and said, "No reason. We're here for the duration. I'm beginning to think we really should take this slow. We aren't a scout ship and we don't have scouters as crew." He paused, "Do we Dawn?"

Dawn tapped on a CRT. "Captain, we do as a matter of fact. We have several: Lieutenant Clark Lewis, Lieutenant Lockley, and Warrant Officer Tanner."

Sean thought for a few seconds, "What I'd like to do is form a committee to look at how we should best proceed. We can do it in route, given that our new engines will allow crew to walk about untrank, which is going to feel strange."

Loggar could only nod. If she protested she would be seen as reckless. She waited this long she could wait longer. "Sounds good," she said.

Sean nodded, "All, meet back here in two hours." He looked around. "Foster, calculate different scenarios and time frames. Pros and Cons. Ensign please stay behind. Same for you Kathy and Dawn. Everyone meeting adjourn until two clicks."

The room emptied out quickly.

Once all four were alone Sean began, "Dawn. Adriana is really my Great granddaughter."

Silence.

"Seriously."

Dawn laughed, "Captain, you're kidding?"

Sean slowly shook his head. "Wish I was kidding, but the Necronians have a very different type of humor."

Dawn nodded and looked at Adriana and smiled. "Nice to formally meet you Great granddaughter of Sean Blakemore."

Adriana blushed.

Dawn said, "Most High?"

Adriana replied, "Not practicing. My Mom was a local Goddess, but she never pushed me to become a follower. In fact, she did the opposite. I always wondered why."

Loggar said, "Adriana, it is nice to have you here."

"Thank you, Ma'am."

"No need to call me Ma'am. I'm civilian. Call me Kathy."

Adriana nodded. Calling The Most High Goddess by her

first name was going to feel weird she thought.

Sean said, "Ensign, your academic record is impressive. Commendations, Honors, envy of all. Nothing the likes the academy has produced in the last fifty years."

Adriana blushed.

Sean continued, "Why Engineering?"

"I like hands on, sir."

"Dawn," Sean began, "Start the paperwork on the Ensign's promotion. The Chief Science Officer can't be an Ensign."

Dawn nodded. "Junior, correct, sir?"

"Absolutely, can't make the jump too far."

Adriana was dumbfounded, "Thank you, sir."

Sean leaned forward, "Don't thank me yet, you may even hate me later, but since you are family I may push the envelope," and smiled devilishly. "You're pushing new territory on board. During our long jumps you'll have a chance to know crew and start a department."

"Sir?"

"Now that you're Chief Science Officer, you'll have to assemble a staff."

Adriana's shoulders dropped slightly. She just uttered, "Sir."

"See you in two hours and the personnel database is now open to your login. No one is off limits, understood, Lieutenant?"

Lieutenant? Surreal. Adriana squared her shoulders and looked Sean in the eyes. "Understood, sir."

Sean smiled as Adriana walked out. "Well, Dawn, what do you think?"

Dawn said, "Seems to be a tough kid. Maybe like her old, old, old man," and laughed.

"That has yet to be seen and I've had my fall from grace before, but she'll do right, I think. How do you think the crew will react?"

Dawn thought for a few seconds, "They'll be some grumblings, of course. I think the crew will accept her. She'll have to do the leg work to maintain, but being the Captain's 'niece' gives her an immediate master status of Command Officer."

Sean pondered, "You think some will treat her roughly?"

Dawn shrugged, "Maybe, but she has to be her own person. The First Officer on board the Barack said in her exit review she was very capable and formed friendship and alliances easily despite being brilliant."

"Merriwether, right?" Sean asked.

Dawn nodded.

"Then that does mean something. Merriwether is a bastard if I remember and praises no one."

Dawn added, "Cold-hearted Fuck is more like it, but yeah, if she got that much from him then she bedazzled them all."

Loggar said, "Sean, excuse me, but why Great granddaughter, you suppose?" The appearance of a Necronian descendant wasn't boding well for her. One just doesn't create a legacy just because. "I mean, wouldn't a daughter or granddaughter been better?"

Dawn answered, "Dilute the influence."

"The influence?" Sean questioned.

Loggar injected, "I understand. Sean, whatever physical traits you would have passed didn't make it to Adriana. She's removed from you far enough that she looks like her own person when standing next to you. She may have more Necronian genome than you would have given her. She also hadn't had the benefit of being raised by you."

"Heh! That might be a good thing. Not really sure if I'd be a good parent."

Dawn said, "Parenting has a way of changing people."

"The question I have," Sean started, "Does she have nanobots?"

Loggar answered, "None, though Karen did find an extra dense mass of muscle tissue near her heart."

Sean nodded and pursed his lips. "Well we have two hours, I need to walk."

Dawn stood up, "Then see you in two hours," she said as she walked out the sliding doors.

Loggar and Sean were alone.

"Sean, love." Loggar whispered into his ear. "Have anything pressing that needs to be done?"

He smiled and knew where this was going. "Not at the moment. You had something in mind?"

She reached down between his legs and started slowly rubbing up and down.

Sean immediately grew hard, "I see. Giving or receiving?"

She kissed him deeply, "Giving this time. I've worked you way too hard. Your turn to receive." She undid his pants and pulled him out. She knelt down in front of him and licked his entire length.

Sean moaned and made himself comfortable. He pulled the rest of himself out and enjoyed watching as Loggar rhythmically sucked up and down. She had a firm grip and stroked him in concert as she motioned up and down from tip to balls. After a few minutes she felt Sean was about ready and she only concentrated on his tip. Another moment later Sean erupted and she swallowed hungrily; making sure none of it stained her outfit or furniture. She cleaned him up and smiled.

Sean, breathing heavily, looked down. "Kathy, my Goddess." He leaned forward and kissed her passionately. He could taste what was left of him on her lips and that excited him. Standing up and collecting himself everything went back neatly into his pants. He lifted her up and maneuvered her into his seat. Now was her turn. As he lifted her skirt up he could see she was already wet. Slipping her panties aside he knelt before her and ran his tongue along her inner thighs. He took his time making him way to her center. Her hood was plump and swollen. He flicked his tongue rapidly, occasionally sucking up her juices, until her legs started to spasm. He sucked harder until she cried "enough," then he licked harder still and sucked until she forcibly moved his head away. He sat in the chair next to her and watched her legs twitch for minutes still.

Loggar was spent. She thought Sean always knew how to drive her crazy and this time was no exception. She leaned over and they both kissed each other.

After a minute Sean broke first, "Game for a snack?"

Loggar nodded, straightened her skirt and she made herself presentable.

Chapter 12

Adriana sat at her CRT. The Captain said no one was off limits, but he also said the Johnson never had a need for a Science Officer. She scanned through a list of names. Nothing. With 3000 on board there would have to be a hand full of personnel who majored in Science. She'd even settle for minor degrees. "Computer, new query. . . "

"Query is . . . ?"

"Sciences majors and minor. Sciences hobby. Data Mine library for books read dealing with sciences. Exclude department heads. Execute."

"120 results." The computer replied.

"Divide results into hard and soft sciences. Execute."

"34 results in hard sciences, 120 results in soft sciences."

"Divide hard science results into micro and macro lists. Execute."

"Five results in micro, seven in macro, 22 in both."

"Of the 22, how many are biology, physics, and astronomy?"

"Five found."

"Display their names, please."

Adriana smiled when she recognized one of the names. Maybe this won't be so hard after all she thought.

***

"Cookie?!?" Sean uttered, "You want Cookie as one of your staff?"

Adriana, Sean, and Dawn sat around the Ready Room table.

Adriana smiled, "Sir, you said 'no one is off limits' . . ."

"I did?"

Dawn said, "You did, sir."

Sean cleared his throat. "Cookie, huh? And he is qualified?"

"Thoroughly, sir. Cookie holds three science degrees and regularly reads a dozen science trade communiques. His emphasis is on biology."

"Does Cookie know yet?"

"No, sir. You are the first."

"Captain," Dawn started, "Biology makes sense. . ."

"I know, but . . . Cookie?"

Adriana remained silent. Her Mother taught her long ago the art of keeping one's mouth shut when wanting a favor. It only took the Captain a few moments to decide.

"Okay, Lieutenant. Cookie is yours."

Adriana smiled.

"If he wants it . . . there's another?"

"Lieutenant Ga Ka from Engineering."

Sean frowned, "Engineering, huh?"

Adriana nodded.

"Not sure if Pulse is gonna like that."

"Sir, Ga Ka and Cookie would still work in their main duties. There won't be a need to use them full time."

Sean's shoulders relaxed.

"We can make formal requests for several Science only recruits and transfers."

Sean's frown line faded and his face visibly unscrunched itself. "That works for me. You and Dawn work out the details. Anyone else?

"Yes, sir. Lieutenant Fielders from Bay Maintenance."

Dawn coughed.

Sean said, "Dawn, not a good choice?"

Dawn replied, "Not a bad choice, but she's got habit established. Might be a work-in-progress."

"Well, Lieutenant, a work-in-progress is not ideal. Might give you a lot of grief and I won't rescue you."

"I understand, sir. I'm not here for rescuing."

Sean replied, "Still want her?"

"I do."

"Anyone else?"

Adriana slowly shook her head. "Not at the moment, but I'm sure I will need more."

"Then I'll expect the transmits by EOD."

Adriana nodded. "Thank you, sir." She got up and walked out the Ready Room.

Dawn turned to Sean once the door slid shut and laughed.

Sean surprised, "Dawn! Laughing at my expense?"

Dawn smiled wide, "She has spunk. Gonna be an interesting mission."

"Bet I get grey hair by the end of this mission."

"Shall I have Kirkland start a pool?"

"Ah, no." but he smiled anyway.

***

Adriana walked back to her shared quarters. One of her Room mates, Karolina from Medical, was sitting at her desk viewing a story Vid. She looked up and said, "Hey, girl! Getting used to the place yet?"

Adriana nodded, "Yeah, lots to do that I can't even think on where to start."

"You've been to Starboard's Bow yet?"

"I have."

"Starboard's Bow is mainly for the Enlisted, but since Cookie became a Warrant there are no longer any restrictions."

Adriana nodded.

Karolina stared into Adriana's eyes for a brief moment, then looked away. "Is it true?"

Adriana asked, "Is what true?"

"You the Captain's niece?"

Adriana paused. Great granddaughter would sound kind of weird. "I . . . am his niece."

She snorted, "Must be nice."

I shrugged, "Wouldn't know. Never met him until today." She stretch out on her bunk bed. She supposed this was going to be the norm. Folks asking if it were true. Then saying how nice it must be. What are they going to say when word gets out that she's a department head and a new minted lieutenant, she thought. Adriana could see a lack of invitations to inner circles now. Or. She smiled. Maybe not.

Karolina said, "You kidding me?"

"Wish I were. I didn't know he was my Gre . . . Uncle until today either. Took a DNA scan to confirm."

"No, shit? I bet he still kicks your ass if you mess up." She laughed.

"He's a hard-ass?"

"Commander Dawn is, but I'm sure she doesn't bite unless the Old man gives the okay."

Adriana thought about that.

"You into outside activity? Like circles?"

That was the same question she got while on the Barack. Are you into circles? "Not particularly so. Nothing wrong with them. I'll wait out a bit and see."

Karolina smiled. "There's a lot of drama on board. I joined a few. Most are not worth it. Quarter D Deck Goddess is a super bitch, remember that."

"Hadn't thought about it. A Local Goddess being a bitch. My Mom was the Local in our colony with less than a quarter the Most High, but everyone in town was civil to us."

Karolina laughed, "Really? I thought it the norm. The one's to form circles. You know the Doc is the Ship's Goddess?"

Adriana sat straight up. "I would not have guessed. She seemed okay with me."

"Probably the only Goddess who isn't a bitch. Word is she didn't even know she was the Goddess until the Commander pointed it out. Probably why she's not a bitch. I think the whole power thing corrupts."

"What about Dr. Loggar? The Most High?"

"Power corrupts absolutely." Karolina said with a laugh.

Adriana faked hers. "Seriously, she is?"

"Girl, she is the worst. Captain's starting to unwrap himself from her . . . "

Adriana said, "And?"

Karolina said, "Maybe I spoke too much. He is your Uncle."

"Of which I just found out, so if you're thinking I'm gonna gossip don't worry. I learned on the Barack when to talk."

Karolina hesitated.

Adriana got up, took a chair from her desk and sat next to Karolina. "Really, I just met the man today. I'm just trying to get into the scuttle before I become center."

Karolina smiled, "Too late for that, Adri . . . " She lifted an eyebrow. "Mind if I call you that?"

"Adri?" Adrianna shook her head. She got a nickname. She smiled. "May I call you Kar?"

Karolina gave Adriana a good look from foot to head to eyes. She liked this one. And only within 30 minutes, too. Gotta be her personal best. "Okay, Adri."

Adriana smiled and thought battle one won. Karolina seemed talkative and personable. She could do worse in finding a good crewmate. Time would tell, of course, but for the moment, Kar was her new BFF. "I met the Most High. She seemed okay. Maybe a bit wound tight, but today could have been a bad day."

"She's a bitch every day. She's the Most High but not the Best High. Collins would be better, but she's also hovering above the atmosphere at L2. If you hang around Loggar long enough you'll learn she's a Snap turtle, not a song bird."

Adriana nodded. "I'll remember that. What about the Commander?"

"Dawn? A bottom abuser, but fair. Do right, she's sweet like candy. Piss her off and you're tasting vinegar for days."

Adriana giggled. She liked this one. "Kar, I have to tell you something and please don't think it's because I'm the Captain's . . . niece."

"Okay. I can't promise but I can try."

Adriana smiled. So far she's a keeper, "You know our new mission, right?"

"Yeah, too seek out new life and such. Alien hunting. Not if I'll see any upfront, but it'll be a change to drifting."

Adriana took a deep breathe, "I'm the new department head of science."

Karolina frowned, thought a moment, then laughed. "Shit, we finally got a Science department."

Adriana nodded. "Science was a major. And since I'm the only one on board with the letters the Captain put me in the position."

"Scared?"

"Not really, but, you know. It's different. Hadn't expected the leap for a while."

"You pick staff yet?"

"Some, there's still slots to fill. Captain gave me a blank roster and said no limits."

Karolina leaned further toward Adriana. Her expression

changed to serious. "Really? You can pick anyone?"

Adriana nodded.

Karolina's face played a multitude of emotions. "What will it take to get on that roster?"

Adriana said, "Any of the sciences. Mostly multiple disciplines. You interested?"

"Goddess, yeah. Medical is okay, but I got three more years until re-enlistment. I was getting kind of bored and had been thinking a civilian tour on a research vessel an option. The Johnson's a great ship, but we either fight or drift. There's not enough fighting and I'm tired of drifting."

Adriana nodded. She could sympathize. She remembered Karolina's bio. It read well, but her focus was strictly medical. "Would you be willing to gain other skills?"

"Hello, girlfriend. You tell me what it'll take and I'm there."

Adriana liked that. And she would need an immediate ally.

"Who's on the list? I pretty much know everyone on board."

"Ga Ka from Engineering . . ."

"You got him?"

"As soon as I put in the transmits."

"I like him. He came in last week with a surface burn. I was gonna ask him out but got cold feet."

Adriana laughed, "You don't seem like the shy type to me."

"I can be! It's the eyes that get me."

"If Cookie wants in . . . "

"Wait, Cookie? And the Captain is going to approve that? The Captain had Engineer construct a special room for Cookie as an incentive to take the Warrant promotion. Nobody bothers Cookie."

"The Captain said he's science if he agrees. Besides he'll be temporary and part time until I fill the ranks in with permanents."

"But Cookie? He's, well, only, into . . ."

"Three science majors and reads trade transmits regularly. His IQ is 175. That more than qualifies him."

Karolina blinked rapidly. "175? You serious about this department?"

Adriana nodded.

"Ummm, what other science would I have to learn?"

"Geology would be nice. You have any interest in sciences other than medical? Specializations not listed in your bio?"

Karolina realized she was being interviewed for a position she wasn't sure she'd qualified for. If she hadn't been roommates with Adriana she'd never known about the new positions. She was certain Adriana had given her a pass. "Xenobiology!"

Both women laughed.

Adriana replied with a smile, "Since we are Alien hunting that qualifies you."

Karolina exhaled and relaxed, "Who else?"

"Lieutenant Fielders from Bay Maintenance."

Karolina exclaimed, "Shit! That's Deck D's Bitch."

"The deck goddess you mentioned?"

Karolina nodded, "Oh, Goddess. She's an arrogant cunt bitch from here to the fringes."

"That bad?"

"If you ever wanted to be tested as a department head she'll be the one to do it. She runs Bay Maintenance like a personal circle and not just for consultation."

"The Captain told me he won't be rescuing me. What I do is what I do."

Karolina shrugged, "Adri, maybe you will be the one, but she'll make you earn it for sure."

Words to heed Adriana thought. Words to heed.

Chapter 13

Sean tapped out a command on his CRT. "Pulse, are you ready?"

Pulse replied, "The Johnson is ready, sir."

"How's our new Lieutenant working out?"

"Captain, we're here aren't we, is all I have to say."

Sean laughed – Lt. Commander Fortshure won a month's pay.

"Very good." He tapped out. "Mr. Kirkland, make announcement please."

Kirkland entered the Shipwide broadcast mode, "Attention all hands, attention. Prepare for Long jump. Prepare for Long jump."

Sean said, "Mr. Foster?"

"Yes, sir."

"Move us out of dock please."

Foster slid a finger along the acceleration strip.

The Johnson slowly moved from the docking station. At twenty klicks the Johnson stopped.

"Johnson is ready, sir."

Sean nodded, "Very good." He tapped out Shipwide broadcast from his CRT. "Attention crew. This is the Captain. Thirty seconds to Long jump. Thirty seconds to Long jump. Two bell rings to ten second countdown." He tapped Shipwide broadcast off. "Mr. Foster, start countdown."

The Johnson moved forward.

Foster entered the Long jump code. "Down to twenty seconds, sir."

Sean turned to Dawn, "We've gonna have to come up with something new."

Two bells rang.

Dawn said, "Should be something easy to remember. . . "

And, the Johnson jumped.

Sean waited and felt . . . nothing special. All the AVs said most likely nothing special would happen. He looked around Top Deck and crew did the same as he was doing. "How are you feeling Dawn?"

"A slight headache, but other than that good. Very good. You, sir?"

"Disappointed."

"Sir?"

"I take that back. All this time, the Johnson could have had the upgrades, but no, we had to keep the older engines, Tranking, all because of some bullshit politics. I'm not disappointed, I'm pissed."

Dawn nodded.

Foster said, "Captain, Long jump ending in 30 seconds."

Sean tapped out Shipwide broadcast on his CRT, "All hands, all hands. Long jump ending in less than 30 seconds. Two bells to ten second countdown."

Two bells sounded.

And.

Nothing. Sean was greatly disappointed again.

"Well, that was very disappointing. I don't feel any different."

"Same here Captain, though that headache got a little worse. I'm sure taking a PAREL will resolve it."

"If that's the worst we get then I'll declare this test a success." Sean said as he tapped out a few commands on his CRT. "Engineering, report, please."

Pulse answered, "Captain, have we started the test yet?"

Sean paused, "Pulse?"

"Captain, the Johnson's engines registered practically nothing. It's amazing. Not sure how above redline we can push the engines but it'll be something when we do."

"Thanks, Pulse, I'll see you in two hours. Debriefing room five."

"Very good, sir. Engineering out."

Sean tapped out Medical on the CRT, "Doctor, report please."

Collin's voice came through the speakers, "Captain, all is well. There are a few reports of headaches and some nausea. I should have some numbers by briefing time."

"Thanks, Doc. Top Deck out." Then, "Mr. Foster?"

"Sir," Foster began, "Still calibrating NAV to the new engines. For some reason the specs are off . . ."

"Off?"

"Yes, sir. The Manual says there should be a 10 point variation from the old engines to the new at point six-zero power. I read an 80 point difference. COMP is still computing."

"Why the difference?"

Foster shrugged, "The Engines, sir. Mr. Landtrap peaked the efficiency."

"Okay, briefing in two hours. Mr. Kirkland?"

"Yes, sir?"

"Broadcast an all stand down. Department Heads to Briefing room 5 at afternoon watch four bells."

"Briefing at afternoon watch, four bells, all stand down,

sir. Will do."

Sean stood up. "Dawn, I'll be in Starboard's Bow. You have the Conn."

Dawn nodded, "I have the Conn." And she watched as Sean stepped into a lift.

***

There was a bowl of Skilly waiting for Sean.

Cookie sat opposite and waved him over. "Captain!"

Sean walked over and sat. The Skilly smelled delicious. There was a tin cup of Rum to one side. Sean lifted the cup to his nose and inhaled. "Cookie? The good stuff?"

Cookie beamed. "Yes, Capt'n. Kind of a tradition."

Sean took a sip of the Rum. The sweet liquid bit at his lips before sliding down over his tongue and down his throat. Sean knew Grog when he tasted it and this was it. "Damn, Cookie! It's been awhile since I had some."

"Captain, Miss Newton stopped by earlier."

Sean nodded. He took a spoonful of Skilly. Magic.

"She says I'd only be on the Science team temporarily . . .
"

"Now, don't worry, Cookie. We'll build the department up with new recruits next inbound and . . . "

"But Cap'n, I was hoping it would be permanent."

Magic gone.

"I was hoping this could be a permanent assignment, sir."

"Serious?"

Cookie nodded.

Sean lost his appetite and drained the cup dry. His stomach bucked.

Cookie noted the look on Sean's face. "Captain, the Skilly was done by Lieutenant Longhorn."

Sean looked down, "Really?"

"I've been coaching the Lieutenant for a while. Both messes are on auto-pilot, now. Haven't you noticed I've been outside the kitchen more often?"

Sean had to think about that. Sure he noticed, maybe. "How long Cookie?"

Cookie laughed, "A while. This group is the best and finest I've had the pleasure to guide. The Lieutenant is ready. She has been for months and if the Capt'n will let me I'd like to step behind the burners and cook up a meal or two on down nights to keep in skill."

Sean stared at the bowl of Skilly. He slowly lifted the spoon and scooped up a piece of lobster meat. He took a bite. The magic was still there. He took another bite and before long the bowl was empty. He wiped his lips with a napkin and stared Cookie in the eyes.

The big man smiled and waited patiently.

"Okay, Cookie. Once Lieutenant Newton finishes the transmits I'll make the transfer permanent . . . are you sure about this?"

Cookie laughed again, "I am. Sir. The Johnson is a great war craft and now we'll have an even better explorer craft. I'd like to be on the front line on this one."

Sean nodded. "Thanks, Cookie . . . Warrant Officer."

Cookie smiled, "Sir, Cookie will always do."

Sean nodded, stood up. "Very well, then, Cookie. Briefing room 5, afternoon watch four bells."

Chapter 14

". . . Okay folks. Pulse gives the Johnson the green light. The transmits from GRID Command make the Johnson officially an explorer vessel. Lieutenant Newton is the new Chief of Science, with Warrant Officer Holloway on permanent assignment to Sciences. We got our first destination that'll take us about a week to reach using long jumps. Dr. Loggar is the lead Scientist and Mission's Chief. Milkens and Herb her staff, will work with Engineering and Sciences. We've replaced half our fighter wings with new shuttle groups. Commander Molino is in charge of Planet Fall and in System Flights. Lieutenant Quock is Chief of Security, ship and Planet Fall. Doctor Collins is Chief Medical Officer and Surgeon. Lieutenant Longhorn is in charge of Food Services and Planet Fall Supplies. Senior Chief Junker is in charge of Ship Maintenance and Sanitation. Senior Chief Goldman is in charge of Bay Maintenance and Control. Any questions?"

No one voiced any.

"Doctor, I'll let you start."

Collins began, "More than half the crew suffered mild headaches. A third suffered nausea with half that group vomiting after the jump. We only had 100 crew effected enough that they'll still have to Trank, but at lower doses to allow them some ability to work and move about ship. Everyone else suffered little or no effects worth mentioning. I've put in place new procedures for future jumps. I've sent the procedures to all department heads."

Sean nodded, "Thanks, Doc." He turned to Molino. "Commander?"

Molino cleared his throat, "Sir. We have a total of ten new Mark Delta Shuttles. Primary pilots have been assigned and simulation training started the moment we got word. I have three qualified pilots now, excluding me. The rest should be qualified within the week. We're ready now."

Sean smiled, "Quock?"

Lieutenant Quock spoke, "Security is ready. We finished a new series of planet fall combat defense and offense sessions. Half of security has been recertified in multi-environment survival tactics and strategies. GRID Command delivered the new MK rifles and Armor suits. That should cover most everything the infinite has to toss our way."

Sean nodded, "Very good." He turned to Lieutenant Longhorn, "Lieutenant? Food Services?"

"We're in good shape, sir. We took on extra supplies and we expanded hydroponics by a quarter deck. We're working out the details to supply each crew quarter with Ponic Pods for Berries and small vegetables . . ."

Sean perked up, "Really?"

Longhorn nodded, "Yes, sir. It'll help stretch out ship supplies. It'll also add to crew moral."

Sean smiled. "Senior Chief Junker?"

Junker cleared his throat. He was from the Faulkner colonies and carried their famous Gothic accent. "Sir, the Johnson is in good condition. All air and water filters replaced. We replaced all fittings over five years old with Level 3 ones. All deck bathrooms now have retrofitted seals in the toilets and shower heads. We squeezed out three percent more in recycling while maintaining water pressure and flush strength. Autosweep bots have been upgraded to the newest model and all lighting elements have been replaced."

Sean nodded, "Excellent, Junker. Excellent. Senior Chief

Goldman?"

Goldman pushed his wired glasses up on his nose. "Bay Maintenance is top notch. Repulsion field emitters upgraded as all armatrons replaced. We retrofitted mounts and grips to accommodate our new shuttles. The replaced fighters have been dismantled and stored as salvage. And, Lieutenant Fielders received her transfer notice." He looked Adriana in eyes and smiled. "Lieutenant Newton will be getting a gifted crewmate, she's also getting a crewmate with habits."

Sean nodded, "Okay, Lieutenant Newton, the floor is yours."

"Thank you, sir." She took a deep breath. "Commander Landtraps group converted part of K Deck as the Science Deck. We're setup to accommodate a compliment of thirty personnel. Computers and labs are set. We're tied into NAV and Astrogation. One new addition to Science is from Medical and Doctor Collins and myself worked out some process and procedures for cross referencing data. I haven't had a formal meeting with staff but will after this meeting. Engineering has also established a permanent Top Deck station near Command. We'll spend the week in transient tweaking and calibrating new sensors and monitors. I've already completed a schedule on training with new equipment, sir."

Sean eyed his new Lieutenant. "Very good, Lieutenant. Okay, Pulse."

Pulse leaned back in his chair. "The Johnson's new engine upgrades are beyond great. They are exceptional. Lieutenant Newton schooled staff," He winked and smiled at Adriana, "on new harmonic gravitational variations. Not only did we squeeze out twenty-three percent more power we used less energy in the process. As a comparison, the old engines would have redlined passed one-seven-five just to achieve what the new engines did at green line four-two point seven-five."

Sean did a quick mental calculation. "Astounding!"

"And that is not all. We left two of Johnson's original engines in place. The computer is running some simulations, but we might be able to push GRID propulsion tech further."

Sean raised an eyebrow.

Pulse nodded. "Thought you might like that one, sir. It'll be another eight hours before the simulation is complete."

Sean said, "Kathy? You get last say."

"Thank you, Sean." Loggar tapped out a command on the table CRT and the lights dimmed. "As you know, the Johnson's new mission is to find Alien life. We know it's out there. . ."

The main vid displayed a starfield with a dozen stars circled.

" . . . The existence of the Necronians proves it. And with Data collected from the Necronians we know there are hundreds of humanoid establishments. How many are at our level or beyond our technology we don't know. Might be many, might be none. Out of all the hundreds of coordinates my team has narrowed our options to a dozen we can reach in a month's time by long jumps . . . "

A flight path dotted across the map. An animated Johnson moved across it.

"Sean and I decided the Johnson's first mission is to visit all twelve planets, survey the area for life, possibly leave a team with supplies, if we find life. The teams will determine if contact is warranted. It's been almost a hundred years since Humanity has done any real exploring for life. We're the first wave and we're starting from scratch. With consultation from Lieutenant Quock and Doctor Collins we decided the team would consist of a five person Security team, one Scout, three medical personnel, and one Science staff. Since we're building science from scratch the medical personnel team will run through a checklist of items from Lieutenant Newton. The team lead will be from Security until it has been determined immediate danger is not imminent. Then, the Lead Medical Office will be in-charge. On teams with Science personnel, science will be team lead. Security will, of course, take charge in an emergency. We'll leave it up to Lieutenant Newton on which planets she'll send personnel." Loggar tapped out a command and the lights came back on.

Sean looked around, "Any questions, people?"

None.

Then he said, "May we have strong winds at our backs and smooth sailing before us. The horizon is far but the stars are bright. We have only a straight line to follow and destination is within reach. May the Johnson see results and reward us for our efforts and will of heart. Eight bells morning watch we begin. Meeting adjourned."

Chapter 15

Cookie placed a stack of raisin oatmeal cookies at the center of the briefing table. He, Ga Ka, Karolina and Adriana were waiting for Fielders. Adriana set the meeting for six bells afternoon watch. It was now seven bells afternoon watch.

Karolina signed, "Adri, the scuttle is Fielders was spitting nails when she got the transmit." She reached across the table, grabbed a cookie, took a bit and said, "Damn, Cookie. How come you never made these for crew?"

Cookie smiled. He had taken a bite of his own cookie. "Been waiting the entire war to break out this recipe. When the war ended I waited for a chance to grab berth with a science vessel. That never happened. GRID stopped running explorers by then and decommissioned all the science fleets."

Karolina said, "What about civilian?"

He nodded, "And compete with young, brighter minds."

Adriana blushed.

"Glad I waited though . . ."

Adriana sat and listened to Cookie and Karolina talk. She could hear the hurt and relief in Cookie's voice. He waited. For years. She reached over and took a cookie. The texture was unreal. She had never touched an oatmeal cookie before. And the raisins, plump, dotted the surface like embedded meteorites. She took a bit and tasted . . . ecstasy.

Then Fielders walked into the conference room.

Adriana had made up her mind minutes ago. Her Mother prepped her for moments like this. She said, 'Never give a selfish person a chance to be selfish a second time.'

Adriana and Fielders locked gaze.

"Lieutenant, you're late."

Fielders walked up to the table. She hadn't known Cookie to be a science type. She was thinking how easy it'll be to run this new department. In one week's time she'd be running this operation like her personal circle.

Adriana sized Fielders up. Selfish.

Fielders was about to sit when Adriana cleared her throat.

"No need to sit, Lieutenant."

"Pardon, me?" Fielders answered.

"Late and you can't hear. I will repeat myself." And she slowly said, "No. Need. To. Sit."

"What?!?" Fielders frowned. She hadn't anticipated a challenge. She heard that Adriana was the Captain's niece and that he handed her the command to the new science division. Scuttle was nasty, but the Captain had too much credit for it to turn bitter. There were more protectors than protractors and the scuttle moved on. As a new officer she figured Adriana would make the mistake of a noob. "I'm sorry, I'm late. I won't . . ."

"Do it again? Not with me you won't." And Adriana finished her cookie and took another one.

Everyone stared at the smaller mound of cookies. The room was thick with tension.

"Look, I really am sorry, ma'am. I just . . ."

" . . . does not matter, Lieutenant." Adriana rapidly tapped out a transmit to personnel. "I'm rescinding your orders. You may go back to Bay Maintenance."

"But . . . "

Adriana stood up and summoned all her will to stare Fielders in the eye. Fielders, to her credit, stared back. Adriana leaned forward and lowered her head slightly. She was determined to win this battle. "Lieutenant, you're dismissed."

Fielders dropped her gaze. Battle lost. This Lieutenant just handed her a spanking and wasn't going to give her an inch of movement. She did what she could and collected what dignity she had left.

As the door slid closed on a receding Fielders did Adriana allow herself to relax and sit.

Cookie pushed the tray of cookies toward Adriana, who took another cookie.

"Okay, everyone," Adriana began, "Let's get started."

The door slid tight behind a furious Fielders. She told herself she only left because of Cookie. Then reality stepped in. She was rejected. "Fuck!" Fielders spat. "Fuck!" She said again as she stomped her way back to her quarters. Dismissed by that bitch. Captain's niece or not she was going to pay. She had all of Bay Maintenance at her disposal, where accidents can happen at any time to anyone. Fielders smiled as she had some solace in her revengeful thoughts. Adriana crossed the line and that was unacceptable.

Karolina said, "Adri, shit! You just kicked her ass with a look! Priceless!" Her laughter was infectious.

Ga Ka nodded, "She had it coming. I'm glad you released her. I was worried she'd damage another department." He let out a nervous laugh.

Adriana nodded, "She was very selfish. Not just to me, but to you guys as well. I should have listened to everyone who warned me about her, but I just didn't know."

Cookie said, "Lieutenant, you gave her the most important test of all and she failed. Her arrogance did her in. Now, will she learn from this? Probably not. Should you worry? Maybe a little bit . . ."

Adriana scowled, "Worry?"

Cookie answered, "Yes. All organisms potentially carry cancerous cells. The Johnson is no exception. Lieutenant

Fielders is cancer. Right now it's contained in her circle, but like cancer she may not be thinking rationally. If, for whatever reason, you have to go to Bay area, bring one of us."

"Cookie! What are you saying?"

"Bay Area is a dangerous place. Shuttles and vehicles moving about. Accidents are not common but they do happen."

Adriana nodded. She won the first battle. Could she win more and survive the war? "Thanks, Cookie."

Fielders stormed through the door. "Fuck!"

Stane was relaxing on his bunk. He sat up with a start. "Goddess!"

"That bitch is gonna pay, and pay, and pay!"

Stane sighed. This wasn't going to end well he thought. "Goddess, what can I get you?"

"Get me? Get me?!?"

Stane swallowed. It had been a long time Gibrealla was this mad.

"Get me?!? Get me the box."

Stane swallowed again, hard. He walked over to her desk and keyed in the passcode on one bottom drawer. It popped opened. A black box sat in the middle. Stane reached down and lifted it up. He walked over to Gibrealla, handed it to her and knelt down.

Fielders took the lid off and pulled out a large black strap-on dildo. She looked down at his submissive face and said, "Who am I?", as she effortlessly slid into the harness. She turned on the tiny vibrator motor that rested on the end touching her. Even through layers of clothing the little engine would do its magic.

Stane faced the large dildo.

Fielders grabbed the back of his hair, but he said nothing. She liked it when he resisted a little. "Who am I, bitch?!?"

Stane didn't say a word. He could feel himself getting hard. He liked this as much as she did. They both knew it and it made for better sex.

Fielders gave him a back hand across his jaw. "Bitch, say it! Say it!"

The inside of his mouth stung from the blow. She really was mad and might possibly hurt him. She struck again and yelled. He had to time it just right before she went over the edge.

Fielders lifted him up and shoved him onto his bunk. She snatched his uniform neck latch off and forced his top down. "Who am I?!?"

Stane said nothing but took another slap to the face. When Fielders yanked his uniform down to his knees his hard-on was rock solid and he knew his was close.

Fielders was about to punch Stane when he softly said, "Goddess." She relaxed her hand and said, "I didn't hear you."

Stane answered, "Goddess. You are my Goddess. There is no one more beautiful." She gave him another slap and he moaned. She grabbed his jaw hard and kissed him. His lip was cut from a tooth.

Fielders straightened up and stared down, "Eat it." She demanded.

Stane pressed his lips tight.

"Eat it you god damn fucking twink lady boy!"

He refused. She would have to do better.

She pulled hard the back of his head by the hair and gave him two quick slaps to the face. "So fickin, to me, I will beat you senseless. Eat it!"

He briefly opened his mouth then shut it again.

Fielders rapidly slapped him twice again. "Eat it or I swear I'll force you to eat this meat!"

He opened his mouth slightly.

"Eat it Lady boy! Eat it!"

He pressed his lips to the dildo's tip. Testing its feel.

Fielders yelled, "Eat it!" and she shoved the dildo passed his lips, nearly gagging him.

Stane sucked hungrily.

"That's right ," She said, "Suck this bitch and get it wet."

Stane licked the length of the shaft and deep throated the dildo.

Fielders grabbed the back of Stane's head with both hands and rapidly pumped hard. She imaged she was gagging Adriana. "What's my name, bitch?"

Stane tried to slow Fielders down.

"What's my name, you little bitch?!?"

Stane tried to talk but couldn't. He gagged and coughed up mucus.

Fielders relaxed her grip and pulled the dildo away. "Slut bitch, what's my name?"

Stane coughed. He took a deep breath and coughed up mucus again.

"What's my name?!?" Fielders screamed.

Stane whispered, "Goddess."

"What?"

"Goddess," he said louder.

"What?!?"

"Goddess! You are Goddess!"

Fielders smiled. The tiny dildo motor hummed nicely and she was building to a good climax. She rolled Stane over. "Spread those cheeks, bitch."

On his knees, with his face on the bed, he grabbed his cheeks and spread. He could feel the dildo's tip. He relaxed and it slipped in effortlessly.

Fielders pumped slowly at first. The motor hummed bringing her to the edge. She grabbed Stane's hip and rapidly pumped as the little motor did its job and took her over the cliff.

Stane grabbed himself and furiously stroked. When Fielders screamed from her orgasm he squeezed himself tightly as his hand pumped harder and within seconds jismed on his bedding.

Both collapsed exhausted.

Fielders pushed herself up. She slipped out of the dildo and staggered over to her bed. She started to drift off to a blissful sleep when she said, "Tomorrow I'll be bottom."

Stane muffled, "Bottom you. Me top. Fuck yeah Goddess."

Both fell promptly asleep.

Chapter 16

"All hands, all hands, this is the Captain speaking. Prepare for long jumps. Repeat, prepare for long jumps. Two bell ring to ten second count down." Sean cut Ship broadcast off. He turned to Dawn, "Not sure about you, but I wonder if we should be making this 'prepare into' and 'prepare out of' long jumps so dramatic."

Dawn laughed, "I was wondering the same thing. I think we should give it a few more times. Maybe just announce two bells ring to ten second count down."

Sean nodded, "I like that."

The bell sounded two times.

"You think of anything yet?"

Dawn shook her head, "Not yet."

And . . .

. . . nothing again.

Sean got up, "You have the conn Dawn, I'm going to chat with Collins."

Dawn said, "I have the conn, sir."

Sean stepped into the lift. "Med Deck."

The lift started and hummed to its destination.

Sean stepped out and headed to Medical Complex.

Collins was at her desk when Sean stepped in. He was deep in thought and absentmindedly stepped over a scrub bot.

"Captain, "She said, "How can I help you?"

"We need to talk in private."

Collins nodded, "Walk with me, Captain."

Sean followed Collins to one of the VIP examine rooms.

Once in the room Collins gestured for Sean to have a seat on the examine table.

Sean sat and stared at the floor.

"Captain . . . Sean, I can see something is on your mind."

"Why am I feeling so . . . so . . . off?"

"Pardon?"

"I'm actually missing Trank."

Collins nodded. Sean wasn't the first person to say that.

"We've been Tranking and STIMing for years. So long that it seemed normal. Now we got nothin'. Is there something wrong with me?"

"Nothing wrong with you, sir. A fifth of the ship has been saying the same thing."

Sean was shocked, "That many?"

Collins answer, "That few. Modest compared to what the other ships had to go through during their conversion. There's one report that says one ship had to replace the entire complement due to Trank and STIM addiction. Trank supplies dwindled to nothing in days and multiple fights broke out often."

"Goddess, we can't have that!"

"I'm putting together a program and vid to address that issue. I was going to talk to you later about it."

"Which one?"

"Sir?"

"Which ship had the addiction problem?"

She smiled, "The Webster."

"Really?"

"She was the one command staff that didn't get addicted." Collins walked over to a cabin. She tapped in a command and the doors unlocked. She then pulled out a bottle.

Sean watched and was hoping for a Trank spray but instead he saw Collins pull out a bottle of pills.

"Here, take one now and one every four hours. Take one

just after we drop back into Now-space."

Sean did so and started to feel better. "What is this stuff?"

"A fix. You'll need to do this for a while. At some point it'll make you jittery. That's when treatment is done."

Sean nodded, "Works for me. Thanks, Doc." And he caught her eye. She was radiate and he suddenly had the urge to kiss her. Sean cleared his throat, "Are there side effects?"

Collins caught Sean's change of expression. "Just one, if any."

"One?"

She nodded, "Your sense of smell."

He so badly wanted to kiss her and he couldn't get it out of his mind. "I've got this serious aggressive urge, and I was hoping it was from the pill."

"And it is," she said as she leaned toward Sean.

"You have very lovely lips."

She smiled, "You are smelling my pheromones, possibly."

Sean's eyebrow lifted. "And they smell just oh so lovely."

Collins blushed and smiled. A strand of her hair slipped down in front of an eye. "How are you coping with this serious aggressive urge?"

Sean leaned in close, "This," and kissed her gently. He wanted to crush her in his arms, but decided gentle would make both of them feel better and after a long moment he pulled away. His heart skipped and he swallowed hard. "I think I should get back to Top Deck."

Collins slowly nodded but that was not want she wanted. As Sean got up off the examine table she grabbed his hand and squeezed tightly. She pressed herself close to him. The warmth from his chest felt like a snug comforter. She placed the side of her face against his chest and hugged him.

Sean was nearly overcome with emotion. He hugged back in kind for he couldn't remember how long. Then moments later the embrace slowly broke. He smiled at her and kissed her lightly on the lips. "I think we may have a problem."

She nodded, "And not an easy one. Can you visit me tonight?"

"Maybe, I'll have to come up with a lie or maybe we'll get lucky and Kathy will summon a circle tonight."

"We could only hope. Sean, I'm fal . . .'"

He placed a finger on her lips, "I beat you. I'm there already."

The examine room door chimed.

Both broke their embrace and Sean sat back up on the table.

Collins said, "Enter."

Loggar stepped through the door. "Sean, I was looking for you. You okay?"

He lifted the bottle of pills, shook then, and slowly nodded. Kathy wasn't so lovely anymore.

"Sean, what's the matter?"

"Hard time coping with these new engines."

Loggar said, "Oh, you poor dear," while wedging in front of Collins to hug Sean.

Collins took an involuntary step back. "Excuse me."

Loggar nodded. "Sorry, Karen. I was just concerned."

Sean stepped off the table and started walking toward the door. "Kathy, I'm fine, really. Taking one of these did the trick.

Loggar gave Collins a quick glance.

"Treatment," she said and smiled.

Loggar's smile never reached her eyes.

The examine room door slid open and the rush of noise burst through.

"Sean, love," Loggar said, "Dinner?"

Sean nodded, "Sure."

"But I want to go to the Officer's Mess."

Sean stopped. "You do?"

"We always eat at the Starboard's Bow. I was hoping to try something a little different this evening."

Sean thought a moment. "Kathy, later after Dinner I'll be working late."

Loggar flashed a quick glance at Collins. It was brief but Sean and Collins caught it.

"I want to talk to the Crew and get their feel for this trankless travel."

Loggar's features relaxed, "I think it's wonderful. I so hated Tranking."

Sean listened as she droned on and on. At some point Sean and Loggar said bye to Collins. He was preoccupied by thoughts of her soft lips and how nicely she smelled. He smiled and wished he were elsewhere. Was this the treatment he wondered?

"Sean, are you listening to me?"

Sean shook the bottle and said, "Of course I was, Kathy, but I was just wondering about these pills. I feel remarkably calm. . . and yes I was hearing you. You were telling me about Suptka accidentally corrupting data and how Olivia was able to backdoor it into something useful. I also heard you telling me that Kate might be able to add some intelligence to the Stupinates by using buckyball clusters as registers."

Loggar rapidly blinked several times. He was listening.

He hurriedly kissed her on the lips, "Kathy, I just remembered something I have to do on Top Deck. Dinner after four bells first dog watch, I'll come get you." and darted into a lift.

Loggar felt . . . something. Anger? Hurt? Panic? Maybe all of the above. Maybe something else. Sean had been acting strange. More pre-occupied. She walked back to her office and retrieved several messages. One read, "Captain at seat. All is well." Another read, "Newton not on Top Deck. Not in Mess. Blow out with new transfer. Nothing else."

Chapter 17

Sean found Collins at her desk working late. She looked up and smiled.

"I was hoping to see you tonight."

He smiled back. "I wasn't lying when I told Kathy I wanted to survey the ship."

She nodded.

"And it would make sense if you'd accompanied me, maybe bring some staff as to make it seem proper."

She nodded again and saw the bulge in his pants. "Sean, but I'm not sure that would be proper." And she pointed.

Sean coughed, "Yes, I agree. I was hoping for some medical advice on this. I have a question."

"Yes?"

"Is this a side effect?"

Collins got up and motioned Sean to one of the examine rooms. She called out, "Barthy, watch the boards for a moment."

A dark skinned woman looked up from her CRT, "Yes, Doctor."

"Also, you and Underwood are going to accompany the Captain and myself through the ship. We're going to survey crew. Take a Med bag and a dozen pack of Trankless pills."

Barthy nodded. She typed a quick message to Underwood. He was one of the Psych Doctors on duty tonight. She also sent a brief message to Kirkland. Within minutes a new pool started up.

Sean walked over to the examine table and sat on it.

Collins locked the door and walked over to Sean. She leaned into his arms and kissed his passionately.

Their tongues excitedly touching. Sean unsnapped his pants and pulled himself out. He was rock stiff and felt relief now that he was unconfined. Collins grip was firm. She leaned down and licked at his tip.   His head was sensitive and his stomach tightened. She engulfed him entirely and worked her mouth up and down the length. Sean moaned and reached over to lift her dress up. He felt between her legs. She was wet and his fingers easily slipped in. He worked two fingers in and out as he played his thumb near the top. She rhythmically gyrated her hips until she started to climax. Sean orgasmed a moment later. It took less than three minutes and both were exhausted.

Chapter 18

Sean tapped out the command for ship wide communication. "All hands, all hands, this is the Captain. Prepare yourself for Now-Space. Repeat. Prepare for Now-Space."

The Johnson dropped back into Now-Space with a flash. Momentum sped the Johnson an additional twenty kilometers before coming to a rest.

Sean reached for his bottle of pills in his shirt pocket. He looked around and noticed all of Top Deck did the same thing.

Everyone looked around, saw the bottles. Laughter erupted. "I'm gonna miss Sharp-vision." he told Dawn popping a pill into his mouth. It was sweet sour, but he felt good.

Dawn, smiled after taking her pill, stood up, "Look alive people! This is still a GRID ship."

Deck Chatter slowly replaced a spontaneous lapse of discipline.

Sean said, "Mr. Kirkland, signals?"

Kirkland responded, "None sir. There's some background noise, but nothing to suggest advanced tech."

Sean nodded, "Very well, continue monitoring. Lieutenant Newton?"

"Yes, sir." Adriana answered.

"Anything special?"

She stared into a thin rectangular CRT. She was looking at images from Optics. She scanned normal light, infrared, ultra, violet, short and long radio, nothing to suggest an advanced civilization above ground. It would take 30 days to receive deep scan radar, but passive readings looked good. "Sir, there are no detectable advanced tech signatures. Passive data looks clean. Initial optics shows a world rich in resources. Spectral analysis indicates a world rich in oxygen, nitrogen, some rare elements. Traces of CO_2 but in low quantity. Methane is also in low quantity. Oxygen is at 32% with Nitrogen at 65%. Median temperature is 24 Celsius."

"Mr. Foster."

"Yes, sir?"

"Short jump to three-days light, please. Give two bells ring at ten seconds."

Foster replied, "Moving Johnson to within three light-days distance, sir. Sounding two bells at 10 seconds before jump."

"Very good." Sean tapped out Ship broadcast, "Attention, attention. Ten second count down at two bells sounding. Ten second count down at two bells sounding." He turned to Dawn, "Think of anything yet?"

"Not yet, sir." She smiled and pulled out a pill.

Sean watched most of Top Deck pop a pill into their mouths. A crew of addicts he thought.

Two bells rang, and then . . . this time it didn't matter.

Minutes later the Johnson dropped into Now-Space.

Foster reported, "Captain, 3.287 light-days from planet."

Sean said, "Newton? Anything?"

Adriana scanned the area. The results were pretty much the same as before. "Nothing's changed, sir."

Mr. Kirkland, Relay all data to Scout one and tell her stand-by to launch."

Kirkland keyed in several commands, "Scout one, stand-by to launch."

"Roger," was the reply.

Molino would be piloting the shuttle himself. Cookie sat Observer Station two, behind co-pilot. His co-pilot was Evans. Medical sat behind Pilot, with two others in the rear with a six-person security team. At first, Molino wondered what a fighter wing commander could possibly do on an explorer craft. He had mixed emotions about this whole operation until one of his pilots pointed out that the Johnson was going out into unknown territory. The bogeyman was out there more so now than ever. Molino reluctantly agreed. It would be the bogeyman months in between.

"Mr. Foster."

"Yes, sir?"

"Short jump to three-hour light, please. Two bells sound to ten second countdown."

"Sir, I will be moving Johnson to within three light hours of the planet. Sounding two bells to start ten second countdown."

"Very, good. Proceed." Sean said. "Dawn? Anything yet?"

Dawn answered, "Still thinking."

Sean smiled and nodded.

Two bells sounded.

Then, the planet floating on the main view screen went from a small dot to a large disk set center. It was a beautiful world with white clouds, green landmasses and large pools of blue water. There were no snow caps.

Sean said, Newton?"

"Readings coming in, sir." Adriana's CRT was flooded with dense data streams. She switched over to optics. A spectral analysis of one particular region looked promising. She saw signs of carbon. She scaled up magnification and got a surprise.

Sean leaned forward and said, "Lieutenant? Pardon?"

"Life, sir." She looked up, "Signs of life."

Top Deck went silent.

Sean walked over. "Humanoid?"

Adriana switched to infrared. There, a heat signature like fire. She switched back to optics. Crude shelter. Then, people. Lots of people. Human looking people. "Yes, sir. Streaming data to shuttle." She clicked on communications to the shuttle craft. "Cookie, I'm sending you data now."

Sean stood straight. It was happening. Life. Alien life. "Mr. Kirkland, get Dr. Loggar to report to Top Deck."

Kirkland keyed in Dr. Loggar's room and lab office. "Top Deck to Dr. Loggar, please report to Top Deck. Please report to Top Deck. Your presence is urgently needed." He tapped out.

Loggar was at her desk when Mr. Kirkland requested her presence on Top Deck. She was reviewing the latest findings in Sean's last test. So close, so close. She got up and hurried to Top Deck. It really could be only one thing. Our first contact with Humanoids other than the Necronians.

Sean said, "Lieutenant, please, place optics on view screen."

"Placing optics on view screen, sir. Compensating for rotational drift."

Sean took a sharp breath in when he saw a large mass of humans assembled around a large fire. He could make out animal skin clothing. The scene skewed and drifted then stabilized.

Loggar stepped out of the lift just as the image of similarly looking humans crowded around an elderly male. He had his hands spread wide and was talking. She stepped up next to Sean. He looked at her and smiled.

"Kathy, amazing. Looks like we hit payday early."

Loggar nodded. The scene to her was beautiful.

Sean said out loud, "Kirkland, pipe this through ship

broad Vid. Give the crew a look."

Kirkland responded, "Sir, giving crew a view of main screen." He noted the time. Midshipman Curtis won the main pool. Half-a-year salary.

Adriana had placed the vid stream with a 15 second delay. She gasped.

Sean said, "Lieutenant, something wrong?"

"Sir, maybe. Look."

Sean stared at the view screen. The older male was gesturing wildly. His hands started glowing blue and he flashed his hands upward. The area was washed in pale blue light and suddenly the entire crowd turned and faced the view screen.

Sean held his breathe, "What the . . . ?"

The view screen drifted, skewed and stabilized. The crowd collectively raised arms toward the Johnson and dropped to their knees. The elder glazed into the view screen and Sean felt a chill down his back. The view drifted again, skewed, then disappeared.

Foster said, "Sorry, sir. Line of sight lost. The area dipped below the horizon."

Sean nodded and started walking toward the main conference room, "Kathy, Lieutenant Newton, meeting please. Kirkland, tell shuttle to stand-by. Dawn, Top Deck is yours for the moment." The door slid shut.

Seam sat at the head of the conference table. "What the hell did we just see?"

Adriana replied, "Two things, sir. An assembly of humans and the display of magic. Possibly."

"Possibly?" Sean said.

Adriana nodded. "We won't know for sure until we investigate."

"And were they really looking at the Johnson?"

Adriana shrugged, "Still hard to tell. We were seeing something that happened three hours ago. Coincidence? Not enough data."

Sean turned to Loggar," Kathy? Thoughts?"

"Sean, we definitely have to investigate. Adriana hypothesized that the SI are either here or not. So far there is no evidence of their presence. Could it be that this world has Necronian nanobots and some of the inhabitants are able to use it? Sean, this would help us answer more questions about the Necronians."

"Newton? Have you had a chance to review the nanobots?"

"Not yet, sir."

"Kathy, give Newton everything you can on the nanobots and . . ."

"Sean, I'm . . . "

"Kathy, I don't want to send personnel down unprepared. Newton can analyze and relay vital info to Cookie and the others."

"Sean, I know, but, I'm . . . I'm torn?"

"Torn? How so? Wait." He turned to Adriana. "Newton, could you excuse us for a moment."

Adriana nodded and backed out the conference room. At first she wasn't sure how to really feel about Loggar. Now she knew.

Sean turned back to Loggar. "Kathy, give."

"Sean, should we slow down a bit . . ."

". . . slow down? You wanted to rush headlong. Why the hesitation now?"

"I just have a feeling about Adriana. Not sure she can be completely trusted, and she hasn't been tested."

"Tested? For what?" Sean sucked in his lips.

"She's part Necronian. We don't know her true intent here . . ."

Sean gave her a cold stare.

". . . I just want to make sure we are making the right decisions."

"Kathy, I'm not sure I'm liking what you're telling me. Paranoid?"

"Of course not!"

"Jealous?"

Loggar tried to keep from shrilling. "Of what?!?" She failed.

The cold stare continued.

"I'd just like to watch her. I just can't reveal everything."

"How about what would make her job easy? Specs, maybe? Test results would be nice. Okay, you don't want her to see what you deem too sensitive. Fine, just don't treat her like a mushroom."

"Sean, aren't you concerned that your Great granddaughter transferred to your ship. Someone you never knew existed. Someone who happens to be a super-genius. Someone that's very attractive. We have to question her motives. We have to wonder what the Necronians are up to?"

Sean took a deep breathe. "Adruqu, wrote that Adriana would help us. And I believe her. Adruqu has her motives and I'm sure most of it is in our best interest."

"How do you know the poor girl isn't being lied to or manipulated?"

"I don't, but I've also learned my gut feeling is almost always right. And, it is telling me to trust her. Watch her if you want, but don't impede her ability to perform her job."

Loggar frowned and gave an equally cold stare.

Sean had more practice. His record is five minutes without blinking.

Loggar gave up after thirty seconds. "Sean, I hope you are right for all our sakes."

"Kathy, and I hope you are wrong for all our sakes." He

got up and walked to the door.

Adriana was talking to Dawn when Sean emerged from the door. He walked over to his Command chair and tapped out a special access code. A few seconds later he looked up. Kathy had walked out the conference room just in time. "Newton, you have command level access, now. Get what info you need and proceed accordingly."

Adriana caught Loggar's stare. "Thank you, Captain."

Loggar walked over to the nearest lift and took it to below decks.

Kirkland immediately started a new pool. He could see this being one of the biggest pools ever. Within minutes it reached a mid-grade level year's salary.

Cookie looked out the side window and saw launch tube. Not his idea of a first adventure. So far the Captain had them on standby. The minutes ticked away to hours. Cookie looked over to Molino who had his eyes closed. "Commander, you asleep?"

Molino smiled, "Just writing myself a Vid."

"You are? Is that how you fight the boredom?"

Molino nodded. "Yeah, then when I have downtime I enter it into a storage disk. Maybe one day I'll see one of my Vids made."

"How many?"

"That I have written? About 300."

Cookie whistled.

"I've had a lot of standby time and . . ."

Kirkland called over the net, "Scout one, download new orders and study."

Molino tapped at his CRT and he began to read new mission orders. He tapped out a new command. "Cookie, new orders for you."

A blinking light appeared on his console CRT. He tapped

out the access code and read his new orders. He laughed when he saw schematics of the Necronian nanobots. Tears started to stream down his cheeks. This was happening he thought. This was finally happening. He continued reading. It only took five screens to understand what happened to the Captain. All the rumors about Loggar and magick and snippet Vids the Captain had graced the crew with coalesced into a revelation.

Thirty minutes later Kirkland announced over the net, "Scout one. Launch when ready."

"Hot Damn!" Evans exclaimed. She never had the patience Molino had. Standby always sucked and it never got easier to go through.

Molino kicked into action. "Guys ready and secure back there? Evans, move us out of launch tube."

Evans replied, "Roger, that."

Scout one emerged from the launch tube and headed for deep space. Once cleared of the Johnson, it banked sharply and headed toward the planet. A hot burn would get them there in twelve hours.

Cookie held his breathe as the shuttle launched. It had been on very rare occasions he had a chance to venture outside the Johnson. Now he was in planet fall. He thought about singing a shanty but changed his mind. The old Mess Hall Cookie would've done that. He was the new Explorer Cookie. A different Cookie. A Cookie that waited nearly twenty years to be here. A happy Cookie.

Kirkland reported, "Captain, Scout One launched."

Sean nodded, "Very good," and keyed in a command on his CRT, "Captain to Scout One."

Molino answered, "Scout one, here."

"Molino, wish I could have given you something with

immediate action."

Molino laughed, "No worries, sir. There's a big unknown in front of us. I just may get that immediate action yet with the new orders."

"Good luck. We'll do regular audio checks every four bells."

"Very good, sir." Molino replied.

"Dawn," Sean began, "Fighter wing on alert?"

"Yes, sir. Wing groups twelve and eighteen are hot with groups six and two on stand-by."

Sean nodded. There was nothing else to do but wait for planet touch and subsequent reports afterward.

***

Sean couldn't remember the last time he ate in the Officer's mess. The interior reminded him of a Spaceliner. Opulent and trendy. Nothing like Starboard's Bow, which had a home diner feel. He looked over to Loggar. She was just finishing a Lobster Thermidor. She ran two fingers along the inside of the shell and placed them to her lips. A faint moan escaped her lips. Sean opted for lobster bisque and was still nursing the last half dozen spoonfuls.

"Sean, you seem preoccupied lately."

He nodded. "A lot of things to do. And now with this new discovery, a lot of things to consider."

Loggar sipped at her glass of white wine.

"Kathy, they looked at us. From about three billion kilometers it seemed like they were looking at us."

"But, Sean, that image was over three hours old."

"Which makes it all the more odd. And Magick?"

Loggar nodded, "I'm hoping yes. None of the recent scans revealed nanobot signatures. Sean, that's the most exciting thing of all. Necronian magick without nanobot."

"That we know of."

Loggar smiled.

"Magick without technology." Sean lifted his hand in from of his face. Then he frowned, "That may not be such a good idea,"

"How so?"

"Are we ready for it?"

"I would say most assuredly. We've been looking for this for centuries."

"The Most High has been looking for it, not GRID population as a whole."

She nodded, "True, The Most High is also the most deserving. Human expanse into space was mostly pushed as a Most High Agenda."

"Would that include responsibility of war?"

"Nonsense, Sean! The SI war was not our objective or agenda."

"Records show the SI were created in a quest to help humans explore."

"Yes?"

"To explore for intelligent life or intelligent life that had magick?"

Loggar clenched her jaws.

"If it were The Most High's agenda to push for exploration, then it would be the Most High who embraced or endorsed SI technology."

"Sean, The Most High never intended . . ."

". . . the SI turning on their creators?"

She nodded.

"Kathy, I agree with you. It is imperative we understand Magick. I get that now. This is SI territory for a reason and we are out here for a reason. I stopped really believing in coincidence with Necron and Necronian time travel. And I am absolutely convinced that Adruqu knows something about

Humankind's future and is working behind the scenes through proxies to an end point. My gut tells me she is helping us survive."

"I really wish I felt the same, Sean, I do. My thoughts are she is experimenting with us. Tossing us random variables to see how all this falls into place . . ."

"But Kathy, she gave me the means to bring you back. . ."

"Which further convinces me she is manipulating us to her end game."

"An end game of what?"

Loggar shrugged, "Lab rats, but on a grander scale."

Sean slowly shook his head, "So why us? Why not the people below us?"

"Maybe they have. We saw some display of magick. Maybe this planet is a grand experiment . . ."

" . . . and we happened to come here first?"

"As you said, Sean, the Necronians can time travel. This could all be just one big manipulation."

Sean nodded. His bisque turned cold, however, he still finished off the last spoonful.

***

Adriana stared into her desk CRT. The nanobots were fantastic. It felt weird looking at tech a once unknown ancestor created. Part alien. A chill traveled down her back and she began to wonder about the whys. Was this the reason for her existence? Begin a full circle of unlocking the mysteries of a dead alien race, which bizarre at it could get was not actually dead, but traveling through time doing all sorts of mischief, mayhem, and possibly malice with humankind? And this new discovery of an alien race. Adriana wondered, is one really alien when the discovered looks just like you? Possibly, identical internal organs in the correct slots? "Computer, region Y12X05Z83 please."

The screen zoomed to a cluster of buckyballs, hanson cubes and piper tubes. She was able to quickly conclude this was the memory assembly. "Computer, zoom to fit screen, please."

The screen shimmered to show a nanobot in its entirety. Ten multi-jointed legs attached to an inverted tin pie pan shaped body, which seemed strangely odd. There were numerous antennas that covered its body with the bulk of them clustered thickly underneath the concaved belly. She typed out a message to Cookie. He replied back that he was studying the body shape, too. He added that as a chef he sees things concaved to be filled or used to make as a mold. Since the legs were attached toward the bottom a swag would be that the nanobots sat on top of something or that something would use it as a top. Adriana glanced over to another work station across the room. Karolina and Ga Ka were talking in whispers and smiled often. She tasked Karolina with producing a checklist Cookie should use on Planetside. It took her an hour and it was thorough. Two hundred and ten items to confirm or class as not present. Ga Ka had studied Geology and produced another hundred items for Cookie to check. She thought Cookie would have a heart attack when he saw the list. Instead he squealed un-Cookie like and hugged everyone.

Chapter 19

Sean began, "Scout One reached the planet several hours ago. Currently, it is surveying the land in high orbit. We're hoping the Scout will find the same settlement area. It'll scan and take optics, relay the data back to us. They'll land at a distance, set up camp, and start ground survey. They'll treat the area as hostile friendly. Instead of moving on to other planets on our list the Johnson will establish high orbit and monitor. We'll stay long enough to collect ground, air, water samples. We'll observe the settlement and see if we can get info on language, customs, and norms."

Cookie was in high elation. Scout one had been in orbit for several hours now. The Security team, medical, and Evans were asleep. Only he and Molino remained awake. "Molino, can you move us over to sector Gamma-twelve, please?"

"Sure thing, Cookie. You got a hunch?"

"I do. I noticed what could be a road leading to a large pit. Here, take a look." Cookie tapped out a command on the CRT.

An image of a wide groove appeared on Molino's CRT. There was very little vegetation in the area. He could see small pockets of dark circles around the pit. He eased Scout One out of its orbit and followed the groove. Thirty minutes later he came across what looked like ruins. Massive blocks seemed to have been tossed randomly. Further up there were smaller blocks scattered. He could see piles of rubble placed neatly along a mile stretch. Suddenly he saw a makeshift wagon. Two kangaroo looking creatures were pulling the wagon with several humanoids walking on either side on the wagon. "Cookie, you streaming this back to the Johnson?"

"Done and done."

Molino keyed in radio comm. "Johnson, this is Scout One, come in."

Loggar sat uneasily in her seat. Last night Sean didn't visit, which is not all that strange. Sometimes he works late and elects to sleep in his own room. She told herself he is the Captain, who is very hands-on, and he can't cater to her sexual needs all the time. But still, they were approaching their one year anniversary and he had been increasingly distant. She knew Sean was his own man. He was strong and could be very charming. He was funny and self-confident. She liked that. She also thought him handsome and loved looking into his sometimes brooding eyes. His face was very expressive and even though they disagreed on some issues she loved him dearly. Of late it was the differences that seemed to be providing the divide between them. He had power, yet he was reluctant to use it. The only human in all of GRID who had instant magickal powers elected to keep his powers at bay. He could do anything he wanted. He could be part of GRID Command and yield a considerable amount of power. He could be a God. A God, if he wanted. Without her. Sean could change the face of The Most High, forever. And that bothered her. Is that why Adruqu gave him magick? Because somehow he demonstrated restraint?

"Kathy, your take?"

"My take?" She couldn't remember the question. "Sean, sorry. What was the question again?"

Sean frowned, "Kathy, the vid from Scout One?"

She looked over to the Viewer. Ruins. Fascinating she thought. She kicked herself for missing most of it. "Roll back to the beginning please."

The groove leading up to the pit appeared.

"Freeze."

The image froze and Loggar stood up and walked closer to the Viewer. "Magnify, please. I want to see the pit."

The screen filled with blackness. Loggar peered intently at the center. She could make out some sort of faint outline. "Can we zoom in a little bit more?"

The outline increased in size. It had a humanoid shape but with sharp angles at each joint.

"Computer, increase exposure and decrease dark levels."

The image brightened to furry jigsaw puzzle shaped outlines.

"Increase contrast and sharpen."

Dawn snapped, "Shit!"

Sean's heart sank. SI.

Loggar kept her composure. Something just didn't seem right. "Computer, infrared."

The image turned blue.

"Computer, can you count the number of SI units?"

Within a second the computer replied, "Three hundred sixty-four. The pit is about one hundred meters deep. Very few units are intact."

Loggar turned to the table and sat down. Her smile was wicked and she understood what happened.

Sean turned back to face the others. He too understood the meaning. "Folks, now we know why the SI never conquered this world."

Loggar said, "We can speculate that Necronian magick is strong here, yet the absence of nanobots makes this a mystery."

Sean nodded, "Going to give new orders to Scout One."

Molino had woken everyone else up.

Evans sat next to him, "Fuck. I hate the SI, but look at that." The wagon was full of SI body parts. "How in the world did these people beat them?"

Kirkland came in over the speakers, "New orders Scout One."

Molino here. Johnson, go ahead."

"This is no longer a life discovery mission . . . "

Molino whispered, " . . . no shit. We hit the mother lode."

" . . . This is now a reconnaissance and intel mission."

"Understood, Johnson." Molino turned to Cookie. Sorry, Cookie, looks like ground survey is going to have to wai . . . "

The Shuttle shook violently. Warning alarms sounded.

Molino tapped Emergency Comm. On his CRT "Mayday, mayday, mayday. Johnson, we got warning alarms and losing attitude fast."

The Shuttle shook several more times. Port engine sheared off.

Molino shouted, "Crash position."

Starboard engine tore away.

The ground came up rapidly.

Sean leaned back in his chair staring at the scene. He could hardly believe it. The SI. Here. But defeated. Then there was a flash of blue light. The image jumped. Then . . .

"Captain," Kirkland piped in, "Scout one losing attitude. Telemetry shows loss of engines. Cabin pressure still holding, but no power. Emergency repulsor fields activated. Signal lost."

Sean raced out the conference room. "Mr. Foster, how close can you short jump us to the planet?"

"Five hundred thousand kilometers, sir."

"Make it two hundred thousand."

"Kirkland, emergency jump. Sound alarm. Two bells to jump."

Kirkland entered the appropriate code in his CRT. Five new pools started. One of which no one would collect if there was a winner.

The alarm sounded throughout the ship.

Sean tapped out Ship broadcast on his CRT, "All hands, all hands, crash stations. Emergency short jump to planet mass. Repeat, emergency short jump to planet mass. Two bells ring to three second count."

Foster had already worked out the details hours ago. He tapped in the code. "Ready, sir."

"Do it!"

Two bells sounded. The view screen switched to a starfield with a blue disk dead center. Seconds later it filled the screen.

Foster said, "Sir, One hundred thousand kilometers from planet."

Sean smiled, "Very good, Mr. Foster. Two-days off once we are out of this." He tapped on his CRT. "Quock, meet me in Bay launch. Shuttle two. Bring a platoon. Dawn, you got the Conn. Newton, you're with me."

Adriana found herself running after the Captain. Things moved fast but she caught on soon enough. The Johnson was in rescue mode and the Captain was leading it himself. She darted into the lift just before the door closed. "Bay Launch," Sean said. Then, "Comm to Collins." He ticked off several seconds. "Collins, assembly a team and met me at Shuttle two. Ship down."

Collins grabbing a Medpack. "Running out the door now, Sean."

When Sean reached the Shuttle the others were waiting. Just as the last person boarded Loggar stopped breathlessly at the door. "Kathy, this is a rescue mission."

She answered, "I'll stay out of the way, but by the chance we encounter the natives I might be able to help."

"Natives? Kathy . . . "

"Sean, please, not here. Time."

"Alright get in."

She hurried in and found a spot. Sean took pilot seat with Quock taking co-pilot.

"Everyone secure? This is not going to be one of my joy rides. Johnson from Shuttle two, launching."

Fielders answered, "Captain, Bay Launch prepped. Launch when ready."

Sean pulled back on the controls and pushed the engines toward redline. The shuttle zipped out of its launch tube at a harrowing speed. "Quock, you got a fix on last location?"

"I do. Coordinates on screen and laid in."

Sean pushed the engines to one-two-zero percent. He toggled forward shields on maximum and punched through the atmosphere. A moment later they picked up the distress beacon. Another moment he spotted the downed shuttle. The main fuselage was broken in three pieces. A few bodies lay scattered nearby.

Sean came in hard next to the debris field. A cloud of dust bellowed up and out from Shuttle two. "Everyone, alright?" Sean asked as he unbuckled himself and headed toward the door. Quock reported that the area was clear for about a mile with some animals dotting the landscape. She and her security team were lined up and ready to go. Sean punched the door release with an open palm. A warm waft of sweet fragrance hit Sean in the face. Other circumstances he would have enjoyed the sensation. This moment he rushed out, weapon drawn, with security behind him. Quock had her team quickly fan out, covering the area. Medical came out later and approached the fuselage. The bodies scattered over the area had been part of the security team. Molino, Evans, Cookie, and two others were still buckled to their seats. Evans had a deep gash across her head, Molino only scratches, Cookie not a mark. Minutes later Scout one personnel were aboard Shuttle two.

Collins stepped down the ladder and walked over to Sean. "Four casualties. One was critical but stabilized. The rest shaken but okay."

Sean said, "Damn! What a mess . . . " His communicator chirped. "Blakemore here."

One of the security guards called in, "Sir, we got movement about three hundred met . . ."

A bright blue blast.

Sean detached his blaster from his hip. He spotted Quock running toward the Security Officer's location. He followed. A large blue fuzzy ball of light flashed by once they cleared the ridge top. The elderly man Sean saw earlier was approaching. A mass of humans were behind him. "Auferte malum ex inferno daemones. Iubeo!" The elder man yelled and shot another blast.

Sean caught the blast and tossed it to the side.

The Elder looked perplexed, "Quid hoc est fallacia. Recéde mones. Recéde!" Another blast emerged from his hand. Sean brushed it off easily this time. His nanobots studied the blast and adjusted to it. Messages had been relayed to Sean's brain and somehow he knew just how to deal with it.

Loggar had just stepped out of the shuttle when she heard, " . . . Recéde mones. Recéde!" Impossible she thought. Latin! She saw Sean and Quock disappear behind a ridge.

"Non pertransibis!" She heard as she got closer. "You shall not pass!" The speaker yelled. A moment later she reached the top. The Elder was casting fuzzy fireballs at Sean. The mass of humans standing behind the Elder seemed to be distancing themselves. They started to fan out hoping to flank Sean. Quock had been on the communicator. Her security team covered the natives. Loggar smiled. Latin. And she yelled,

"Nec hostis nos!"

The Elder looked up at Loggar.

She walked down the hill, "Nec hostis nos!" Once she got next to Sean she said, "Non sumus hostibus."

The Elder yelled! "Vos moneo, daemones. Volumus terram nostram defendere possimus!"

Loggar replied back, "Non sumus hostibus. SI autem sunt inimici nostri."

The Elder dropped his arm.

Loggar wasn't sure how long he stood there in silence.

The Elder turned and said, "Deinde sequatur me."

Sean turned to Loggar.

She said, "Follow me."

"Quock, secure the area. I'll keep the comm line open."

"But Captain, how about I come with you?"

"I need you here for the moment. Look at them. The Natives are scared. And scared folks can do dumb things." Sean took out his communicator. "Newton."

"Yes, sir. Come with Dr. Loggar and myself."

The Elder waited. Once Sean, Loggar and Adriana started following he continued along the path. Thirty minutes later they reached a cliff.

"Aperta, ego præcipio." The Elder said.

A small portion of the cliff face gave way, then lifted. The Elder walked in. Sean, Loggar, and Adriana followed. The rest of natives stayed behind.

Once through the threshold the Elder clapped his hands. The ends of embedded thick sticks along the wall suddenly glowed and washed the room in pale blue-white light.

The Elder walked over to a large wooden trunk. He lifted the lid and pulled out an object covered with a cloth. Placing the object on the table he withdrew the cloth.

Loggar gasped when she recognized the head as a SI warrior.

Sean said, "Kathy, what is this?"

She looked at the Elder. "Ecce caput hostis. This is the head of our enemy."

He looked at her, then Adriana, then Sean. There was something about the young one he thought. Something very familiar.

"Quis enim es tu?"

"Magna sumus exploratores. We are great explorers."

He stared at Sean. "Quis enim us tu?"

Loggar answered, "Ipse est ductor noster. Captain est nomen eius. Ut ipse habet. He is our leader. His name is Captain. He has power such as yourself."

The Elder grasped the mechanical head. Blue light surrounded the head and after a moment the light blinked out. "Omnia possum in eo est tollo. Non possum perdere."

Loggar figured out exactly what he was getting at. He wanted Sean to prove himself. He wanted Sean to destroy the metal head to prove he was not a foe. "Sean, my love. He wants you to destroy the head."

"What?!?"

"Sean, please show calm and destroy the head."

"And how do you propose I do that?"

"Magick, Sean. Magick, my love, just simple magick."

Sean walked up to the head and concentrated. He wanted not one atom from that thing inside him, so he willed the nanobots to break it down to a pile of metal filings and dust.

The Elder watched as Sean's nanobots did short work of the SI head. Within seconds a pile of dust with small piece of metal and glass lay before the Elder. He stepped back and bowed to Sean. "Legenda vite." he whispered. "Legenda vite."

Loggar smiled. This was moving along better than she had hoped for. Sean seen as a legend, she as his Goddess, perfect.

Adriana watched in amazement. She heard the Captain

had abilities, but never saw them in action. She also was surprised that the first encounter she'd have would be people who spoke Latin, a language her Mother insisted she learn fluently. In fact, she knew a half dozen dead languages fluently. When pressed, her Mother would be tight lipped about the reason for her learning. She did eventually say, "Because one day it'll save your life." She gave Adriana a bit of advice regarding her skill. "Hide it", she said. "Tell no one you know it. Keep this secret close to you." Adriana responded, "You said knowing the languages may save my life. How can it, if no one else knows." Her Mother smiled, "You're a brilliant young woman. I'll give you this to think about. Ipsa scientia potestas est."

What to do, Sean asked himself. Yet again, Kathy seemed to be in control. And yet again he followed. Hadn't he learned his lesson? Apparently not. His gut was telling him something was wrong. Not the Elder. He seemed as is. The leader and protector of his people. He didn't want to admit it, but there it was. The seriously simple ugly truth. Kathy was changing and not for the better. Sean noticed the change in her eyes first. Eyes he fell in love with so very long ago it seemed. They stopped smiling a while back and that was sad.

Adriana had drifted while Loggar and the Elder talked. The talk was mundane. Occasionally Loggar would speak in English for Sean's benefit. Sean, himself, nearly nodded off. He'd check in every half-hour. Then the Elder asked Loggar's role in the group.

Loggar answered, "Ego principium nostri instituti. Dea sum Altissimum."

I am our people's religious leader. I am The Most High Goddess. Two simple statements that were true yet somehow they sounded wrong coming from her lips. The Elder beamed and bowed. He clapped his hands and a tall man wearing a long robe appeared. The Elder whispered in his ear. The man looked at Adriana and the others, turned and walked out.

"Veni mecum, obsecro." The Elder said.

The group stood up and followed the Elder into a large chamber. A large wooden table was at the center with about a dozen chairs around it. He gestured for everyone to sit. He placed Sean on one side near the head of the table and Loggar on the other side.

The tall man brought out a bowl of fruit, something that looked like cheese, and a pitcher of liquid colored brown.

Loggar said, "An permittenda sit religiousus quaerere quod populus tuus? Offendere nolumus, sed ad audiendum. Et re quidem ut a nobis recepit."

The Elder beamed and said, "Joiada. Habeo multas quaestiones. Nos autem vos estis eros. Ut in machinis hostes versaris. Quomodo duci tuo, non solum verbis loquimini?"

Loggar turned to Sean. She said, "He is asking why I am able to speak Latin and not you?"

Sean smiled and replied, "I thought it sounded familiar." He pursed his lips, "Never had a reason to. I'm comfortable to have you do all the translating. Besides, this is fantastic. Humans, who speak an old Earth language. Amazing."

Loggar nodded, "Sean, one of my theories is that certain old Earth languages had been given to us by the Necronians. Latin is the only one to have survived. Their language is close enough to our Latin that I'm having no problem communicating with The Elder. . ."

". . . The Elder? That's his title?"

"It is. He's their religious leader, which I still haven't figured out yet, but you can appreciate the back and forth we are doing." Loggar turned to The Elder and said, "Placet, ignoscant. Im 'iustus ad explicandam Captian nos sunt questus ad invicem novimus. Habeo sumendi eam tardus interdum."

He nodded and smiled. "Ut maiore natu. Simpliciter autem vir simplex occurrat."

Sean lifted an eyebrow but said nothing.

Loggar said, "Interesting. Sean, there is a hierarchy here. Wonderful!"

"You fill in the details later, tonight."

Loggar nodded and started chatting with The Elder.

Sean reached over and grabbed a fruit from the bowl. To his surprise it was similar to a Dukufa.

Adriana watched Sean as he held the fruit in his hand. He seemed to have recognized it.

Sean sniffed the fruit. It had the same sweetness as a Dukufa. "Dukufa lup aba ca na dabra."

The fruit split in a half-dozen pieces.

The Elder stopped in mid speech. "Te lingua primum seniorum?"

Sean was about to say something. He turned to Loggar.

"The Elder asked if you know the Necronian's language."

"Tell him some."

"Seniorem principem faciéndam sciat simplices dolis appositi."

Sean placed some of the pieces in front of The Elder and gestured what he hoped was universal as 'join me.'

The Elder's eyes suddenly moistened with tears and he bowed his head deeply. He took three of the pieces and carefully carried them to a gold colored tray on top of a small dresser. He knelt and began to pray.

"Kathy, what just happened?"

Loggar was just as confused. She and Sean looked to Adriana, who shrugged.

The Elder rose and slowly walked over to the three. "Secundum seniorum placeat sequatur."

Loggar said, "He called us Second Elders and he wants us

to follow him."

Sean got up and followed The Elder out a door on the far side of the room.

Adriana and Loggar hastily followed the two down a hallway that opened into a large room. Along the walls sat rows of tables and chairs with a man or woman sitting. On top of each table was a crystal marble ball the size of a skull. It sat on a gold and silver stand. The Elder walked to a young woman sitting at one of the tables. He whispered in her ear. She stared at Sean for a moment, smiled, and placed her hand on the marble ball. A few seconds later she nodded to The Elder.

"Senior Elder meam suscepit invitantis. Erit in decem soles."

Loggar told Sean, "The Senior Elder will be here in ten days. The Elder said suns." She turned to The Elder, "Sic et reliqui presbyteri et loqueris?"

He nodded, "Vos dont 'utor psychicae iunctio?"

"Alia ratione utimur, et similia." She answered. "Sean, this is fantastic. This is how they communicate between villages.

Adriana took out her scanner. The Marble ball had a quartz center. A deep scan made the center glow slightly. Adriana stopped scanning.

Sean said, "Ten days? Here?"

Loggar nodded.

"What if we went and picked him up?"

Loggar gave Sean a double take.

"Damage has been done in exposing them to technology. Even though ten days is not that long I'd rather deal with this now than later."

Loggar turned to The Elder and said, "Africanus Maior Vivamus deducere poterimus quam hic ad diem novissimum."

The Elder looked at Loggar incredulously.

"Volans nostri plaustrum."

The Elder looked worried.

"Nos tibi ut quis te veniat. Hic nostri Quisque aliquam."

He turned to the woman in front of the marble ball and whispered in her ear.

She closed her eyes and concentrated. The Marble ball's center glowed bright blue. Moments later she whispered something into The Elder's ear.

He said, "Senior Elder concordat. Et ingrediemur in plaustro volanti."

***

Sean and the others approached the Shuttle. Quock and Collins met them halfway.

"Captain," Quock began, "Got your message. Shuttle prepped. Shuttle twelve left a few minutes ago with Scout One crew. Molino decided to stay.

Sean looked at Collins.

"Molino is fit to fly?

Collins said, "He was lucky. Not a scratch."

Sean nodded and gestured toward The Elder. "Quock, Collins, this is The Elder."

Loggar translated, "Quock, Collins, hic est maior."

Collins said, "Latin?"

Loggar nodded. "Hoc est nostrum Doctorem. Id nobis maxime securitatem."

"Deae accessisses, tot mulieribus principatum."

Loggar nodded, "Ita etiam modo operatur in nobis."

The Elder laughed, "Ut est apud nos."

***

Sean sat in the Pilot seat with Molino Co-pilot. The Elder sat behind Molino with Loggar behind Sean. The rest sat in mid deck and aft. Sean slowly lifted the shuttle.

The Elder clenched the arm rest and exclaimed, "Senior senior! Da mihi virtutem!"

Loggar looked over and said, "Senior, id est tutum."

Little comfort it gave The Elder as they passed the Scout One's debris field. The very craft he himself brought down so easily. "Tantum populum meum ut salvum fecit." He said.

Loggar saw the debris and said, "Ad quartum dicendum quod bonum et malum non vos vel vestros portus. Nos ita egisset."

Collins listened. 'We would have done the same thing in your position.' Loggar told The Elder. Maybe, maybe not Collins thought, but fear does have a way of distorting perception and judgment. The Shuttle banked twice momentarily interrupting her thought. Collins looked out the window and saw a precession waiting below.

Sean swung the Shuttle around and landed neatly in front of the gathered crowd.

Dust kicked up as the metal wagon landed and the Senior Elder shielded her eyes. A moment later a door opened and The Elder stepped out. He was followed by a woman and man in strange clothing. Once The Elder was close he said, "Seniorem principem et dea est."

She sniffed, "Tu es?"

Loggar translated, "You are the one?"

Sean replied, "I am no one special."

Loggar frowned, "Sed sum princeps. Populus meus, et protéctor meus Deae. Honorati sumus occurrit vobis."

Sean smiled and said to Loggar, "That sounded pretty long for 'no one special.'"

"Sean, my love, I gave your title along with our honor. Trust me. I feel good about this."

He eyed her suspiciously.

Loggar turned her attention to The Senior, "Gratias tibi, quia dato ad te princeps ad urbem."

The Senior nodded deeply toward Sean. He returned the favor and gestured for them to board the Shuttle. The Senior stepped up cautiously. Once inside the Shuttle she looked around. Collins and Adriana stood up and bowed. Sean gestured for The Senior to take the seat behind the Pilot chair. The Elder sat behind Co-Pilot. Seconds later Sean had the Shuttle powered up and lifted off gently.

"Summum enim maior!" exclaimed The Senior Elder.

"Affectum transibunt. Sit normalis." The Elder said.

Loggar smiled, "Lorem ipsum plaustrum eget elit."

The Senior looked out the window and started praying. Loudly.

Molino looked over to Sean, "Not fast enough, sir."

Sean nearly laughed as the Town appeared. He landed the Shuttle near the main gathering area as most of the townsfolk gave the craft a wide berth. He set the Shuttle to standby mode and helped the Senior Elder down the ladder. Once on the court yard The Elder lead everyone into a large stone building. Its interior was cool despite the numerous smoky torches that lead the way to a large room. A large door was at one end and benches at the other. The Elder gestured everyone but Sean to sit and said, "Dux sequetur nos in cubiculum Magiæ."

The Senior Elder and The Elder motioned Sean to follow them into the Chamber.

"Sean, you'll need someone to translate."

Sean smiled. He kissed Loggar on the forehead, "Kathy, don't worry. I'll manager."

Then the doors closed. Sean on the inside, she on the outside. Her planning, her guiding hand, her efforts, her hard work, all for nothing. Hate would not have been the word she would use at the moment, but Loggar thought it was close enough.

Collins approached Loggar. "Kathy, are you okay?"

Her brooding expression revealed a part of her not pretty. "I am not okay. This is not fair."

Collins guided Loggar over to a set of chairs. Both sat holding hands with Loggar staring at the large imposing wooded doors. Tears welled up in her eyes. "Not fair at all. He didn't even want to be a Most High. I found him shattered and gave him purpose. A reason to go on . . ."

Loggar hadn't noticed when Collins slowly released her grip and placed her own hands into her lap. Collins scooted away from Loggar a tad bit as she droned on about her accomplishments, her achievements, how she was the one who single-handedly brought The Most High to the brink of epic proportions. She alone sacrificed years to bring this very moment about. She should be behind that door not Sean. "Besides, he doesn't speak Latin, he . . ."

Collins coughed. She said softly, " . . . speaks it fluently."

Loggar continued" . . . it must be embarrassing. Sean trying to follow and . . ." She looked up. "Karen, what did you just say? Something about Sean and Latin?"

Collins nodded, "He speaks it fluently."

Loggar remained speechless for several moments. "Fluently?"

"Ut sicut volubiliter loquor," was her reply.

"That was never in his records? When did he learn Latin. He has . . ."

" . . . a past," Collins finished. "The Captain is complicated."

Blood drew to the surface of Loggar's cheeks. Her blush was deep and she wasn't sure whether to feel silly or furious. "Why would he hold something like that from me?"

"You probably never asked, assumed some things you shouldn't have, or he never thought it important enough." She shrugged, "I'm sure he thought it a tactical advantage not to say something."

Loggar frowned. She decided on feeling silly.

Chapter 20

The great doors closed behind Sean. The chamber was smaller than the massive doors would indicate. A small table in the center had a clear decanter of iridescent blue liquid placed in the middle. It was surrounded by three plates. On each plate lay one of the three pieces of dufuka fruit The Elder had taken earlier.

The Elder motioned for Sean to sit. "The Captain, I know you understand our tongue."

Sean smiled, "You found me out. I do understand."

The Senior Elder sat at a place. She lifted her heavy robe enough to get comfortable. "Do I hear deception?"

Sean answered, "No intentional deception Senior Elder." He looked at The Elder, "Please accept my apologies for not being forthright. I decided to let our Goddess speak for us. She after all really is the head of our religious group."

The Elder nodded. "Accepted The Captain," he said as he sat behind a plate.

Sean took his place.

"You are your people's protector?" The Senior Elder asked.

"One of many. I am the leader of this quest to find places the First Elders visited. To form an alliance and allegiance."

The Elder said, "To fight the Metal ones?"

Sean nodded. "But I see you won't need our help."

The Senior Elder replied, "The First Elders left us with the Liquid of Magick. They knew one day we would need it."

"How many Elders are on your world?"

"There are one thousand regions spread from the north to

south and from east to west. The top and bottom of our world we leave for the First Elders."

"The First Elders are here? Now?"

"They come and go. Sometimes one will visit to see how our liquid is doing. They've shown us how to increase our supply, but sometimes it's not enough. The canter you see before you is for a special occasion."

"I am honored."

"The honor is ours The Captain." The Elder said. He poured the blue liquid into the glasses in front of each plate.

The Senior spoke, "May The First Elders watch over us and guide us through times that are good and times that are bad. May we display courage when needed, humility when called for, and the guiding thought to know the difference."

Sean took a drink of the glowing blue liquid. It felt surprisingly warm as it made its way to his stomach. It left a bitter aftertaste and suddenly his mouth felt dry. He started to sweat.

The Senior Elder and The Elder had just finished their glasses. They popped the dufuka piece into their mouths and chewed slowly.

Sean did the same thing. The dufuka took the bitter edge away, but he continued to sweat. He felt hot and his vision started to blur. "I feel strange," he heard himself say but hadn't realized he said anything.

"The Captain," The Elder started, "are you okay?"

Sean heard himself say, "No, I'm not feeling well. Please get our Doctor."

Then blackness.

Collins heard the massive doors opening before she saw them. The Elder hurried over to Loggar and herself.

"Please follow me. The Captain seems ill."

Collins followed The Elder and found Sean lying on the

floor. He was drenched and started shaking uncontrollably. She pulled out her scanner. His body temperature over 105. She pulled a HYPspray from her Medical pouch and slid a small bottle into the hand grip. A moment later Adriana appeared. "What can I do to help?"

Collins pressed the tip of the HYPspray against Sean's neck. "Hold him still please."

Adriana placed a hand on each shoulder and pressed down.

Collins pushed the trigger release and a stream of fluid flowed into his neck. Seconds later Sean stopped shaking and his temperature dropped to 99. He's normal was 97.1.

Adriana ran her scanner across Sean's body.

Collins stood up and faced The Elder and the Senior Elder. "What happened?"

The Elder bowed deeply. We didn't know this would happen.

"Didn't know what would happen?"

Tears welled up in The Elder's eyes. "He drank the water of Magick."

"Pardon?"

Loggar had lingered by the door out of the way. She watched everything and heard The Elder mention " . . . the water of Magick."

The Elder gestured to the clear decanter.

Collins ran her Scanner over the decanter. She reviewed the readers and her eyes grew wide. "Adriana? You have to see this."

Adriana stood up and walked over to Collins. Loggar was close.

"Take a reading."

Adriana did so. The tiny display screen flowed numbers and symbols. The flow stopped on a wireframe image of an organic version of the Necronian nanobot.

Collins said, "nanobots?"

Adriana answered, "Organic bacteria with a similar structure as the nanobots."

***

Loggar approached The Elder and Senior Elder. "The Captain will be okay."

The Elder looked at Loggar, "But how could this happen?"

Loggar answered, "Even though we may look the same there may be some differences. The First Elders visited many places and may have made us all a little different."

The Elder was mournful.

"The Captain's power was given to him by a First Elder named Adruqu, he . . ."

"Directly?!?" Replied The Elder.

The Senior Elder came in close, "By the Holy Supreme Elder?"

Loggar nodded, "As I was. "

Both Elders dropped to their knees. "Forgive us, Goddess." Both said in unison.

" . . . I am alright." Sean said behind The Elders.

Both stood up and bowed deeply. "The Captain, please forgive us. We are deeply . . . "

Sean interrupted, "Forgiven."

The Senior Elder fainted.

Collins rushed to her side and ran a scanner over her. "She'll be fine, from what I can tell. As a people we are very similar, with some slight differences."

Adriana stepped up next to Sean. "Sir, how are you feeling?" She ran the scanner along the length of his body.

"I feel surprisingly well."

Collins ran a scan. She looked at Adriana who nodded. Collins turned to face The Elder. "The Elder, may I move this object across your body. It will not hurt and you will not feel a thing."

The Elder looked at Sean and Loggar.

Sean said, "Please."

The Elder bowed deeply and tears welled up in his eyes.

Collins and Adriana both started taking readings. After a few minutes Collins said, "Sir, I'd like to get back to the shuttle and input this data into the computer."

Loggar turned to The Elder, "Elder, may we have a small amount of the liquid?"

The Elder was torn emotionally from saying yes and holding onto the sacred liquid. After a moment he nodded. He went to a small closet and pulled down a medium jar. The liquid glowed blue. He handed it to Loggar ceremoniously.

Loggar said, "Thank you and don't worry. We will protect it."

The Elder warily smiled.

Chapter 21

Loggar, Collins, and Adriana huddled around one of the Shuttle's work stations. The monitor displayed nanobots taken from Sean's blood.

Sean hovered in the background looking over everyone's shoulder. The image of his familiar looking nanobots on top of a semi-translucent organic looking nanobot made the hair at his neck stiffen. "That's inside me?"

Adriana answered, "Yes, sir. Not this one but many others."

Loggar said, "Sean, the Necronians engineered bacteria to work similar to the nanobots in our bodies. It's fantastic. Living cells that can manipulate electromagnetic fields? This is beyond fantastic. This means that anyone can potentially become powerful."

"Which may not be a good idea."

"How so?"

"Kathy, we're on a planet full of people and only a handful have the power. The Necronians control the upper and lower half of this planet . . . "

"How'd you find that out?"

"The Elders told me. But the point is, not everyone of this planet can do magick."

Collins spoke up, "It makes sense to keep the numbers down, otherwise there would be those who would abuse the power."

Loggar gave Collins a scowl. "Okay, of course that makes sense. What I was getting at is there would be no limits. Not just the few who could do magick, but more. Like the planet. Their Elders help protect their regions. No SI."

Sean nodded.

Collins said, "There's also their body make up. They are human, but genetically and chemically slightly different. Not enough to be called human but not enough to be called Alien either. We have more in common than the Necronians have with Sean."

"But, Karen, I drank the liquid, and I . . ."

" . . . was dumb. Sean, one should not drink glowing blue liquid from total strangers."

"Okay, a bit reckless . . ."

"A bit?"

"Alright, Doctor, very reckless, but I am here feeling pretty good."

Adriana stepped in, "Which I've been meaning to talk to you about."

"Yes?"

Adriana tapped in a command on the work station CRT. "Some of the Elder nanobots and your Necronian nanobots are working together. The Bacteria nanobots are using the others like some sort of armor."

"Or augmented like a cybersuit?" Sean asked.

"Or like commanders."

"Those things are sentient?"

"I don't think so. I think more like complex programming. There's probably a few hundred, maybe a few thousand subroutines programmed."

"What about his immune system." Loggar asked.

Collins said, "I can answer that one. I thought it interesting your immune system to be programmed to accept bacteria you never encountered. Apparently, some of the specialized nanobots are programmed to learn the immune system and mask all the Nanobots against white blood cell attacks."

"Let's get back to this command thing."

"Having only one or the other they act as a unit controlled by you. Introduce both to together then you create a second layer of control. They'll still act as a unit but now you have augmented coordinators, which can also do specific tasks."

"But to what purpose?"

"That, sir, is a very good question."

"What about dormant nanobots?" Loggar said.

The other three looked over to Loggar.

"What about dormant nanobots?" She repeated. "We know what happens with active ones."

Sean faced Collins and Adriana.

Adriana said, "Unknown. I suspect your reaction to the bacteria nanobots was because of an internal struggle." She shrugged. "Both types are clearly capable of Magick. It was just a question of who would control whom."

Loggar said, "So, in my case, I would feel nothing?"

Collins spoke up, "I'm not sure about that and I see where you are taking this. We . . ."

"Taking this where Doctor?"

"We'd be introducing foreign objects into your system. We have no idea if the dormant nanobots had time to program your immune system to accept the bacteria."

"Give me worst case scenario?" Sean asked.

"Death."

Loggar said, "I don't think so."

Collins replied, "Genetically engineered alien foreign bacteria. Hello!"

"I already have engineered alien foreign objects still in my body. The Necronians had tens of thousands of years to perfect this. I'm certain this was a scenario they considered."

Collins thought a moment. "Point. But still." She turned to Sean. "We're not supposed to rush blindly into the unknown."

Sean grimaced.

"This is no longer the unknown. Sean crossed that line and now we have data."

"I strongly stress you wait for further testing of . . ."

"Of what, Karen? We know what they are. We know what they do. We can infer how they work. We either do or don't. I'm not . . ."

"But . . ."

"Nothing. I'm not about to pass this up. I'm already established as the religious leader. They've accepted Adruqu as giving me magick."

"What are you saying?"

"We either do this here or I walk into town and do it."

Collins stared hard into Loggar's eyes. Neither blinked for a full twenty seconds.

Sean coughed, "Adriana. Please give us your take."

Adriana took a deep breathe. "Sir, as much as this goes against protocol, I agree with Dr. Loggar."

Loggar and Collins both replied, "You do?"

Adriana continued, "Procedure is lost. And Dr. Loggar could do as she says she would, but only by the Captain's grace. Sir, you are curious as to what you can do now. You are also curious as to what would happen to Dr. Loggar." She paused.

Sean said, "Go on."

"Sir, I believe the bacteria went through a DNA change to be compatible with your body. As Dr. Loggar pointed out, the Necronians had tens of thousands of years to perfect the bacteria."

Collins frowned. "Fine! If you want to do this then do it. If you die . . ."

Loggar smiled, " . . . you will bring me back, Karen."

***

It took Loggar seconds to up end the cup of glowing blue liquid. It tasted sweet with a bitter aftertaste. Collins and Adriana were actively monitoring everything: heart, pulse, blood pressure, brain wave, white blood cell, everything.

Collins asked, "How do you feel?"

"I feel well . . . no wait. I'm feeling warm."

Sean nodded, "It's beginning."

Adriana watched an infrared image of Loggar on a monitor. Loggar's image went from a deep blue shade to green to light pink to red to deep red. She looked up just in time to see Loggar lose consciousness.

Collins didn't feel the need for urgency this time. One, partly because she knew Loggar's body temperature would drop back to normal in a minute and two, she wanted her to suffer just a little bit. Just a little you smug bitch she thought.

Sean sat and watched how Collins did nothing special. She and Adriana monitored Loggar's condition. They watched over her with clinical indifference and it seemed to him they would still be indifferent if Loggar's condition went from bad to death.

A moment later, Loggar's temperature started dropping. Sean himself felt a twinge of guilt from being disappointed in there being a less than dramatic outcome. He thought Kathy got what she wanted. Her obsession finally satiated. Now what?

Chapter 22

Loggar opened her eyes and saw . . . no one near. She helped herself up, still wondering why no one was near. She looked around at the dimly lit shuttle interior and heard the sounds of soft snoring. She got out of bed and walked to the front of the shuttle. Sean was sitting at the controls staring out the window. He turned when she was near.

He gave her a small smile. "Kathy," he started in a low voice, "you're awake. How are you feeling?"

"Tired."

He nodded and remembered the way he used to feel about her. The dim interior lights cast a lovely glow over Loggar's face. "I can imagine. What do you feel like doing?"

Loggar sat in the co-pilot chair. "I'm not sure. I suppose I should wait until daylight."

He nodded. "I still have another two hours before Molino will relieve me."

Loggar got up and kissed Sean on the cheek. She couldn't put her finger on it, but he changed. He accepted the kiss but it wasn't like old times. She sighed and went back to the bunk she had been laying in. Collins and Adriana slept in two of the other bunks. Sean would probably sleep in the fourth. Nearby was better than forever far she thought. She pulled the blanket over her body and minutes later she was asleep.

Sean watched her walk back to the sleeping area. Not the same anymore he thought. We just started this mission and nothing will be the same.

***

Loggar woke up with a start. She felt strange, but in a sort of good way. Despite the Shuttle's cool interior temperature she felt warm. She remembered using a blanket last night but couldn't find it now. Part of her body was covered in a very fine layer of cloth. She brushed it off and held out her hand and thought 'flame.' Seconds later a tiny red flame appeared in the middle of her hand. She nearly squealed with delight. Bigger she thought and the flame covered her hand. Her first impulse was to scream, the second to try and blow out the flame. Then she realized her hand was not burning. It was the nanobots. Her nanobots! She finally got what she wanted. The ability to do magick anywhere, anytime, anyway she wanted and the weight of it all settled squarely on her shoulders. Her mind raced with jumbled thoughts on what to do next. Go outside and blast a few rocks and trees? Scientifically and painstakingly measure, test, and hypothesize a wonder of science? Flame-off she thought. The intense red glow faded.

"Happy?"

Loggar turned her head. It was Sean. "Yeah I am."

Sean stared.

"Sean, now I can be a true Goddess."

"Kathy, you were . . . "

She shook her head, "I pretended. We all pretended. Except for you . . ."

"Of which I never really wanted. I just wanted . . ."

"Sean, how can you say that! You have power very few humans have. How can you not want the power and how can you not want to use it?"

"Because, magick is not the person. It's a tool I choose to use when absolutely needed. And it is something I don't need to use as a crutch."

"Crutch? What are you trying to say?"

No reply.

"Is this something that'll divide us?" Loggar asked. She was uncertain she had wanted to ask that question.

Sean, poker faced, stared at Loggar's face. "I'm not liking what has been coming over you this last few weeks."

"Me?" She said, angry that Sean could believe that she was the one who changed. "Me? You're the one who changed . . ."

Adriana woke up to what sounded like an argument. She heard Dr. Loggar tell Sean he was the one who changed. She got up and approached the two. Then without warning Loggar turned on her.

"You! Why are you really here?"

Adriana, still drowsy, said, "To help the Captain . . ."

Intense anger flowed from Loggar's lips. "I think it's more than that. You want to . . . "

Sean interrupted, "Kathy, I think you should . . . "

"No, I won't let it lie. She is here because of Adruqu. Why are you here?"

Adriana was confused. She thought it all settled. "To help the Captain."

Loggar stepped in closer. "I don't believe you!" She screamed.

Sean wedged himself between Loggar and Adriana. The hell he was going to let Kathy treat one of his crew like this.

Loggar gave Sean a hard looked but didn't blink. "Why are you protecting her?"

"She's crew," was all he said.

"She is Adruqu's Great granddaughter and . . . "

"She's crew. And family. And you think I'm going to stand here and let you yell at her?"

"But . . ."

"Back down, Kathy. Nothing good will come of this."

Loggar took a deep breath and let it out slowly. She

realized how foolish she looked. She turned and faced Collins. New emotions built back up. She suddenly felt hatred. Pure and intense. "You! Bitch! I hate you!"

"Kathy!" Sean exclaimed. "What is wrong with you?"

"She is trying to take you away from me!"

Sean stepped up close to Loggar. He sighed and leaned close to her ear. "She is not trying, Kathy."

Loggar turned. "What are you saying?"

"I'm saying she is not trying to do anything."

She leaned in and kissed cold unresponsive lips. Bastard she thought. "Sean?"

"Kathy, I'm not liking this changed you."

"Changed me? How dare you!" Anger spilled out. She hissed, "I made you."

Sean stared.

"Without The Most High you would still be a Commander drinking your career to hell."

"Because of The Most High I was punished for doing the right thing. I was drinking my life away because of your Most High. I remained a Commander because of the Most High."

Loggar felt her heart race. Her blood pressure increased and the only clear thing she could think of was using her new powers and ending this argument.

Sean shook his head. "Kathy, don't. Just don't."

"Or else, what?"

"Just don't."

She glared into his eyes. This time she went two minutes without blinking, but in the end, Sean won. He always won. "Now what?"

Sean exhaled, "We say our goodbyes, head back to Earth, and reconsider things."

"No," she said.

"This mission is a failure on some levels. We can't continue given what just happened."

"I am in charge of this mission."

"And the Johnson is under my command. I also have full backing of GRID Command."

"You . . . you . . . fuck! We can't stop now. We . . ."

" . . . will turn back. You can get another ship for your quest. I don't care how or who, it just won't be the Johnson."

Loggar clenched her hands into a fist. A red glow surrounded her hands.

Sean slowly shook his head, "Kathy, don't. As I stand here before you, don't." His hands started glowing blue.

Loggar suddenly felt scared. She couldn't possibly fight Sean and win. And the idea that she had taken a step to commit an act of violence sickened her. The red glow faded. She dropped to her knees. "I am sorry. I am so sorry."

The energy around Sean's hands faded. "So am I, Kathy. I really am." He turned and walked out the Shuttle.

Loggar looked up at Adriana and Collins. "Sorry. I just . . . don't know what came over me. It was like someone else." She sighed. Even that sounded lame to her ears. Loggar got up and walked out the door. She headed toward the main courtyard. There she found a bench and sat. So much planning, so much time, energy, and effort.

***

Sean stood in front of The Senior and The Elder. He bowed deeply hoping the gesture would be taken as a sign of respect. The Senior and The Elder returned the gesture.

"The Captain," The Elder began, "I sense some turmoil within you."

Sean nodded. "There is so much we can learn from one another, but things have changed within us that compels me and my crew to leave."

The Elder's face contorted to distraught. "We did not

mean to offend The Goddess, The Captain. We had no idea she was given magick from the Ultimate Elder Adruqu." He bowed deeply several times.

Sean stopped him. "The Elder, it is nothing you have done. Believe me. Your people, you and The Senior Elder, have been very gracious to us. I thank you. But, The Goddess . . ."

" . . . would like to stay." Loggar finished.

Sean and the Elders faced Loggar. "Kathy?"

She replied, "I want to stay, Sean."

Sean did not attempt to stare her down. "Kathy, you understand what this would mean?"

She nodded.

"We may not return to this planet, ever. You understand that?"

She nodded. There would be no way she could weather this storm. The Most High council would do a vote of confidence. Things would come out she had held from them. They would call witnesses. It would be ugly. "I understand, completely."

The Elder said, "Our people will have to vote. Goddess, you'll have to address the town and they will decide. It is the way of our people." He bowed his head as in deep shame.

"I understand that Elder. Of course, I will make my case to the people."

He looked up and smiled. "I will call a meeting this afternoon."

***

Loggar stood on top of the raised rock platform. She cleared her throat. "Good Town's folk. I'm asking to stay with you. To be a part of your Town, your culture, your belief. I can offer much in new tools. I've learned much in my travels. I can help the Elders fight the Edged Monsters, of which we call, the SI." And as a demonstration she made her hand glow.

There was a collective gasp and the entire front row of folk stepped back.

Loggar heard a murmur through the crowd, "Red glow. . . she has the red glow. . . she is not the one." The crowd took another step back.

Loggar's heart sank. Her thoughts swirled into a frenzy of panic. "Town folk, please. I can help the Elders."

The space between her and the gathering grew wider and a path opened up and The Senior Elder and The Elder walked through. They stopped in front of Loggar.

The Senior Elder spoke first, "You have the red glow. You cannot be among us."

Loggar pleaded, "Why? I have magick too."

The Elder spoke, "Those with the Red glow always turn evil."

"But I'm not of your people?"

"Always." The two turned their backs on her. "Please leave, now. Or the Town will rise against you and we will be forced to fight you and the Captain."

Anger boiled up from Loggar's heart. Hatred grabbed at her throat and she hissed out, "FINE!" Her hands started glowing red. Her voice was hollow sounding as it broadcasted loudly over the gathering. "Reject me!" She stepped off the raised rock.

The gathering began to disperse.

"Reject me!" And anger consumed her. Thoughts deep with murder rose to the surface. "REJECT ME!!!"

A wave of energy spread across the area knocking people down.

"I. Am The Most High. Goddess!"

The Senior Elder stepped forward, "Begone, evil one. Begone."

The Elder shouted, "Begone! Begone!"

The Townsfolk shouted, "Begone, begone, begone."

Sean stood at the back row. Collins and Adriana were beside him.

Collins leaned over to Sean, "Captain, this is going to turn ugly."

Sean nodded, then projected his voice, "Enough!"

Everyone became silent and turned toward him.

Sean really had no idea what he was going to say, or how he could make an impact on the situation. He just knew something had to be done. "Please, hear me." Then an idea hit upon him. His hands glowed blue and he told the nanobots to lift him a meter into the air. "We will leave. We will leave your good town and home alone. We will not come back unless your enemy which is our enemy returns. We are sorry."

Loggar watched in horror. The pain of rejection, the embarrassment it caused, and the rage it forged was too much. "I will not be chased off!" Her hands glowed an intense red. "I've come too far."

Sean shook his head quickly. "Kathy, let's leave in peace."

Loggar couldn't believe it. Mission failure. On her watch. And nothing made sense. She fired two red glowing energy balls into the gathering. Another ball at The Senior and The Elder. The Fourth at Sean.

It happened fast. Adriana felt the wave of intense heat slam into her. She was knocked back several meters and collided into Collins. She looked up and saw The Senior Elder vanish in a poof of pink mist. The Elder saved himself by projecting an energy ball at Loggar. She brushed it off. And sent another energy ball toward the Elder. It pushed him a dozen meters and slammed him into a tree. He lost consciousness. Sean maneuvered his way between The Elder and the rest of the townsfolk. Bodies lay strewn across the immediate landscape.

Another blast hit Adriana. She blacked out.

Loggar shouted, "Never! I've waited all my life for this and you want to take it away?" The foliage around her turned black, wilted, dried up, dead. Her hands aglow in red flames. She launched a fireball at Sean.

He took it full force and fell back. His clothing singed. Anger now started to boil deep inside him. She had to be stopped and his heart sank as he realized what he had to do.

Loggar turned to one of the natives lying face down in the dirt. His death was quick, but no matter. His fate had been sealed the moment he raised arms against her. She grabbed his hair and lifted the lifeless face up. The eyes were still open. She looked over to a watching Sean stand. Her face contorted into an ugly mix of hatred and anger. She willed her nanobots to consume the native's flesh. The body dried up in seconds and turned to dust.

Sean witnessed in horror what Loggar had done. She crossed the final line and now had to pay. Before Loggar could unleash her newly fed energy he leaped the long distances between them. She was caught off guard and nearly fell back. Sean grabbed her arms and whispered, "Sorry, Goddess. It stops here." His kiss was tender as he tightened his grip around her arms.

Loggar suddenly felt weak. Her arms couldn't move and her legs gave way.

Sean clenched her arms harder as his nanobots worked. He stripped her on everything. Her nanobots, her power, her life. Nothing can be left.

Tears welled up in her eyes as she realized Sean would not hold back. She committed so many atrocities today her crime must have one payment.

Sean cried as his nanobots methodically and effortlessly impoverished Loggar's body into a blackened mess of remains.

His tears streamed uncontrollably down his cheeks and he stumbled back. His knees buckled as his consciousness accepted his act. Kathy, dead. Dead beyond returning. He released what was left of her and crawled over to Adriana and Collins.

Collins woke up to a crying Sean. His eyes red and puffy. He was trying to steady his breathing. She looked about and spotted a blackened mass of something some distance off. She looked at Sean and tears began to flow down her cheeks. She knew how hard his choice had to have been. Kathy, dead. By the very thing she tried to control.

Epilogue

Sean was staring out the conference room window watching the planet slowly rotate. So many regrets he thought. He stared down at his hand and commanded the nanobots to generate a red flame in the center. They did. He thought blue and the color changed quickly. It would have been that simple. Just on a thought. His thoughts were broken by a chime at the door. "Enter."

Milkens and Herb walked in with Dawn and Adriana following.

Sean turned. "Gentlemen, please have a seat."

They settled in, but looked nervous.

"You read the unofficial report?"

Both nodded.

"You understand your options?"

Herb said, "We do, Captain. Milk and I discussed our options . . ."

Sean raised an eyebrow.

" . . . we'd like to stay with the Johnson as part of the Science Team."

Sean nodded. Good he thought. "Glad to have you on board. Your decision places you under Military rule. Subject to rewards and punishments. You're okay with that?"

"We are."

Sean looked at Milkens.

He said, "Yes, sir. We are."

Sean said, "Very well. Officially, our mission is to still discover alien life-forms and form alliances. GRID Command has been slowly releasing info to the general public about the Necronians. It's now nearly impossible to keep this a secret, but we can put our own spin on it."

Both nodded.

Sean continued, "In the coming weeks GRID Command will be sending a diplomatic ship to this planet. The Elder assumed The Senior Elder position and has agreed to meet with a Diplomatic delegation. That's good. Unofficially, we're still tasked with specifically looking for Necronian seeded worlds. Everything else is extra. That's not so good."

Herb bit the bottom of his lip.

Sean noticed, "Herb, something on your mind?"

Herb cleared his throat, "Why not so good?"

Sean said, "Magick. Are we ready? Some things are just a very bad idea. Down below mission gone wrong is a case in point."

Herb nodded. It had been a worst case scenario nightmare. He was going to miss Dr. Loggar terribly. Not necessarily the one of weeks past, but of the eager super-genius not so obsessed with magick and power. "I understand, sir."

Sean nodded. "Adriana, your new staff."

Adriana smiled. "Gentlemen, follow me please. Science Team is on K-Deck. Your new home."

The three walked out.

Dawn turned to Sean, "What did you not tell them?"

"I'm still part of The Most High and until a new Goddess has been decided upon, I'm the leading voice."

"My Goddess, sir! You are GRID Command."

"As long as I have full backing by them . . ."

Dawn laughed, "And who is going to challenge you?"

Sean's smile was slight but Dawn saw it.

"And you've already sent in your recommendation as to the new Most High Goddess?"

The smile increased.

Dawn laughed, "Does she know?"

He shook his head slowly with an exaggerated movement.

"Are you going to tell her?"

"I'll leave that to The Most High Council. By the time we reach Earth she should know."

Dawn smiled. "Sir, the pool had started minutes after word about Loggar was made."

"Cold-hearted," Sean nodded, "I had to recuse myself from it."

The two remained silent for a moment, staring at a lazily rotating planet. Sean sighed, "Ready, Dawn. Earth is not going to wait forever."

"With what has happened in the last few months, I think she will."

Sean tapped out the comm command to Top Deck. "My Foster. Take us out of orbit and head back to Earth, please. No rush."

"Course laid in and set, sir. How does fourteen days travel sound?"

"Very good. Give the two bell ring warning."

"Yes, sir."

Sean gave the planet one last look. The Elder allowed him to bury Kathy's remains on the Planet. He couldn't think of a better place. A planet full of life and hope and magick. All three things she wanted.

Two bells sounded.

The End

ABOUT THE AUTHOR

Born and raised in Southern California, J Carrell Jones has worked in the Customer Support field (private and Government) for over 30 years. His current position as a Technical Support Manager for a Digital Telephone Service Provider allows him to feed the family and pay some bills. He is an Army Veteran, where he worked in Computer Operations – last active duty mission served was for Project Restore Hope. Currently, he lives in Inglewood, California with his wife, a beautiful daughter, a female cat named Perilous and a dozen fish.